BEYOND control

KIT ROCHA

BEYOND CONTROL

Edited by Sasha Knight
Cover Artwork by Bree Bridges

ISBN-13: 978-1-942432-31-9

To You-Know-Who

*For all the reasons she knows, and
a few she hasn't figured out yet.*

1

The night was on fire. Lex could smell it, wood smoke and plastic burning in barrels and trash heaps. Gas, coal—anything that would take flame and light up the darkness.

A shatter of glass accompanied by victorious shouts echoed close by, maybe only three or four narrow streets over, and Lex lifted a hand instinctively to the pistol nestled under her jacket. It was the worst thing about these nights, the crime that swept through like a plague when the sectors went dark. People stole without thought or discrimination. Being disgusted by that might have made her a hypocrite, except that she never did either.

There was nothing *elegant* about looting.

The marketplace had been stripped of its wares, and the stalls stood like skeletons in the moonlight as she wound her way through the narrow street. Smart of the vendors to take their goods home with them, because boards and locks wouldn't keep out prying hands, not on a night like this.

Lex ducked into the alley behind Walt Misham's shop, sidestepped a pile of rotting trash, and knocked on the dented metal door.

Chains rattled on the other side before a rough voice challenged her. "Whoever it is, you should know I'm armed."

"I should hope so, Walt," she shot back. "Let me in."

The door creaked open an inch. "Lex? What the hell are you doing out on a night like this?"

"Business," she answered. He peered at her, one rheumy blue eye appearing out of the darkness, and she tilted her head to meet his gaze. "I finally got my hands on something you've been looking for."

"Let me see it."

Lex shoved her hands in her jacket pockets and squinted at him. "You know better. Mad's bringing it. He's on his way."

Walt's bark of laughter turned into a wracking cough as he pulled open the door far enough for Lex to slip inside. She had to ease carefully past a six-foot stack of crates in one corner, and a jagged wooden edge still snagged her hair.

She yanked it loose and followed Walt deeper into the back room of the shop. "You'll be glad to get out of here, I bet."

"Past time, to be sure." His breathing was raspy, and he led her toward a candlelit table before lowering himself heavily to his chair. "If these blackouts don't kill me first."

"The solar converter will help." She sat across

from him and studied his face, which was heavily lined and shadowed in the dim light. "I tested it this afternoon, so it should be fully charged. You can try it out tonight."

His lips twitched. "If I meet your asking price, of course. You'd best give me a good deal, girl, if you want me around to buy your stolen goods."

"You're not my only customer," Lex drawled. "Still, it'd be a shame not to have you screeching at people in the market."

"Don't tease an old man, Lex." He grunted as he lifted a lockbox onto the table. "Name your price— unless you'd like to trade."

"Ten." A few grand less than she could get elsewhere, maybe, but Walt had cut her plenty of deals in the past based on her association with Dallas. Besides, it seemed wrong to play hardball over something like this. A pretty bauble, sure, but not a legitimate medical need.

Walt groused—he always groused—but fumbled with the lock on the box. "You want cash or clean city credits?"

"Half and half. And bust the credits up onto a couple of different sticks."

A hollow knock sounded on the front door as Walt pried open the box. "Drag your young body over there and let your friend in, if that's him. I'll load up your creds."

"Cranky ass." But Lex crossed the room and peeked out the dirty window. "It's him."

It took a solid minute to disengage all the locks and chains, but Mad didn't seem impatient. He smiled as if the night wasn't alive with the threat of violence and held up a crinkled brown paper bag. "Old man willing to deal?"

"I'm very persuasive." She opened the door far enough to admit him, then glanced around the square outside before securing the locks again. "Show the man what he's bought, Mad."

"The finest tech money can't buy." Maddox was nearly twice Lex's size, but he moved with deceptive grace, claiming a chair across from Walt. "I'll have you know, old timer, that these aren't available to private owners. City-issue, strictly reserved for councilmen and military police. I still don't know how Lex managed to find one, but it's a thing of beauty."

"Never you mind how I found it." *Stole it,* she corrected silently. Not that it mattered.

Walt's gnarled hands shook as he reached for his breathing device. "Flex those clever fingers, girl, and help me hook it up. If it works, the money's yours."

Walt's assisted breathing device delivered oxygen through a simple set of nasal tubes. The complicated part was the apparatus itself, a small black box that worked as a conductive purifier. The small intake drew air in, filtered it, and both isolated and concentrated the oxygen content. It worked without power, but barely any more efficiently than simply breathing.

Lex slipped one of the small rechargeable battery cells from the solar converter and fit it into the slot Walt indicated. A tiny light on the side of the purifier flashed blue and then a solid green, and an almost imperceptible hiss filled the room as Lex helped Walt loop the tubes over his ears and fit the points into his nostrils.

Walt closed his eyes and inhaled deeply. Mad watched them both, a tiny smile curving his lips. "See, old man? Tech so smooth it's almost magic."

"Hush," Walt grumbled in between more of those relieved breaths. "This one, Lex—he has no trouble getting air, and he wastes it on so many words. Does he ever stop talking?"

"Nope." Mad talked all the time—and mostly, Lex suspected, to convince people he was simple. Shallow. "Don't let it fool you though, Walt. He's sharp."

Walt huffed. "The whole lot of you O'Kanes are sharp."

"That we are," she teased.

The old man squinted at her. "I heard Dallas had himself some trouble, though. Should I be worried about moving out to the edge of the sector? Is the place coming down around our ears?"

"No more so than usual." Lex gathered the cash and credit sticks in one hand. "Anything else you're on the lookout for? Just in case I stumble across it?"

"I've got a new customer, a collector. He'll pay top credit for pre-Flare videos. Westerns, he wants. Cowboys and outlaws." Walt showed his disdain for that preference with a loud sniff. "Fools with more money than sense. But fools make my living, don't they?"

"We've all got our something." Some people wanted porn, others wanted priceless art. And others wanted vintage Clint Eastwood. "I might be able to scrounge up a few. Keep in touch."

Walt followed them back through the labyrinth of crates and boxes to the back door, and Lex lingered outside long enough to hear the click and scrape of every lock and chain. "Got plans?" she asked Mad, her hands in her pockets.

"That's what I was about to ask you." He nodded to her jacket. "I saw you got credits."

She still had her fingers wrapped around the paper and plastic in her pocket. She pulled out the handful and shoved it at him. "You and Doc can split it. You know the drill."

"Doc's got a girl who can use some of this tonight." He folded the bills before dumping the credit chips into his pocket. "Pregnant. She almost drowned in the river trying to get out of Two before—"

Lex closed her eyes, as if doing so would shut out the words, as well. "It's better if I don't know, Mad."

"You're doing good work, honey, helping people who need it. Why don't you ever want to hear that?"

Because it wasn't her job. Because it wasn't enough. Because Dallas would make her stop—or worse, try to throw in with her and do more. "This is the way I want it."

"Ah, Lex. All right." Mad threw a friendly arm around her shoulders and tugged her to his side for a brief hug. "You gonna let me walk you back to the compound?"

"That wouldn't be very sneaky," she demurred. "I've got to slip by Dallas somehow. I'm not supposed to be out after dark."

"Well, be good and sneaky, then." He squeezed her shoulders. "I know you can take care of yourself, girl, but have some pity on the rest of us. Dallas roars around like a lion with a thorn in his paw when he thinks you've been putting yourself in harm's way."

She'd planned to wait until morning to run her errand. She'd tried, even, but in the end she couldn't. "Was I supposed to let a sick man huff and puff all night just to keep Dallas from flipping his shit?"

"You snarl and snap all you want, Lex. I know your dirty secret." Mad laughed and poked her in the chest. "You have a heart."

Now *that* she couldn't let stand. She grabbed his finger and bent it back until he winced. "What I have is money, along with a tiny bit of a conscience. That's not the same thing."

"We live in the slums of paradise, sweetheart." Mad looked down at the O'Kane logo tattooed around her wrist—the same logo inked around both of his. "Do you know what the street value is on a tiny bit of conscience? Don't undersell it."

"I only have it because I can afford to." She hated the almost frantic edge that tinged the words. "If I couldn't, you'd better believe it'd be gone."

"You can afford it." His words were intent, a quiet answer to the desperation she wanted to hide. "You're an O'Kane. Hell, you're the next best thing to *the* O'Kane."

"Don't let him hear you say that." Lex took a step back, then another. "If Dallas finds out we were out tonight, do me a favor, huh? Don't tell him anything."

"You asking me to lie to the king of Sector Four?"

"Hell, no. Just keep some shit to yourself." She flashed Mad her most irreverent smile. "Buck up. I've been doing it for years, and I'm still kicking."

If Dallas O'Kane had an ounce less self-control, he'd have found a way to plant a tracker on Lex to preserve his peace of mind.

The tech existed, though most people would have to give up eating for months to get their hands on it. In the four decades since the solar storms had obliterated life as humanity had known it, technology had become a luxury enjoyed by the privileged and the powerful—or those willing to cater to vices the powerful were privileged enough to be allowed to enjoy.

Dallas had gotten rich off other men's vices, for all that he allowed himself only a few. The fantasy of tracking Lex was one of them. Eden was the morally righteous city of the future—they must have come up with a hundred ways to keep tabs on the many sins of their citizens.

Not that they needed to trouble themselves with covert surveillance. The Council tracked their sheep right out in the open, like any self-respecting theocratic oligarchy. No one dared to breathe a word of protest, even when the councilmen parked their intrusive little spy drones right up some poor bastard's ass.

Sometimes Dallas envied them the bliss of blind obedience. Sometimes.

Liar, whispered a taunting inner voice. Dallas ignored it and dropped the butt of his cigarette to the cracked pavement, grinding it under the heel of his boot. He was all but invisible in the shadow of the garage, but from here he had a good vantage point of the side gate. If Lex was going to sneak back into the O'Kane compound, this was the likeliest place.

Blind obedience would never be a problem for Dallas as long as Lex was around, so any tracking mechanism he planted on her would *have* to be covert. Something unobtrusive that could be sewn into her favorite leather jacket or those shit-kicking boots with the heels that made her legs go on forever.

If she found out, he'd be the one getting kicked, and the fantasy of Lex coming at him with violence and passion all twisted up was a vice he didn't have time to indulge.

But fuck, it was a hot fantasy.

The scuff of boots interrupted his reverie, and Jasper's face flared out of the darkness as he lit a cigarette. "Last shipment's on its way. We had to siphon one of the trucks for enough diesel to run the club's generators, but we managed to keep the lights on 'til closing."

"Good work." Keeping the club open on blackout nights was worth the hassle. Anyone who wasn't out looting or had finished lining their pockets showed up to watch the girls dance, or to pickle their livers on the lifeblood of Sector Four—O'Kane liquor. "How's your lady handling her first night without lights?"

"Noelle's all right. She doesn't love it, but hey. The sectors are already darker than Eden, right?"

"Damn near every day." Dallas reached into his vest for his battered cigarette case as he studied Jasper. His right-hand man had the easy smugness of a guy getting laid well and often, a fact Dallas might have resented more if Jasper and Noelle hadn't been willing, even eager, to include him in their sexual adventures.

But he wasn't the only one they included. And if Lex had drifted back into the compound through the main doors, Jasper's girl was the one most likely to know where she was. "Don't suppose Noelle's seen Lex?"

Jas shook his head. "Nah, not tonight. But I can let you know if she shows up at our place."

Dallas paused with his lighter open but unstruck. "Does that happen a lot?"

"Often enough." The corner of Jasper's mouth quirked up. "Had to get a bigger bed."

There was a mental image to give any man a raging hard-on. Sleek, hungry Lex climbing into bed with dreamy-eyed Noelle. A sexy, gorgeous sector woman and a soft, curvy princess out of Eden, tangled together. Naked.

And Jasper, the lucky bastard, getting to have them both in his damn bed. "What a hardship," Dallas drawled. "Must be rough."

A creak interrupted his reply. "You bragging again, Jas?" Lex closed the side gate and fixed the man with a challenging look. "Whatever happened to not kissing and telling?"

"Guess I'm not as well-mannered as you thought." He grinned at Dallas as he turned back toward the garage. "Good night. To both of you."

Dallas took his time lighting his cigarette, waiting until the door shut behind Jasper to click his lighter closed. "I'm surprised you're not curled around Noelle right now. You know city folk don't like the dark."

"She has Jasper." Lex was dressed in head-to-toe black and zipped up all the way to her chin. "Besides, I was busy."

"Mmm, busy." Even though his eyes had adjusted to the dark, she was barely more than a shadow. He couldn't see her face or judge her expression, which would have been a disadvantage with anyone else. With Lex, it never mattered. She'd been trained from the cradle to show the world only what she wanted it to see. "We're not under lockdown anymore, love, but you picked a hell of a night to go for a stroll."

"I know. But I brought you something." She stepped into the center of the courtyard and held out her hand. Moonlight glinted off her hair and the small glass jar in her palm. "It's strawberry."

"Jam?" Something that cost more than liquor or tech. Fresh produce was always at a premium in the sectors, since it had to be lovingly cultivated in dry, scorched earth or shipped in from the rustic communes far beyond the city. "Where in hell did you find this?"

"I have my methods." She wiggled the jar teasingly. "Well, do you want it or not?"

Dallas caught the jar and her hand along with it, folding her fingers under his. "Tell me you had backup, Lex."

"I'm not dense, Dallas."

Dallas, not his given name. Not *Declan*, the two syllables he only heard from her. Tenderness and rage brought them forth, and it was no wonder he had a hard time separating the two. At least now he knew she wasn't completely pissed. Yet.

He could fix that. "Good. Then I won't take you over my knee for sneaking out."

She stiffened, and a rueful, mocking smile curved her lips. "I almost forgot. Property of Dallas O'Kane, whether I like it or not."

Yes. Not a civilized thought, but this wasn't a civilized world, and he'd never pretended to be a civilized man. Letting his cigarette fall to the ground, he snatched the jar out of her hand and twisted her wrist until the moonlight spilled over her tattoo cuffs with the O'Kane logo. "Damn straight, honey. You and everyone else."

"Me and everyone else," she echoed flatly.

He ran his thumb over the skull etched into her skin. "You regretting taking ink, love?"

"No." She hesitated. "But would it matter if I said yes?"

His blood chilled. "O'Kane for life, isn't that the promise?"

"From the day I first darkened your door." Lex tugged at her hand. "I'm tired. I want to go to bed."

Resisting the urge to ask whose bed, Dallas released her and took a step back. Personal space, it turned out, wasn't optional when it came to Lex and his self-control. "I'll find out when the power's coming back on. We'll need to push Jas and Noelle's party back until it does."

"I'll take care of it." Lex cradled her wrist, rubbing it gently, as if to erase his touch. "I always do, don't I?"

"You always do," he agreed, closing his hand around empty air. The harder he clutched at her, the faster she slipped away. It had always been true, but it had gotten worse since she'd been shot. Money could buy regenerative technology that healed flesh, but nothing could rid him of the image of her bleeding out on the club's stage.

He couldn't stop tightening his fists, even when he threatened to crush her.

2

"You heard me." Lex took one last gulp of her water, capped the bottle, and tugged on the oiled leather of her waistband until her pants were riding low, almost off her hips. "Right across here."

Ace wheeled his stool closer and studied her bare abdomen for a moment before flicking his dark gaze up to meet hers. "Lex, honey. You're the light of my life, so I ask this with love. Are you fucking high?"

O'Kane for life. Dallas's words, and they hadn't stopped reverberating in her head for three goddamn days. "Just showing my dedication to the cause."

"Uh-huh." Ace folded his tattooed arms across his chest. "And what cause is that, sister? Giving our fearless leader some sort of cardiac event?"

"Why would it do that? It's not a mark." Though it'd serve him right if she went ahead and had Ace wrap the ink around her throat for all to see. "Call it a tribute."

"A tribute." Ace huffed and smoothed his thumb over her belly button. "You're asking me to ink Dallas O'Kane's name into your flesh without his knowledge. May not be a mark, but it's still some kind of ballsy."

She'd rather chew off her tongue than discuss her reasons—her highly fucking personal reasons—with anyone, even Ace. "You don't want to? Okay." She sat up on the table. "I can think of three guys right off the top of my head who'd probably do it for free, anyway."

He stared at her, his handsome face slightly less appealing with his mouth hanging open. "You're fucking serious, aren't you?"

She opened her mouth to say yes, but what came out instead skirted uncomfortably close to confession. "He's been threatening me with it long enough. I can't go a damn day around here without him reminding me that he owns me, so I think it's time *I* reminded *him*."

Ace's brow furrowed in a frown. "Threatening you?"

Not quite the right word. "Warning me, maybe. Just give me the ink, Ace."

As careless and vapid as he could be at times, there was nothing shallow in his eyes now, just affection and concern and a steely sort of resolve. "I don't lay marks on women who don't want them, Alexa, not even for Dallas. Tell me this is all your own idea. Swear to me."

He couldn't help the concern, as misplaced as it was. She sighed and laid her hand on his cheek. "You're sweet, but you know I wouldn't let him strong-arm me into this. I'd strangle him with his own belt first."

"Maybe you would, at that, doll." He caught her

hand and laid a smacking kiss on her knuckles. "But you owe me for threatening to let someone else defile one of *my* canvases with inferior work."

"Great, now I'm an inanimate object." Lex pushed her pants low again and lay back, pillowing her head on her arm. "You know I'd never actually let anyone else near me with a needle."

"I should hope not." Ace studied her for another moment before spinning his stool to rummage around on the table behind him. "Fine, girl. Did you have any ideas about the particulars, or are you going to let me do my thing?"

"I want his name. The rest is up to you."

"Which name?"

Lex stilled. Oh, it was tempting to take things all the way, to write his given name on her skin. But there was a difference, subtle but certain, between belonging to Dallas and belonging to Declan. One was simple, a role she should have already taken on officially. The other...

The other was forever.

"Dallas," she whispered.

"Dallas, it is." Ace rolled back to her side with a fistful of pens and markers. "So. Dare I ask what the lug did to piss you off this time? Seems like he's been too busy to get in trouble."

"He always finds the time." She tugged at a short, dark lock of hair that curled over Ace's ear. "What about you? You've been hiding out lately."

"Busy, love. That's all." He uncapped a pen and frowned. "Nope, the angle's wrong. Hop into the chair so I can make myself comfy between your thighs."

Ace's flirting was far more forced than his usual casual overtures. Lex arched an eyebrow at him as she slid off the table and shimmied out of her pants. "You're trying to change the subject."

"There's a subject more interesting than your thighs?"

"Hard to believe, but yes."

Ace swung around to tilt the chair back, then situated himself on the rolling stool between her knees. "You missed a show in here yesterday, sister. I laid the last of Noelle and Jasper's marks."

Lex curled her fingers around the leather armrests. "How did you pry them apart long enough to finish the tattoos?"

"It was damn near an act of God, I'll tell you that." His pen tickled her skin with the first slow stroke. "Not that I mind the show. But why am I telling you? You know how hot they are together."

"If you like the idea, you should try it again for real." Lex licked her lower lip. "Noelle's getting so bold. She doesn't even whisper anymore when she asks Jas to hold me down and fuck me."

"Fuck *me*, Lex." Ace glared at her from under the rakish fall of his hair. "You trying to get my hands shaking? I'm making art, here."

"You deserve a little teasing now and then."

"I suppose I do." He edged the lace of her panties down and continued his sketching. "Oh well, we'll all get a show in a couple nights. How's the party planning coming along?"

"Fine." Everything exactly the way Jasper and Noelle wanted it, a fitting celebration to the beginning of their life together. "You bringing a date?"

"And deny everyone their chance at me? That would be selfish."

"Uh-huh. You're not nearly as convincing as you think you are, you know. At least, not to me."

Ace tried to scowl at her, but the expression didn't fit his face. By the time he capped the marker and reached for one with a finer tip, the corners of his mouth were curving up again. "Didn't there used to be a saying about glass houses? I always wondered about that, to be honest. Was life really so easy before the storms that people lived in glass houses?"

"It's a metaphor, honey. About hypocrisy." She winked at him. "Not that I would know anything about that."

"Mmm." He bent over her abdomen, his brow furrowed with concentration as the narrow tip of the pen glided over her skin. "Don't throw stones, Lex. I'm busy building your glass house."

That was one thing she'd always liked about Ace—he didn't judge, but you sure the hell couldn't put one over on him. "You really think it's a mistake?"

He shrugged. "Depends on what you're trying to accomplish, doesn't it?"

"I don't know," she admitted. "Maybe...I want to show Dallas that he should be careful what he wishes for."

Ace pursed his lips and said nothing.

Fine. "Maybe I want to show *myself*, too. Fair enough?"

"I think it'll be educational all around." He flashed her a wicked grin. "And, sister? Between your body and my art? It's going to be fucking *fantastic*."

Educational, he'd called it, and she suspected he

was right. Dallas would lose his shit, of course—good or bad, that much was a certainty, not a possibility. Either way, things would *change.*

They had to change.

Lex leaned her head back and closed her eyes. "Here's hoping."

"Oh, *Lex.*"

At least Noelle was laughing. Lex cocked her hip and studied her healing skin in the full-length mirror. "Don't sound so scandalized. It's just a tattoo."

Noelle rested her chin on Lex's shoulder, her gaze fixed on the mirror. Dallas's name stretched between Lex's hipbones in elegant, intricate calligraphy, the swirls and flourishes melting into thorny vines. Tiny rosebuds nestled amongst the sharp points, some caught on the edge of bloom but most still tightly furled.

"It's beautiful," Noelle said, her voice thick with amusement. "And clearly Ace's work. The thorns are so real, you'd think you could prick yourself on one."

"So it meets with your approval?"

"I didn't say *that.*"

Lex turned and eyed the fresh ink winding across Noelle's throat and collarbones. "It's not something settled," she murmured. "Not like yours. But it's a push, one he can take however he wants."

"Mmm." Noelle's fingers drifted up to brush her new tattoo, almost as if she couldn't help the gesture. "Did you guys have another fight? I heard you went out the night of the blackout."

"I had something to unload." Lex eased by her and dropped to the bed. The little orange kitten curled on a pillow mewled his protest at being jarred, and she soothed him by stroking one fingertip in a tiny zigzag between his ears.

"To sell, you mean." Noelle tilted her head. "Something from your closet?"

"No, something new." She told Noelle about the deal, and about the solar converter she'd nicked from a loudmouthed drug dealer from Sector Three. "I figure Walt needs it more than that asshole. But I had to sneak around because I don't want Dallas to know, *especially* that I was in Three alone."

Concern filled Noelle's eyes as she settled cross-legged on the end of the bed. "I don't like it, either. Jasper said everything's breaking down over there now that there isn't a sector leader."

"Not you, too." She nudged Noelle with her foot. "I was in and out before the lights went off. No big thing."

Noelle returned the nudge. "I'm a worrier. I know you need to do it, but promise you'll be careful, okay? I'm not ready to see you hurt again."

Hurt. Shot. Bleeding out from a sniper's bullet. Lex didn't like to think about it, and luckily she didn't really have to. All she remembered was a fleeting moment of pain followed by darkness, and then waking up to solicitous concern from damn near everybody.

Noelle and Dallas had both had a hard time dealing with it. Noelle had grown clingy in her worry, something Lex only managed to indulge out of affection—and with Jasper's help in distracting his lover from the worst of her fretting.

And Dallas... Lex brushed aside the memories of him holding her, stroking her hair, breaking the silence only to assure her that she'd be all right.

Noelle nudged her again. "Lex? *Did* you guys have another fight? Is he being awful?"

Lex shook herself and laughed wryly. "He's being Dallas. He's being..." She let the words trail off. He thought she didn't know what he was doing. That he'd been spending time and resources looking for a way to get to Gareth Woods, the councilman who'd sent a sniper into their sector.

Part of her wanted to encourage the hunt—the man had, after all, hurt Noelle—but she knew Dallas too well. He didn't want to stop Woods because the man had proven himself a danger to the gang.

He just wanted the fucker dead.

Lex rubbed at the goose bumps that rose on her arms. "Are you ready for tomorrow night? Ace is going to cry if you and Jasper don't get it on and let him watch."

Noelle still blushed as pink as any innocent city girl, but the low laugh belonged to the woman Lex had watched bloom in the freedom of the sectors. "Ace doesn't want to watch, he wants to *help*. That's where he likes to be, isn't it? Right in the middle."

"Mmm, he's very jealous of me and my standing invitation into Jas's bed."

"Only because he loves having Jas boss him around."

Lex would be willing to bet Ace found corrupting Noelle an equal or greater thrill. "You like him?"

"Sure." Noelle shrugged and toyed with the hem of her jeans, folding and unfolding the denim. "I like Ace. I like messing around with him. I like that it can be about joy and pleasure." Noelle smiled self-consciously. "But he's not Jasper."

Not just someone special—*the* one. Lex funneled her tiny spark of jealousy into a groan. "It's a good thing you went and got marked, baby girl, because you're hopeless."

"Uh-huh." Noelle traced one of the small rose-buds on Lex's hipbone. "Talk to me after you've rubbed

Dallas's nose in this." Her smile widened. "At least that'll put his face right where you want it."

"Dirty, but effective. He likes eating pussy almost as much as you do."

Oddly, the tease sobered Noelle. She caught Lex's hand, her blue eyes deadly serious. "No, I like *you*. You know that, right? I don't care if Dallas is the boss or the king or a god. You always have a place with me and Jas, and Dallas can go—" Her lips pressed together and her brow furrowed, as if the effort to find words to encompass her anger actually *hurt*.

Lex had to swallow around the tight lump in her throat. "Oh, honey, I know. And you and Jas are great—I love you both—but you have your thing. I'm glad you let me in for a little while now and then, but you're not *less* when I'm not there. And that's okay. It's good."

"All right." Noelle released her and flopped back on the bed. "You need to teach me some new words. Not dirty ones—angry ones. I could use a few for my shifts at the Broken Circle."

Lex curled up beside her. "Believe it or not, foul language that's not about sex? Not my best area."

"So who can teach us? Amira? Nessa?" Noelle laughed. "I bet Rachel knows how to outswear all the men. Just like she can outdrink them."

"She's kind of busy these days. That new guy— Bren's friend from the city."

"Cruz?" Noelle propped her head up on her hand. "You know, I'm not surprised. Not even a little."

"She wanted a prince," Lex agreed softly. And who better than a man who'd given up his life in Eden to bring a sniper to justice, to avenge attempted murder? "All the more reason to be a bit gentle with Ace right now, yes?"

Sympathy narrowed Noelle's eyes. "I thought he was into Rachel, but I can never tell with him. Sometimes I think he's just half in love with everyone."

Lex knew better. She and Ace were more alike than either of them let on, and maybe that was ninety percent of the problem—that they never let on.

She sat up with a sigh and rubbed her hands on her jeans. "I've got to get going if I'm going to find someone to cover my shift tonight. If I go on stage and flash this goddamn tattoo, there'll be fireworks. The wrong kind."

Noelle leaned up and kissed Lex's cheek. "We'll have a girl's day soon, okay? Next week, after Jasper comes down from the high of seeing his ink on me."

"You know it." If things went south with Dallas, Lex would need them more than ever.

cruz

It wasn't the first time he'd had to fight for his place, but it had to be the most honest.

Cruz easily avoided a telegraphed punch and used his opponent's momentum to swing him toward the edge of the cage, face first. Dominic slammed into the steel bars with a grunt of pain before staggering back.

Out of respect to the O'Kane logo wrapped around the other mans' wrists, Cruz didn't press the advantage. There was a delicate balance to this sort of battle, a line to walk between scorn-worthy weakness and too-dangerous strength. If he wanted to find a place among the O'Kanes, he had to prove he could hold his own, but he couldn't humiliate them.

Not even this one, who whirled around with eyes brimming with cruelty and rage. He swiped the back of his hand across his mouth, streaking blood across his cheek. "Cheap shot, city boy."

The jab didn't sting like it had at the start, if only because Cruz had heard it so many times. Sometimes fond, sometimes suspicious, and sometimes—like now—practically an expletive, but always the same. *City boy.*

Cruz didn't let his irritation show. Bland would piss the man off worse, but it might bring the fight to a close. "I thought there were no rules in the sectors."

"Not a rule. Just shows what a pussy you are."

"No rules means no such thing as a cheap shot."

Dom grinned blood. "So you're stupid *and* ugly."

It was so sad an attempt, Cruz almost felt bad for him. Stock insults, spit out in fear and desperation, but it was the hot anticipation in Dom's eyes that wiped away any pity. He wasn't like the other O'Kanes, fighting for fun or glory or competition or even just for the hell of it. Dom wanted to hurt someone. Physically, mentally, it didn't matter.

And with that realization, Cruz had had enough of playing and verbal banter. He struck, lashing out so quickly his opponent didn't have a hope of blocking. A fist to the solar plexus, a blow to the face, and a swift kick to the side of Dom's knee, and the bastard crumpled into a heap.

The warehouse went silent, except for Dom's pained groan.

Cruz had moved too fast. Usually there were cheers when one of the fighters went down, but the onlookers hadn't caught up with what had happened yet. The people in the sectors were used to street brawlers and cage fighters, hard, hungry men who'd grown up malnourished and scraping to get by. Not men who had been taken from their cradles, handed over to soldiers and given perfectly calibrated nutrition, carefully planned training...

Eden had spent twenty years turning him into a lethal weapon and another ten honing his edges. Now he was fighting in cages. It didn't seem fair. To anyone.

The silence broke on a female cheer, swiftly joined by two more. The O'Kane women, making their appreciation known from the couches where they held court. As if they'd popped a bubble, sound rose all around him, shouts and cries and dozens of people fighting over bets placed and lost.

The cage door rattled, and Cruz turned in time to see Rachel pull it open. She carried two bottles between the fingers of one hand with an ease that spoke of practice, and a pleased smile curved her lips. "I came to rescue you."

Beyond her stood a tight knot of women, each one eyeing him with greedy assessment. Nothing personal there, merely the desire for a hard body and expensive presents. He knew the type because they'd made up the bulk of his bed partners over the years. Faced with the choice between using a woman and letting one use him, he'd always opted for the latter. In the end, they cost as much as the hookers, but at least they had a choice.

It was all still empty. Shallow sensation, and nothing compared to the way Rachel could warm his body with just her smile. She knew him, talked to him. *Liked* him. Accepting one of the beers, he smiled back. "Can we get out of here? I need to cool off."

She glanced down at the motionless man on the mat with an exaggerated wince. "Sure. I don't think Dom'll mind."

Dom would be lucky to get that knee under him in the next hour, and Cruz couldn't stir an ounce of guilt as he stepped from the cage and swept up a towel. "Maybe outside?"

She folded her fingers around his. "I know a place."

Rachel pulled him through the crowd and down a back hall, which was thumping with music and lit with red light. The darker corners writhed with moans and flashes of bare skin, people who preferred a little privacy over the open main floor. To Cruz, even the shadows seemed criminally indiscreet, but he was starting to suspect most of Sector Four considered sex less fun behind closed doors.

"This way," she murmured, staring straight ahead until they reached the end of the hall—and a door that led out onto a set of pitted exterior stairs.

Cruz followed her up three flights and found himself on the roof of one of the tallest buildings in the sector. In the darkness, he could see twinkling lights for what seemed like miles in either direction. "Not a lot of original buildings in this quadrant, are there?"

"No." Rachel leaned against the low wall edging the roof. "When I used to look out toward the sectors when I was a kid, all I could think was how dark they were. Now it all seems so bright."

"They're a lot brighter than they used to be." He tossed the towel over his shoulder and leaned next to her, close enough to brush her arm with his own. "I used to see them from the air. They flew us in one weekend a month for classes inside the city, but only at night."

She looked up at him, her eyes brilliant in the moonlight. "Do you miss it?"

It wasn't the first time someone had asked him the question, but it was the first time he really thought about the answer. A lock of blonde hair slipped across her forehead, and he echoed a gesture he'd seen once, reaching up to tuck it behind her ear. The cook at the training base had always done that when his wife's hair escaped its braid, but Cruz had never understood why brushing it back made the man smile.

He got it now. An excuse to touch, affection, and the warmth that came from being trusted with something precious.

He gave her the same in return—the truth. "I don't know. Some of it. I miss flying. No chance anyone in the sectors will get the resources together to get a helicopter or plane off the ground in our lifetime."

"You never know." Her breath blew over his skin as she turned her face into his hand.

He knew. He knew it the way he did most things— because it fell within the parameters of knowledge necessary to complete certain mission objectives. He could recite the dangers each sector represented and list the tools and materials each required to obtain or build various weapons, but he didn't know how to contain the feeling of this woman's face cradled against his hand.

Unacceptable. He wasn't the only one whose pulse raced when she smiled. Bren had warned him of as much the first time he'd caught Cruz's gaze following Rachel across a room. The gang's tattoo artist had been circling, sizing up Rachel like a fortification he wasn't sure he could storm, but Cruz had crashed into the middle of the game before Ace made his move.

And now this. It felt like racing toward a target, knowing that stumbling could give your enemy the lead. Ace was the one with the experience wooing women. He wouldn't be thinking about mission objectives and weapons if he had Rachel alone on a rooftop, nuzzling his hand.

Cruz moved his thumb to touch the corner of her

mouth and trace the full bow of her lower lip. "I don't miss it right now."

"Good." She stretched up on her toes, but even that only brought her mouth in line with his throat, and her lips brushed his collarbone. Heat threatened to consume him. His blood boiled and his dick hardened.

A thousand things he could do to her rose up from that dark place inside him, all the things the men he'd worked for had condemned in rough, angry voices before slinking into the shadows to indulge themselves with men and women who couldn't say no.

He didn't want any of those things, not yet. Tonight, he wanted to be soft, slow. He wanted to kiss her knees weak and know what it felt like to have her tremble between him and the wall. Carefully, he cupped the back of her head. "Look at me."

She was already shaking, but she met his eyes boldly, without shying away, and it hit him almost as hard as her touch. People in Eden never really *looked* at each other. Not like this, open and without shame, daring the other person to see into them, through them.

Cruz didn't want anyone seeing through him, so he was the one who broke, sweeping down to catch her mouth with his own.

She made an encouraging noise in the back of her throat as her lips parted and her hands slipped around him to tease just under the waistband of his jeans. A heartbeat later, her tongue touched his.

The darkness rolled up again. He could have her. Turn her around, bend her over the low wall, and fuck her fast and hard until her screams floated all the way to Sector Three. He could urge her to her knees, twist all that shiny blonde hair around his fist and find out if she still stared at him, open and brave, while he pushed his cock between her lips and jerked off in her mouth.

No. Kisses. He concentrated on kissing her, licking her, learning the taste of her lips and what made her moan. He'd do this right. Slow and hot and respectful, with no stumbling. Not when he could feel Ace dogging every step, waiting for him to fail.

3

No one knew how to put on a party like Lex. Hell, no one knew how to put on a *show* like Lex.

The party room had never been subtle, because Dallas had never been a subtle man. It was a room furnished for sin—for one kind in particular—and he spared no expense in indulging this vice. He'd built a playground for adults, with a hundred accessories to spice up sex and every surface begging to be defiled.

Lex had turned that blatant offer into a silken promise. Dallas wasn't sure how—something with the softer lighting, new decorations. Hard leather benches with heavy D-rings were now buried in soft cushions, the sumptuous fabrics alongside the harsh silver chains somehow a perfect celebration of the couple of honor.

Noelle and Jasper were enthroned next to Dallas on the plush couch that dominated the raised dais.

Jasper looked smug as hell in leather and denim, and Noelle was taunting every man in the room with a frilly scrap of white lace that bared endless skin, framed her gorgeous tits, and showed off the intricate black tattoo wrapped around her throat.

Ace had outdone himself with that one, working Jasper's name into a delicate web of lacy curls that looked like an expensive choker from ten feet away. Every time Dallas glanced to his left, Jasper was staring at the damn thing like a dying man catching a glimpse of salvation.

Jealousy formed an ugly knot in Dallas's gut, especially with Lex holding down the opposite end of the couch, sleekly beautiful in a little red dress and acting like Dallas didn't fucking exist.

That was fine. That was just *fucking* fine. Dallas could have any woman in the room on her knees for him by twitching a damn finger. For all the soft-focus lighting and pretty hors d'oeuvres, the night would devolve into fucking soon enough, and that would take the edge off his temper.

It *was* an O'Kane party, after all.

Noelle's soft laughter washed over him from where she leaned away from Jasper, her head tucked close to Lex's. Dallas nudged his friend. "How you holding up, old man?"

Jasper finished his drink before answering. "Parties aren't my thing. But this is Noelle's night."

Dallas eyed the fresh ink on the inside of Jasper's arm. Noelle's name, in Ace's inimitable style. "Not just hers."

Jasper followed his gaze and nodded, though his words contradicted Dallas's. "The ink is mine. The party's hers."

That, Dallas supposed, wasn't worth arguing.

People had been drifting up to the dais all evening long with congratulations and gifts, and most of it had been heaped on a glowing Noelle. "Fair enough."

Movement at the door caught Dallas's eye—Bren, with his seemingly ever-present shadow trailing him. Jasper was Dallas's right-hand man, and Brendan Donnelly was Jas's mirror. The strong, silent man who stood at Dallas's left, his cold-blooded intellect a good balance for Jasper's more tempered compassion.

The girl hovering just behind Bren's left shoulder might as well have been Noelle's mirror. They'd come under Dallas's protection within a week of one another, but Noelle had fallen from the privileged grace of the city, and Six—if the girl had another name, she refused to give it—had been dragged out of the hell of Sector Three. Noelle was sweet softness in white ruffles, and Six was nothing but wary, hard edges and baggy clothes that covered her from her chin to her borrowed boots.

Her eyes were wounded. Broken, maybe. Sometimes Dallas woke from nightmares where Lex stared at him like that, shattered and hurt because the need inside him had crushed her.

Bren grinned as he approached the dais, one arm behind his back. "Especially for you, Noelle," he said, presenting her with a small flogger festooned with a red bow.

It had a multitude of tails, all light, butter-soft suede, and Noelle flushed a pretty pink as she caught one of the tails and rubbed it between her thumb and forefinger. "It's beautiful."

Lex leaned forward to peer at the whip. "Stuart make this?"

"He did." Bren dipped his head. "Thanks for recommending him."

"No problem." She brushed the back of her hand

over the braided handle, her expression contemplative. "He does good work."

"That he does," Dallas agreed, watching one tail slither over Lex's skin. Wrapping leather around that woman's body could be a full-time hobby, one to which he'd gladly devote himself. It was an effort to tear his gaze away and smile at Noelle. "Bren knows his toys, kitten. I think you'll like this one." Jasper would like it too, once he had Noelle stretched in front of him, writhing through the pleasure she took from pain.

Jasper set aside the flogger and folded his hand around Noelle's. "Should we ask Bren to dance?"

"It's only polite." Noelle dropped a kiss to Lex's cheek before hauling Jasper to his feet. "Six, do you want to dance?"

Her dark eyes widened just a fraction, and then she was giving Noelle that look, the one Dallas had seen on the poor girl's face a dozen times. It screamed, *You* cannot *be for real,* and sometimes it seemed like that was the only look anyone got from Six.

Except Bren.

Dallas gestured to a chair tucked in a dark corner on the dais. It was far enough out of the way to give the wary woman a little privacy, but not situated so that she'd have to worry about being cornered. Not with him—and Lex—between her and the rest of the room. "Why don't you park yourself over there, Six? Watch until you feel like joining in, eh?"

After an awkward moment, she nodded jerkily and mumbled something that sounded like a congratulations as she slipped past Jasper. Dallas arched an eyebrow at Bren, who threw a wave over his shoulder as he followed Noelle out onto the floor.

"They left you alone with me," Lex muttered. "I guess you'll be making them pay for that later."

Dallas laughed and stretched his arm across the back of the couch. "How do you know this wasn't part of my plan?"

She moved fast, and her hair spilled over her shoulders to tickle his cheek as she straddled his thigh. "Was it?"

It didn't matter what his plan had been. When Lex's perfume hit him, his cock got hard and his plans got muddled. He slid one hand up her leg, edging his fingers under the hem of her dress. "It sure as fuck is now, love."

She slapped his hand away.

He couldn't help his grin. "What's the matter, Lex? Don't want to ride my fingers?"

"Mmm." She leaned down until her lips grazed his ear. "I'm not that easy."

Nothing about Lex ever was. "Congratulations on your protégé's big debut. You were right, back when we took her in. She's gonna settle down and make Jasper real happy."

"Told you so." Lex slipped a hand between them, pressing her fingernails to his chest through his shirt.

Her dress rode up her thighs, and Dallas braced both hands on her hips and raised his leg, grinding up against her. "And you don't get tired of being right, do you?"

"With you? I've learned to take what I can get."

It was a challenge, one he couldn't keep himself from answering with one hand cuffing her throat. Gently, so gently, but he liked the way his fingers looked wrapped around her neck, with his thumb along the opposite side. A collar of his own making and a gesture of dominance, even with his grip soft enough to caress. "You should be careful what you wish for."

For some reason, it made her laugh, though the

sound melted into a moan.

That was better. "Keep rocking. I like having you squirming on my thigh."

Her eyes drifted open, oddly intent as they focused on his, and the rest of the room vanished. Lex's clever, intimate lighting, her carefully set stage, the heat in his blood—all of it conspired to melt everyone else into the background. "Gonna slap my fingers again?"

"I think..." Her throat worked under his hand. "I think I'm going to go dance."

He could tighten his fingers. Keep her with him. That was the eternal battle, the constant temptation. "You could do that."

"What do *you* want?" Lex reached down and rubbed her palm over the hard bulge of his cock through his pants.

People were watching them. Friends, members of his gang that might as well be family but would always be *his*. He was Dallas O'Kane, leader of Sector Four, and he was expected to get everything he wanted.

Which meant he was only allowed to want what he could get. Easy things. Casual things. Her fingers around his dick, her mouth, sucking him deep.

Not enough. Not tonight. "I want you to take off your panties."

She rose with a shiver, hesitating only a heartbeat before easing her thumbs under her skirt. The fabric rucked up a little, and she dragged her panties down. The skimpy black lace fell to her knees and then her ankles, tangling around the high spike heels on her shoes.

For one breathless moment, Dallas could only stare at her, high on the thrill of this woman's obedience.

"Hell, yeah! Throw me your underwear, Lex!"

Lex started, as if Ace's drunken words had drawn

her out of a fantasy, and she threw him a glare that was more flustered than angry as she kicked free of the lace. "You don't deserve my panties, jackass."

When Ace jerked to a halt two steps from the dais, Dallas realized he was glaring at him, too. Belatedly, he smoothed his features, but it didn't diminish his urge to smack the irreverent artist. "You're pushing your luck, Ace."

"I'm too pretty to kill," Ace drawled, full of fake bluster and confidence as he sprawled on the edge of the platform. "But if you two were having a private party..."

"If it were private, we'd go someplace else," Lex said quickly.

She was right, much as Dallas hated it in this moment. Just beyond Ace, Noelle was pinned between Jasper and Bren, their dance a slow grind. She looked blissful under their attentions, her skin already flushed with the slow heat of arousal.

The highlight of any party celebrating a couple taking marks tended to be the couple taking each other, a public consummation played out in loving, explicit detail. This wasn't a time for private moments. It was a time to celebrate Jas and Noelle and their crazy, dirty love.

Telling himself it *was* about them and not the buffer they provided, Dallas grinned up at Lex. "Think we can lure the happy couple back? Or should we start without them?"

But the moment was gone, and Lex's answer was light, breezy, with no hint of her previous intensity. "Why don't we just play it by ear?" she asked as she stepped off the dais and headed into the crowd.

Ace flashed him an apologetic look. "Sorry, boss."

Dallas sighed. "Get lost. Go find some woman

dumb enough to let your face between her legs."

"Oh, you mean damn near all of them?" Ace sprawled back on his elbows. "The trick is having a dexterous tongue, you know. If you brooded less and talked more, yours might—"

Dallas raised an eyebrow and *dared* Ace to finish the thought.

"...I think Amira's flagging me down," Ace said instead, coming to his feet in a rush. Before Dallas could say another word, the smartass disappeared into the mass of dancing bodies, vanishing as surely as Lex had.

Dallas tensed to follow, but forced his muscles to relax. He stretched both arms across the back of the couch and sprawled out his legs, every inch the lazy king surveying his court. Dallas O'Kane didn't chase after women who ran. Dallas O'Kane lifted a finger and women came running.

"I don't know how you're still in charge," a quiet voice murmured from behind him.

Craning his head, Dallas met Six's gaze and stilled his angry retort when he saw the honest bafflement in her eyes. As clumsy as the words were, there was a bone-deep need to understand hidden beneath them.

She'd come into adulthood under the brutal hand of a man too weak to hold his people without abuse and violence. Of course she didn't understand the obedience that came from loyalty and respect instead of crippling fear.

So he tried to explain. "This is my family, sweetheart. These are my people. I'm in charge because they trust me to make life a hell of a lot better for them than it would be without me. I don't need to beat them into line, and I don't need to prove I'm the strongest."

She blinked at him, her eyes huge and painfully

wary. "Everyone needs to prove they're strong."

"The truly strong only have to do it once." But no comprehension showed in her eyes. Maybe you couldn't explain safety to someone who'd never experienced it. Dallas contented himself with a smile and a shake of his head. "Stick around, Six. We'll revisit the topic every couple months and see if you've changed your mind."

From the way she watched him as she curled deeper into the chair, she thought he was insane. She probably wasn't wrong. As he settled facing forward again, his gaze caught on Lex moving toward Noelle, and his dick strained against his fly.

He was a liar. If he didn't have to prove he was in control, he'd be down there already, sliding a hand under Lex's dress while Noelle writhed against them both.

Strength. Control. Two things he needed more than life. Two things Lex shattered when she was around.

God help him, Six was right. He *was* insane.

"You're in my spot."

Bren laughed at Lex's words and lifted his head from Noelle's shoulder. "Pardon me."

"Lex, you have to share." Noelle's scolding tone was ruined by her smile as she stretched up and kissed Bren square on the lips. "But I've been waiting for my dance with you, so Bren and Jas will just have to deal with it."

"I don't share," Lex grumbled as the men melted away, headed for the bar in the corner.

Except the words weren't true. Share—that was one thing she always did, without fail. It was the secret to maintaining the harmony in their little gang, sexual freedom and pleasure without jealousy. Lex had always excelled at it, getting close but never *too* close.

So what the hell had happened?

She pressed her face to Noelle's cheek. "I'm losing my mind. I don't know if I'm cranky because I'm horny or because Dallas is driving me nuts."

"Aw, honey." Noelle wrapped her arms around her. "What did he do *now*?"

"I don't want to think about him." Lex drew her thumb over the new tattoo framing Noelle's throat. "This is beautiful on you. Did I tell you that?"

She shivered. "Ace works magic. I swear, it feels like more than just ink."

It must, because it seemed to have changed the way Noelle and Jasper looked at one another. "I'm happy for you."

Slender fingers tangled in Lex's hair, and Noelle pulled her down for a long, slow kiss. "I'm horny too," the other woman said against her lips. "You know Jasper's going to spend all night letting me stew before he gets around to fucking me."

"And you'll love every second of it," Lex said. Noelle was already soft against her, open and hungry in a way she recognized.

"Especially if you help him." Noelle dug her teeth into Lex's lower lip. "Are you going to help him?"

The two of them together burned so hot, and it would be easy to fall into them, to borrow a little of that fire for a while. Easy to walk away when it was over, too, secure in the knowledge that Jasper and Noelle had each other to hold.

As simple as it was arousing, as satisfying as it was *safe*. "Help him fuck you?" Lex asked softly, drawing aside the lacy white strap of Noelle's dress, baring her shoulder. "How would I do that?"

Noelle arched her neck, putting all of that gorgeous ink on display. "I was thinking we could be bad girls. Sometimes that inspires Jasper to hurry."

"So I'm a means to an end?" Lex couldn't keep her amusement out of the words. "I see how you are."

"I'm wretched." Noelle teased her hands over the curves of Lex's breasts. "A wicked, wicked girl."

"More like delicious." Lex watched as Noelle's dress slipped low enough to bare one hard nipple, then bent to circle it with her tongue.

"Oh, *oh*." Noelle clutched at her shoulders and moaned. "God, I love your tongue."

"More than mine?" Jasper stepped up behind Noelle, wrapped his arms around them both, and stroked Lex's cheek.

Noelle laughed and raised her arms, curling them around Jasper's neck. "Don't be jealous, baby."

"Oh, I'm not." He cupped her breast and met Lex's eyes. "Suck."

A command, but Lex was already so wound up she parted her lips without thinking. Pleasure thrummed in her body, a quick pulse that left her pussy aching as she drew Noelle's nipple deep into her mouth.

Noelle's soft cry drowned under dark laughter. Familiar fingers slid around Lex's waist, strong hands that found the flare of her hips as if every curve belonged to him. "I love watching you make her writhe," Dallas murmured against Lex's ear.

She shuddered. Her and Noelle, sandwiched between Jasper and Dallas. Lex had been here before, and she knew how it would end—with all four of them naked on the floor.

And she was helpless to stop it, helpless in a way she never was when Dallas wasn't part of the equation. Lex tilted her head back on his shoulder, both making room and inviting him to lick the taste of her mouth from the tight, slick peak of Noelle's breast.

And he did, flicking his tongue over Noelle's nipple. When she gasped, he gave her teeth, more than Lex would have used so soon. But Dallas had a rougher touch, and Noelle seemed to like it.

"Fuck," Jasper rasped. He combed his fingers through Noelle's hair and urged her head to one side, baring her neck for a slow, lingering kiss. "I'll fuck you, sweetheart. Nice and hard, the way you like it—" he glanced at Dallas, "—but only if you make Lex come."

Sleepy eyes met hers. "Do you want that?" Noelle asked, already tracing the neckline of Lex's dress. The words held a breathless undertone, a plea for her to play along with the fantasy, the one where Jasper withheld satisfaction until Noelle satisfied every one of their lurid demands.

Oh, the hunger. Lex swallowed a moan and nodded. "I won't make it easy, either," she lied. "You'll have to be so, so good."

Noelle actually shivered, and Dallas chuckled again as he caressed Lex's cheek. "She'll have to be so, so bad. Put her on her knees, Jasper."

He did it with nothing more than a twist of his hand in her hair, as if Noelle's body had been finely tuned to his touch. He sank to the floor behind her, one hand already sliding the ruffled hem of her skirt up. "Fingers or tongue?" he asked roughly, then swatted Noelle's ass without waiting for an answer. "Tongue tonight, I think."

No straight-faced adherence to fantasy could keep the glee from Noelle's eyes as she eased her hands under the hem of Lex's dress. But there was something else there too—awareness. Noelle bared only Lex's thighs, holding the fabric tight across Lex's hips, shielding the new tattoo on her lower abdomen.

If Dallas noticed Noelle's precision, he didn't understand the significance. He was too busy wrapping a hand around Lex's throat and whispering silky commands. "Part your legs, love. Let Noelle and her sweet tongue at you."

Lex knew she'd fall without Dallas holding her up. She leaned back, sliding her hands into his pants pockets and drawing in a shaky breath when her ass rubbed against his erection. "This makes you so damn hard," she said softly.

"Of course it does." Dallas stroked the top of Noelle's head. "I love watching her bury her face in your pussy. Tonight everyone's going to love watching it."

They'd drawn stares already. Part of it was the attention due Jasper and Noelle, but Lex knew the rest revolved around morbid curiosity. They were watching her and Dallas. Probably had a fucking pool going. *Fifty credits says they blow up tonight.*

Lex laid her hand over Dallas's. "You feeling a little wild, Declan?"

He tensed behind her, and the fingers around her throat tightened. "When am I not?"

"Mmm." She eased her legs apart. Noelle was there in the next moment, lips soft on the skin of her inner thighs. A tease, nothing more, sweet kisses that tormented Lex and taunted Jasper with the barest hint of disobedience. When Noelle's gaze met hers, there was mischief there, an awareness of her own power.

Jasper pushed Noelle's dress higher, revealing the bare curves of her hips. His hand slipped past the fabric, up to her hair, and he turned her head, guiding her mouth.

Her tongue grazed Lex's clit, wet and rasping. The

sudden sensation rocked Lex onto her toes, arching against Noelle's mouth and Dallas's hand, which was still caged around her throat.

He laughed near her ear, breath tickling heat over sensitive skin. "Look at her, Lexie. Those big eyes aren't so innocent anymore." Dallas's fingers covered Jasper's, tangled in Noelle's hair, and he braced the back of her head before rocking his hips, forcing Lex closer to her tongue.

He was in control. The thought flitted through Lex's mind faster than the helpless zing of pleasure that shook her. And just like the pleasure, it circled around, tighter and tighter. Dallas had the control, and even though she reveled in it, she also wanted to take it.

One day, she would.

Noelle moaned helplessly, and Lex opened her eyes just in time to watch Jasper slide home, his jaw clenched. Noelle's eyes fluttered shut as bliss rolled over her features, and she renewed her attentions, slicking her tongue into Lex with quick, hungry thrusts before sliding up to work her clit with newly inspired dedication.

Dallas flexed his fingers around Lex's throat, but his next rock was more of a grind, rubbing his caged erection against her ass. "They make a pretty picture, don't they? Except..." He moved his hand from Noelle's head to Lex's dress, winding the fabric higher, giving Lex an unobstructed view of Noelle's lust-clouded eyes.

"Better." Dallas slid the slinky fabric over Lex's skin.

Jasper wrapped his fingers around Noelle's wrists, one after the other, and pulled them behind her back. It left her balanced on her knees, rocking precariously as he eased his cock in and out of her pussy. Every thrust jolted her just a little, pressing her mouth more firmly to Lex's wet flesh, turning her gentle, eager caresses into hard swipes of tongue and the barest graze of teeth.

The room might as well have dissolved in a haze. The mounting heat reduced Lex's vision into a series of flashes—ink on skin, pink lips, the wet glisten of Jasper's dick as he fucked Noelle faster. Harder.

"So fucking beautiful." Dallas muttered the words against her cheek, his lips brushing the corner of her mouth. He had her pinned against his chest, her legs splayed wide, held up by the brutally gentle hand at her throat and one iron forearm across her hips. "Come for her, Lexie," he whispered. "Show her she's a good girl and come all over her hungry tongue."

"No." The denial was as much for her as it was for Noelle.

His growl vibrated through his chest, more amused than irritated. "Are you teaching her to be as disobedient as you are?"

"Never," Lex panted. For Noelle, disobedience was a means to an end, a reason for Jasper to punish her until she came.

Jas slowed his thrusts and shifted both of Noelle's wrists to one hand. He leaned over her, pausing to slip his thumb into her mouth before massaging it in a firm circle over Lex's clit. "Get her off. Now."

Noelle hummed her agreement, her tongue slicking over and around Jasper's thumb and then lower, moving in the rhythm Lex had taught her over lazy nights curled together, with or without him, the one Noelle knew twisted her into dizzy knots.

Lex gave up trying to still her hips. They rocked in anticipation of every lick, and the world narrowed even more, shrank until the only things that existed were touching her. Her dress, chafing her nipples with every movement. Noelle's mouth. Jasper's fingers. Dallas.

She came with a cry she could barely hear through the buzz in her ears, but it had to be loud because it burned her throat like whiskey. Like a scream. Pleasure and relief, and beyond it all a hunger Lex couldn't quite understand. A need for more, for less, for *something*.

The world tilted and took her along for the ride, and she realized belatedly that Dallas had spilled them both to the floor. He knelt a foot in front of Noelle and Jasper, with Lex sprawled across his lap, her knees on either side of his and her face level with Noelle's.

Noelle licked her own lips with a husky laugh before straining forward to kiss Lex. "You didn't make me work for it."

"I tried." Dallas's hands were sliding up Lex's thighs, and she tried to wiggle away.

He laughed and hauled her back, splaying one hand across her belly as he lifted the other to Noelle's mouth. "Jasper?"

"His turn," Jasper whispered, and Noelle parted her lips without looking away from Lex, even as she swirled her tongue around Dallas's fingers until they were slick and wet.

Lex was still squirming when he dropped his hand and stroked her clit. "I told you you'd get a chance to ride my hand. Think you can come again before Jas fucks her over the edge?"

He knew the answer. Sometimes she felt like he knew everything—the only explanation for his raging arrogance. Lex spun around and crawled onto his lap, folding her arms tight around his neck. "You have to make me," she challenged, her mouth close to his. "Can you?"

Hunger tightened his eyes. And something else, too—a hint of danger. She'd challenged him, and he wouldn't back down. Not here, surrounded by his people. It wouldn't matter that most were glued to the spectacle of whatever Jasper was doing to drive those crazy, desperate noises from Noelle's throat.

Dallas O'Kane never let a challenge lie.

He gripped her bare hips and dragged her against him, aligning the unforgiving steel of his cock with her clit. There was nothing slow or easy about his movements as he caught her gaze, held it, and rolled her hips in even, brutally direct circles. "I could make you come so many ways."

"Not with a little dry humping," she lied. Her hands itched to slip between them, to open his pants and bare his cock and *then* ride him. "Noelle fucked me with her tongue. You have to do better than this."

He just smiled and leaned closer, until his lips brushed hers. "Noelle needed her tongue *and* Jasper's thumb. I don't. All I need..." He caught both of her arms and crossed her wrists at the small of her back before pinning them with his hands. "Just like this."

The silent, imperious command inherent in the position made her shiver as the ridge of his erection nestled between her pussy lips. Too much, too direct. If he'd been wearing denim, it would have hurt. But he'd donned soft, supple leather tonight, and she was wet, so wet. She took a deep, shaky breath, and even that was enough to slide her over the hard line of his cock through his slippery pants.

Her inhalation caught in her throat, turned into something low and hungry.

Dallas captured her lower lip between his teeth and teased his tongue over it. Nothing else—no movement, no rocking, just the tip of his tongue, sliding back and forth and back and forth, slick with suggestion even before he closed his mouth on her lip and sucked softly.

A taunt and a promise, and it wasn't *fair* that he could do this to her with the tiniest of touches. Lex trembled through another blinding spike of sensation and tried to free her hands.

He held tight.

She struggled without thinking, lightly but still enough to shift her on his lap. Wet leather stroked her clit, and she bit her tongue trying to hold back a moan.

His gaze held more than a hint of danger now. His cool detachment had shattered, leaving behind a hot-eyed man who bared his teeth in a feral grin. "You want to get away, love?"

Yes. "No." Both answers were true, but neither was quite enough.

He tightened his grip on her wrists and watched her face as if the rest of the room had simply dissolved. Even Noelle's throaty cries of release drifted away as he lowered his mouth to her ear. "But you want to try."

Telling, not asking. The words shivered over her, his voice like fingers on her skin. Truth, but he didn't understand. "I want you to stop screwing around."

"You are so fucking bossy." Rough words, but they came out edged with affection, and he started that steady rock again, grinding her clit against slick leather. "Ask for it. Ask me to get you off."

She wouldn't. She *would not.* Then the vise twisted, a tense ache that enveloped her. "Please," she ground out. "Please—"

He soothed her with low murmurs against her cheek and moved faster, his fingers clenching every time he rocked her against his cock. He kissed her jaw and her cheek before his mouth found her throat, his lips parting only so he could close his teeth with a hiss of triumph.

The bite was just as delicious as the heat that swept through her. She wanted it all—pain, pleasure, even the anger.

The passion.

Lex closed her eyes as the sensations collided, blistering and undeniable. She came again, and this time it was with Dallas's name on her lips.

Her back hit the floor as pleasure ebbed, and Dallas loomed over her. Noelle sat curled in Jasper's lap a few feet away, both of them as lost in their own world as Dallas seemed lost in her.

He reared back and reached for his belt, but his hands froze as his gaze swept down her body. The ragged hunger gripping his features twisted as his lips curled down and his eyebrows drew together.

Lex followed his stare. Her dress had ridden up, revealing her new tattoo, dark and damning against her skin.

He didn't look happy. He didn't look anything but confused, and she swallowed, suddenly feeling just as spun.

Then she whispered the only words that came to mind. "Happy birthday."

He blinked, but that was the only reaction she got before his face smoothed into lazy amusement, the king of Sector Four at his finest. He might as well have been sprawled on a throne instead of kneeling over her, his hand still crushing his belt buckle. Arrogance rolled off him, and the dangerous promise from before seemed tiny and harmless next to what filled him now.

"You're a few months early," he drawled, tracing his finger over one of the thorny vines. "But that's all right." He lifted his gaze to hers, and the easy warmth in his voice didn't reach those predatory eyes. "I'll take it."

Oh, *shit*.

Seemed like miracles could happen outside the walls of Eden after all, because he'd rendered Lex speechless.

Not that she needed to talk. Her actions were speaking loud enough all on their own, and so was that ink etched from one hip to the other. Ace's work, without a doubt, recognizable not just by his skill and style but his stubborn adherence to the idea of truth in art.

Trust Ace to turn a simple name into a maze of subtext and hidden messages. Like the rosebuds, so tightly furled, except for the one wrapped around the *s*. That one looked like it was struggling to bloom in the shadow of his name. The vine climbing the *D*, on the other hand, was thick with thorns, more than one jabbing into the calligraphic letter. One thorn glistened with a barely visible drop of blood.

That felt about right. Sharp edges and blood, and dragging his gaze from the tattoo only showed him Lex, staring up at him in some confused tangle of brashness and nerves. She might well be too scared to speak— God knew she *should* be—but she wouldn't show terror with everyone watching.

She wouldn't scratch his face off, either. Probably. Without taking his eyes from hers, he unhooked the carabiner from his belt and held it out. "Bren. My desk, top drawer on the right. Bring what's there."

Bren moved to obey, and the jangle of keys almost eclipsed Lex's words, ground out between clenched teeth. "You wouldn't."

A glance around the room showed plenty of people

scurrying to find a way to seem occupied. Half of them were probably straining to hear their words over the music, but most couldn't without edging closer than they were willing to get.

Well, they'd get their show soon enough. He stroked a lock of Lex's hair away from her cheek and wondered if he'd end up bitten for his trouble. "What wouldn't I do, Lexie?"

She struggled beneath him and tried to sit up. "It's not funny—"

He caught her throat, laying his thumb over her rapidly beating pulse as he closed his fingers. Not hard enough to choke, but the precise gentleness of it shut her up faster than roughness would have. She was frozen, half-raised on her elbows, and he leaned down to whisper in her ear. "I'm not joking."

Lex shuddered. "Don't," she rasped. "If you do, you can't take it back."

"Can you take the tattoo back?"

She bit her lip. "I guess I deserve it."

"A fate worse than death, huh?" She'd etched an invitation into her skin, but now *he* was the monster, dragging her to certain death by the hair. It stirred a dark frustration that spiked when Noelle made an angry noise and reached for them. Before she could open her mouth, Dallas jabbed a finger at Jasper. "You keep your woman out of shit that doesn't concern her."

Jasper locked an arm around her and pulled her back. "Not our thing, remember?" he whispered. "Theirs."

"That's right, baby girl. This is me and Dallas." Lex pushed up into his grip, challenging him not only with her movements but with a bold stare. If he didn't pull back, she'd end up grinding bruises into her own skin, forcing him to leave the mark of his hand around her throat.

No winning there. He loathed the idea of leaving marks on her flesh that weren't purposeful and planned. But the only other choice was retreat, and he didn't know if he could back down with her staring at him. *Daring* him. She'd get what she wanted one way or another...and maybe that wasn't a bad thing. Not with all he was about to take.

He gave her the lingering victory and locked his arm. He didn't need to tighten his fingers, not with her shoving up into his hand. If she wanted bruises, she'd get them.

After too many long moments, she relented, easing back to gasp for breath. The delicate skin of her throat was red, but she acted as though he'd answered a question. "The collar better not be one you've put on anyone else."

He smoothed his thumb over her ravaged skin. "Look at you, jumping to conclusions. You knew what would come of this tattoo, didn't you?"

"Am I wrong?"

"No. Am I?"

But she wouldn't give in, not that much. She averted her eyes. "Your boy's back."

Bren must have run *and* taken the stairs three at a time to get to Dallas's office and back so quickly. But he wasn't out of breath, and his expression remained calm as he held out the collar. Dallas accepted it with absent thanks and held it up.

It was some damn expensive custom work, made from smooth, supple leather. Flat at the back, it split into four narrow cords on each side, the top and bottom lengths forming a frame for the pieces woven in and out of sterling silver Celtic knots. And at the front, carved with amazing precision, the O'Kane logo, situated where it would nestle in the hollow of her throat.

A far cry from the plain black leather he'd buckled around women's throats in the past, and Lex would know it.

She swallowed hard and met his gaze. Waiting.

No one interfered. No one would, and that made him move slowly. He swept her hair aside, twisting it around his hand and then up. "Hold this, love."

She kept her eyes locked on his as she braced her hands on the cushion and crept out from under him just far enough to sit. She lifted her hands, fingers sliding over his as she took over holding up the mass of her hair.

He'd seen that look in her eyes. The one that said he'd pushed her past fear or anger into driving, vengeful lust. Never before had he taken what that look offered. Blowjobs and spankings were good clean fun, but he didn't fuck a woman he had to share. Not even Lex.

If he wrapped this scrap of leather around her throat, he wouldn't have to share her—and if he dwelled on that, his hands would shake before he got it fastened. Still moving carefully, he laid the etched centerpiece against the hollow of her throat and admired it for a moment before fastening the collar.

"How does it look?" she asked—low, breathless.

He told her the truth. "Beautiful."

She glanced around, taking note of all the rapt stares, and her voice dropped even lower. "What now?"

Dallas smoothed her dress down before rising to offer the silent crowd a lazy smile. He held out one hand and waited for Lex to take it. She was still wary, unsure of what she'd gotten herself into.

Good. He wouldn't be the only one, he'd just hide it better. He tugged her to her feet and draped an arm over her shoulder. "Now we let Jasper and Noelle have their moment back."

"I don't think it'll matter. Noelle wants your blood." Lex shook her head. "I'll have to talk to her. Later."

A glance at Noelle proved the truth of that. She didn't look like a soft little city girl now. With ink around her throat and her eyes burning with protective anger, she looked like an O'Kane, one who might not be satisfied with his blood if she could get a knee—or something worse—close to his balls. Jasper was talking to her in a low, even voice, but the words didn't seem to be banking that inner fire.

Jasper was either going to have the hottest time of his life tonight trying to tame that, or he'd end up sleeping alone. If he found himself in a cold bed, Dallas really would owe him for fucking up what should have been a good night. "Think Jas can handle her?"

Lex flashed him a look of sharp rebuke. "If you had any question about that, you should never have let him mark her."

He bit back his retort—that the girl who'd stumbled into their midst wasn't the same one slowly bending under Jasper's words and touches, and Lex should know since she'd been partly responsible for that transformation. But he'd seen the hints of this fierce tiger in the clumsy kitten Noelle had been a month ago, and he was confident Jasper could handle anything she threw at him.

It didn't mean he'd always *enjoy* it, though. "Collared all of two minutes and you're already second guessing my decisions, huh? You could at least get me a drink first."

She exhaled—it could have been a laugh or a scoff—and nodded once. "Yes, sir." Then she headed in the direction of the bar set up along one end of the room.

Prickly. That was fine. The full impact of what he'd just done was starting to catch up with him, which made the walk back to his couch take forever. The dais was empty, and even Six had abandoned her spot. No one would tread too near with his temper presumably still close to the surface.

If only they knew. The momentary flash of outrage at Lex's presumption had vanished under the gut instinct to turn it to his advantage. He'd missed his window of opportunity on collaring her during the Wilson Trent blow-up, but this time he wouldn't give her a chance to get skittish.

It was a pity that pressing this particular opportunity involved skipping a few key steps. Discussion. Negotiation. The setting of guidelines and the drawing of boundaries. Collaring was ownership, however temporary, and a smart man made sure his idea of ownership fit before trying to shove a woman into it. Doing otherwise tended to end badly.

Lex came back to the dais, a whiskey triple in one hand. The ice clinked as she held it out to him, the perfect picture of submission, ruined only by the glimpse of fire he caught before her lashes lowered.

She reached up, and the collar shifted as the top of her halter dress loosened and fell to bare her chest. The slinky red fabric slipped down to her hips, then the floor, and she stood there, clad only in his ink, his leather, and her high-heeled shoes.

So much for giving Noelle and Jasper back their spotlight. "Thanks," he drawled before patting his thigh. "Care to sit?"

"We can do better than that." She dropped to her knees.

He'd lost count of the number of times she'd blown

him right here, just like this, and every memory paled beside the reality of having her on her knees. Burning, like that collar was the only thing holding back the kind of explosion that would singe a man to ash.

Sometimes she was a little scary when she looked at him like that, and fuck if he didn't like it. "I don't know, love. The way you're looking at me, I don't trust you not to use your teeth."

She laid her hands on his knees, slid them up his thighs. "Has that ever stopped us before?"

"Not really." He rested the hand holding his glass on the back of the couch and slid the other into her unbound hair. "Is this what you were going for, Lexie? Is this what you wanted?"

"I always do." His belt buckle clicked, and leather whispered over leather as she drew open the belt. She reached for the button on his pants, the zipper—all by touch, as if she knew this moment too well to even look down.

He tightened his fingers in her hair, a quick tug of warning. "So you're going to swallow my dick like nothing's changed?"

"You want something else?" she asked, pulling against his grip as she leaned over his legs. Closer. "Is that why you asked me to sit on your lap? So I could ride you right here? Now?"

The first time he buried his cock in her, no one else would be watching. He'd been waiting too long to share *any* part of that first time, even the sight of her coming for him. "No," he murmured, pulling her hair hard enough to edge her chin up. "But being collared means you get my dick when I give it to you."

"Oh." Her hands stilled. "So that's how it's gonna be."

He left his drink balanced precariously on the back

of the couch and stroked his thumb over her lips. His skin was chilled from the ice, and her breath burned as hot as her gaze. "Is that a surprise? I remember you saying you knew all about what gets me off."

"Of course." She smiled, easy and bland.

Sometimes it amazed him, how fast she could shutter her eyes. A product of her training from Sector Two, no doubt. Sighing, he released her hair. "That ain't it."

Lex sat back on her heels and folded her hands in her lap. Waiting, silent and obedient and so sweetly submissive they were attracting stares again. Lex on her knees was nothing new, but Lex in a posture of surrender...

This is what he got for trying to play the game without discussing the rules first. She was gazing at him like an empty-headed doll, and he had no one to blame but himself. "Get dressed, Lex. Tomorrow we'll have a talk."

She snatched up her dress but didn't bother slipping into it before she stalked off, through the crowd and out the door.

"Well done, old man," Dallas grumbled before draining his whiskey. The party would go on, and he'd sit and endure their looks and their barely concealed speculation, but by God if one of them dared pity him—

Well fucking done, indeed.

Jasper stared at him in sympathy. It wasn't overt, but Dallas had known him long enough to see the commiseration beneath his seemingly impassive features. Then he broke the awkward near-silence with a muttered question to Noelle, one she answered with an eager nod.

At some point, the flogger had found its way from the dais to the main floor. Bren handed it over to

Jasper, who tested its weight and balance in his hand before drawing the suede tails slowly through his fingers—and then across Noelle's bare, upraised ass.

The crowd fell silent, and even Dallas held his breath as Jasper began to twirl the flogger, rotating his wrist until the tails swirled in a smooth figure eight. The tense silence broke when he let the first hint of suede thud against Noelle's skin, and her grateful moan ripped through the room.

A show. The kind that would please his woman but also distract a drama-hungry crowd from gossiping about Lex's sudden departure.

It was working, too. By the time Jasper began to intensify his efforts, landing harder and faster blows on Noelle's reddening skin, people had either gone back to screwing each other, or they were watching with a rapt attentiveness that left no room for thoughts about Dallas.

And fuck if Dallas didn't owe him for it. Big time.

4

Lex had a splitting headache, a sore neck, and a powerful urge to crawl back under the covers and hide from the world. All three were her own damn fault, and irritating enough to drive her from her bed and into the shower.

Ten minutes to linger under the steamy water, and she forced herself out. She dried her hair first, then wound the strands into an intricate mass of braids, a style she hadn't worn since her days in Sector Two. More than a decade, and her fingers still moved automatically, smoothing every hair into position.

She'd never be rid of that goddamned place.

The last thing she did was fasten Dallas's collar around her neck. It was exquisite, easily the most beautiful thing she'd ever owned, and the weight of it threatened to strangle her. But what had she expected?

That he'd lock her in a collar and suddenly *change*, read her mind and give her exactly what she wanted?

Maybe she *had* expected that, and why not? Fuck, if a man wanted to own a woman like her, he'd damn well better earn it.

With that rebellion fresh in her mind, she wrapped herself in armor—a boned leather corset and jeans that sat low enough on her hips to bare her fresh ink. Every bit of ownership carefully framed, from the tattoo to her collar to the darkening bruises on her skin.

Let him look at what he'd bought.

He answered on her second knock with a muffled, "Come in," and she pushed open the door to find him bent over the desk with a stack of papers under one hand and his hacked computing tablet under the other.

His scowl faded when he glanced up, but frustrated tension still knotted his shoulders. "Lex."

His gaze raked over her, and she welcomed it. All the other bullshit aside, she turned him on, quick and hard, so at least she wouldn't be the only one twisted up. "I came to discuss my duties."

He frowned. "Duties? Really?"

"Hmm, maybe not." She dropped into a chair and crossed her legs. "You made it pretty fucking clear last night this is all about appearances."

"Is that what I did?" He shoved the papers aside. "Why don't we back on up to the beginning of this tangle?" He pointed at her tattoo. "Don't pretend *I'm* the one who set this off."

After the humiliation of the night before, she'd pretend whatever she pleased. "I got a little ink, and you jumped at the chance to put me in my place."

"No, I took you up on your invitation."

"Did you?"

"Yeah. But I made a mistake." Dallas jerked open

his desk drawer, rummaged around, and pulled out tobacco and rolling papers. "We skipped right over the important part, and I know better."

She watched his hands, mesmerized by the leashed strength there. "The negotiation, you mean."

"Mmm." He measured out the tobacco with easy, absentminded movements, most of his attention focused on her. "You put me in a hell of a spot, love. Normally, I'd tell you to take that collar off until you agree to what comes along with it, but you forced my hand a little, didn't you?"

Lex would have admitted as much—hell, she *had* the night before, but now... "I didn't force you. You had other options."

"Forced my hand, not me." He paused with the tobacco-filled paper pinched between his finger and thumb and gave her a level look. "Let's cut through the bullshit. We've been dancing around this for years, but until last month, I never thought you'd consider a collar. Because you don't get to be just another girl in my bed, Lexie. None of the others has been one of us. You know where this puts you."

He'd had women in and out of his bed, always collared and always outsiders, women who came and went like clockwork. *Shift change,* Lex had ruefully called it.

No more.

"It means I have *duties,*" she said, feigning a patience she didn't feel. "Is it the word that offends, or the fact that I'm not slobberingly focused on the many things I get to do to your dick once you deign to let me touch it?"

His gaze dropped to her throat, where her fingers had come to rest on the collar. Lex tensed but refused to jerk them away, and he clenched his jaw as he turned his attention back to his task. "All right. Duties is fair enough, as long as touching my dick isn't one of them."

As if she'd been the one to deny him. "That's the funny thing about these collars." She scratched one fingernail over the rough surface of the O'Kane emblem. "Most men put them on women they plan to regularly fuck the shit out of."

His lips twitched. "I put them on women who get off on having me fuck the shit out of them however, wherever and whenever I want."

Even the words tightened her nipples, raised goose bumps on her skin. "But you think that isn't me."

"You can flip the submission on like a switch, darling, but you sure as fuck weren't getting off on it last night."

She crossed her arms over her chest. "Noelle likes punishment. I don't."

Dallas finished rolling the cigarette before offering it to her. "That wasn't punishment, which proves my damn point. We both know better than to play games when no one knows the rules."

He kept talking in circles, and they were getting nowhere. "Okay, I'll play along." She leaned forward and snatched the cigarette. "If keeping me off your dick wasn't punishment, what was it?"

His lighter was shiny silver and etched with a skull, and it reflected the light as he swept it up and flicked it open. "Foreplay."

Lex glared at him over the flame. "We've had six years of that. Do we really need more?"

Dallas grinned. "And here I thought you girls trained us this way on purpose."

She rolled her eyes and lit the tip of the cigarette, puffing until it caught in a gentle smolder. "Rules. You show me yours, and I'll show you mine."

"Control, Lex. I want it." He snapped the lighter

shut to emphasize his point before starting to roll a second cigarette. "Sometimes I'll want you to give it to me. Sometimes I'll want to take it. You need to be right with both."

It pulled the air out of her lungs. Part of her wanted to blame it on the smooth tobacco smoke, but she couldn't, not with her attention riveted to the lines of his face as he stared down at the paper in his hand.

Control. Oh, how she'd hungered to let go for a little while, to have Dallas hold it all, but the way he spoke proved he didn't know. Maybe not how much, or maybe not at all.

She opened her mouth to say something, anything remotely coherent. Instead, she sucked in a rough, ragged breath.

He lifted the second cigarette, and his gaze flicked to hers as he drew his tongue along the edge of the rolling paper, licking it like a lover.

"I don't know if I *can* give it," she said in a rush. "Not entirely. But you can take it. Me."

After a pause, he nodded. "Here's what we're going to do. You're going to take a day and think. Really think. And then you're going to tell me what you like, what you don't like, and what's straight-up off-limits."

There were no such things as boundaries, no limits when it came to Dallas. "And if I don't need a day?"

He lit his own cigarette and exhaled toward the ceiling. "Take it anyway. Seriously consider it—for me."

"You want me to...what? Make a list?"

"Yes," he said without hesitation. "An honest one."

"Of things I don't want you to do." Jesus, it'd take her all day to think of *one*. "All right. You, too."

He smiled and nodded, then changed the subject. "Tell me what you've heard about Sector Three."

"What everyone's heard—that it's falling apart.

Wilson Trent may have been a piss-poor leader, but he was a leader. Now they don't have anybody calling the shots." Lex tilted her head. "You're not thinking of staging a takeover, are you? The other sector leaders might not want Three and all its problems, but if it looks like you're expanding your power base, they'll flip their shit. Guaranteed."

"It'd mean going back to late nights and double shifts," he admitted. "The money might not make up for it at first, especially if we have to bring in new bodies to hold the territory. And we'll need real friendly neighbors in Two and Five." He paused. "So, no. No takeover. Not yet, anyway."

Lex stiffened. "I wouldn't count on Two. Cerys is only *real friendly* when it serves her purposes. And who the hell knows what Mac Fleming's doing half the time over in Five."

"He's cooking drugs," Dallas replied, his mouth twisting around his distaste. "Getting as rich as we are too, and maybe richer, since he plays both sides. Medicinal and recreational."

Dallas hadn't minded availing himself of Fleming's regenerative technology when Lex and Noelle had both had bullet holes in them. "He keeps to himself. No reason to cause trouble—but no reason to throw in and back you on anything, either."

Clamping his cigarette between his lips, Dallas shoved everything on his desk to one side with a careless sweep of his arm and unrolled a meticulously sketched map of Eden and the surrounding sectors. The city walls formed a near-perfect circle in the middle, with the eight main roads out of the city thrusting out like spokes on a wheel.

Dallas thumped an ashtray down in the corner near Sector Seven to secure the edge and frowned at the map. "Mad brought back some updates," he muttered around the cigarette as he jabbed his finger at an area marked with fresh ink in a slightly darker color. "Seven's in trouble. Eden seized two-thirds of their fields. Mad thinks the city's building more wind farms."

Lex rose and bent over the map, bracing her elbows on two of the other curled edges. "The ones they've already got plus the solar arrays aren't enough?"

Dallas bit off a bitter laugh. "Probably. But hell, what are a few potato farms compared to the ladies in Eden getting to use their fancy hair dryers whenever they want?"

No wonder people had been flooding into Sector Six and pushing outward, toward the wide, empty spaces away from the city. "I wonder what Eight'll do when Seven empties."

"Eight's always tricky." Dallas traced his finger over the manufacturing district that made up a healthy part of that sector. "They have to walk the line. If they don't provide Eden with the supplies they want, the city'll seize those factories. And if they make it look too profitable..."

Most of the sectors had buildings that predated the Flares—tenements for workers, factories, and warehouses that had been built to support the day-to-day functioning of Eden. But Eight and Five were the only ones with facilities that still ran, industries deemed too valuable to destroy—for now.

Three had had one too, once upon a time, a sprawling plant that produced electronics. Lex still remembered watching it burn from the top floor of the Orchid House in Sector Two, the night sky alight with flames and intermittent explosions—like the fireworks she'd read about, only deadlier.

She straightened and propped her hands on her

hips. "It's all conjecture. But you know what comes next."

Dallas crushed his cigarette into the ashtray hard enough to slide the heavy glass three inches across the desk. "Yeah. I get a pretty invitation from Cerys. And the meeting will go pretty much however she wants it to, once she's buried all the sector leaders in booze and beautiful women."

"Don't hate the player," Lex teased with a wry smile. "Stay on her good side and it won't matter. Remember—she's brilliant *and* ruthless."

"Oh, I think I know something about women like that," he drawled, rolling up the map again. "Speaking of brilliance, turn a little of yours toward Six, huh? The girl, not the sector. Bren seems to think she's trustworthy, but maybe he's not seeing clearly. Dragging Wilson Trent back here for her to kill doesn't fit my definition of a courting gift, but his idea of flirting might be as twisted as his sense of humor."

"Does everything have to be about fucking?" Lex straightened with a shrug. "Maybe he just wanted to do something nice for her."

Both of Dallas's eyebrows swept up, but a moment later he was grinning at her. "You beautiful, bloodthirsty bitch."

"Mmm. Remember that when you think about pushing my buttons." Lex brushed against him as she leaned over to put out her cigarette in the ashtray. He was warm and solid, the kind of hard that came from working and fighting in equal measure. "Your place, this time tomorrow. I'll bring my list."

She got the satisfaction of hearing his breath catch, but he managed his warm, easy drawl. "I'll clear my schedule."

"Hell yeah, you will."

ace

Jared's loft might have been wall-to-wall bare brick and exposed steel beams, but it was the swankest place in Sector Four that didn't belong to an O'Kane, and the only place outside of the compound that Ace had ever felt at home.

Sprawled on the expensive leather couch, he eyed the new sculpture of a frolicking couple that dominated one corner. It wasn't bad, for a post-Flare carving, but more loving detail had been given to the man's undeniably impressive cock than to the rest of him. The woman was a masterwork of tits and ass, with a rapturous look on her face that skated close to being comical.

Not refined enough for Jared's tastes, which could mean only one thing. "New patron's giving you gifts already, eh?"

"She's eager to please." Jared handed him a

whiskey on the rocks. "But then, she'd never had an orgasm before."

So few of the women in Eden had, even the ones who moved in less elite circles than Noelle once did. Ace took a sip before gesturing to the statue with his glass. "If you put that look on her face, I'm not surprised she's buying you presents."

"Better." Jared dropped to sit in the chair opposite the couch. "I taught her how to get there herself, too."

Which was one of the many reasons he was a more successful whore than Ace had ever been. Ace's artist-in-search-of-muse shtick had opened plenty of pocketbooks and parted more than his share of trembling Eden thighs, but Jared's reputation as a connoisseur of female pleasure earned him mindless devotion and gifts that pushed him past well-off and straight into obscenely wealthy.

There'd been a time when Ace had envied his friend that success, a time before he'd fallen in with the O'Kanes and learned to untangle sex from competition and desperation. "You and Lex should exchange pointers. Have you *seen* what she's got Cunningham's daughter doing on stage at the Broken Circle?"

"Not yet, but I heard it was positively stunning."

Stunning was a pale word to describe what Noelle and Lex got up to. "If one of Eden's angels making Lex scream for mercy turns your crank, hell yeah. You should come around next week and watch."

"And get the hard sell on signing up with the O'Kanes?" Jared shook his head. "I'm not a joiner, Ace. I don't play well with others."

He waved a hand. "Don't worry about Dallas. Didn't you hear? He finally collared Lex. We've all got a month, minimum, before he even comes up for air."

"Really now?" Jared swirled the ice in the bottom

of his nearly empty glass. "Is he still interested in information about Councilman Woods?"

The question brought a pang of guilt. He came to hang out with Jared because he enjoyed the man's company, and had spent years ignoring Dallas's increasingly pointed suggestions that he leverage that friendship into a source of information. But asking about Woods hadn't been a suggestion, it had been an order.

Even Ace didn't ignore orders. "Yeah," he admitted. "Full disclosure, brother. I'd have asked eventually—the boss told me I had to. But I can tell Dallas you don't have anything, and that'll be the end of it."

Jared looked away and finally said, "He doesn't keep to Eden. Might find him out here in the sectors sometime, if you figured out where to look."

It felt carefully phrased. Deft, though Jared was always deft. Ace wasn't a fan of having to pick and choose his words or when to let his silence do the talking, so he filed the tidbit away and changed the subject. "If you don't want to swing around the club, I could always bring a party to you."

His friend ignored the offer. "He'll owe me one. Your boss."

Ace's blood chilled. "Is it that dangerous? Fuck, man. I'll go to my grave for O'Kane, if that's what I have to do, but the gang's got my back. Don't go out on a limb for him if you're not gonna take protection."

"Relax. At best, I might spook a few rich ladies." Jared grinned. "The city has them to spare, and so do I. But he'll owe me, all the same."

"Gladly, if you can give him anything. Dallas wants to spike his morning whiskey with this bastard's blood."

"Then I'll keep it in mind." Jared finished his drink and clinked the ice in his glass. "Another?"

It'd take two, minimum, to get the taste of politics out of his mouth. "You know it," he replied, holding out his glass. "Now, about that party. You have got to meet this new girl who's doing shows with me. She's got a dirty fucking mind *and* she's inventive."

Jared poured the refills with a chuckle. "I'm sure she's wonderful, but is there any particular reason you're dying to bring her around here? You O'Kanes have plenty of filthy parties."

Plenty of parties he spent watching Cruz count Rachel's teeth with his tongue. "What, I can't miss hanging with an old friend?"

"I can't help but be curious as to the source of this sudden nostalgia."

Ace produced his best leer. "Maybe I miss refined debauchery. We can do wonderful things to a lady when we work together."

Jared wasn't fooled. "Does it have anything to do with how studiously you've avoided talking about Rachel lately?"

"Have I?" He hadn't thought he'd been that obvious, but he'd mostly been trying to avoid thinking about Rachel at all. Life was better simple, and there was nothing simple about the tangle of emotions evoked by her and Cruz and their fucking tongues. "Nothing to tell. She's making big eyes at Bren's military police friend."

"That's not exactly nothing," Jared replied.

His friend's voice held an uncomfortable edge of sympathy, and Ace needed more whiskey. "Nothing to *do*, then," he said as he leaned over to snag the bottle. "City boy doesn't share, and I don't play that game. I gambled on a slow chase, and I lost. So it goes."

"As you say. I am sorry, though. I liked her."

"You can still like her. She's not dead." Ace

knocked back the whiskey, enjoying a brief moment of comfort as it burned its way down his throat and kicked him in the guts. Or maybe that kick was this conversation, battering away at his determined denial. "Sorry, brother. I'll replace your booze."

Jared snorted. "Fuck the booze. I buy it by the case, and Dallas cuts me a sweet deal."

Of course he did. "Then screw you. I'm drinking it all."

"Good." He abandoned his glass on the coffee table and leaned back in his chair with a slow smile. "Drink it all, and then tell me about the redhead who works at the bar. The tall one."

Feeling like he'd just stepped clear of a minefield, Ace relaxed into the couch cushions and began to extol Trix's many, *many* charms. But somewhere in between a loving description of the busty redhead's glorious tits and her deliciously spankable ass, he acknowledged that his reprieve was likely to be short-lived.

The O'Kanes lived in close quarters with high stakes. Sooner or later, someone was gonna stomp on one of those mines, and the whole thing would blow up in their faces.

5

She could hear him grunting.

Lex stared at Dallas's door and ran through the incredibly short list of activities that could result in rhythmic grunts drifting from the other side of it. Fucking, obviously—easily set aside. Even if he wanted to be a pig, he wasn't a stupid one. If anyone was getting in his pants today, it was her.

Of course, he could have started without her, a mental image that curled her toes in her heeled sandals and stopped her just shy of a knock. She licked her lips and rubbed her thumb over the inside of her thigh as she tugged the hem of her skirt down. An intoxicating possibility, but unlikely. Dallas wouldn't begin this discussion at a disadvantage, even one borne of pleasure.

Working out, then. Probably doing pushups, and

enough of them to leave his skin sheened with sweat and imminently lickable. Enough to distract the hell out of her.

"Fuck you, O'Kane," she muttered, then banged on the door with the side of her fist.

The grunts paused long enough for him to say, "Come in," before resuming.

Not pushups, after all. He was hanging from the bar in one corner of the room, his shoulders flexing as he pulled his body up and then lowered it again. The sweat was there, of course, dampening his white wifebeater just enough to give an impression of the ink beneath. He kept going, every movement a controlled concert of muscle and power—and tailor-made to leave Lex weak in the knees.

"Fuck you," she said again, this time plenty loud enough for him to hear.

He grinned at her and paused with his chin above the bar. "Says the woman who makes us all watch while a fallen angel from Eden licks her pussy on stage."

"You love it." Lex held up the folded paper between her fingers. "I have something for you."

Still grinning, he dropped to the floor and reached for a towel to wipe his face and neck. "I wasn't sure you'd do it."

"Then maybe you don't know me very well," she said innocently.

"Uh-huh." He tossed aside the towel and walked toward her. No, not walked. *Swaggered*, every line of him dripping self-confidence. "We'll see."

Damn him, and damn his swagger, too. "Did you make a list?"

"I know my list." He stopped in front of her and touched her chin. "You want to hear it first?"

"Sure, why not?"

He nodded toward the couch and waited for her to sit before sprawling out beside her. "First rule. No sex without me."

A command that echoed the one scribbled on her own list. "I figured as much. Next?"

"The shows." His gaze darkened a little. "Though God only knows how much we'll lose if I pry Noelle off you."

Plenty enough for them all to feel the pinch. "You don't act like it bothers you."

"Mmm, things change. But I'll let the shows stand for now. Just the ones with her, though." Leaning in, he traced a fingertip along the collar before catching her chin. "No one with a pulse will wonder why I haven't put a stop to that."

But he wanted to. She could hear it in his voice, a low hum of tension and something else, a deeper rumble almost like possessiveness. "Anything else?"

"No lying to me about sex." He held her gaze, his own firm and unwavering. "If I ask a question about what you can handle, or what you need, that means I want the truth, not what you think I want to hear. Because believe me, I'll be taking plenty without asking."

Unbridled honesty, no matter what. Lex had been taught never to give it, because revealing too much led to deadly weakness. "I can try." The admission alone made her gut tighten. "I can't promise. Not always."

His jaw tightened, but the frustration in his eyes didn't follow through in the soft way he stroked her jaw. "Do you trust me?"

Honesty. "As much as I trust anyone."

It seemed like he studied her forever, his gaze roaming her face, his fingers still stroking. The silence stretched on long enough to make her want to look away before he jerked his head in a short nod. "If that's what I've got, I'll work with it."

It sounded too much like a concession, and she bristled. "I am what I am, Dallas. If you don't like it, I can find the door."

That fast, his fingers clenched on her chin. "Don't you snarl at me. If I didn't want you, you'd already be out of here. But if you think I'm not going to fight to turn that answer into *yes*, then maybe you need to rethink what you're walking into. I'm not a man who stops at *almost*."

In that moment, she hated him. Her eyes and throat burned, and she ached to throw it all back in his face and leave, just to prove that she could. Not even to him, but to herself.

She told her brain that it was time to move, but words spilled out instead as she shoved her crumpled note into his hand. "You want the truth? I don't know why I'm here, but I don't know how to leave. Not until I find out what this is."

He released her with a deep breath that turned into a chuckle. "I guess we'll learn whether I can handle the unvarnished truth, won't we? Not many people will give it to me anymore."

Lex pushed her fingers through her hair, bereft without his touch. "Do you blame them?"

"Sometimes." He smoothed the paper out on his thigh and glanced at it. A frown creased his brow as he studied what she'd written. "What is this?"

"It's my list. My rule."

He read the words aloud, all seven of them. "*Whatever we do, we do it together.*"

No inflection, nothing. She shifted on the cushion and cleared her throat. "That's all."

"What happened to not liking punishment like

Noelle?"

"It's not my thing, but it's not a deal breaker, either." Lex arched an eyebrow. "If you expected me to list everything that gets me hot and everything that doesn't, forget it. You can figure it out like any other mere mortal."

For a second, he looked so irritated she thought he might snap. His hand clenched tight around the paper, and that dangerous heat she knew so well gathered in his eyes. "So you're saying I can do any damn thing I want to you."

The pendant woven into the center of her collar was warm on her skin, warmer still when she touched it with nervous fingers. "That's what it means for me, wearing this."

"Stand up."

It sounded different from his usual commands, softer and harder at the same time. She rose and faced him, standing with her hands in fists at her sides.

He shifted into a pose she knew well, settling in the center of the couch with his long legs sprawled out carelessly. The lazy king at his finest, except he usually had plenty of people to demand his attention. Now there was only her, shivering under the weight of his gaze.

He was looking at her like he owned her, and that was all he needed.

Another long moment, and he smiled slowly. "What's under the dress?"

"Not a damn thing." This was more familiar territory, and Lex clung to it as she gathered her dress an inch higher on one leg. "Want to see?"

"Dirty girl." The words held nothing but sincere approval. "Show me. Take it off."

With every nerve on high alert, the fabric sliding

over her skin felt like hands. Lex eased it up, over her head, and dropped it on the floor at his feet.

He gestured again. "Shoes, too."

She nudged his knee with one toe. "The buckles are tricky. Help me?"

"Maybe if you bend over, you can see them more clearly."

Grinding a spike heel into his balls would be counterproductive, and not nearly enough payback for this arrogant performance. Instead, she pulled away and turned. One slow, deliberate bend from the waist later, she unbuckled one shoe, then the other.

"That's my girl," he rasped. "Always fighting dirty." She hadn't heard him move, but he was there, suddenly, hands on her hips. "Don't move."

She swallowed hard. "Not even to take off my shoes?"

He splayed a warm hand across the small of her back, traced the curve of her ass and lower, along the inside of her thigh and the back of her knee. When he spoke, his breath spilled hot over her pussy. "You can do that."

Only long years of practice allowed her to keep her balance. She kicked off the shoes and stilled. "Like this?"

"Mmm." He edged his hand between her legs and stroked her, slicking past her outer lips to tease one finger into her, and her inner muscles clenched at the invasion. "I thought I might have to eat this pussy to get you wet enough to fuck, but you could take me right now, couldn't you? I think you like being pissed at me."

As hard as she tried, she couldn't swallow her moan. "I know your game, honey. You're not fooling me."

"Is that so?" Another finger joined the first, broad

and sure, working into her with the confidence of long familiarity. This, he'd done plenty of times, getting her off in a hundred ways.

She choked on another moan as heat tingled outward from her core, curling through her like ink in water. "You have to keep up the cocky act, or you'll blow."

"Oh, I'll blow either way." He whispered the words against the curve of her ass, her only warning before he bit her with a dark laugh. "The only question now is where my dick's gonna be when it happens."

There was only one thing he refused to do to any woman who didn't wear his collar, the real reason behind the parade of random women in and out of this very room. And every instinct she possessed screamed that he'd been dying to do it to her.

Lex arched her back, staying bent at the waist but leaning up far enough to peer back at him over her shoulder. "You scared? Afraid I won't live up to the fantasy, Declan?"

Leather whispered over denim, his belt sliding open as he slipped his fingers from her body. Without taking his gaze from hers, he lifted his hand and licked his finger. "Not even a little."

She faced him. "Then what are you waiting for?"

Instead of answering, he left his belt hanging open and plunged his fingers into her hair, jerking her against him hard enough to suck the air from her lungs. His mouth landed on hers, stealing all the air she had left as he wrenched her head back and drove his tongue past her lips.

The answer to more than her question. Lex moved closer, despite the sharp tug of his hand in her hair. He'd kissed her before, but never like this, with a fire that threatened to consume. They'd always kept the need between them so carefully banked, painfully aware of the lines they could cross so easily.

That need sizzled to life now, like something had been unleashed. She scratched him, bit his lip, hissed his name when he hoisted her off the floor and slammed her against the closest wall.

No more waiting.

"Now." His shirt ripped as she wrenched it over his head. "Fuck me now."

"Not like this." He snaked an arm around her, pivoted, and thumped her down on the arm of the couch. Strong fingers dug into her hips and sent her sprawling back, falling until her shoulders hit the plush cushion.

Dallas loomed over her, his hands curled around her thighs. His gaze swept up, lingering on the tattoo of his name, on her tits. Her collar.

Lex squirmed. She'd expected a submissive position—on her knees, maybe, with Dallas gripping her hips—but this wasn't symbolically helpless. She couldn't move or control anything, was completely at his mercy...and he knew it.

He didn't seem to have the patience to savor it. He all but ripped his jeans open and freed his cock, fisting the shaft with a growl. "Pinch your nipples."

"No." Despite the refusal, she was already lifting her hands to obey. Instead, she grazed them lightly, teasing the hard peaks with her thumbs.

His cock ground between her pussy lips as he leaned down and closed his hand around hers, forcing her finger and thumb together on her nipple. "Yes."

Rough and sweet. It set off a shudder, and Lex dug her teeth into her lower lip when the reflexive movement rubbed her clit against the hard ridge at the head of his erection. *Fuck.*

Dallas laughed and forced her to tug at her nipple,

guiding her fingers in short, rough jerks that skated close to pain. "That's right, love. Control, not obedience. If I have control, I can get obedience, whether you give it to me or not."

"Only if you take it," she managed to rasp.

A rock of his hips rubbed his cock over her clit again, but it seemed unconscious, instinctive. His focus was on *her*, his eyes dark as he moved his hand. "Pinch those tight little nipples, Lex. Do it, and I'll fuck you."

Another denial sprang to her lips, but she held it back, held his gaze as she cupped her breasts and slowly squeezed her fingers together. The denial melted into a moan as pleasure and anticipation tingled up her spine.

Dallas straightened, sliding his hand down her body as he went. Her hip, her abdomen, soft touches, almost gentle. They might have been too gentle if he hadn't gripped her inner thigh, his fingers biting into flesh with impatience as he thrust her leg wide.

And thrust into her.

The sensation that rocked her was more than physical, an awareness of the harsh stretch and hardness of his cock. It wasn't new, not exactly, but oddly familiar. This was how he would own her, with a possession so complete it had always existed, in glances and whispers.

He'd never been in her like this, but he'd always been in her.

For once, Dallas was as speechless as she felt, his face slack and his eyes almost closed. He dug bruises into her leg as he stilled, buried deep in her body. Neither of them spoke. Neither of them *breathed.*

Before she could get air into her lungs, his eyes snapped open, searing the space between them as he skated that hand from the tender flesh of her inner thigh to her even more sensitive clit. His thumb slicked in one slow circle, then another. "I've been waiting forever to feel you coming on my dick."

"Oh, God." She tried to keep from moving, but her shoulders pressed into the couch cushions as she arched against him. "Not too fast."

His thumb stroked faster. Harder. "You trying to tell me what to do again?"

"No, I—" Control. She needed it, but her body didn't care. It cared about *now* and *fuck* and the way his hips flexed, grinding his cock deeper inside her.

"Give me this, Lexie." His voice was a coaxing rumble, the gentleness a thin mask over hard command. Each time he rocked into her was a little rougher as his patience unraveled. "Tell me my cock's the hottest thing I've ever fucked you with."

"You know it is." She barely recognized her own voice, low and strained. Every muscle trembled, as much with tension as with bliss, a heavy anticipation that tangled her in knots.

He rewarded her confession with a long thrust that drove a cry from her throat. "Next time, I'll tie you open like this." It sounded like a promise—to himself or her, she couldn't tell. "I'll fuck you slow."

Next time, because this had to be fast. Lex drew in a shaking breath and clenched her fists, digging her nails into her palms. "Dallas."

Another thrust. "I'll tie you up and suck your clit." Again, harder. "Fuck you with my fingers, or something bigger. Maybe I'll let you choose. Wood or glass or steel."

Every word was a tease, a weapon, and knowing he was desperate enough to use them shook her restraint. One more quick thrust destroyed it, curling her toes as a throb of pleasure tore through her.

The noise that escaped her was barely human, all primal need and naked desire. Too much, too *open*, but she couldn't think enough to care, not with Dallas riding her release, dragging it out with the kind of fucking she'd always imagined he'd like. Hard and demanding, their hips slamming together, the sound raw and slick.

Better. It could get even better, and all she had to do was reach for it. "Please." Lex clawed at his arms and bucked, sheer animal hunger driving away everything but *him*. "Please, baby—"

He hauled her half off the arm of the couch and cupped his hands under her knees, pushing them back toward her chest.

It should have been impossible to feel more pinned, more helpless, but the new angle was brutally sharp, and so goddamn deep. So *full*, and nothing held back. Lex opened her eyes and focused on his face, on his almost pained expression as he sped his thrusts, rough and frantic, his balls slapping against her ass.

The world was hazy around the edges, dulled by ecstasy—but not Dallas. She could see him as clearly as she could feel him—intense, fierce.

Hers.

He came with a snarl, his rhythm faltering, bleeding to quick, jerky thrusts before he slammed home with one final grunt and froze. A sound rattled free of him, barely coherent, but it echoed in her bones. "Lex."

She couldn't move, couldn't breathe. The trapped feeling that had been so delicious only seconds earlier now tripped off panic, rising in her throat to choke her. It didn't dissipate when he lowered her legs and pulled her close to his chest, lifting her with him as he straightened.

"Lex?" His fingers smoothed through her hair, slow and gentle. "You with me?"

"I'm here." Here—and with no idea what to do next.

Dallas caught her chin and tilted her head back, but as soon as his mouth opened, the door rattled under a brisk knock. His brow furrowed as he glared past her. "If someone's not bleeding or invading, go the fuck away."

Bren's low voice drifted through the door. "You're gonna want to see this."

Sighing, Dallas swung Lex up in his arms. He crossed the wide room to deposit her on the edge of his bed, then fastened his pants and swept up a discarded T-shirt for her. "Sorry, love. You know how it goes."

"It's business," she murmured, grateful for the distraction as she drew the soft cotton over her head.

Dallas didn't bother with a shirt or even buckling his belt. She could read his irritation in the muscles of his back, tense under his tattoos as he stalked to the door.

On the other side, Bren leaned against the doorframe, an ivory-colored envelope in his hand. "Messenger delivered it just now."

"Great." Dallas glared at the envelope like it contained live explosives, but after a moment he plucked it from Bren's hand. "Well, we knew it was coming. Have Rachel make us something to eat and pry Jas out of Noelle. Tell him I need him in my office in an hour."

"Anyone else?"

"I need you to stick close. And find Mad."

"Will do." He glanced past Dallas, and a hint of a smile curved the corner of his mouth. "Hi, Lex."

Dallas slammed the door in his face.

Lex didn't have time to be pissy about Bren's amusement. She couldn't stop staring at the envelope in Dallas's hand, at the thick but graceful slashes of royal purple ink across the front. "From Cerys?"

He returned to the bed and flipped the envelope, revealing an intricate orchid seal imprinted in purple wax. "Guess so."

The tattoo, the collar, the fucking... "You'll want me to go with you, I guess."

Instead of answering, Dallas pulled a switchblade from his back pocket and flicked it open. The sharp edge sliced through wax and the envelope alike, and the scent of orchids assaulted her as he withdrew the letter and unfolded it.

It was concise, to the point. His gaze traveled from the top to the bottom of the letter twice before he turned it over to her wordlessly.

A summons, as she'd suspected. "It was inevitable."

Dallas dropped his knife on the dresser and reached for the whiskey. "Doesn't mean I have to like it." Forgoing glasses, he took a swig directly from the bottle before meeting her gaze. "I can't imagine you like the idea of going back to Two, but I need you with me."

For so many reasons that were strictly political—for her knowledge, for the sake of appearances. To watch his back and fight if necessary. But she suspected those reasons had little to do with *why*. "I understand."

He offered her the whiskey. "I'm going to be dealing with this most of the day. We'll leave tomorrow afternoon, with Bren and probably Mad."

"Anyone I should bring?"

"The queen of Sector Four." Dallas grinned at her before hauling on a shirt. "Anything we do, we do together, love. I agreed to it."

She realized with a jolt that he was right. She'd been thinking of sex when she'd written the words—hadn't she?—but they applied to everything. As far as the world was concerned, their names went together, and so did their authority. They still had personal shit to muddle through, but that took a back seat. They had to present a united, harmonious front, to their own people and everyone else.

Anything else meant weakness, and weakness in front of the other sector leaders meant death.

6

Rachel was the only woman Dallas knew who could chastise with food. The stack of grilled cheese sandwiches at his elbow was stingy on the cheese and generous with the grilling, resulting in charred edges that tasted like crap. *I ain't your woman, and I've got actual shit to do* was the message, reinforced by the lack of fries and the absence of any of Rachel's homebrew. She wouldn't turn down a direct order, but she had no trouble letting Dallas feel the bite of her irritation.

As Jasper sat, Dallas shoved the plate across the table. "Good thing I'm leaving. Give me another day and I'll have all the girls pissed at me."

Jasper held up his hand with a shake of his head. "I'll eat later, thanks."

"Good call." Sweeping the whole mess off the side of the desk and into the garbage was worth the hell he'd get for breaking a plate. "I'll just lay this out. You're not coming to Two with us, not this time."

"Guess you're gonna have a full house with Lex along."

"That's not why." Dallas offered Jas a cigarette before pulling out one of his own. "Shit's a mess, man. We've got enemies on all sides. Gareth Woods in the city, the usual scum trying to bite bits of the sector off when we're not looking. Whoever supplied Wilson Trent with those explosives. Hell, even Dom's getting to be more trouble than he's worth. I can't leave for a couple days and trust the place to be standing when I get back. Not without help."

Jasper seemed to consider that. "I can hold it together. Depends, some, on how long you plan to be gone."

A usual meeting between sector leaders dragged through at least two days. One evening for them to indulge in whatever vices Cerys had arranged to put them all in an agreeable frame of mind, and one wasted morning with everyone poking and prodding, feeling out weaknesses and strengths. Only then could they get down to business—and that was under usual circumstances, not with a sector leader dead and his territory dissolving into anarchy.

Dallas lit his cigarette and inhaled deeply before shaking his head. "Figure three nights, at the least. Maybe a week, if nothing goes sideways. They won't want to leave until they've figured out what to do about Three."

"You mean besides burn it to the ground?" Jasper groused.

"Tempting, isn't it?" Not that their own sector had much in the way of elegance. Not like Two or Five or even the nicer parts of Eight. Four took its style from the

O'Kanes as much as it took its temper—rough around the edges but solid. Three was straight up broken, just like its leader had been.

But the potential was there.

"There are things we could salvage," Jasper admitted, "but I'm not sure it'd be worth thumbing our noses at everyone else to do it—unless they want you to. It wouldn't be stupid. You clear the place, divide the spoils, and take a finder's fee."

"It'd take a lot of work to enforce some fucking order over there. And probably a fair bit of blood." Perfectly reasonable words, but work and blood had never stopped him before. And staring at all that unclaimed territory on the map stirred the sort of excitement he hadn't felt in too long. "But if we had the manpower... the money could be nice."

"We'd need more people." Jasper leaned forward and braced his elbows on the desk. "I'm talking serious membership drive."

Just the thought splintered pain behind his eyeballs, a headache begging to split open. "Only if you're willing to break them in and weed them out. I don't have the patience for that shit."

"Just let me know. I can start with the fights, the guys who've been around on the fringes for a while."

"Might as well start while I'm gone." Dallas blew smoke at the ceiling as a scowl twisted his lips. "Doesn't really matter who ends up in charge of Three, does it? We need to be stronger."

Jasper grunted.

Dallas glanced at him and got a speculative, curious look back. Jasper didn't sit around and gossip like the women—or Ace—but that didn't make him any less nosy. "You looking for the stab wounds?"

"Dunno." He shrugged. "Figured Lex might take a

chunk out of you after the other night."

"We worked it out." Dallas quirked an eyebrow. "Did you and Noelle?"

"We're all right."

Not exactly the words of a man with a newly marked woman bouncing excitedly on his dick. "Sorry for pissing off your girl on your night."

He just shrugged again and, for a moment, Dallas missed the Jasper who'd been utterly his man. As loyal as Jas still was, Noelle had his heart in her perfectly manicured little hands now. She was the one he protected, even if it was just with silence.

Dallas sighed and stared at the ceiling. "I'll make it up to both of you when I get back. Lex is wearing my collar. We've still got shit to figure out, but I'm not enough of an asshole to try to keep her away from Noelle."

Jasper finally chuckled. "I don't think you could, man, even if you wanted to. With a thousand collars. Not even with ink."

That was the truth, and it pinched. "Then I guess it's a good thing I don't mind your ugly face."

"Would you rather have a woman who didn't give a shit about anyone?"

He'd had plenty of those. Cold women, hard women, even broken ones. At times, Lex could seem to be all three, but she wasn't really, and he was glad. He'd never want to strip away that caring core.

Not even if he couldn't own all of it.

Straightening, Dallas snuffed out his cigarette. "Since we're stuck together for the time being, I'll make an effort to play nice with your kitten. Unless you like getting scratched up when I piss her off."

Something clouded Jasper's eyes, but he blinked it away. "I'd threaten to kick your ass if you upset her, but I don't think it'd do any good. You always do whatever the hell you want anyway."

"That's pretty much how this works." But it wouldn't hurt to ask Lex to talk Noelle down. The girl would have to learn sooner or later that courtship in the sectors sometimes came with bumps and bruises. For now, the best thing Dallas could do was change the subject. "Go stick your head out—"

A knock interrupted his words, and Mad slipped through the door. Bren followed, rubbing his hands together. "All the deliveries and collection runs are set up. Should flow smoothly in our absence."

"Good." He waited for them to drag up chairs before looking to Mad. "Have you talked to your cousin yet?"

"I sent a message," he answered, dropping into the chair. "Gideon will probably reply by carrier pigeon or some bullshit. Depends on how much he's buying into the grandson-of-the-Prophet mystique this month."

Mad's grandfather had been the first leader of Sector One, a spiritual man elevated to legend by followers who wanted a religion to replace the stifling edicts of Eden. "Either way, you'll see him tomorrow. You'll be Lex's bodyguard while we're in Two. I don't want you leaving her side unless I'm stuck to it."

"Got it," was all Mad said, though the man was smart enough to know Lex wouldn't appreciate having no say in the matter. Too fucking bad for both of them. Lex wouldn't be allowed to participate in the daily negotiations, and Dallas wouldn't be able to concentrate on them with her flitting around her old sector unprotected.

Jasper grinned at Bren. "Bring Dallas back in one piece, huh? I'm not ready to be king."

Bren rescued the cigarette languishing in Jasper's

hand and finished it off in one long draw. "He's too stubborn to die."

It was Dallas's place to grin, to give them their cocky leader, even if he wasn't feeling it. "Yeah, I am. So get comfortable in my chair, Jas, but not *too* comfortable."

"Wouldn't dream of it."

The fact that he really wouldn't made Jasper the rarest of things—a truly trustworthy second. "Things should be quiet. Cruz seems to be settling in okay."

Bren tipped his head. "He is. Getting some shit in the cage, but that's to be expected. As far as most people are concerned, he's still got to make his bones."

Cruz hadn't taken ink yet, but he'd lost his place in Eden while bringing Dallas the man who'd pulled the trigger on Lex. For that, and with Bren's word, Dallas would have given him cuffs on the spot, tradition be damned.

But it was smart of the man to wait. Normal recruits had plenty of time to find their place in the pecking order and earn respect by tolerating a little friendly hazing, and most of them hadn't started out as elite members of Eden's military police.

Speaking of which... "That was quite a show he put on in the cage the other night. He makes you look clumsy, Bren."

The man's brows slashed down in a frown. "The fuck he does."

Jasper chuckled. "Now don't get your little feelings hurt—"

Bren punched him on the shoulder. "Cruz is good, and maybe he *is* smoother in a fight. A clean fight. He's gonna have to learn how to fight dirty."

"He's gonna have to learn a lot more than that," Mad said, shaking his head. "He's wound tighter than

Bren was. It doesn't matter how many fights he wins, no one will accept him if he can't drink a few shots and relax."

"Or a few beers," Jasper muttered.

That momentarily distracted Dallas from his mental checklist. The O'Kanes didn't make beer, and they didn't drink alcohol produced by anyone else—with one exception. The same exception who hadn't given him anything to drink with his lunch. "So that's actually happening? Rachel and the city boy?"

"Loudly and frequently," Jas confirmed. "If the rumors are to be believed."

Some rumors were easier to believe than others, and Dallas would wager this one held more salacious curiosity than truth. "I'll believe that when I see it. Even Ace couldn't score any alone time with Rachel, and all the women love him. God knows why."

Bren and Jasper both turned to look at Mad, who snorted. "I should let you all wonder if it's true. If you want answers, listen to what people are saying when you haven't asked them a question."

"Pithy," Dallas grumbled. "Is that some wisdom of the Prophet?"

Mad tapped the side of his head. "That's advice from a spy. And the answer to your question is...it's none of your damn business."

Figured. Mad knew everything because people trusted him, and people trusted him because he didn't spill secrets. "Fine. We gonna discuss anyone else's love life before we get back to actual business?"

Bren regarded him with a bland look. "Is yours on the table? 'Cause I had to stand outside your door for a good ten minutes this afternoon before I fucking *dared* to knock."

Dallas had fucked women in front of Bren before.

Hell, he'd fucked women *with* him and had never felt the slightest bit possessive or self-conscious.

But that moment of Lex melting beneath him—that tiny crack in her impenetrable fucking façade—that should have belonged to him alone. Bad enough that he'd been dragged away before he could savor it, but knowing Bren had been witness to it infuriated him.

Fucking irrational, but damned if he cared. "That's what an orgasm sounds like when you do it right, asshole," he snapped, anger turning his tone ugly. "Jas can show you."

He wasn't playing, and they all knew it. Jasper and Mad exchanged an uncomfortable look, but Bren only lowered his gaze. "Message received. Not on the table at all."

Dallas got the message, too. *Too far.* There was a line between strength and abuse, and he'd been walking the wrong side of it more often than not lately. It was one thing if he needed to be vicious for their safety, but not when it was all about his own stupid pride.

Grinding his teeth, he forced himself to take a breath. "I don't like this. I don't like dragging her into Sector Two, and I don't like having to go there now, when I'd rather be figuring out how to put an end to Gareth Woods. I'm pissy."

"Then you get through it," Jasper said evenly. "As quick and easy as possible. Then you can get on to more important things."

Unless the whole meeting exploded in his face, or they ended up at war with whoever had backed Wilson Trent's attack. Both seemed equally probable, at this point.

What a grim fucking future for him and his newly collared queen. "Recruitment drive," he told Jasper. At least with that rolling, he'd feel like he was preparing for whatever came next. "Make it a priority. When we get back, we'll all sit down and figure out the quickest way to bring up our numbers without taking on any dead weight."

"Yes, sir."

Mad and Bren were still silent and stone-faced. Dallas tried to lighten the mood with a crooked smile. "Cheer up, boys. You're headed to one of Cerys's parties. Expensive pussy *and* someone might try to stab you. Can't get more exciting than that."

"It's not a party until someone pulls a blade." But there was a rough edge to Bren's voice, with no trace of his usual quirky humor.

Mad stepped into the awkward silence with his easy smile, but Dallas had the distinct impression that Mad was rescuing Bren, not him. "Bren will handle the knives, and I'll take care of the hookers. It'll be a regular shindig. Is that all you needed, boss?"

It was a question, but it also wasn't. Mad had a look in his eyes, a set to his jaw and brow, one that told Dallas that it had better be enough. "Yeah, you two go pack."

They filed out, but Jasper stayed behind, rubbing at his eyes with his thumb and forefinger. "Jesus, Dallas."

The bottom drawer of his desk held rum, whiskey and two glasses. Dallas dropped all of it on his desk and poured himself a triple. "I know, I know. But I thought the bastard would laugh. We've all watched him get off how many chicks in the damn cage alone? What's got him so defensive?"

"Maybe he can take some good-natured ribbing, but doesn't like having his head bitten off."

"Is that what I did?"

Jasper arched an eyebrow. "What would you call it?"

He didn't have an answer for that—not an honest one he wanted to give. Dallas drained his drink and slammed it down. "Fuck, Jas. She's got me turned inside out, and I can't afford that right now. None of us can."

"That's not Bren's fault. It's not mine, or even hers." Jasper rose and shoved his hands in his pockets. "Get it as right as you can before you leave, because if you lose your shit in Two, you make Lex a bigger target than she already is. Truth."

"I hear you." But hearing wasn't enough. Somehow, he had to get a chokehold on his own base reactions, along with the fucking temper that ran too close to the surface where Lex was concerned. "I'll make things right, too. With Bren, with you and your girl."

Jas shook his head. "First order of business—stay alive. Everything else can wait."

Dallas almost laughed. "That's the one thing you don't have to tell me, man. I always stay alive."

"You've never done this before. Watch your back."

"I'll do you one better. I'll let Lex watch it." Dallas smiled wryly. "You don't think she'd let anyone else sink a knife in it, do you?"

But Jasper didn't smile. "No, I don't. I wonder if you do, though."

No, that was one thing Dallas had always been certain of, whether Jasper believed it or not. Lex was fully capable of trying to tear out his heart with her bare hands if she thought he deserved it, but she reserved that right for herself.

And if he didn't get his temper under control, she'd be trying sooner rather than later. "I'll see you after dinner. We can walk the warehouse and check the next shipment."

"I'll take care of it." Jasper turned the knob with a grin. "Bren and Mad aren't the only ones who have to pack." He slipped out and closed the door behind him.

No, they weren't, and they had the easier task. Bodyguards faded into the background. Dallas would be front and center, and he had to look the part. Deadly and uncivilized, the living embodiment of why no one should fuck with Sector Four. Truth in advertising—the only political game he actually liked to play.

He'd done it before, always with Lex's advice. Now he'd have more than that. He'd have her at his side, his dangerous, beautiful queen, and together they could present a united front of strength that should keep anyone from stepping so much as a toe in Sector Four.

Lex juggled the bags in her hands as she opened the door to Dallas's suite. He usually asked for her help with his wardrobe when he had to visit another sector, and this time was no different. It was damn hard to walk the fine line between dangerous criminal and civilized businessman—especially when, by his very nature, he tended to veer toward the rough-and-tumble side of the equation. So he relied on her to put the finer touches on his image, little things that screamed money and class without also screaming, *I give two shits what you think.*

A noise drew Lex's gaze, and she stopped short just inside the room. The bags slipped from her fingers and hit the floor with a thump.

He usually had her help him pack. What he didn't usually have was a naked woman in his bed.

Six rolled from between the sheets before the door clicked shut, the wide, wild look in her eyes betraying her panic. Her gaze darted from her clothes to Lex and back as she shifted self-consciously, like she was trying to figure out if she could reach the tangle of fabric before Lex reached *her*.

She looked tensed for a fight. A beatdown.

The spot right behind Lex's eyes had already started to ache, and she pinched the bridge of her nose. "Put your panties on, honey. We've got to have a little talk."

Six lunged for her clothes and held them against her chest as she straightened, her gaze locked on Lex. "Is that code for sticking a knife between my ribs?"

"I don't speak in code. If I wanted you to hurt, you'd know it."

After a moment, Six nodded and wiggled into her underwear and pants. She pulled the shirt over her head last, tugging it down to hide her scarred torso. "You've always been pretty upfront about what you'll do to me if I betray Dallas. Guess you wouldn't bother lying now."

"No reason to. Especially since this whole thing?" Lex gestured to the girl's rumpled clothes. "It's not a threat to me."

She stiffened, and the emotion that finally broke through her desperate attempt at a stoic mask wasn't offense or anger, but a dark amusement. "That was going to be my argument. I'm not much competition for someone like you."

The words irritated Lex, and she spun away and stalked to the bar. "It's not funny. O'Kane women don't sell out like that. Lesson number one."

Silence greeted the words, stretching long enough for Lex to pour a drink before Six whispered, "I don't have anything else to sell."

"You look able enough." Lex poured a second drink and held it out. "You saying you can't work?"

"I wasn't—" The girl grabbed the glass and drained a double of Dallas's oldest and best whiskey. "I wasn't expecting to stay in his bed. I just needed something to offer now. I needed a trade."

To a man she'd already assumed didn't really want her. "A trade for what?"

She rubbed her thumb over the inside of her wrist, over unmarked skin, as if she could feel the lack of ink there. "Bren said he's leaving tomorrow."

"He is. We're going to Sector Two."

"I wanna go."

It was Lex's turn to smile in dark amusement. "No, you don't. I grew up in Two. You want to stay your ass right here."

Six stared into her empty glass. "I'm not an O'Kane. I'm not saying that to be a smartass, like I don't have to try'n follow your rules. It's just the truth. You might be safer here, but I don't know if I am. Not without..."

"Without Dallas around." Lex plucked the glass from Six's hand and refilled it. "Or is it Bren?"

That put her on the defensive. She muttered a curse and glared at the floor. "He's the one vouching for me, isn't he?"

"Don't be so touchy. I have a right to ask, especially if you think Bren's the one protecting you."

"Isn't he? None of the other guys have fucked around with me."

It made sense for the girl to assume that was Bren's influence instead of standard operating procedure on the O'Kane compound. "Is that what things were like with Trent in Three?"

This time Six sipped the whiskey slowly. "If you weren't his piece of ass, you were anyone's toy," she said finally. "Bren's not the leader, but I see how the guys watch him."

Reassurances were just words, and words meant jack shit. Lex drained her own glass. "Jasper'll be handling things while Dallas is gone. If you're not comfortable going to him and Noelle if you have any problems, then stick close to Rachel. Anyone tries to mess with you, she'll bite his dick off. Good enough?"

Six looked up. "When Dallas brought you in to talk to me after I first got here, I thought he was running some sort of stupid game. That he was an idiot, or took me for one. But he really fucking expected it to work, didn't he? He thought I'd trust you, because all the women trust you."

Lex gave her a slow grin. "Sometimes it takes a while, but yeah."

A flicker of amusement crinkled the corners of Six's eyes before she schooled her features. "You really don't fight over the men? Ever?"

"I didn't say that. People want what they want, even if other people have it." Lex paused to consider her next words. "But we don't lower ourselves. It's beneath you to chase after a man who belongs to someone else."

Six's gaze fixed on Lex's, and she swallowed. "I wasn't chasing him. I just figured—I mean, he's the leader of Four. Even when Trent had a woman, he still took his..." Her lips twisted. "His *tax*."

"Dallas gets enough ass. He doesn't need to coerce women who don't really want to fuck him."

The younger woman flinched, but didn't try to deny it. She didn't say anything until she'd finished her second drink and offered the glass back to Lex. "I don't get the rules here, and I don't think Bren can teach me the ones I need to know. Can Rachel?"

The truth was stark and uncomfortable. "You'll probably have to pick them up as you go along. But

Rachel can get you started."

"All right." She hesitated. "What about Bren? Do you think—?"

Before she could finish her question, the doorknob rattled and Six's teeth clacked together. Dallas pushed open the door, his frown melting into confusion as he took in both women. After a moment of tense silence, he quirked a brow at Lex. "Everything all right in here?"

"Fine." Lex didn't bother with a smile he would see through anyway. "Six was a little worried about Bren leaving. I told her Rachel'll take care of her."

That cleared Dallas's expression. He patted Six on the shoulder like she was a puppy who needed encouragement before moving to pour himself a drink. "That'll be good. Rachel can put you to work in the bar."

Six glanced from Dallas to Lex and back and barely managed to stammer out her agreement before flying out the door. It swung shut smartly behind her, and Dallas sighed and doubled the amount of liquor in his glass. "Do I want to know?"

"Only if a little useless, impotent rage would make your day complete."

"You okay?"

The covers on one side of the bed were still drawn back and rumpled. Lex busied herself with straightening them. "I'm good. Everything arranged for the trip?"

"Just about." He unzipped his jacket and edged a hand inside. "I got you something."

It made her smile, but she had to ask. "Gift or weapon? With you, I never know."

"Gift." He returned her smile and pulled out a black velvet bag embroidered with a familiar logo.

"Stuart's sister." Lex took the bag and rubbed her thumb over the velvet. Stuart made exquisite leather goods, while his sister worked mainly with metal and jewelry, but sometimes they combined their efforts. "Another collar?"

He grunted as he shrugged out of his jacket, his movements too forcibly casual to be entirely at ease. He seemed nervous, and even more so when he spoke. "Whenever the leaders meet in Two, Cerys makes us all suffer through some fancy fucking dinner party with the wives and escorts. Stuart said this'll match that fancy corset he made you a few months ago."

She offered him a smile as she undid the strings on the pouch. "I know the one. Don't worry, we'll both look damn good."

Dallas didn't answer, all of his attention fixed on her face as she slipped the choker free of the velvet. It was breathtaking—a wide strip of supple leather edged with lace and set not only with another pendant like the one she already wore, but also with jeweled chains.

"It's beautiful." And it would have taken weeks to craft, if not months. She met his gaze, unable to keep the question out of her eyes. "Dallas?"

"It'll look good on you," he replied as he sprawled out on the bed. Not exactly an answer, but not an invitation to keep asking, either. "Fit for a queen. Isn't that what they used to say?"

"Yes." She glanced at the couch. It had been on the tip of her tongue to mention that afternoon, to open discussion about the things that had changed between them, but he obviously preferred avoidance. "I know how to handle myself at one of Cerys's gatherings."

"I guess you do." His brow furrowed. "You don't expect trouble, do you? I thought you told me you'd made your peace with her."

Paid her off was more like it. Lex had left Sector Two without earning a dime for Orchid House, which meant she owed them for feeding and clothing her for years. But that money could only be collected if you could be found, and Lex had managed to stay off the radar for years.

Until the leader of the O'Kane gang had plucked her off the street and taken her under his wing. It hadn't taken Cerys long to come knocking, looking for payment, a fact that Lex had managed to keep from Dallas. If he'd known, he'd have ponied up the cash, and her pride never would have recovered. She would have become something else then, another bauble he'd bought and paid for, not a woman standing on her own feet.

Dallas had both hands tucked behind his head, but his easy, relaxed posture was a lie. The look in his eyes had turned dangerous. "Lex?"

"Relax." She laid the bag and collar on the bar and crawled onto the bed. "I've got no problems with Cerys."

"Uh-huh." He extended one arm in commanding invitation. "Cerys will just have to get right with the fact that you're an O'Kane. For life."

Lex curled up beside him, her head on his shoulder and her hand clenched in his shirt. "I don't think she's in danger of forgetting."

His arm folded around her, tucking her close. He'd never had any trouble with the physical displays of affection, and she knew what would come next. Sure enough, his fingers drifted through her hair a moment later, absently stroking the strands.

"I know you don't like this," he said, quiet but firm. "I don't, either. But I'll be stronger with you there, and you can read Cerys in ways I can't. It could make a difference this time, especially since one of those bastards may have been working with Trent—"

"You're preaching to the choir, Declan." She closed her eyes. "Just...shh."

His chest rumbled with his amused noise, but he went silent. He fondled her hair as his chest rose and fell in slow, even breaths.

They still needed to pack. They still needed to *talk*. But, for now, the quiet suited her just fine.

7

No matter how many times he visited Sector Two, the one thing Dallas could never get past were the fucking angels on the ceilings.

Every sector enjoyed its own degree of wealth. Four was no exception, and a man who kept carpenters and leather workers busy creating custom sex furniture didn't have a lot of room to judge how other people wasted money. He'd come a long way from scrabbling for food and shelter, and paying for creative sex toys was as frivolous a use of his fortune as Dallas could imagine.

But fuck, at least he had *fun* with them. The painted angels just glared down at Cerys's guests in prissy judgment, which was rich, considering how the woman had amassed her fortune. *No innocents here.*

The reminder made him tighten his arm around

Lex's waist. "Here we go."

"It's a party," she whispered in response. "Not a firing squad. Everyone's just gonna flash their feathers and compare dick sizes, and you've got nothing to worry about on either count, all right?"

His lips twitched, trying to form into a smile that would surely ruin his glaring barbarian image. "Fine, but it's an insult to fun to call this a party."

"You're above it all," Lex told him firmly as they made their way down the wide marble staircase to the main floor. "If you forget everything else, remember that."

Dallas didn't know about that, but they were sure as hell at the center of everyone's attention, and he'd bet his next batch of corn liquor that no one was staring at *him*, not with Lex sultry and deadly at his side. The leather pants were hot, and so were the heels that brought the top of her head level with Dallas's eyes. But everyone gaped the first time they saw that corset, a masterwork of stamped leather and shining rivets. The fastenings began beneath her breasts, which were on glorious fucking display behind nothing but crisscrossing ties.

Someday, he was going to pull a knife and slice through those taunting laces. Maybe tonight, as a reward for getting through this without pulling a knife for a different reason.

Cerys crossed the floor, her feet silent and her lavender robes flowing behind her. The tall brunette was still stunning, her pale skin showing only the vaguest hint of lines, and a fierce intelligence sparked in her amber-colored eyes, as sharp as the calculating smile that curved her lips.

She stopped in front of Dallas and bowed slightly. "Welcome, Mr. O'Kane."

"Cerys." He inclined his head—as close as he was planning to come to bowing to any of these people—before tilting it in Lex's direction. "You remember Lex, I guess."

"Of course." Her gaze lingered on Lex's throat as she held out her hand. "Alexa."

She ignored the proffered hand. "You heard the man. It's Lex."

"Lex," Cerys corrected, her smile widening. "Yes."

Dallas knew what held the woman's attention. The fancy collar, the one he'd set Stuart's sister to work on the morning after Noelle's welcome party. Not a subtle symbol, dripping as it was with rubies and diamonds he'd pried out of a dozen pre-Flare trinkets. It was a statement of wealth as much as ownership, and Cerys was unlikely to miss any of it.

Dallas laid his hand on the small of Lex's back and tried to smile without baring his teeth. "Lex has settled into being my better half. Isn't that right, love?"

Lex focused on his mouth, a tiny, secret smile playing at the corners of her lips. "That's right."

He wanted to kiss the hell out of her. He could probably get away with it, too—no one expected him to be polite—but something about the glint in Cerys's gaze made him hold back. Instead, he smoothed his hand to Lex's hip, splaying his fingers wide in a grip no one would mistake for anything but possessive. "Seems like most everyone's here already. No stragglers this time?"

"Everyone arrived promptly." Cerys gestured behind her to the long table set for dinner. "No business, as usual. There's plenty of time for that. Tonight, we enjoy ourselves."

"Always do." Spotting a familiar figure leaning against a marble column, Dallas nodded again. "Mind if I go say hello to your neighbor?"

"You're a guest," Cerys murmured. "You do as you please." With that, she turned her attention elsewhere.

"Dismissed," Lex teased quietly. "She has that way about her, doesn't she?"

Dallas snorted and guided Lex past a young girl holding a tray of drinks. She was wearing a simple, gauzy gown that floated around her like a hazy promise, one that drew men's gazes as she passed. That was Sector Two in a nutshell—hazy promise. Never overt, never blunt, but always seething just under the surface of everything, from the decorations to the girls serving punch and champagne.

The man by the column was the only one who seemed oblivious to that promise. Gideon and Mad might have been cousins, but they didn't look much alike. They both had that same relaxed smile, though, the one that made Mad so easy to trust. Dallas had seen wary men and women alike give way to Mad when he flashed that charming grin, and usually he appreciated its effectiveness.

Not so much when it was directed at Lex, though. "Gideon. Quit ogling my woman."

Gideon ignored him completely and kept grinning at Lex. "It's nice to see you, sweetheart. I imagine things will run a lot more smoothly with you around."

"I know my way around Cerys's games." But the sharp look she flashed him belied the tranquil words and triggered a warning instinct in Dallas. She'd gone tense against his side, and there was no reason the leader of Sector One should present a threat to Lex.

Even more unsettling, Gideon seemed to have no trouble interpreting the sudden tension. He sighed, and if Dallas hadn't known better, he'd swear the man looked disappointed. "Still, Lex?" Gideon asked softly.

"Even with his collar around your throat?"

She leaned in and kissed the man's cheek. "You talk too much."

"And still manage to avoid the things that truly need saying." Gideon finally turned to acknowledge Dallas. "You're a lucky man, O'Kane. Congratulations."

After a strained moment, Dallas let the odd comments slide. Demanding an explanation would only underscore his ignorance—a weakness he couldn't afford tonight. "Luckier every day, it seems. It's invigorating to have a lady who can keep you on your toes."

She made a soothing noise, but a moment later a booming voice drowned it out. "O'Kane."

Dallas turned to see Mac Fleming bearing down on them, his tailored suit a stark contrast to Gideon's denim and homespun and Dallas's own leather. The man who ran Five moved more illegal drugs than anyone else in a thousand miles, but he liked to play legitimate businessman almost as much as Cerys liked to play well-bred lady.

The games were exhausting, but Dallas knew his own role: thug. Hopefully one they underestimated. "Fleming. Been a while."

"Not nearly long enough, judging from your tone." The man straightened his cuffs. "Introduce me to your lady."

Dallas would eat his own boots if there was anyone in the room who didn't know who Lex was, just like he knew Mac had a long-suffering wife pregnant with her seventh or eighth kid—Mac's way of flaunting his access to the fertility drugs that counteracted the birth control Eden fed into every available water supply. Dallas had met her twice in ten years. Mac was far more likely to show up with a sleepy-eyed mistress on his arm, some pretty, barely grown girl willing to trade her body for a high.

Drawing Lex back to his side, Dallas bared his teeth. "Lex, this is Mac Fleming, head of Sector Five."

Lex offered her hand. "How do you do?"

He smirked at the equally smarmy bodyguard lurking behind him. "Manners, and from Sector Four, no less." Then Fleming stopped short and lifted a hand. "Though you were raised here, yes?"

"Yes." Lex smiled, sweet but somehow icy. "I was Cerys's best pupil, but only in certain subjects. Oral sex and improvised weaponry, for example, though rarely in conjunction."

Dallas damn near choked on his own spit. Fleming's bodyguard spluttered, though Mac only sighed and shook his head. "And there's your rough influence, O'Kane."

Grinning, Dallas smoothed a proprietary hand over Lex's hair. "What can I say. We like our women only mostly tamed. Where's the fun in a woman who'd never stab you just a little, if you pissed her off bad enough?"

"You like to live more dangerously than I do."

Dallas patted her hip. "No danger. You wouldn't stab me anywhere important, would you, love?"

Before she could answer, a melodious chime rang through the hall. The call to dinner, and whatever entertainment Cerys had devised. It was guaranteed to be illicit—Sector Two took cultured debauchery to heights unimagined even by most of the O'Kanes. For once, Dallas wasn't relieved to be spared more conversation. Watching Lex sharpen her tongue on bastards like Mac Fleming revved him harder than anything Cerys could have planned.

Fleming and his bodyguard drifted toward the long table, but Dallas slid his hand around Lex's abdomen to hold her back. He splayed his fingers wide over the skin bared by her corset—the skin marked with his name—and lowered his mouth to her ear. "I should have brought you with me years ago."

She dug her nails into the back of his wrist. "I'm here now."

Two steps to the left and he had her up against one of those ridiculous columns. It seemed a lot less ridiculous when he had Lex pinned to it, her hands trapped under his, her leather-clad ass rubbing against his cock. He found her ear again and bit it roughly enough to draw a moan from her. "If you were wearing a skirt, I'd be in you already. I'd fuck you right here, while they sat down to dinner."

She wiggled and moaned again when he held tight. "Why? To show them what a big man you are?"

"No." He swept her hair aside and bit the back of her neck this time, setting a mark in her smooth skin. He'd have Ace do it for real someday—that much he'd already promised himself. For now, he used his teeth before licking the ravaged spot. "Because watching you wield a verbal knife gets me hot. Slice up that jackass from Seven over dinner, and I'll make it worth your trouble tonight."

"You're gonna do that anyway."

He knew Lex. He'd paid attention to all those trysts he'd pretended not to notice, had filed away the pleasures Lex pursued again and again. He knew how to stir fantasy to life. "Maybe I'll invite Bren or Mad to help me. Maybe both."

Lex shuddered. "You're a dirty tease, Declan."

"Only I get to fuck you." He tugged at her hair, arching her head back until she had to meet his eyes. "But they're creative. They'll think of a dozen ways each to get you off."

Her eyes fluttered shut, and she snapped them open again. "And you, telling them what to do, every step of the way."

He kissed her, hard and abrupt, a promise more than anything else. Her lips tasted too good for him to linger, or he really would decide fucking her was better than gritting his teeth through awkward dinner chatter. He stepped back and smoothed her hair back into place. "I *am* the king, darling."

Her gaze raked over him, head to toe. Her breathing was just short of steady, and a delicate flush colored the skin above her corset. "I hope that means you can fake dinner conversation with my hand around your cock. You deserve the distraction."

He almost thought she was joking, but he shouldn't have. They'd only been seated for a few minutes when Lex landed her first verbal blow on Sector Seven, undercutting Colby's crudely leering greeting with cool ease. The lights dimmed before the man could recover, and a dozen of Cerys's girls glided into view, draped in transparent scarves and enough sparkling jewels to impress men used to pretty things.

Dallas appreciated the beauty of woman debauching each other, but Cerys's little show always lacked heat, honesty. The girls were pretty, no doubt, and flexible in ways some of the dancers at the Broken Circle would envy. But there was an emptiness to their movements, almost an innocence, if you could call a woman innocent as she was spread wide and stroked by a half-dozen hands before being flogged to supposed ecstasy.

For all their artful moans and graceful thrashing, Dallas couldn't see past the choreography. The other men never seemed to notice, but they weren't used to watching Lex and Noelle crawl all over each other, their tongue-tangling kisses hot because they weren't really meant for anyone else. Even on a stage, with a crowded bar of men riveted to her every move, Lex never let anyone forget she owned her own pleasure, and anyone who got to see it should count himself lucky.

So should any man seeking to tame her. As a second girl submitted to a whipping that turned her ass pink, Lex's hand settled in Dallas's lap. The theatrics planned by Cerys had done little enough to stir his blood, but Lex got it raging with a few clever strokes. If she'd started teasing him already, she no doubt meant to drive him crazy by the time dinner ended and they returned to their rooms.

When this was over, he'd have time to teach her the truth. He was always crazy when it came to her.

8

Their guest suite had been modeled after a nine-teenth-century Parisian brothel, complete with wide, velvet-covered chaises, elaborate crown moldings, and gilt-edged wallpaper. Everything was decorated in shades of red and gold, opulent in a heavy, desperate sort of way, and Lex hated it on sight.

Cerys had chosen it purposefully, of that much she was sure. The woman never did anything by accident, but always by design. This room, with its low lighting and furnishings that looked cheap no matter their extravagant expense, was meant to remind Lex of her origins. Of her place.

No matter how far she ran, it said, she would always be a whore.

Mad was sitting on one of the sofas, smoking. Lex dropped beside him, kicked off her shoes, and plucked the cigarette from his hand. "I hope you had a better evening than we did."

"Hard to tell, sometimes, with Bren." Once she'd taken a puff, Mad rescued the cigarette and took a long drag. "Sometimes I think he's ready to blow a vein, and it turns out he's having the time of his life."

Bren glowered at them from the bar across the room. "This is my relaxed face."

Lex laughed. "Mad's right. It looks just like your *I'm about to rip a bastard's spine out through his ears* face."

"And all of his faces are a little busted." Mad tossed the rakish fall of hair from his eyes and grinned at Lex. "He wishes he was pretty like me."

"Mmm." She ran her thumb over his lower lip. "And you wish you were pretty like Dallas."

Mad bit the pad of her thumb and caught her wrist. "Where is our fearless leader?"

"On his way." She did her best to look innocent as she tilted her head. "The guy from Eight won't talk in front of simple-minded females like me, you know."

"Lucky you. He's more boring than God and all the angels." Mad dropped her hand back into her lap with a wink. "Speaking of higher powers, you keep your pretty little hands to yourself. I'll cuddle you all night long, but this—" his finger brushed her collar, "—means I'll answer to one vengeful motherfucker if I get too friendly."

"You could help me blow him." The mental images were more reminiscence than imagination. "Wouldn't be the first time you'd licked my tongue *and* his cock."

"Sweet words won't change my mind," Mad informed her with mock severity, but she could see the heat of memory in his gaze, as well. He'd always taken pleasure as freely as he gave it, and the more warm bodies around him, the better.

"Too bad." She shifted on the couch until she was leaning against the opposite arm with her feet in Mad's lap. "I think Dallas is feeling a little wild tonight. But if you don't want to play..."

Rolling his eyes, he dropped his hands to her feet. He was clever with his fingers and knew how to push his thumbs right where her foot ached from her shoes. "Don't be dense, lovely. If Dallas is feeling frisky, even Bren and his busted face will jump in the pile with you."

Bren grunted before draining his drink. "You're sure as hell not getting any of this, though," he told Mad.

Mad winked at Lex. "We'll see, won't we?"

Spoken as if he had no doubt Bren would fuck him, given half a chance. Then again, few people in the world had proven immune to Mad's charms. "You're terrible," Lex proclaimed. "And delicious."

"We're all—" The door crashed open hard enough to make him jump, and he jerked his hands away from Lex's feet as if he'd been caught with them down her pants.

Dallas was too furious to notice. He slammed the door shut behind him and kicked it for good measure, his face carved in forbidding lines. "I *hate* these motherfuckers."

Whatever the bastard from Sector Eight had said to Dallas, it hadn't made him happy. Lex made a soothing noise and beckoned him. "Time to hide from them for a while."

Mad abandoned the sofa to make room for Dallas, who dropped to the plush cushions with a groan. "That's how I kept from wringing his damn neck. I thought about how disappointed you'd be if we had to waste the night shooting our way across two sectors to get home."

"What the hell did he say?" she asked.

Dallas snagged her with one arm and hauled her into his lap so she was straddling his thighs, her face level with his. Still scowling, he traced his thumb along her jaw. "He was impressed with how neatly you cut Colby's knees out from under him. He wants to buy a girl from Cerys and have me train her up like I did you."

A notion almost as laughable as it was horrible. "Someone doesn't understand how the concept works, hmm? A woman who'll speak her mind?"

"Like he could handle one." Dallas let his head thump back against the sofa and grinned up at her. "Besides, there's only one Lex."

"Only me." The tension started to seep from his muscles, and she stroked her hands up his arms. "Did you tell him to go fuck himself?"

"Worse. I told him Cerys sent you to me just the way you are." He stroked her throat and the soft lace edging her collar. "I hope she sends him a clever little spy who jerks his territory out from under him. I don't care if it makes her stronger."

Bren couldn't let that stand. "You can't afford not to care," he told Dallas firmly. "Cerys is ruthless."

"Fine, I don't care *tonight*," Dallas amended. "He's already got it in his head to take one of Cerys's girls, and I was too fucking pissed to talk him out of it."

Lex nuzzled his cheek. "Don't listen to Bren. You need to relax for a while, or you'll drive yourself nuts."

"Mmm." His hands fell to her hips, edging her closer. "You gonna help me relax?"

No matter what he'd promised before dinner, he couldn't mean to include Mad and Bren—especially since at least one of them had to pull first watch. Still, just knowing the other men could hear the gentle command was its own measure of arousal. Her skin prickled, and her nipples tightened. "Is that an order?"

He kept one hand on her hip and caught her chin with the other, his thumb coming to rest against her lips. "All night, all those bastards' eyes on you. They wish they owned you, even Cerys. But they don't, do they?"

She couldn't move her mouth under the bruising pressure of his thumb, so she shook her head.

"That's right. You're an O'Kane." He eased his thumb down, forcing her lips apart. "And you had your hand on my dick half the night. Get on your knees and finish what you started."

The urge to obey trembled through her. She wanted him in her mouth, but not as much as she wanted to challenge him with a little bite. So she did it literally, closing her teeth sharply on his thumb.

He laughed and drove his other hand into her hair, twisting as he surged to his feet and spilled her to the floor. "Fine, Lexie. I'll get just as hard putting you there myself. Maybe harder."

He held tight to her hair, the delicious pressure skirting close to pain, and her hand brushed his erection as she reached for his belt buckle. "That's how I like it. Hard enough to be a little rough."

"I know." He gave her hair an extra sharp tug as a fond smile curved his lips. "You got a taste of what you like. You want more? Give me what I like."

She glanced over her shoulder. Mad quirked one eyebrow at her from a large cushion, and Bren's fingers had constricted around his glass. "You're a tease, Dallas," he muttered darkly.

"I'm a selfish bastard," Dallas corrected, dragging Lex's head back around. "Ask them if they'll watch, Lex. Ask them if they'll do it because it makes you hot."

"I don't ask anyone for anything." She pulled his belt buckle open. "Nobody but you."

His eyes sparked, and his slow smile promised sex, the kind where you came so hard you'd ache for days. "That's my girl." He looked past her. "You two can make yourselves scarce or park your asses on the couch and enjoy the show. I'll return the favor when Cerys sends a girl around to bounce on your dicks."

Bren set his glass on the bar with a gentle thump. "Someone has to make sure Cerys doesn't send bullets or blades instead. I'll man the door."

"All right." Dallas stroked Lex's cheek. "And, Bren? Don't let anyone in. Not even one of the girls. I'm not in the mood to be interrupted."

"Yes, sir."

The door clicked shut, and Mad rose before circling to stand next to Dallas. For once, Lex couldn't decipher the odd look in his eyes. Assessment, maybe, or anticipation. "Sure you don't want a hand, boss? Or two? I'll put 'em wherever you want 'em and keep my dick to myself."

"Stay close," Dallas murmured, still caressing Lex's face. "If she doesn't get my fucking pants open in the next ten seconds, I may have you spank her ass."

Not quite a tease, because he was fully capable of doing it. Lex turned to lick his wrist, running her tongue over the ink marking his skin, and jerked at his zipper. Her fingers shook when she wrapped them around the thick, hot length of his cock to guide it free.

He shuddered before easing her hand out of the way and gripping the shaft. "Hands at the small of your back, Lex. Mad, find something to tie them there."

He walked away, and Lex leaned toward Dallas as she crossed her wrists behind her back. "I thought you liked having me touch you."

Challenge didn't transcend the lust in his eyes as he stroked his fist up the length of his erection, but it came close. "You need your hands to get me off?"

There was no part of her she wouldn't use, her hands or voice or tongue. She rubbed her cheek against his fingers and licked them before continuing on to his hard, pulsing heat.

He groaned with the first touch of her tongue, and her victory was the involuntary twitch of his hips, pushing the crown of his cock past her lips. Rough fingertips dug into the back of her head, and Dallas's voice dropped to a low rumble. "I thought about this during that whole stupid show. I could've shown them a Sector Four barbarian. Demanded you blow me right there at the dinner table."

That and more, anything to draw those harsh noises of pleasure that echoed inside her, left her wet and desperate for relief. Lex pushed on, taking him deeper without his urging.

"Fuck." The word seemed torn from him against his will, but more followed, gruff and intense. "You would've done it. You would have let me fuck your face, and they would have thought I owned you, because they're stupid fucks. They'll never get it."

Cerys would. She understood the power a woman could have on her knees, the intense give and take of control that made a man like Dallas so dangerous.

And so delectable.

She didn't realize Mad had returned until his fingers slid down her arms. Silk followed, a sumptuous length of fabric that had undoubtedly been left for this purpose. Mad tied her wrists with a few deft movements and released her, but she could still feel him behind her, an extension of Dallas's will.

Delectable.

With her hands bound, she was finally free to move. Lex flexed her fingers, testing the silk. It held fast, and she turned her attention to licking the ridge around the head of Dallas's cock with her tongue. She flicked the sensitive spot just under the crown, tapped it with her tongue, and looked up to meet his eyes.

"Suck me," he whispered, the softness of the command not blunting it in the least. "Deep and hard and fast. Get me off."

A shudder tore through her. Maybe she'd exhausted his patience already, driven him past the point of prolonging his pleasure.

Or maybe he wanted to come because he couldn't wait to get his hands on her.

She moved—quick and deep, just like he'd said— her own excitement speeding her movements. He wanted *so much*, and she felt it all, especially when he growled and pushed against the back of her head.

"Take off her corset," he growled, and Mad reached around to tug at the laces crisscrossing her breasts.

So heavy and full. Lex moaned in the split second before one more thrust took him all the way into the back of her throat. She swallowed, held him there, her breath cut off as surely as her resistance. Arousal thrummed in her veins, bloomed within her until she was certain the rigid leather was all that held her in check. Without it, the cool air and Mad's hands and Dallas's eyes would drive her over the edge, and she'd explode.

Dallas snarled and dragged her head back, and the latches on her corset gave way just in time. Mad pulled it wide, and Dallas jerked his hand roughly over his dick before groaning his release. Semen spilled across her breasts, a primal mark of possession every bit as real as the collar and the ink—and as subtle as a hard left hook to the jaw.

She licked the corner of her mouth and tried to catch her breath. Dallas's gaze was riveted to her breasts, which heaved with each panting breath. "All yours," she rasped. "Is this what you wanted at dinner?"

"For starters." Dallas continued to watch her as Mad eased the corset out from under her bound arms. His hands were warm and strong but carefully, deliberately impersonal. Not even Ace would have tested Dallas with that possessive glint in his eyes.

When the fabric slipped away, Dallas touched the corner of Lex's mouth. "Mad?"

"Yeah, boss?"

"Go jerk off on your own or wait for the hooker. I'll make it up to you."

Mad leaned in just enough to whisper against Lex's ear. "Have fun, honey." Then his heat vanished, and there was no one left but Dallas, looming over her with an insatiable hunger in his eyes.

She didn't speak. There was nothing to say—not yet.

Dallas took his time refastening his pants and shedding his vest. He looked out of place in the delicate surroundings, his broad, tattooed chest too raw and unrelentingly uncivilized.

He didn't match the polite lie of a fancy French whorehouse, but his sudden, cocky grin flipped that thought on its head. Then the *room* looked out of place around *Dallas*, as if he was the one who truly belonged and the whole place was flawed for not bending reality to suit him.

Everything else did. Even her.

After an endless silence, Dallas traced her jaw and put the tip of his finger under her chin. "I'm feeling possessive tonight, Lexie love, so here's your choice. I can untie you and we can have a little tease and cuddle... or you can stand up and go into the bedroom. If you do that, I'm going to play with you until you think you can't take it anymore, and then I'm going to ride you so hard your legs won't work in the morning. Pick one."

"Just cuddling?" She managed to climb to her feet. "Don't be such a girl, Declan."

"Hey, I already got mine." His gaze flicked to her chest, and she could taste the smugness in the air. "If you want your turn, less backtalk, more walking."

As if he didn't know the truth. "There's more to sex, the really good kind, than orgasms." She turned for the bedroom, but instead of his steps trailing hers, he veered off into the washroom.

Lex waited, one knee propped on the velvet-covered bench at the foot of the bed. Mirrors lined the walls, inset into the panels laden with delicate, fussy woodwork. Each one was framed with drapes that could be released to cover the mirrors.

They were open now, and reflected Dallas in dizzying multitude when he returned with a damp towel in hand. He swiped it over her breasts with a teasing tenderness that undercut his low, intense words. "Obedience, Lex. I'm going to take it tonight." His knuckles grazed one nipple, and he paused to tug on it. "But you go ahead and be as sassy as you want. I'll get off on shutting you up."

She shivered, as much from the dark look in his eyes as the sensual contact. "You always do."

His brows drew together as he tossed aside the towel and grabbed her hips. He hauled her off the bench, then jerked her pants open roughly. "That's my girl. Always going for blood."

Because she couldn't stop, even when her words kindled that stormy frown. "Why don't you ask yourself why you like it so much when I hiss at you?"

"Who gives a fuck why?" He hooked her pants and underwear and dragged both down her legs. "I'm not worried about psychology with your pussy two inches from my face, love. Lift your foot."

She began to obey automatically, and that alone was enough to slam her heel back down on the floor.

"No?" No anger in the word, just amusement, so she wasn't ready when Dallas lunged. His shoulder thumped against her abdomen as his hand slapped down on her ass, and then he was on his feet with her dangling over his shoulder.

Instead of a shiver, this time it was a shudder, one that shook her whole body and left her nipples in hard points that got even harder when they rubbed against the hot, bare skin of his back.

Dallas circled the bed and dropped her onto her stomach with her feet on the floor. Nothing had been left to chance in the design of the furniture, even the height of the bed. It was high enough to support her upper body once Dallas stripped away her pants and nudged her feet apart, and no matter which way she turned her head, she was treated to her own reflection—her body bent submissively in front of him and her wrists deftly bound at the small of her back.

With her heels gone, Lex stood stretched up on her toes, naked and helpless. She turned her cheek to the soft fabric covering the bed and closed her eyes, waiting for the slow burn of continuously flexed muscle to start.

"You gonna let me be sweet to you now, Lexie?" His fingertips grazed the curve of her ass. "I don't think you are. I don't think you like it as much when I'm sweet to you."

He didn't wait for an answer—not that she was

willing to give one. He crossed the room, footsteps fading bit by bit as he moved, and she kept her eyes shut. Waited.

It didn't take long for him to return. Sensuous silk slithered over her back, more like the fabric looped around her wrist. Dallas left it there and smoothed both hands down her sides until his fingers dug into her hips. One foot nudged the inside of her ankle. "Open wider."

It left her even more exposed, with cool air on her heated flesh and the teasing promise of Dallas's touch. "Like this?"

"Good girl." He slid one hand between her legs, fingers slicking over her pussy before he spread her outer lips wide and plunged one broad finger inside her. Pleasure buzzed in her ears, and she clenched around him. "How long have you been wet? Did it get you hot, fondling my dick under the dinner table?"

"Yes." She could barely move, but it didn't stop her from trying. "I wanted to fuck you then."

"Not much of a show, was it?" He worked his finger in and out, shallow, lazy strokes that brushed over sensitive spots without enough pressure to do more than taunt. "Those bastards couldn't handle watching you and Noelle writhe on each other."

"Neither can you."

"Smartass." He swatted her ass with his free hand, a mere warning slap before his hand fell again in earnest.

The third blow left her skin burning, and she bit her lip to hold back a moan. "Fuck."

"You'll have to settle for my hand tonight," he murmured as his finger resumed its leisurely thrusting. "Unless you come without asking. That might earn you a round with my belt."

Would he do it while he fucked her, lay the leather across her back every time an orgasm swept her into its clutches, mixing ecstasy and pain until she couldn't separate them anymore? "I don't need permission to find pleasure. You wouldn't stop me."

Rough fingers twisted in her hair, and he dragged her head up until she was forced to meet his gaze in the mirror. His expression was rough, a short step from wild. "I never used to." It was barely more than a whisper, but the words were stern. Hard. "But then, you weren't wearing my collar before, were you, love? You ask permission now."

It was instinct to struggle, to make him earn that control. He clenched his hand, his grip steady and implacable, and when she twisted he pulled his finger out of her and slapped her ass again. "Tell me you understand. I want to hear it. If you come without asking, you might get my belt." He leaned over her, his breath warm on her cheek. "Or maybe I'll just stop altogether. You'll have to take that risk if you're feeling bratty."

Lex met his eyes in the mirror without guarding her own hunger. "I understand."

"Good." He tugged at her hair, sending another jolt through her, before releasing it to fall around her face. "Because you're mine, honey. And I'm not in a sharing sort of mood tonight."

She bowed her head to rest her forehead on the bed. "I didn't ask you to."

Dallas dragged his hand from the nape of her neck to the small of her back. "I know, but I promised. I thought I'd be able to go through with it, but I couldn't. Not tonight. Not here."

Not in someone else's territory, when everything else was far from under his control. Lex hummed softly and rocked up against his hand. "You have me."

She watched his reflection as he retrieved one swath of silk and smoothed it between his fingers. "Crawl up on the bed. Kneeling, legs together."

She wiggled her hands in their bindings. "I can't. It's too high without my hands."

Dallas dipped into his back pocket and pulled out a familiar knife. The blade caught the light, twinkling dangerously, as he flipped it open. "Be still," he warned her, then slipped the steel beneath the silk. The flat of the blade brushed her arm, cool against heated flesh, but the sharp edge sliced through the fabric before she even thought of moving.

Her hands slipped free, and Lex rubbed her wrists. "Kneeling, legs together?"

Laughing, he eased the knife shut. "For now, love."

She climbed on the bed, knees together, but instead of leaning forward on all fours, she sat back on her heels. It wasn't what he'd meant—he wanted her bent over, so he could touch her pussy even after he tied her up—but he wasn't the only one with demands tonight.

He'd get exactly what he commanded. No more, no less.

In the mirror, his reflection watched her with an impassive expression and unreadable eyes. Anything could have been going on behind that blank mask as he put his knife away and reached for the silk again. He lifted it...

And settled it across her eyes.

She closed her eyes and took a deep breath as he tied it, his knuckles brushing her hair. The world drew in on itself, condensed until the only thing that existed was *waiting*. Anticipating the next touch.

It came in the form of roughened fingertips tracing

along the front of her throat. "You see everything, don't you?"

"I—" Her voice broke, and she had to clear her throat. "I try to."

"You've had to."

"Yes."

His hand closed around her throat, over her collar. Not tightly enough to restrict her breathing, but his grip was firm. Possessive. "Not anymore. Not with me."

A lifetime's habit didn't stop like that, with *words*. "You'll have to show me how."

He laughed right next to her ear before his touch disappeared. Steps circled, soft and muffled. The next time he spoke, he was somewhere to her left, and she turned her face toward the sound of his voice. "I'm going to show you a lot of things, Lexie."

She bit her lip to hide a smile. "Like what?"

No answer. Leather whispered over leather—his belt pulling free of his pants—followed by silence. Then he said, "Hands and knees, Lex. Crawl toward my voice."

Right in front of her.

They'd flirted with this game before, and Lex knew how it went. Soon, her body would respond effortlessly, without thought. For now, she'd have to make the conscious decision to obey.

She reached out, creeping forward until her hands hit the bed. Then she began to crawl.

He stopped her with a hand in her hair. He wrapped the length around his palm this time and used the grip to haul her head up until only her fingertips brushed the mattress.

His mouth on hers was a shock, as much a shock as the gentleness of his kiss while he held her neck craned back at such a severe angle. She barely remembered to leave her hands on the bed as she parted her lips and traced her tongue over his lips. He caught the tip of it between his teeth in a warning bite, and his groan vibrated through her as he chased her tongue back into her mouth with his own.

Harder now, almost punishing. Lex whimpered as thought vanished, and she reached up to thread her fingers through the hair at the back of his neck.

Dallas bit her lower lip as he eased back, but only far enough to whisper a rough directive. "Fuck yourself with your hand. Not slow, either. I want to hear that slick, delicious sound. Fingers shoving deep into a hungry pussy."

Not being able to see magnified everything—the sound of his breaths, slow and measured, and the smell of him, leather and spice. Even her own touch, cool fingers on warmer skin. She started at her throat, slipped over the collar that marked her as his and down, pausing to brush one nipple as she eased her knees apart.

Stomach, hip. She tracked her progress with a shiver and then a startled moan when she reached her pussy, wet and aching with the kind of arousal that took only a touch to spin off into desperate hunger.

Quickly, she circled her clit, but just once, and moved on, low enough to slide inside. She thrust two fingers deep and held them there, the heel of her hand pressed hard against her slippery flesh.

"No wonder Noelle's such an unrepentant brat. You're a bad influence." Disapproving words, wrapped in amused warmth. Dallas jerked on her hair, hauling her fully upright. "Maybe I should ask Jas how he feels about that."

As if she gave a damn. "Should I care what he thinks about it?"

Suddenly, Dallas was *there*, his breath against

her ear, his free hand covering hers where it pressed between her legs. "What if he wanted to take his belt to your ass for it? Would you want the collar gone if I tied you over my bench and let him whip you over the edge? Or maybe Mad or Bren. Or all three of them."

She wanted to say yes, to give him a line he couldn't cross—but this wasn't it. "No," she whispered. "I wouldn't want it gone."

He sucked in a sharp breath, and the hand blanketing hers trembled. Simple words of submission, but if his groan was any indication, they inflamed him. He cupped her breast, his thumb and forefinger closing on her taut nipple. "Fuck yourself, Lex. *Now.*"

She moved, rocking her hand in a grind that gave way too quickly to *fucking*, sharp, hard thrusts of her fingers that splintered tingles up her spine until only his grip on her hair kept her upright.

That, and the fact that he hadn't yet given her permission to sink to the bed.

She had no warning before his mouth closed around her nipple. He was simply there, rough heat, his teeth digging into soft flesh and his tongue lashing back and forth, flicking over her in time with her thrusting fingers.

Her shaking legs would barely hold her. She gasped his name, and the sound was still dying on her lips when she orgasmed. It singed her all over, a burning pleasure quick enough to wrench a cry from her throat but deep enough to curl her toes. Lex crooked her fingers, desperate to prolong it.

He let her ride the waves, but when the final one shuddered through her, he gripped her wrist and dragged her hand away. "Looks like you need a lesson in asking first, don't you, love?"

Fuck. She swallowed hard. "I forgot."

"I noticed." His lips brushed her ear in a teasing, reassuring kiss before he planted one hand in the center of her chest and pushed. "Fold your arms behind you and lie back."

She was still kneeling. Bending back on the bed, especially with her arms beneath her, would leave her helpless and at his mercy. "I'm trusting you," she murmured, then yielded to the pressure of his hand.

Once her head and shoulders rested on the bed, Dallas drew both hands down her body, pausing to tweak her nipples before his fingers came to rest on her upper thighs. He circled his thumbs, stroking her pussy before spreading her outer lips wide.

Not just at his mercy. On display, open and bare. Helpless. He gave her a silent eternity to feel it before answering, "Trust is the point, love."

His tongue found her clit.

Her legs flexed, but he held her hips still. She was still buzzing, and the inexorably direct contact almost hurt...for a heartbeat. Then the buzzing mellowed into heat, and Lex moaned. "Dallas..."

No reply beyond the clever swipe of his tongue. He knew how to toy with her, when to ease off and build anticipation with slow licks that dragged the rough flat of his tongue over every sensitive spot, and when to return to hard and fast to work her clit with arrogant assurance.

He hauled her closer and closer to the edge, until it was sharp enough to cut. Heat built in her belly until her entire body tensed in anticipation—

And he lifted his head.

She groaned and gripped the bedspread in one fist. "Don't *stop*, damn it."

His chuckle flowed over her. "I'm saving you from yourself, Lexie. I don't think you were about to ask if you could come."

She'd thought that his reasons didn't matter, but the knot in the pit of her stomach said otherwise. "Tell me why first."

The bed tilted by her head, and she could feel him looming over her, his weight braced with one hand on the mattress. He tugged at the silk, lifting it up and away from her eyes. His face filled her vision, a strong jaw with a day's worth of stubble, his crooked nose and those dark, dangerous eyes.

"Because I'm a selfish bastard," he answered, stroking her cheek. "When a woman's mine, she doesn't take pleasure. I give it to her."

Selfish, yes, and conceited. But she'd half expected him to need to prove there wasn't anything he didn't own, including her, so the answer filled her with relief instead of rage. "Then give it to me." Her gaze locked with his. "Let me come. Please."

"Mmm." He straightened and stroked her trembling inner thighs. His thumb touched her clit, jolting her back toward arousal as he worked two broad fingers into her body. "Not yet. Remember to ask when you're close this time, and I'll consider it. Or we can do this all night."

Lost in desire, she rocked her hips. "I will. I'll ask."

"We'll see." The tattoos wrapped around his arms rippled with his flexing muscles, each one working in graceful concert for the sole purpose of fucking into her, faster and harder with each advance, but when she tried to push up, he planted his other hand on her belly and pinned her against the bed.

Caught again, and this time Lex didn't hold back. Waves of hot, insistent bliss began to build, teasing her with how very, very good she could feel—if she'd only let go.

"Please," she whispered, writhing against his hand. "Can I—holy fuck, *please*. Please let me come—"

"Who gets to decide, Lexie?"

"You." She squeezed her eyes shut as her breath tangled on a sob. "You do, you decide."

"That's right." His fingers crooked, working her G-spot, shoving her toward oblivion. Testing her. "Why, honey? Tell me why."

She barely had the wits to answer, and her voice sounded far away and strained. "Because I'm yours."

"You're mine," he agreed. So warm, so approving. His voice wrapped around her as his thumb settled on her clit, the perfect, piercing counterpoint. "So come for me."

Lex tensed, and her eyes snapped open. How did he do it, have her body responding to the words as if triggered for exactly that? Her arms were going numb, her muscles were cramping, and she didn't give a flying fuck. All that mattered was his hand, his fingers, and the sheer, overwhelming ecstasy flooding her.

"Just like that, love." He dragged her through her climax with relentless stroking and his thumb working in circles that wouldn't stop. "Feels so good to let go, doesn't it?"

Good didn't describe the torturous pleasure. "Dallas—" Her voice shuddered, broke.

"Want something, honey?"

So satisfied. So smug. "Fuck you," she panted.

Laughing, Dallas pulled his fingers free of her body. "Not unless you ask nicely." He traced his slick fingertips over her nipple. Before she could respond, he bent to capture the stiff peak between his lips, sucking the taste of her from her skin with an appreciative rumble.

She'd given him so much, and still he wanted

more. Everything. "I won't ask."

"You will." Rough hands closed around her shoulders without warning. She barely had time to smack his arm with one numb hand before he dragged her from the bed and flipped her to her stomach.

The edge of the mattress bit into her abdomen as he braced his thighs on either side of hers and pinned her in place. Lex struck at him, but he caught her arms and held them tight. "You will," he echoed, "but maybe not tonight."

He'd fuck her like this, pinned down and protesting. He'd do it.

The thought shuddered through her, echoing in rhythmic pulses of hunger that left her wetter than ever, her pussy swollen and her upper thighs slick. "No." Another pulse as she breathed the denial. The plea. "Don't."

Dallas gripped both wrists in one hand. The other trailed up her spine as he ground his leather-encased cock against her ass. "I know this is the game you want to play, but that's not how it works, honey. You don't get to skip straight to this. You're not ready."

She had to bite her lip to hold back a cry of sheer frustration. He not only craved her submission to his touch, he had to define exactly how she gave it to him— and her clumsy offerings always seemed to be wrong. "Then can I get up now?"

"No." He stroked her back. "I want to fuck you, just like this. I wanna hold you down and ride you so damn deep we're *both* screaming for mercy. You don't have to beg. You don't even have to ask, not tonight. But you have to tell me you want it, because you're not the only one who isn't ready for that game."

The hint of vulnerability in his words melted her resistance. "How can you still wonder? I want you. I always want you—I always *have*."

The backs of his fingers grazed her ass as he jerked at his pants, and she knew she'd won. Maybe more than one battle, judging from the rough way he pushed her feet wide and repositioned himself between her thighs.

"Someday." He guided her arms down to her sides and folded her fingers around the edge of the mattress. She had no warning before his fingers twisted into her, driving a cry from her throat, pushing deep as his thumb teased between her ass cheeks. "Someday, we'll play your game, Lexie. Right out to the edge and over it. That's a promise."

A promise, and Declan O'Kane never went back on his word.

Lex gripped the mattress. "I need you with me this time."

He pumped his fingers lazily—once, twice—only to withdraw them and trace one slick fingertip up to push against her ass. "You'll get my cock as soon as I decide where I want to put it."

She hissed in a breath. "Anywhere."

"That's what I like to hear," he whispered as the blunt head of his cock prodded her pussy. One long rock took him inside, thick and hard and stretching her inner muscles, and he groaned and wrapped both hands around her shoulders. "You'll let me fuck you any goddamn way I want, won't you?"

Lex couldn't answer, not with Dallas walking the edge of her darkest fantasies. She tried, went so far as to open her mouth, but all that emerged was a pleading whimper. In response, he tightened his grip on her shoulders, holding her in place for a single hard thrust—rough, claiming.

Fire.

Her pulse pounded in her ears as she tried to center herself, but Dallas stripped it all away with another deep drive of his hips. Fast, faster than her racing heart.

Exactly what she wanted.

His satisfied groans rose behind her, raw animal sounds that prickled over her skin and punctuated his speeding thrusts. He cracked his open palm across her ass with his next advance and growled. "Up on your elbows," he commanded, pulling back on one shoulder to lift her upper body. "I want to watch your tits bounce in those ridiculous fucking mirrors."

He wanted *her* to watch, to see the quick slam of his cock into her pussy. To watch him take her.

She arched her back and gave it to him—but not too easy. "Mother*fucker*." Reaching up, she slipped her fingers into his hair and pulled. *Hard.*

Dallas just laughed and fucked her faster. Oh, he liked the hint of pain, almost as much as he liked the control.

And he had it. He shifted her hips with one hand, guiding her back into a deeper arch. He always knew just how to fuck her with his fingers—when to hold off and when to drive her higher—but this was different. Possessive. Desperate.

Fierce.

When she found his reflection in the mirror, the truth hit her as hard as his next thrust. He was wild, his lips parted in a needy snarl, his eyes narrowed and dark, so dark. Every inch of control he gained over her stripped away a layer of the control he had over himself.

Give and take. Not about bodies, or even the breathless ecstasy lighting her up from the inside out. Suddenly, it made sense, and she knew what he really needed.

Every thrust bordered on pain now, grinding her against the bed. She could barely speak, but she managed to hold his gaze in the mirror and let him see *her* truth. "You have me," she rasped. "I'm yours."

He shuddered, his fingers digging bruises into her skin. "Come for me. Come all over me."

Her head hit his shoulder. She couldn't stop shaking, but there was something, *something*— "Harder."

"No." One hand caged her throat as he slammed into her with a grunt. "Just like this." Another thrust, angled just right and riding the sharp edge of too much. "Just hard enough."

His hand tightened a little, and Lex shuddered. She gripped his wrist, her nails digging in to his skin. "More."

"Filthy girl." His lips crushed against her ear, teeth scraping her lobe as he carefully, oh-so-slowly tightened his fingers. "You want it rough and raw," he rasped in a low whisper. "I'll give you that, love. I'll give you the fucking world."

Yes. The world he spoke of, beautiful and bright, spun around her in dizzying, white-hot circles. The pressure of Dallas's hand collided with the pressure building inside her—until it all exploded in a blinding, choking rush. And this time he was there, riding her ecstasy, his obscene torrent of words reduced to a guttural snarl of her name as he came inside her.

Her knees wouldn't hold her. As soon as the hand around her throat eased, Lex stumbled. Dallas caught her and swung her up onto the bed, though he didn't seem particularly steady, either.

It didn't stop him from pushing her hair back from her face and brushing a soft kiss to her lips. "You with me, darling?"

Her tongue felt thick, useless, but she managed a

slow nod.

"Good. I'll be right back."

The mattress shifted, Lex opened her eyes and watched the low light gild the hard, muscled lines of his Dallas's body as he stripped off his clothes. "The lamps should have voice controls."

"Damn waste of resources," he grumbled, but she noticed he still took advantage of it, sliding into bed beside her before ordering the lights to a bare glow.

His warmth bolstered the soft haze of pleasure that still blurred the world around its edges, and Lex curled up in his arms. "The big meeting's tomorrow?"

"Mmm. A few hours of backbiting and arguing while everyone circles like stray dogs. And, if we're *really* lucky, maybe an assassination attempt by lunch."

She might have laughed—if it hadn't been so terribly likely. "Watch yourself, okay?"

He curled a hand around her rib cage, spreading his fingers until his thumb brushed her breast. "You, too. And don't you try'n ditch Mad, either. If he loses sight of you outside this room, I'll beat his ass down."

"I wouldn't." Wandering around Sector Two with no backup appealed to her about as much as sticking her hand in a snake pit.

"Good. I don't like this place. Don't like letting you out of my sight." His sigh tickled her temple. "Not just for your benefit, either. I don't have a damn clue how I'll keep my temper tomorrow."

He'd do it, like so many other things, because he had to. She turned her face and kissed his jaw. "It'll be over soon."

"Yeah? Do I get a reward for getting through the day without stabbing anyone?"

She rubbed one bare leg over his. "I'll think of something creative."

His laughter was a low rumble that vibrated through her as he rolled her beneath him. "I like you like this," he murmured against her lips. "Sleepy and sweaty and disheveled. Sexiest fucking thing in the world."

Any other time, she might have fought the pleasure that rose with his words. But here, now, the satisfaction seemed not only acceptable but *necessary*.

This was what it meant, the collar. The marks.

She didn't hold back the slow smile that curved her lips. "Don't you forget it."

rachel

You can do this. Rachel wrapped her hand around the slightly crooked door handle and hesitated. She'd wanted this tattoo for too long to punk out now, just because Ace was the man for the job. She was an O'Kane, and he laid O'Kane ink.

Pure and simple.

The door creaked as she pushed it open. Ace stood next to a table, straightening his pens and markers. He didn't turn or even look up, but his voice washed over her, warm and wry. "Rachel."

"It's two o'clock." She dragged her gaze away from the muscled lines of shoulders, bare under his white wifebeater. "Are you ready for me?"

"Of course." He glanced back with one of those easy smiles she hadn't seen in too long. "Hop up on my table, angel, and tell me what your heart desires."

For a moment, all her heart did was shudder to a halt. She shook it off and climbed onto the table. "The tattoo we talked about—the O'Kane emblem across my chest."

His gaze settled on her chest, and his smile took on an edge of teasing. "How big are we talking?"

Her cheeks heated, and she cursed herself for wearing the sexy retro getup Trix had picked out for her. The capris were okay, and she'd worn the outfit specifically for the tight strapless top, since it meant she might not have to strip half-naked for her tattoo.

Right now, though, it just felt like she'd tried too hard.

She cleared her throat. "You're the artist. You know what would look good."

"Damn near anything." But he relented and dropped to his stool. "Hanging out with that city boy's bad for your constitution, angel. I haven't seen you blush that pink in years."

"Maybe you haven't been paying attention."

"You think not, huh?"

He'd been paying attention. Watching. Biding his time, and that was the part that made her irrationally angry—because now it was too late. "I think I want my tattoo."

Ace sighed and rolled his stool back to the table that held his pens. "I can do a sketch on paper first if you want, but if you just want our logo..."

"That's all I want."

"Message received, angel." He rose and returned with a collection of blue markers clenched loosely in his fist. "Wiggle that top down. I need to see what I'm working with."

She glanced down. "It's not low enough?"

He didn't touch her, not with his fingers. Instead,

he took the capped tip of the marker and set it against her skin, just beneath the hollow of her throat. "The logo's shaped kind of like an inverted triangle." He dragged the tip of the marker along her collarbone and down the inside curve of her breast. "The hilts of the daggers stick out a little, but for the most part it'll nestle nice and sweet, right between your tits."

He'd need room to work, and the way he traced the pen over her flesh made her realize something else—the shirt would pull at her skin, distorting the tattoo.

It had to go, and making a big deal out of that could reveal far more than her body.

Wordlessly, she tugged the fabric down, doubling it over the wide belt cinched around her waist.

"There we are." His gaze was tangible, a warmth that prickled over her skin as he studied her. It wasn't even all that lascivious—she'd seen Ace ogle women's breasts plenty of times. This was something else, something more. This was the deadly serious artist who lived beneath Ace's joking exterior, studying her like she was a masterpiece he intended to improve.

The intensity drew her attention to his hands. Strong, but capable of such tiny, intricate work. And skilled in other ways—ways she couldn't afford to remember just now.

Not that she could stop. The memory seized her, more sensation than recollection, of hot breath on the side of her neck as those hands roamed her body, eased under denim and lace to tease and then demand. She could still hear the music, feel the way he'd matched the rhythm beat for beat with slippery circles on her clit.

She'd danced with him exactly once, a harmless encounter that had turned into something else entirely, a grinding, pulsing need that had culminated in a single perfect orgasm—

—and had ended with him walking away as if it had never happened.

Rachel looked away again, fixing her stare on the corner of the table behind him. She had to break the silence, but safe topics of conversation were practically nonexistent. "How long will Dallas and the others be gone?"

"A few days, tops." He caught the cap of one marker between his teeth and pulled it off, his gaze still riveted to her chest. "No way will Dallas keep Lex in Two a minute longer than he has to."

"No, I guess not."

"Big, I think." He didn't offer a segue, just traced one fingertip beneath her collarbone, from one shoulder to the other. "Following all these pretty curves. Make a statement, eh?"

She hadn't thought this through. Ace was touchy-feely anyway, but when he was in the zone, he got downright pornographic. "Don't you have a stencil for it or something?"

"What, that fancy city shit?" He touched the cool tip of the marker to her skin and drew the first line, a swooping curve that must have been the top of the skull. "I save the tech for the ink, honey. You know that."

"Sure." If she shivered, he'd have to wipe away the lines and start over. The threat of it kept her still, silent, and she closed her eyes.

One large, warm hand folded over her shoulder, bracing her body as he leaned closer. His breath skated over her when he exhaled, tightening her nipples to aching points. "So tell me what gossip I've been missing lately. I hear you're showing Bren's wildcat around."

"Six." Rachel cleared her throat. "Her name is

Six."

"I know." He edged the marker lower, dipping between her breasts. "Is she as snarly as she looks? I don't even dare smile at her. She looks like she'd gnaw my face off."

Six was scared, out of her element. Traumatized. "If you smile at her, she'll probably think you're about to eat her. Face it—she might seem snarly, but *you're* the big, bad wolf."

"Me? Never." He peeked up with a teasing grin. "I'm bad, and sure, I'm big...but I'm harmless as a kitten."

Rachel grimaced. "Everything's a dick joke to you, isn't it? You couldn't hold a serious conversation if I put it in a fucking bucket for you."

That wiped away his smile. "I didn't think you were serious. Shit, Rachel. That girl beat Wilson Trent to death with her bare fucking hands. *I'm* a little scared of *her*."

God, she didn't want to *talk* to him, to get wrapped up in trying to figure him out again. "It's complicated. Don't give her a hard time, all right?"

"All right, angel." He settled back into sketching, working in silence beyond the rasp of the marker and the slow, even sound of his breaths. Every once in a while he switched to a different pen, laying thick lines around the edges and going back with a fine-point pen to tease out details.

He finished the guide sketch quickly and turned back toward the low table, and Rachel took advantage of his distraction to rub the goose bumps off her arms. "Can I lie down? The needles make me woozy."

Ace tilted his head toward the chair. "Why don't you sit there? It'll make it easier to move around, if I need a better angle."

A casual request, but everyone knew what kind of shit went down in Ace's tattoo chair. She swallowed hard, pushed away the mental images, and slid off the table. "Fine."

He sighed as she settled onto the leather. "Now *you're* looking at me like I'm the big bad wolf. You don't have to worry about me, and neither does your city boy. I don't play that dirty."

It stung, but only because it was so far from the truth. "I'm not arrogant or vain enough to think you can't keep your hands off me."

"It wasn't an insult." He slid into place in front of her, scooting his stool between her legs. "No man with a working dick wouldn't be tempted, angel. Trust me."

"Why should I?" Rhetorical enough to be safe...and earnest enough to be dangerous.

Ace stared up at her in silence for a moment—long enough to remind her that he was mere inches away and her shirt was wrapped around her waist. If he bent his head, just a little, he could have his mouth on her bare skin, her breasts, and something about the tightness in his eyes and the sudden unsteadiness of his breathing made it seem like a possibility.

But when he leaned in, it was only to reach past her for a mirror.

Jesus, she was a mess. Her skin was flushed, from her cheeks down under the sketch he'd inked between her breasts, and even her hair was disheveled.

She looked like he'd fucked her already.

Ace held the mirror steady and dipped his head to catch her eyes. There was something profoundly gentle in the way he smiled at her, not wicked or teasing, and all the more dangerous because of that tenderness. "Does the sketch look all right?"

"It's fine," she murmured breathlessly.

"Good." Once the mirror was back on the table, Ace returned with the tattoo gun and brushed a stray lock of Rachel's hair out of the way. "This is bigger than your last one, but it's simpler. Just the black. I'll go easy, but if it hurts or you need a second, you ask, all right?"

"Okay." She clenched her fists as he poured out the ink caps and turned on the machine.

Pain came with the first touch of the needle. Not much at first, just the initial shock that almost vanished in the next moment. Then it bloomed into a burning ache, a low-level irritation that couldn't quite distract her from the hand he placed above the spot he was working on, his fingertips brushing her throat and his thumb riding the curve of her breast.

He'd said something to her months ago, when she'd first mentioned the tattoo. That laying ink over sensitive skin and bone could be excruciating. This was sharp *and* dull, throbbing through her slowly at first and then swelling into a prickling wave.

She almost begged him to stop, had to dig her teeth into her tongue to hold back the plea. Then the edge of pain subsided, a wave flowing back out to sea only to be replaced with the crash of something else, hot and blurry.

"Stay with me, angel." A gloved finger touched her cheek, tilting her head. "I need to know what kind of fuzzy you're getting."

She rubbed the back of her head against the chair and tried to bring the room back into focus. "Ace."

"Still good?"

No, not good, but somehow she knew it could be. "So easy," she whispered.

Concern furrowed his brow, and the buzzing of the machine cut off. Ace filled her vision, patted her cheek.

"Look at me, Rachel."

She couldn't. Instead, she squeezed her eyes shut and tilted her head back. "Just finish. Please."

The buzz resumed a moment later, followed by the brain-scrambling, blissful pain. "I'll take care of you, Rachel. Doesn't matter what's between us or why. Or who. I've always got your back. You hear me, girl?"

"Yes." But it didn't mean anything. The real problem was why she couldn't seem to let go.

"If you want me to keep going, you're going to have to talk to me. Prove you're not about to pass the hell out." He wiped at her skin, then moved his hand down, cupping the outer curve of her breast. "I don't care if you sing or recite the alphabet, just talk."

"I can't." She tried to drag in a breath, but it sounded more like a sob. "I don't ever know what to say to you."

He made a soothing noise as the pain spread along her shoulder. "Then I'll talk."

He did, of random things like Noelle's dancing and the bar and what was happening in Sector Three. About the latest gossip out of the border whorehouses and who was favored to win the next round of cage fights.

Nothing too heavy, nothing personal. Nothing *real*.

Cruz talked to her, told her about the pain of his past and his hopes for the future. He was honest in a way she wasn't sure Ace knew how to be for longer than a few stolen moments at a time. Cruz was good, *decent*—

And only the worst kind of woman would be sitting there right now, wishing Ace would kiss her, just once.

A tear seeped out of the corner of Rachel's eye, and she let it track down into her hair as she breathed deep and focused on the pain instead of letting it fuzz away into the dark corners of her mind.

She deserved to feel every single sting.

9

By the time the elaborate grandfather clock in the corner of Cerys's meeting room chimed to announce an hour of Dallas's life wasted, he was starting to think longingly of those assassination attempts he'd joked about.

The ridiculous clock aside, the room where the sector leaders met to plan—and argue—was probably the starkest in Sector Two. It was dominated by a solid table, ten feet square. Just enough room for suspicious men to spread out, two on each side, but not enough to really keep them safe from one another. And they all knew it.

They were arranged by sector, by unspoken agreement. Or maybe the original agreement had been spoken before Dallas's time, when the first group had tentatively gathered, mistrustful leaders of the strongest factions, the ones who were smart enough to realize the truth that kept the sectors alive. Too much organization, and the men who controlled Eden would sweep out from the city, use their superior technology to wipe away the threat that unified sectors could represent. Too much chaos, and Eden would be forced to exert a different but equally destructive kind of control.

Everything depended on balance. Balance between the sectors and Eden, balance between the leaders of each sector. Seated next to the empty chair that Trent had occupied during their last meeting, Dallas could *feel* their carefully won balance tipping.

Not that they were talking about Three. No, they'd blown the last hour listening to Timothy Scott and Richard Colby argue over the new wind farms going up in Seven. Both ruled their sectors like petty kings straight from a goddamn fairy tale, relying on greedy retainers to suck the land and the people dry while they lounged in modern-day palaces, and both seemed perpetually convinced the other was conspiring with the city.

Dallas glanced at Cerys, who had humored them thus far but was obviously running low on patience. She rose and held her hands wide. "Gentlemen, your concerns about Eden's new construction are valid, but hardly actionable. Not here."

"The lady has a point." Jim Jernigan, hard-ass leader of Sector Eight, rubbed the bridge of his nose. "How about we discuss something that affects us all?"

"The empty chair," Gideon agreed from his seat beside Cerys. He met Dallas's gaze with a small smile of apology before continuing. "Wilson Trent made a stupid move out of greed. Dallas was well within reason to put him down for it, but it leaves us with a mess to clean up."

A pretty little speech, but not without a chiding edge. Or maybe Dallas was still irritated with Mad's cousin. He couldn't forget the moment between Gideon and Lex the previous night, that awkward, halting conversation that had implied the two shared secrets.

Secrets were intimacy, and God knew he was jealous as fuck of Lex's intimacy. It lent his voice unreasonable bite as he drawled his response. "If I'd set about cleaning up that mess, you'd all assume I was aiming to expand operations."

"Someone will have to," Cerys observed. "Leaving a power void in that sector could hurt all of us."

"You most of all, eh, Cerys?" Fleming noted idly. "After all the effort you and the other ladies have gone to, buffing and shining Two until it's as pristine as Eden itself. You've got leaderless barbarians on your doorstep now."

"And I don't like it. I like order, just as you do."

Scott barked out a laugh. "Fleming likes *money*, not order."

"Money comes from order," Colby intoned piously, unable to pass up the chance to land a jab on his enemy, even a ridiculous one. Dallas had seen Colby's sector, and Seven was damn near as chaotic as Three.

Scott opened his mouth to retort, and Dallas cut them off before they could start another fight. "We all like money, and we all like not having our sectors fire-bombed. Or have you two forgotten how Three got so damned fucked up to start with? The asshole before Trent let his ego get ahead of him, and Eden blew up all his pretty factories."

"Which is why I'll gladly let someone else take on the risk of developing Three." Jernigan leaned back in his chair and shook his head. "The place is a pit. It's not worth losing my manufacturing capabilities over."

Dallas studied Jernigan, trying to see past the man's businesslike façade. All the people around the table were dangerous to one degree or another—even Gideon—but none of them were as tough to read as Jim Jernigan. He was the only original sector leader left, one of the first who'd helped carve out the eight territories and set down the rules for survival. A dangerous man, to have held on to his sector while his contemporaries lost their places to internal struggle, one after another.

He had a poker face that'd make Lex weep with envy.

"Dallas."

He started at his name, and for a moment thought he'd missed part of the conversation. But everyone else was peering at Gideon in confusion, too. Fleming frowned and leaned forward. "Dallas, what?"

"Dallas can do it without attracting attention." Gideon rolled a cigarette between his fingers without lighting it. "It's not just about location. It's about style, and keeping things running without too many changes, so no one in Eden decides they need to poke their noses in. Three and Four have always been similar."

Scott's face drew into a disbelieving grimace. "You want to just *give* O'Kane a fucking sector?"

"No," Colby corrected in a withering tone. "Gideon obviously wants to give it to his cousin. Maddox. O'Kane even brought him to the damn summit."

Holding back a sigh, Dallas flashed Gideon a dark look and received an enigmatic expression in return. Gideon was playing a game all right, but Dallas would bet his boots *and* his balls that Mad wasn't in on it. If he didn't trust in Mad's unconditional loyalty, the man wouldn't be guarding Lex right now.

Fleming scoffed. "If we're offering up our

subordinates, my second-in-command could work wonders with the sector."

Cerys smiled. "Let's be clear what we're talking about here. A seven-share split of whatever profits come out of Three, less a small percentage. We'll call it a management fee."

"Profits meaning income after expenses," Dallas cut in. Gideon had started the ball rolling, but Dallas could feel excitement prickling along his skin now. The promise of power in the air, if he worked it just right. "How many of you have been to Three? There are some decent crafters in there, but the sector's a damn mess. Most of the roads were wiped out when they torched the factories. Travel is a nightmare, which makes business a pain in the fucking ass."

"You and Cerys are the only ones close enough to make it practical." Jernigan's gaze roved over Dallas, assessing and cold. "And Cerys—God love her, but her skills run toward a more refined sort of enterprise."

The observation drew a few chuckles from around the table, and for one split second, Dallas could see behind the ever-present solicitous courtesy she wore like a mask. Cerys played her part, trading on the flesh of her girls, her own sensuality, and the ignorance of men foolish enough to underestimate her.

She played her part, and she hated it. Just like Dallas did.

How many times had he gritted his teeth through jokes about O'Kane, the ignorant barbarian? How many times had he fought to keep understanding from his expression when Fleming or Colby insulted him to his face with esoteric references from pre-Flare literature that an uneducated thug from Four wasn't supposed to understand?

How many of them would choke on their own

damn spit if he admitted he knew what the word *esoteric* meant?

Oh, he knew how hot frustration burned when an idiot smiled smugly, confident in his superiority. He knew the temptation to throw away everything just to rub their noses in how stupid they were. He had no doubt that Cerys would slit the throats of every last man in this room and feel nothing but pleasure.

Him included, which was a good thing to remember before sympathy made *him* a fool, too.

Gideon was looking thoughtful now, but Fleming wasn't giving up the fight. "Five's not that far from Three, and my man's familiar with the territory. Dallas has built himself a pretty little empire, but let's be honest. He runs a *gang*. If you want profit, you need a businessman."

Cerys arched an eyebrow. "It may be a gang, as you say, but he didn't take his business from someone else. He built it from the ground up, which is exactly what needs to be done with Three."

"A self-made man," Gideon agreed, casting such a sly look at Mac Fleming that Dallas almost resolved to forgive him. "Those of us who inherit our power and influence lack an advantage the less fortunate have in abundance."

Fleming stared back across the table coolly. "And that is?"

"Hunger." When Fleming opened his mouth, Gideon held up a finger. "Which is not the same thing as avarice or envy."

"Your second. The one who can't wear a suit without looking like a little boy playing dress-up?" Jernigan turned an old coin over and over on the backs of his fingers. "Is he hungry, Mac?"

When Mac didn't answer, Gideon chuckled. "Not

hungry enough, or Mac would have bigger troubles. Or maybe he's starting to wonder if he already does."

Jernigan dropped the coin on the table with a sharp, metallic ring. "More money beats less every damn day of the week. All I've seen your man do is fake confidence and smiles, Fleming, but O'Kane's proven himself. If we're voting, he's the one I'll back."

Colby stirred in his seat next to Jernigan, leaning away as if to distance himself from the other man's words. "I lodge a formal protest. If O'Kane wants to be considered, the rest of us should have a chance to present candidates of our own. My younger brother—"

"Spends all his time finding farmers' daughters to add to his harem," Scott sniped. "If you want a grunting lecher, you might as well vote for O'Kane."

"Gee, thanks," Dallas drawled, grinning at them both, an expression that wasn't fake at all. With the chair beside him empty, a simple majority required no more than four votes. Jernigan and Gideon and Cerys...

And him.

Oh, it was moving fast. Too damn fast. He thought of Jasper discussing recruitment and Dom slavering over the idea of moving into virgin territory. They'd be stretched thin, trying to exert order over chaos...but they had more than a few promising allies. More would come running, gambling on their ability to earn places of power and influence.

The smart, careful move was to say no. To deflect. But Dallas could *taste* the power, the thrill of owning more territory than anyone else. More chances to turn opportunity into profit, more chances to create something resembling civilization instead of brutality. A chance to stamp out the worst of Trent's abuses, the girls being sold as virtual slaves. The ones like Six, being tortured in spirit and body.

No doubt *that* was Gideon's endgame. Jernigan's could be as simple as easy money. It wasn't like he could risk his factories on a gamble, and he wouldn't profit if someone else took over.

No, Cerys was the enigma—and the hidden danger. Ignoring the bickering as Scott and Colby started at each other again, Dallas met Cerys's gaze over the empty seat between them. "You sure you're not interested in expanding operations south?"

She answered first with a barely perceptible shake of her head. "I have plenty to occupy myself at the moment, not to mention the hard facts. In my particular business, establishing a base of operations and a solid clientele could take years." She leaned closer. "Years during which no one would be making any money."

Silence settled around the table as men measured greed against laziness, and Dallas weighed his own ambition against the risks inherent in tackling a new territory. He had enough to keep himself neck-deep in toys and trinkets, enough to keep his men happy and his women independent.

But he could have more. They could all have more, including the sorry bastards dying while Trent's men ripped each other to pieces, fighting for scraps.

"I'll do it," he said abruptly. "If we can agree on a percentage worth the risk I'm about to take, I'll do it. And make you all a fuckton of money."

Colby spat a curse. "This is bullshit."

"This is math." Gideon held up his fingers. "Four makes a majority now. Me, Cerys, Jernigan, and Dallas—"

"He can't vote for *himself*, for fuck's sake," Fleming snarled. "That's ridiculous. O'Kane should abstain, which makes this three against three."

Dallas wasn't surprised when Scott shook his head. If Colby called the sky blue, Scott would die claiming it was red. "Four in favor. Four against two. A majority by any reckoning."

"Then it's done." Cerys gestured toward the two silent servants near the door. "Drinks, gentlemen?"

"Only if it's some of O'Kane's famous whiskey," Scott said, and from the gleam in his eyes, Dallas wondered if the man was envisioning getting a cut of that along with his share of Sector Three.

He could dream.

As the taller server started toward the table, Colby shot out of his chair, upending it with a clatter that made Fleming jump. "If you're going to waste time celebrating this ridiculous, hollow victory, I'll be leaving. Some of us have work to do in our sectors."

The door slammed, and Jernigan snorted over the glass one server had already slid in front of him. "Someone's got his panties in a bunch."

Fleming met Jernigan's gaze coolly. "You don't have to be ridiculous to think this all happened too fast. Quick decisions make for deep regrets."

"Not for me. If this goes south, I've lost nothing." He smirked at Dallas. "No offense."

Dallas lifted his own glass and faked his way through a barbaric grin. "What could go wrong?"

10

Most people in Sector Two would say Avery had done very well for herself.

It was true—if you judged such things by luxury and opulence. Lex perched on the edge of a damask settee and tried to study the receiving room objectively. The furnishings were expensive in an understated way that spoke of money and taste, never veering over the line between tactful and tacky. The floor-to-ceiling windows looked out over a small but lush garden, and even through the sheer drapes obscuring the glass, she could see at least four gardeners busily tending the foliage.

They had to be finished, after all, before the master of the house arrived home for the day.

Lex would have rather been sitting on a wooden crate back home, getting splinters in her ass.

The servant who'd answered the door reappeared,

edging into the room holding a silver tray laden with an elaborate tea set. The delicate porcelain cups rattled on their saucers as she hugged the wall, her gaze darting nervously to Lex—and Mad, who lurked behind her like a dark shadow decorated with menacing tattoos and deadly silver knives.

"Lady Avery will see you shortly," the old woman murmured, scurrying forward to drop the tray on the carved table in front of Lex. It thumped down on the wood from two inches in the air, and the servant was out the door before the cups finished rocking.

"Maybe we're overdressed," Mad said, his tone amused.

"Dangerously uncultured is more like it." The nervous fluttering in Lex's stomach had kicked up into a rolling boil, and she clenched her hands around the edge of the bench. "The knives are a great touch, though."

Mad dropped one hand to her shoulder. For only a moment, long enough to squeeze encouragingly, but that one touch said it all. He wasn't just her bodyguard, he was her brother, her *family*, bound by ink instead of blood, but bound every bit as tight.

He released her with a chuckle. "The knives are useful. People are so busy staring at them, they don't notice the gun until I've already shot them."

"Violent misdirection. Nice."

"Lovely to be appreciated. Are you—?"

He cut off abruptly, and Lex heard the sound a heartbeat later. The creak of an old hardwood floor under hurried footsteps, and Mad hissed out a surprised breath when a woman stepped through the door.

It had been twelve years since Lex had seen her sister, years that had turned a confused child with skinned knees into a woman. The resemblance was still there, though Avery was taller, softer around the edges.

Lex rose. "Hey, kid."

Avery's gauzy white dress brushed the floor as she rushed across the room. Ignoring Mad completely, she stopped a few short steps in front of Lex, her hands trembling as she lifted them to cup Lex's face. "It's you. Oh, Alexa..."

Forget the butterflies. The bottom dropped out of Lex's stomach, and her throat squeezed tight with tears. "You grew up."

"So did you." Avery's worried gaze roamed Lex's face, as if drinking in every detail. "Are you all right? Are you safe?"

Christ knew what she thought about Sector Four and what went on there. What she'd been told. "It's not like that. I'm good."

Uncertainly, Avery glanced to Mad and back, but she'd been trained every bit as thoroughly as Lex. With the first shock out of the way, she schooled her features. "Will you introduce me to your companion?"

The way she said it made it clear she thought he was the one who'd put the collar around her neck. "This is my friend, Maddox. Dallas has him on guard duty today."

Out of the corner of her eye, Lex caught Mad's gentlemanly bow and devastating smile. "The queen can't wander around outside her sector without a bodyguard."

"Mad."

"Yes, ma'am?"

"I don't need your protection. Not in this."

He sighed softly, but after that he kept his mouth shut.

Avery wet her lips before inclining her head. "Maddox. Any friend of my sister's is a welcome guest in my patron's home. There are tea and refreshments, or I can have a more substantial meal brought for you. I only ask that you pardon my rudeness in inviting Alexa alone to walk in the garden with me."

Leather creaked as Mad shifted behind Lex. "Technically you're not out of sight if I can see you through the door, I guess."

Or the walls. "He'll wait," she told her sister. "Lead the way?"

Avery turned so sharply that her white gown flared around her ankles. The sliding door squeaked as she pulled on the handle, and the sound sent the gardeners scurrying toward a break in the hedge.

Lex's sister led her to a padded bench wrapped around a pool dominated by a large stone fountain. It was cleverly designed, with water cascading over rocks stacked one upon the other with careful artlessness.

Avery settled on the bench and held out a hand to Lex. "I can hardly believe you're here."

"No fu—uh, no kidding." Lex sat without touching her sister's hand. The distance was vital, because her brain couldn't catch up with reality.

Her last memories of Avery were shrouded in darkness and secrecy, one last clandestine meeting during Lex's flight from Orchid House. She'd been barely more than a child herself, but already so, so old. And Avery...

Lex spoke without thinking, the words tumbling out across her clumsy tongue. "If I'd known they were going to sell you too, I'd have dragged you with me."

"I know." Avery smoothed her hands over her silken skirt before settling them in her lap, her fingers laced together. "You were my big sister, my protector. I always knew you'd walk barefoot through flames for me."

"I should have known." And she had, enough to

realize that Cerys would never take on Avery after Lex's defection. What hadn't occurred to her was that her parents would be able to sell her sister to another house.

"Don't borrow regret, Alexa. I won't claim I wasn't frightened when I was taken to Rose House, but training as a rose is less...intense than as an orchid. I received an incomparable education, and I now live in more luxury than we could have imagined as children."

"With a man you didn't choose."

"With a man who doesn't dare mistreat me." Avery's eyes were suddenly so old, older than Lex felt. Ancient. "We're clinging to civilization after the end of everything. After the end of the *world*. At least my patron cares about being seen as civilized."

Silly, *stupid*, but Lex couldn't help how the words rankled. "Appearances don't mean shit, not when you get right down to it."

Avery's eyes widened. "Oh no, I didn't mean—" She shook her head and closed her eyes. "I'm making a mess of this, because I don't know where to start. I don't know the truth of your life, only what the head of Rose House told me, and I'm not so simple as to believe those stories unembellished. They watched me, because I'm a Parrino. You're practically a fairytale, Lex. A myth. Cerys doesn't often lose control of her girls."

A question hung in Lex's throat, the one she hadn't thought to ask until just now because it had seemed impossible. Unthinkable. "Are you happy here?"

A broken laugh spilled free of her sister. "I've been working up the courage to ask you the same thing. What does that say about us?"

"I have everything." Lex wondered at how hollow the words must have sounded to someone who considered her way of life horrifying and deviant. "You heard

Mad, right? Queen of Sector Four."

"So it's true?" Avery's gaze dipped to Lex's wrists, where her ink flashed beneath the cuffs of her jacket. "You belong to one of the sector gangs?"

"*The* gang in Four. The only one."

"And the leader, O'Kane. He's...kind to you?"

"Dallas is—" Belatedly, Lex remembered she bore faint bruises on her throat, not only from Noelle and Jasper's party, but from the night before. She fought the urge to lift her fingers to her skin, but she couldn't, not entirely, so she compromised by touching the lacy edge of her collar. "He gives me everything. He—"

It was no use. Nothing she could reveal without scandalizing her sister sounded like more than a man lavishing meaningless, material gifts on his property. Dallas was so many things—maddening, lovable, *hers*—

And none of that could be conveyed with simple words.

The door whispered open before she could find more complicated ones, and Avery flowed to her feet as a man joined them in the garden. Tall and solid, he looked like a distinguished businessman sliding into middle age with grace. His suit was carefully tailored, his silvering hair neatly trimmed, but his face was lined with stress and worry, and his gait was uneven, like he fought to hide a limp.

Not an unattractive man, not a monster. Avery hurried to his side, pulled by a force stronger than gravity. "Gordon, I didn't expect you back so soon."

"I decided they could do without me for the morning. I didn't realize you'd have company." He was tall enough that Avery fit under his chin, and he tugged her into an absent embrace as he studied Lex over her sister's head.

One look into his eyes and Lex saw his words for a lie—the man knew exactly who she was, knew her relationship to the woman tucked against his chest. The hand he settled on Avery's hip was as proprietary as the way he stroked her hair, running his fingers over the unbound length as if petting a cat.

When Avery leaned into the touch, all but purring, Lex had her answer. Her sister wasn't just happy. She was blissful. The warm, relaxed tone of her voice almost shouted it as she turned her cheek to Gordon's hand. "It's the most wonderful thing. My sister Alexa has come to visit me."

"She has, has she?" Perfectly polite words, but when Avery turned to face Lex, the wary protectiveness returned to Gordon's eyes. "Welcome to my home, Alexa. I assume the man in the receiving room belongs to you?"

The way he said *man* meant something else altogether: *thug*. "Not quite, but close. He's my guard." A word this man would understand more than *friend*.

"I see." He guided Avery back to the bench and urged her to resume her seat with a gentle hand on her shoulder. "Do you plan to stay for dinner? I'm sure the cook can make accommodations."

His hand slipped back into the dark, unbound mass of Avery's hair, and Lex stared. So easy to see in that gentle touch clear echoes of the way Dallas touched *her*. Absently but constantly, movement without conscious choice, his hands resolving to stroke through need and sense memory alone.

And Avery worshiped her patron, pure and simple. Her regard was a shining, tangible thing, comforting and repelling Lex all at once.

Did she stare at Dallas like that, blind with something beyond adoration?

"I have to go." She'd come fully prepared to enlist Mad as an accomplice if she needed to drag her sister away from this damn place...but she hadn't prepared for this.

The pleasure vanished from her sister's face, all that light snuffed out by her words. "So soon? I thought we could spend time together."

"I can't." The truth, for what it was worth. "We're leaving tonight after Dallas's meetings."

"A pity," Gordon murmured, and he sounded earnest. Maybe he was, if only out of concern for Avery. He bent to kiss her brow. "I'll leave you two to the time you have, pet." Straightening, he nodded to Lex. "Alexa."

The way he said her given name straightened her spine. "Gordy."

His lips twisted in disapproval as he turned away, but Avery didn't notice. She watched, tense with concern, as his uneven strides took him back to the house. "His knee bothers him when he's tired," she whispered once he'd disappeared through the door. "He was only a boy when the lights went out, but he was injured in the riots."

You could leave. Come with me. Lex bit her tongue. Avery would no sooner leave Sector Two than she herself would stay.

"Take care," she whispered instead. "And remember your training. What to do if he hurts you."

Avery blinked and turned to meet Lex's eyes. "He won't," she replied just as quietly. "He's not a perfect man. But I've seen my house sisters go to men who work them or hurt them, who call them whores and break their souls. Gordon wants a pretty girl in his bed and someone to dote upon. How selfish would I be to ask for more in a world where so many have nothing at all?"

"Maybe *more* isn't selfish at all. Maybe it's what you deserve."

"Deserve?" After an uncertain moment, she looked away. "I don't like to imagine a world where we all get what we deserve. I think my heart would break to imagine most people deserve what they have gotten."

She had it backwards, had twisted the words into something damning. Lex released a slow breath—a goodbye. She and Avery shared more than blood. Once, they'd shared the same origin and ultimate fate, even the same values.

But exile had changed Lex in ways she couldn't articulate. Here, in some of the poshest surroundings Sector Two had to offer, Avery heard words of hope as condemnation. Back home, in grungy, dirty Sector Four, the same observation would have been met with indignation. Fight.

She missed that fire already.

"I have to go." She clasped her sister's hand for a moment and rose. "Be happy, Avery."

"I will, if you promise the same."

Mad was staring through the glass, agitated and intent. "I promise," Lex whispered.

Avery smiled and let her go.

Mad all but dragged Lex through the house, past the relieved servant and out onto the cobblestone sidewalk. His arm slid around her waist as soon as they were around the corner. "You okay, honey?"

Honest concern demanded an honest answer. "No. Let's get the fuck out of here."

11

"It's not my secret to share," Gideon said for the third time, leaving Dallas to wonder if punching the grandson of God's supposed prophet was blasphemous enough to endanger his already questionable place in the afterlife. After all the effort it had taken to convince Bren to lag behind while he walked with Gideon, *this* was the only answer the damn man would give when it came to Lex, over and over like some broken pre-Flare toy.

It's not my secret to share.

God damn the bastard, anyway. Him and his meddling and his morals. "Fine, let's talk about some secrets that *are* yours to share. Like what you're hoping to get out of Three."

"Who says I want anything?" The man's wide grin belied the innocence of the deflection.

Dallas didn't hide his snort of amusement. "Yeah. Try that on someone who doesn't know you."

Gideon sobered. "I want my Warriors to have full access to Sector Three."

Christ, the man didn't ask for much, did he? Just motorcycle-riding vigilantes for God rolling through a sector that might as well be hell on earth. "You want them there as helpers or hunters? Because if I'm running Three, my men need to be the law. End of story."

"Hey." Gideon held up both hands. "Feed the hungry and heal the sick. Everything else is your show."

There were benefits to letting Gideon's men in, coldly practical ones. Hungry people were desperate, dangerous, but charity and compassion had a tendency to erode the fearful respect Dallas depended on outside of his gang. He didn't *want* to leave kids hungry and their parents suffering, but he couldn't save them all. And the slightest show of weakness could kick off a territory war that would leave those same children worse than hungry. Innocents were the first to die when bullets started flying.

But if he could keep them safe and let Gideon feed them... "One month trial," Dallas said finally. "But only if they agree to answer to Maddox. I can maybe even find them something in the way of resources, but the lines have to be drawn. You can be the carrot, but I'm still the stick."

"How very manly."

"Hey, some of us aren't coasting on the reputation of a higher power. Us mere mortals gotta do what we can."

Gideon laughed. "If I promise not to make your life harder, will you stop pretending you can't afford to give a shit about people who don't wear your ink?"

That stung, but he supposed it was meant to.

"Afford's a funny word. Some prices I'll pay happily. Others...not so much."

"That's the tricky part—figuring out what'll make you shell out. You did it for Edwin Cunningham's daughter." Gideon tilted his head. "Or was that Lex's influence?"

"Maybe you give me too much credit," Dallas countered, unwilling to give voice to the depth of her influence. Not here, with enemies on all sides. Besides, he didn't have to twist the truth much to come out looking bad. "Maybe I'm just cold-blooded enough to recognize all the ways I could use a councilman's daughter."

"Now, *that* I believe."

"And she has great tits."

"Mmm, there you go. Make love, not war, my friend."

So much for offending the delicate sensibilities of a holy man. Gideon's grandfather may have styled himself a modern-day prophet, but his life's work had been preaching against the strict values enforced within Eden. Love was high on the list of things celebrated in Sector One, and it damn sure wasn't all fraternal or platonic.

Dallas clapped Gideon on the shoulder. "I keep telling you, man. Choosing one over the other's boring. You haven't lived until you've made love and war at the same time."

"I guess that's why you—" A noise interrupted the words, and a man whipped around the corner in a flash, knocking Gideon aside. Silver glinted in warning, and Dallas wrenched his body out of the way fast enough for the switchblade to slice across his vest but miss skin.

The rest was muscle memory. He'd instinctively twisted to put his body to the outside of the attacker's arm—and to get a grip on the man's wrist. A hard yank and a heel planted against the side of his knee, and the man staggered with a grunt of pain.

Only staggered. If he'd gone down, maybe Dallas would have checked himself, would have kept the man alive to ask questions. But a clatter behind him indicated Gideon was wrestling with an attacker of his own, and Bren—orders or no, Bren would be here by now if he wasn't fighting his way clear of *something*.

Dallas kicked him again, popping the man's knee with a solid hit from one steel-toed boot, and snapped the bastard's neck on the way down.

Dallas spun to see Gideon punch a second struggling attacker in the lower back—hard. The man hit the wall face-first with a sickening crunch and slumped toward the floor, but Gideon hauled him up with a curse. "Colby's man."

"Fuck." Dallas whirled, took three loping paces toward the last of a dozen corners they'd turned, and almost slammed into Bren. "What happened?"

"Got jumped." Bren panted a little, and a shallow graze of a cut marred his cheek. "Motherfuckers meant business. You good?"

"We're good." He jerked his head in Gideon's direction. "Colby's thugs. Did you recognize any of yours?"

"Same, but they're dead now."

"Goddamn." Dallas shoved a hand through his hair and let himself sigh. "I suppose I knew what I was getting into."

Bren flexed one scarred hand, eying his busted knuckles. "Shivs only come out when the meetings were productive. I take it everything went well."

"Depends on whether or not you were planning a vacation anytime soon." Dallas swept up the knife that had almost slipped between his ribs and stepped over the limp body of the man who'd been holding it. One of the servants would find the fallen men, and it wouldn't be the first time Cerys had cleaned up an assassination attempt in her hallways. "Mad's crazy cousin here decided to make a power play on my behalf. I'm still trying to decide if I'm going to kill him or not."

"You like me too much for that." Gideon tossed Dallas another knife, this one a switchblade. "Besides, I just saved your life."

"My dignity, maybe," he huffed in return, but he still grinned. "Even if I could have taken them both, I don't want to think about what Lex would do to me if I came back to the room with a hole in my hide."

"You, she'd kiss all better," Bren muttered. "I'm the one who'd have to deal with the queen's rage. Which, come to think of it..."

Dallas slugged Bren on the shoulder lightly. Well, kind of lightly. "Don't get too attached to the idea, buddy. Her rage is mine now, too."

"Uh-huh." Bren grimaced at the men on the hallway floor. "Want me to clean up or make sure everything's ready to go?"

"Leave them. I want to get the hell out of this sector."

"Yes, sir."

He brushed past Gideon, who shook his head. "Shouldn't he be sticking around to guard your back against a second wave?"

"Want a lecture on assassination tactics? Chase him down and ask. Don't blame me if you can't sleep tonight, though." Dallas shook his head and clasped Gideon's hand. "It's time for me to haul ass. I've got to head home and break it to the boys that we're expanding operations."

"Take care, O'Kane. Let me know if I can help."

"Oh, you'll be hearing from me. Believe it."

Dallas watched Mad's cousin turn down the corridor to his own quarters before tucking his new switchblade into his pocket. The second knife he kept handy, toying with it as he resumed the walk to his suite.

At least Gideon's motives were clear now. He was probably hoping to lure Dallas into letting the Warriors move into Sector Four, too. More people to feed, more people to save. More to preach to, spreading their message of love above all else.

Maybe Mad and Gideon's grandfather had truly believed it, but the two of them were more practical. Love was powerful, but it didn't put food on the table or a roof over your head. It didn't protect you against all the assholes with hearts too dead to feel anything but hate.

He could deal with Gideon. And Scott was a nonentity, a spoiled child on a throne he'd built to feel special. He'd backed Dallas just to infuriate Colby. Cerys and Jernigan were the mysteries. Their motives were the ones that could come back to haunt not only Dallas, but all of the O'Kanes.

The risks were worth it. They'd always been worth it before.

He wouldn't think about what had changed in the past week. How much more he had to lose if everything fell to pieces.

The folded paper on the silver tray had been waiting for her, silent and damning, and Lex didn't want it.

But no one ignored a summons from Cerys, not on her compound, so she crumpled the paper in her fist and made her way through the serpentine corridors, with Mad dogging every step.

To her credit, Cerys didn't make her wait. She greeted Lex with a smile and waved her inside. Mad caught Lex's gaze, and she *saw* the protest there, the offer to face this battle at her side, no matter what Cerys wanted.

But Christ knew what the woman wanted—or how condemning it might be. "Wait for me here."

He nodded, and Cerys closed the door, trapping Lex in her domain. The room was dark compared to the rest of them, all heavy woods and deep, rich fabrics.

Cerys moved to a table where an open bottle of wine sat between two crystal glasses. "That one has layers, doesn't he? One might almost think he's not very subtle, but I imagine that's the point."

"You imagine?" As if the strategy was foreign to her. "Haven't you been playing the same game for years, Cerys?"

"Most women do." She poured two glasses of blood-red wine and offered one to Lex. "Subtlety isn't generally the provenance of men, my dear. You can pretend to find that distasteful, if you wish, but we both know the truth."

"Or maybe you hang with the wrong men."

Cerys sighed. "So angry, Alexa? Still? I'm not your enemy. At worst, I'm the woman who took you in and did her best to give you the tools you'd need to survive."

"Not out of the goodness of your heart. And you've been repaid." Lex crossed her arms over her chest, suddenly doubting the wisdom of her decision to bar Mad from the room. "What do you *want*?"

"To see you. To admire the woman you've become. If you can credit me with nothing else, surely you can understand the pride I feel at seeing how much you've accomplished." She held out the wine again. "One drink. That's all I ask. Perhaps you'll discover I have something to offer in return."

Appeased, Lex accepted the goblet. The pride thing was bullshit, but a proposition... That made far more sense. "I'm listening."

Cerys circled to take a seat on a low, sleek couch. "You've come far since I last saw you. For the longest time, I thought you weren't going to make a move at all." Cerys's gaze dropped to the collar circling Lex's throat. "Having Dallas O'Kane in hand makes you a powerful woman. More powerful than you realize, since he's just doubled his territory."

Sector Three. The news only compounded Lex's already surreal disbelief. "You think I'm playing him."

Cerys froze with her glass almost to her lips. "Playing is a crude description of what we do, but yes, Lex. I assumed you were seeing to your own interests as well as his dick."

And of course, those two things had to be intimately connected. "Good thing you're sitting down, because this might shock you, but any attention I lavish on Dallas's dick is for its own sake. I take care of my interests in other ways."

"So defensive. So *vehement.*" Cerys sipped her wine, and from the amusement in her gaze, Lex could tell she didn't believe. Not yet. "You don't need to be ashamed of who you are. You're exactly what I need. A woman strong enough to carry on the work I've started."

Lex's blood chilled. "You've got to be shitting me."

"Your time in Four may have honed your edges, but it's been abominable for your vocabulary."

Fuck my vocabulary. Even thinking the words put a grin on Lex's face. "I ran like hell the first chance I got. What makes you think I'd ever come back here for more than a grudging visit?"

Cerys set aside her glass and crossed her legs,

her posture relaxed and easy. "Because for all that you hate me, you're not stupid. It doesn't matter whether you hold his leash or he holds yours. Maybe you truly love one another, but that's even more reason to consider my offer. Dallas O'Kane is hungry for power, and you could give him an entire sector."

It was what he wanted—he couldn't have worked his ass off for so many years if ambition didn't drive him—but at what cost? "He wouldn't take it. Not like this."

"Not without a battle? Without bloodshed? Wealth, influence and information, served up on a silver platter." Cerys quirked an eyebrow. "Perhaps you don't know him as well as you think you do."

"He knows how I feel about this sector." She took a step closer to the couch. "I can't run it unless I'm here, and I'd rather die."

Cerys's face froze into a polite mask. "I see. I'm sorry you feel that way, Lex."

The words held just enough threat to send a shiver up Lex's spine. "Don't be sorry," she snarled. "Find someone else to carry on your little legacy and leave me the hell alone."

"If you insist." It seemed too easy an acceptance, but Cerys rose and changed the subject. "I heard you visited your sister today."

Rage. Lex went with it, let it explode in a hot rush of temper as she threw her goblet at the wall beside Cerys's head. The delicate crystal disintegrated, raining wine and sharp little shards all over the couch.

Even Cerys couldn't mask her shock. She tried, struggling to compose her features, but her hands trembled and her voice, when she spoke, was strained. "You always did have a temper. It's a pity you've abandoned your lessons in self-restraint."

"I missed on purpose." Lex's voice wavered, and she steeled it before continuing. "My sister. If you fuck with her life, make things hard, even *breathe* funny in her direction, I'll kill you. Slow and painful, with my bare fucking hands. Count on it."

"You've become shrill, darling." Cerys smoothed a hand over her hip and turned away. "It's a sign of a weak will."

"Test me, Cerys. I'm begging you."

"Begging. Another bad habit you've learned from Dallas O'Kane." She'd regained her cool by the time she turned, and her words sounded bored. "If you've run out of things to throw, you may take your leave."

"Gladly." On her way toward the door, Lex ran her hand over a small statue on a side table. It was porcelain, pre-Flare, almost certainly worth more than Cerys had paid to buy her all those years ago.

She took great pleasure in tipping it off the table and listening to it shatter on the floor behind her.

Mad's lips twitched as he fell in beside her outside. Before they'd made it three steps, the door slammed shut with enough temper that the twitching turned into a grin. "Now I'm jealous. You got to break things and I didn't."

"I'd let you go back and break her face, but Dallas would bitch."

"Maybe. Might be worth it, though." He slung an arm around her shoulders. "Until I started a sector war, I guess. Or maybe two of them. That's the best part of being an O'Kane *and* a descendant of Sector One's Prophet. No one knows who to wage war on first."

Lex relaxed into his embrace, allowing herself a moment to indulge in the comfort of it before straightening her spine. "Better to let it slide, then."

They turned a corner, and Mad jerked to a stop

as a brunette stepped out of an alcove in front of them. She was pretty, in a soft sort of way, with a flowing robe that hugged her curves but hung modestly to the floor.

Mad recognized her. He didn't release his grip on Lex, but he nodded. "Jade."

"Maddox." She turned to Lex and bowed as low as most initiates bowed to the head of their house. "You must be Lex."

"Yeah." Lex tipped the girl's face up with two fingers under her chin. "But I'm not in the mood right now. Sorry, honey."

She didn't flinch, but her suddenly slumped shoulders screamed disappointment, along with something worse. Resignation. Jade straightened her back but lowered her gaze. "I only want a few moments. Could I walk with you?"

Damn it. "Five minutes, okay?"

"Thank you." Even her smile, wide as it was, couldn't chase the shadows from her eyes. Mad released Lex and fell back half a dozen paces, and Jade took his place. After a few steps, she glanced at Lex again. "You look so much like her. Avery, I mean. She was my dearest friend while I was in training."

This woman looked years older than Avery. "And you chose to come here instead of taking on a patron?"

"*Chose* is always an interesting word in this place, isn't it?" Jade stared ahead, but her voice turned wry. "I chose to excel at my training. I chose to devote every waking moment to becoming extraordinary, thinking it would bring me more latitude. I miscalculated."

"Let me guess—instead, it turned you into me." Lex smiled a little. "Overachiever and pariah, all rolled into one."

Jade laughed softly. "Your greatest sin isn't

that you're a pariah. It's that you're a legend. Legends are dangerous. They have power over people's imaginations."

"Then the smart thing would be to stay away from me, right?"

"It's too late for me." She lifted one shoulder in a helpless shrug. "I'm a legend, too."

"Kindred spirits, then." Lex stopped and leaned against the wall. "Are we chatting, or are you getting around to asking me something?"

Jade folded her hands together with another nervous glance at Mad. He'd stopped, far enough back to be out of easy listening range, but he made no attempt at hiding the fact that he was watching them both.

Wetting her lips nervously, she turned back to Lex. "I know that he helps women escape sometimes. The ones who are pregnant and want to stay that way, or who've been hurt."

The ones no one bothered to go after because they weren't important or notorious enough to be legends. "If you're talking to me, it must mean you think Mad can't help you."

"When I was seventeen, Cerys needed influence within Eden to keep Sector Two whole. And one of Eden's councilmen needed..." Jade laughed, a sharp, bitter sound. "He needed his ego stroked by a virginal whore. The Rose House specialty, and I have stroked his sad little ego very thoroughly." She looked away. "Every other weekend, for the past seven years."

And she wanted out. "That's a slightly stickier situation than normal. But you know that."

"I do," she agreed, still staring at some invisible spot on the wall beside Lex's head. "Especially since he had me leashed."

Drugs, the kind meant to keep her compliant.

Obedient and helpless. That sort of thing would make a piss-poor leash if getting clean was easy—or even likely. "Your chances are slim, then. You want to try anyway?"

Jade met her gaze, and there was steel in those brown eyes. "I can give Dallas O'Kane plenty of incriminating information. In return, I want a safe place to fight and protection if I make it. I know you can't answer now, but I need to ask. I need to know."

It could be a trap, Cerys's backup plan in case Lex threw her offer back in her face—literally. Or it could have been her way of getting rid of Dallas all along. Spiriting away some councilman's drug-addicted fuck toy guaranteed trouble for him *and* his sector. Cerys wouldn't have to lift a finger to have Dallas out of the picture forever.

But Jade could also simply need help. For every trainee out of the Flower District who was happy with her patron, there were a dozen more who wound up miserable and desperate, and it was that possibility that had Lex whispering, "I'll see what I can do."

"Thank you." Jade stepped back with a sad little smile. "You do look like her. Maybe that makes it easier to trust you. I miss her."

"So do I." Lex caught Mad's gaze and nodded.

Mad swept in, rescuing Lex from further conversation by inserting himself carefully between them. "I've got to get you back to Dallas before he skins me," he murmured. "Jade, a pleasure to see you again."

"And you, Maddox." She inclined her head with a teasing smile. "Give my regards to Bren, would you? He's a fascinating man."

"I'll do that." He sounded almost grumpy, and Mad bustled Lex away with Jade's soft laughter following them around the corner.

Lex caught his hand and held it tight. "Tried to be noble, huh? No screwing women who can't say no?"

He scowled. "I've got no problem with women who sell sex, but it's different when they're *groomed* to think it's their only fucking purpose. Hell, you know that."

"Course I do. So why the long face?"

"She gave me a once-over, said, 'I suppose that was inevitable,' and jumped on Bren's dick." He huffed out a laugh. "Maybe. God knows what they actually did."

"Yeah." Lex brushed back an unruly lock of hair that had fallen over his brow. "If she winds up in Four, you'll have plenty of time to get to know her. If that's what you want."

He snorted. "C'mon, Lex. Not even one joke about my hero complex?"

"Not in the mood," she said again, smoothing his shirt as they reached the guest quarters. "I've decided we need a few more heroes."

He stopped abruptly and tugged her around to face him, his voice deadly serious. "Shit, Lex. Are you all right? I know it's been a long day, but..."

Things had gone fucking downhill when she started scaring people with positivity. "I'm ready to go home."

12

Dallas knew his day had been too fucking long when he was surprised to find Lex in his suite.

Granted, they hadn't had much time to settle into a routine. And he'd always made a point of collaring outsiders before, women who could fit into his life when and where he wanted them and disappear without drama when one of them tired of the arrangement. The woman made that call, more often than not—some because they'd gotten what they wanted, and others because they wanted what he could never give.

None of them had been around, day in and day out, underfoot and there to witness the days he was too tired to play conquering barbarian, too tired to do anything but fall back on the bed and wait for his thoughts to settle enough for sleep to come. Most nights, he drank them into silence, which meant an early morning with an aching head and a vicious temper, and the women who wanted the fantasy of kneeling for the ruthless Dallas O'Kane didn't want Declan groaning about his throbbing temples.

Christ, he should have thought about that before slapping that collar around Lex's throat. He was too exhausted to take off his own boots, and there she sat, curled up on his couch with a book, gorgeous and patient and deserving a hell of a lot more than a man who'd just fall asleep on top of her.

Especially after the last couple days.

She looked up, her brows drawing together as she closed her book. "You look like hell."

"That's where I've been." He kicked the door shut behind him, and damn. Even the four steps to the couch felt like a battle. He dropped beside her with a heavy sigh and stretched out his legs. "Honestly, I expected a hell of a lot more push-back against this. I didn't expect that I'd have to step on half the guy's necks to keep them from charging out tonight to stake their claims on new territory."

"Some of them are hungry. They want to make names for themselves the way Jas and Bren have. And don't forget the money."

He'd bargained hard with the other sector leaders when it came to defining *profit*, hard enough that the men would have their chance to get wealthy, if they worked for it. "Yeah, but money won't do 'em a fuckload of good if they get their brains splattered on the walls by moving too fast and being careless."

"Relax." She slipped behind him on the couch and started rubbing his shoulders. "No one's getting splattered, because you're going to make them understand that wisdom is better than speed."

He snorted but closed his eyes as her fingers dug

into a knotted muscle. It hurt, the kind of pain that came with relief on its heels. "I have my doubts that some of them will understand, but they'll damn well obey either way."

She worked his muscles harder. "The first option's easier."

"If everyone's thinking on the same level. God love some of the guys, Lex. They're good and they're loyal... but they're not all Jasper or Bren or Mad."

"So, you pair them up with ones who'll stop and think. The buddy system. You've been doing it for years, haven't you?"

"I suppose..." He leaned forward as Lex's hands worked lower. "But I don't want *anyone* over there at first except the guys I can trust to keep their heads. We need recon. Intel. If I stuck Six in front of a map, do you think she could figure out what was where?"

Lex brushed her lips over the back of his neck. "Doubtful. She'd do a lot more good on the ground."

"You think she could handle that?"

"She wants to be useful. Let her."

Inside knowledge of Trent's operation and what might be lingering in Three could save him time and headaches. And it wasn't like he'd have to feel guilty about sending her—she stuck to Bren like a burr as it was, and no one would get past him to hurt her.

Lex's lips touched his skin again, and Dallas relaxed into the caress. "Nice to have a second brain to figure this shit out when mine gives up."

"You need sleep." She slid her arms around him. "You've been going nonstop for days. You barely rested when we were in Two."

Sleep. It beckoned with a sharpness that only made his growing erection more ridiculous. "I was thinking about it more seriously before you wrapped yourself around me."

Lex climbed off the couch with a short laugh and pulled at his hands. "No sex until you've slept at least half the night. If you wake up in the middle of it and want to fuck me numb, you be my guest."

"Someone's feeling bossy," he grumbled, but he couldn't sound irritated. There was something fucking adorable about Lex when she was like this. He'd seen it with Noelle before, the open affection, the teasing...

Too bad it only made him harder.

"And if you can't sleep..." She moved in close, pressing her body to his as she spun him around so he backed up against the edge of the bed. "I know how to fix that, too."

That perked up his mood *and* his dick. Amused, he sank to the mattress and lifted his arms so she could drag his shirt over his head. "You gonna read me a bedtime story, Lexie?"

"Better." She dropped his shirt, slid to the floor, and reached for the laces on one of his boots.

He grinned and extended his legs to make it easier. "You're gonna read me a dirty one?"

"Or make one up. This story..." His boots hit the floor, one and then the other. "It's about a king and his concubine."

"Does she have to tell *him* a story every night?"

Lex threw back her head and laughed. "You want me to be your Scheherazade?"

Of course an educated woman out of Sector Two would understand the reference. Dallas hooked his foot behind her leg and tugged her closer. "Could you think of a thousand and one filthy stories about what the king and his concubine get up to?"

Her fingers curled around his belt buckle and pulled it free. "I'll show you instead." She rose, off her knees, and leaned over him. "The first night, she stripped him naked and danced for him."

More than willing to play along, he lifted his hips without looking away from her face. "Watch the goods, love. This king's been hard since you started touching him."

"If you're waiting for me to complain, you'll wait a long damn time." Her eyes glimmered with amusement, but also appreciation. She peeled his pants down his legs and tossed them aside, leaving him nude and ready.

Then she straightened and stared at him.

Grinning, he stared back...and wrapped his fingers around his aching dick. "I'm imagining you dancing," he lied, dragging his fingers up his shaft. Pleasure formed a lazy haze, but he didn't need to imagine her naked. All he had to do was stare at that collar, at her disheveled hair and dark eyes, and know she was here, in his bedroom.

His.

"Mmm." She swiveled her hips in a slow, languorous circle and licked her lips as she grasped the hem of her loose white T-shirt. Tugging it up a few inches flashed the upper lines of her ink, and her tiny, barely there shorts just begged his gaze to follow her endless legs up to her thighs.

Gorgeous. Fucking *beautiful*, and if he didn't watch how fast he was stroking himself, he'd blow before she got her hands on him. "You don't hurry it up with the stripping and I'm gonna make a new rule. No clothes in my bedroom."

But she was shaking her head before he even finished his sentence. "You like it too much when I take them off." She crossed her arms, dragging the cotton up, over her head.

There was nothing under it but golden skin and soft, firm curves. Lex opened the button on her shorts with one hand, then eased her thumbs beneath the denim and shimmied it down.

"Fuck, Lex." Skin. Skin and ink, *his name*, and his blood was fire in his veins. His hand clamped tight, and he shuddered. "I don't suppose the concubine blows the king any time soon in this story."

"You've heard this one." She smiled slowly and kicked free of the denim before climbing astride his legs. "When she was naked too, she sucked him, slow and deep, until he couldn't lie still anymore."

Her hands teased up his thighs. She closed her fingers around his, holding his grip securely in place as she bent damn near in half to flick her tongue over the crown of his cock.

"Christ." Sinking both hands into her hair, Dallas sprawled back on the mattress. Impossible not to clench his hands, not to press up in a silent plea. Maybe he should have demanded, should have fucked up into her mouth and taken control. That was his promise—his dominance for her submission, his careful control for her abdication of responsibility. It was damn near self-indulgent to lie back and let her do all the work.

And he was selfish enough to do it.

"I love looking at you," she whispered. "You're so strong. Solid. A badass fighter with ink and scars, but parts of you are delicate." She feathered a soft touch up the underside of his shaft and swirled her tongue around him again. "Delicious."

Naked words. Unguarded, with none of Lex's trademark sass and prickle, only a breathless warmth that drove him crazy. "Glad you appreciate the taste, love. Feel free to swallow it whole."

"Smartass." She licked him wet, then held his gaze

as she slid her lips down around him.

That never got old.

Hazy pleasure made his eyes droop, but he forced them open. He loved the sight of her like this, glistening lips stretched wide around his cock, staring up at him as she took him deeper and deeper, wrapping him in wetness and heat. Never letting him forget that he could stick his dick in all the groupie faces he wanted, but he'd always come crawling back for this. The moment when he wasn't sure which of them was leading their filthy-hot dance.

Fucking Lex was like driving too fast. Exhilarating. Terrifying. And always a heartbeat away from spinning out of control.

A moan vibrated around him. She changed the rhythm, sucking hard as she drew him into her mouth, and licking as she retreated, over and over.

Worries about the gang and Sector Three vanished under a hum of pleasure. Release edged closer, and he slapped it away, gritting his teeth as he hauled her up until his cock popped free of her lips. "What did the king do next?"

She exhaled shakily and eased up his body. "He gave her pleasure." Her hips aligned over his so that her pussy lips nestled against his shaft, and she ground down with another moan.

Dallas dragged his hands down her shoulders and up to cup her breasts, toying with her tight nipples. "I think you have it wrong. I think he played with her." He closed his thumb and forefinger around one bud and tugged, giving her a hint of pain to balance the gentle stroking of his other hand. "I think he teased her, and told her to ride his dick and find her own pleasure."

One quick shift of her lower body brought the blunt tip of his erection closer to her pussy, almost inside.

"I'll fuck you, Dallas." She rocked her hips, thrusting hard enough to take him into her. "I'll make it good."

His pulse throbbed in his ears as he shifted one hand to her hip. "I'm balls-deep in the hottest woman in any sector. Short of slitting my damn throat, you couldn't make it bad."

"Shh." She braced one hand on his chest and rolled her hips, a slow, sinuous movement that left her gasping. "*Fuck*, yes."

He ground his teeth together and tried to ignore the silky clasp of her body as she rose and fell. Not easy, when she was clenching and moaning and putting on the kind of show money couldn't buy.

He wanted to savor it. He wanted to remember every time she bit her lip, and the way the flush of pleasure stole down her body. He'd drawn her kicking and screaming to this point before, to the place where all of her masks were gone and she was lost in the feeling of his cock inside her.

All he'd done this time was drop his own mask, and she'd melted all over him like chocolate in the summer sun.

The relentless need for release throbbed at the base of his spine, but he tightened his grip on self-control long enough to slide his thumb over her clit.

She shuddered and clenched even tighter around him as her smooth rhythm faltered. "Tell me you feel it." The strained plea gave way to a cry—and another shudder that shook her entire body.

"I feel it," he whispered, giving up the battle for restraint as hopeless. No one could have held on to reason with Lex bouncing on his dick, writhing and moaning and coming all over him.

Dallas snarled and let go, rolling her beneath him in a clumsy move unworthy of his supposed skill. He had to wrench her hips back toward the edge of the bed and push one of her legs up to his shoulder. Half her hair ended up under one palm, pinning her in place as he found his footing and slammed into her. "Feel it. Feel us. Fuck, Lex, feel *me*."

Her fingernails dug into his lower back as she gripped him just as clumsily and arched her back, her skin hot under his. "Declan!"

His name, stripping him bare. Raw. Tenderness and rage. Pleasure and pain. He couldn't separate them anymore when she said his name, so he claimed her mouth in a rough kiss to keep her from saying it again—to keep himself from *begging* her to say it again—and fucked them both into screaming, clenching release.

Lex rode it, clinging to him until her shaking subsided into trembling. Then she wrapped her arms around his neck and held him close, brushing a kiss to his temple. Too much of his weight was resting on her body, and he had to move. He had to.

Damned if he wanted to, though, and the legs and arms tangled around him didn't help. "I'm gonna crush you."

"No." Her arms tightened. "I like this."

He chuckled against her ear. "We're hanging half off the bed, woman."

"Good point." She shoved at his shoulders with a laugh. He hauled himself upright and somehow found the energy to drag her along.

It wasn't until they were both collapsed on the bed that he realized the lights were still on. "Fuck. Sector Two is an evil damn place, but I do miss those voice-activated lights right about now."

"You owe me one." She bit his shoulder and slid off the bed. He watched her cross the room, reveling in those last few moments of admiring her flushed skin and vivid ink before the room plunged into darkness.

Moments later, the mattress dipped again, and she crawled up beside him. Hooking an arm around her, he dragged her into his side with a satisfied sigh. "I'll make it up to you, love."

"I know you will."

His mind should have been cluttered. He should have been staring blindly up into the darkness, running through the eventualities. Marshaling his forces. Making plans he'd have to abandon tomorrow, because no one as exhausted as he was should be making decisions, only he never knew how to make the thinking *stop*.

Fast, dirty sex and a sleepy Lex snuggled at his side seemed to be the secret. He only wanted to work on one plan before giving in to sleep—his plan to talk Lex into exchanging her collar for something a lot more permanent.

Feel it. Feel us. Fuck, Lex—

"So then I decided I didn't care, and something about forgiveness and permission and which is easier, and you are not listening to me at *all*." Noelle shoved a wooden dresser out of the way with a little grunt of effort, endangering a precariously balanced stack of chairs. "This is ridiculous. I know Dallas is busy, but Jas says the new storerooms have been built for years."

Lex forced her mind back to the task at hand and steadied the swaying chairs. "Sorry, I'm being a dick."

Noelle waved one hand with a little *pfft*. "You're daydreaming. Not the same thing."

No good answer to that—nothing that wouldn't make her sound like a kid with a crush, anyway.

"Furniture for Six, right?"

"Yes. Bren moved her into a room of her own before he left, but it's... Well, *sparse* is being kind." Noelle's brow furrowed as she studied the dresser. "I tried to talk her into picking out her own furniture, but that made her freeze up. She keeps saying she's fine with what she has, but she's lying. She's just scared to ask for anything."

Somehow, that possibility managed to perplex Dallas as much as Noelle. "She's having trouble believing hard work and loyalty can be enough. She thinks being an O'Kane woman has to mean selling sex, whether you want to or not."

Noelle's frown deepened. "I remember the feeling, but you and Dallas cleared it up pretty fast for me. Is where she's from so much worse than here?"

"I lived in Three for a while, way back before Wilson Trent took over." The early days, not long after the bombing that had crippled the sector. "I got the hell out as fast as I could."

"God." Noelle shivered and leaned against the dresser. "She breaks my heart, Lex. I caught her looking at a couple of the books Jas got me and offered to lend her one, but I don't know if she can even read. No one's ever taught or given her anything. Maybe I wasn't loved, but at least I was fed and educated."

"Shh." Lex caught a lock of Noelle's hair, wrapped it around her finger, and rubbed it soothingly against the other woman's cheek. "That's why Dallas brought her here. What we'll do for her."

Noelle leaned into Lex's hand with a shaky sigh. "That's what I was saying before, about asking forgiveness. I made Jasper let me into the closet where Dallas stores all the tech. He has a ton of broken tablets in there, and I think I can get one working. If it reads the books to her, maybe she can follow along and learn without feeling self-conscious."

"It'll be fine. And if he gives you shit about it, you send him to me, okay?"

"All right." Noelle dropped a kiss to the inside of Lex's wrist before straightening. "Honestly, I think I make her nervous. After the first day, I let Rachel handle her and left her alone. But this is something I can do to help." Her lips twisted wryly. "And I kind of like it. Is that crazy?"

Even Lex's eyes were burning from the dust, and she was used to far less immaculate surroundings than Noelle. "You like helping, or digging around in this junk?"

"It's not all junk." Wiggling between a desk and a dresser, Noelle laid her hand on an intricately carved headboard, the one piece in the immediate area that Lex would have picked out as extremely valuable—under the dirt. "They're so scornful of anything pre-Flare in Eden, but some of this stuff is just breathtaking. It's from a time when things didn't have to be purely functional. They could be art, too."

"Plenty of artisans left in the sectors," Lex observed. "If there's something you want, take it. If you can't find it, Dallas will get it."

Noelle stroked the high post on the headboard, her gaze wistful. "But isn't it a little sad for so many beautiful things to be tossed on top of one another in here? Why does Dallas keep them?"

Because his mother would have kicked his ass for being wasteful, for not clinging to every single resource that came his way—just in case. "Because he might need them someday. If we can't use it ourselves, maybe we can barter with someone who wants it. All this dusty shit is currency."

Nodding thoughtfully, Noelle turned to survey the room. But her gaze was unfocused, and her next words were a whisper. "I'm almost afraid to ask how you really are. You seem happy…but you went back to Two. Was it hard?"

Lex tensed, afraid of the answer that would come if she didn't force herself to choose her words carefully. "It sucked, and I never want to do it again. But I'll have to. It's part of the deal."

"Do you want to talk about it?"

Honestly, she'd rather chew glass. But this was *Noelle*, who cared so much. "I saw my sister. She's happy—I think. I don't know."

Noelle finally turned to look at her, and she saw a hint of understanding there. "It's hard to imagine people you care about being happy in a place that was killing your soul."

"Shit, it wouldn't even be a thing, except…" Lex ran her finger around the fluted edge of a delicate, dusty vase. "How can you tell what's real in a place like that?"

"I don't know," she admitted. "Maybe nothing is. But that's what the people in Eden say about the sectors."

"Yeah."

Noelle smiled faintly. "Everyone in Two can't be horrible, can they?"

Lex could still see the way Avery's patron had stroked her hair, the protective way he'd tried to edge between her and the possibility of pain. "No. And there are shitty people here in Four. The real question is whether it's the assholes who are in charge, right?"

Noelle pressed herself against Lex's back and wrapped both arms around her waist in a firm hug. "There's an asshole in charge here, but since the woman sleeping with him has been daydreaming about him all morning, I've decided to forgive him."

Lex's cheeks heated in a fierce blush. "Fuck you."

"Right here, in all the dust?" Noelle's chuckle tickled Lex's neck. "No, thank you. Maybe later, so the boys can watch and be jealous."

Lex turned to face her. "Dallas is…Dallas. Even when he's being insufferable, he's still one of the best people I've ever met. You'd have to be an idiot not to love him at least a little."

"I could love him a little," Noelle agreed. "But I love you more, so I reserve the right to be pissed off at him whenever he upsets you." She made a face. "And to get in screaming fights with Jasper about it, too."

The thought of her getting defensive on Lex's behalf was as adorable as it was unnecessary. "Don't—for Jasper's sake. He'd never get any peace. That's just me and Dallas. Damn near how we've always been."

"So he says," she murmured as her cheeks turned pink. "And don't underestimate him. Jasper can get his own peace when he wants it."

So that's how it was. "Well, then. Feel free to fight with him. Just be sure and invite us next time."

Pink brightened damn near to scarlet as Noelle laughed. "Stop teasing. And stop giving me ideas, or maybe I'll reconsider all the dust."

"No, you won't, because we're on a mission." Lex dragged a length of canvas off a square shape. "She'll need a nightstand. And someplace to keep her clothes."

"And a desk." Noelle pivoted back toward the headboard they'd unearthed. "Maybe a couch and a couple of chairs. And a nice bed. Or is that too fancy? Will she think we're trying to force her to owe us a favor?"

"Probably not." As far as Six was concerned, they could force her to do anything they wanted, anytime—and favors likely weren't high on the list of what she expected them to demand. "But it could embarrass her."

"Okay. Nice quality, but understated." She pointed to a solid mahogany dresser built in plain, clean lines. "Stuff like that, maybe?"

"Perfect."

Noelle grinned and started moving dusty cushions off the piece. "So here's the real question. I bet you and I could move all the furniture on our own...but I do so love watching Jasper lift heavy things. Is that wrong?"

You've created a monster. Dallas's voice, amused and a little hungry, but Lex could hear it like he was standing right beside her.

Noelle had taken to life in Sector Four fast, and it would break her heart to realize the truth about Six. The girl had a hard road ahead of her, assuming she ever learned to trust any of them. "Better idea. We'll have Jas *and* Bren do the work, and we'll drag Six along to watch with us."

Maybe she *had* created a monster, because Noelle arched both brows. "No Dallas?"

As if Lex needed the show—or the reminder of what he did to her concentration and self-control. She bumped Noelle's hip with her own. "You're bad. If you want to hear filthy details, all you have to do is ask."

"I always want to hear the filthy details. How else am I supposed to get ideas?"

"You could take him for a ride yourself." Lex mimicked her raised brows and innocent look. "Dallas and Jasper have been known to tag team on occasion."

"Tag team..." Her eyes went even wider. "You mean like Mad and Ace at that party the night before the blackout? Like, both at the same time?"

"Something like that." Judging by her expression,

she was trying to imagine it—hard.

After a long moment of consideration that prompted another adorable blush, Noelle wet her lips. Her imagination had expanded, but Lex could still tell when she was struggling to force her vocabulary to keep up. "Maybe they should both fuck *you* first so I can watch and decide if it's too much for me." She grinned suddenly. "Or just watch."

"Yeah, good luck sneaking that one past Dallas," Lex muttered, then explained, "He's in possessive-caveman mode at the moment."

Noelle hesitated. "Is that bad? I can't tell if you think that's bad."

Because she hadn't decided herself yet. "Here's the thing about men, honey. Sometimes, they're at their most possessive when they think you might walk. But let 'em settle down a while, they loosen that grip, and everyone's happy. Does that make sense?"

"Maybe. I think Jasper would let another guy touch me, but I don't think that makes him less possessive. It's not about sharing. It's just about getting me off. He'll use whips, cuffs, toys...Ace." Her sudden smile was lazily content and faraway. "He'll do anything if he thinks I want it."

Now who was daydreaming? "Yeah, okay. Eyes on the prize, sunshine. You may love the musty smell of all this dirty old shit, but I'm starting to itch."

"You can go," Noelle said quickly, waving her hand toward the dresser. "I can find stuff that matches that and round up Bren and Jas, now that I know what I'm looking for."

"I'd rather help." It would keep her mind off fucking Dallas O'Kane.

Literally.

SIX

It wasn't until they were standing across from each other, seconds from throwing their first punches, that Six realized she'd missed Bren.

She'd expected to miss things *about* him. The security he represented, for starters, both physical and mental. Bren had never been gentle with her, not from that first moment, when he'd wrestled her into submission and shoved a gag between her teeth at Dallas's orders. But he hadn't been rough, either, just been blandly impersonal and efficient. The honesty in that detached competence had soothed her in a way none of Dallas's soft-spoken promises of safety ever could.

She'd expected to miss the way men averted their eyes when she tagged along behind Bren. She'd expected to miss knowing that he'd be a silent wall between her and the rest of the gang, with their curious eyes and their friendly, puppy-dog eagerness. She'd even expected to miss these sessions, the chance to burn through her lingering rage and learn at the same time.

She hadn't expected this weird, tight feeling in her chest, and how much worse it got when he smiled.

Hell, she'd missed him. A *lot*.

One of those smiles curved his lips now. "You're pulling your punches. Afraid you're going to mess up my pretty face?"

He didn't have a pretty face, not like some of the men. Mad and Ace and even Dallas, when he wasn't scowling. Bren's face was rough, all flat, hard lines and crooked angles, like a dozen bar fights had already tried to mess it up but had only made it more appealing.

Appealing. Fuck, she was obsessing over his crooked nose like some soft city idiot. Six tried to summon her usual glower, but it felt wrong, because the corners of her mouth kept fighting to pull up. "Someone beat me to it."

"Pun intended?" He lunged then, grabbing her hand and spinning in an attempt to twist her arm up behind her back. Pivoting with him, she attempted to break his grip by rotating her wrist, but he knew how to press close and kill the leverage she needed. So she kept going, twirling in a dizzy circle as she shifted her balance and freed up one heel to drive toward his ankle.

He caught her leg with his other arm, hooking his elbow under her knee and pulling it high. Pulling her off balance.

Christ, he was *fast*. Squirming only toppled her back against his chest, and her only play there was the back of her head against his nose.

So she took it.

"Fuck." He released her and stumbled back, his hiss of pain turning into a laugh. "That hurt, sweetheart."

"You should have stopped me," she chided, uncomfortable with the flutter of worry in her stomach. She turned to examine his face, but he was smiling through the thin trickle of blood trailing from one nostril.

"I deserved it," he said simply.

"Yeah, a little." Her skin still prickled with awareness, the heightened sense of focus that always came with a fight. She could feel his phantom warmth at her back, the memory of his chest, pressed tight against her, and she hated how much she missed *that*. Clenching her fingers, she buried confusion under action and lunged at him.

Not a graceful attack, and he defended easily, spilling her to the mat beneath him. "You have to take time to think," he whispered, his lips against her ear.

The prickling changed to tingles, and she rasped in a hoarse breath. She didn't like being under him—not when it meant she'd lost—but she didn't hate it as much as she should have. The stinging of her pride was balanced by a deeper satisfaction at his skill.

She'd learn from Bren. She'd get better. And, in the meantime, nothing would touch her because he was magnificently dangerous.

She had to swallow twice to make her voice sound natural. "Speed's the only advantage I have. I need to learn to think faster."

"Couldn't hurt." He shifted his weight and rose on his knees. "But you're being hard on yourself. Fighting me isn't really fair."

"That's why I want to do it." She missed more than some vague impression of warmth this time. She missed the solid weight of him, the feeling of being surrounded on all sides. "I need to learn."

"And I'll teach you. You know that, right?"

She wet her lips, unsure what he was asking.

There was suddenly no safe place to rest her gaze, not with him still straddling her hips and her own disobedient body beginning to take a keen interest in his. "You *are* teaching me. It's helping."

He climbed to his feet. "It's not just fighting. It's understanding when you have to, and when you don't."

"I guess. You have weird rules here. Do any of the other women fight at all?"

He brushed that aside with a shake of his head. "I mean *who* you might have to fight. You're treating all this like an immediate mission goal. Like you're in danger here." A quick nod indicated the cavernous warehouse around them. "Here on the compound."

There was no safe answer to that. The people here were his friends, his brothers. For all the wary respect in their eyes when they watched him, there was also affection. That was as foreign to her as the idea of women having each other's backs because of some crazy devotion to the idea of sisterhood. So she shrugged and stared at his boots. "I guess."

He watched her intently. "Those lessons are important to learn, too."

"I can't—" She clenched her hands until her ragged nails bit into her palms. "He told me it was safe to stop fighting."

"Trent." There was no doubt in Bren's voice, no question.

At least she wouldn't have to say his name. "He didn't lie, not really. It was safe to stop fighting. He just never bothered to tell me how much worse it would be when he got bored of keeping me safe."

Bren closed both hands around hers and tugged her to her feet. "Tomorrow," he whispered. "Same time. We'll fight harder."

No words urging her to trust, or chiding her for

not being able to. Just an offer, the only one that could possibly help. Her heart lurched into her throat, and she spent an endless forever standing there, trembling with the urge to lean in. It wouldn't be hard. Just one step. Only one.

If she did, she could steal a little more of that warmth. Maybe he'd wrap his arms around her. She'd seen him hug others, the back-slapping hugs between the men, the softer, lingering hugs for the women. His arms were thick with hard muscles and solid flesh. He'd had them around her enough times in practice, but never like this. Just two people, standing oh so close, trading warmth and comfort and the air between them.

Her heart hammered hard enough to make the room throb with it as she eased his hands apart and stepped between his arms. He stood there for a moment, unmoving, then slid his arms around her with a low sigh.

This was a different hug than the others she'd seen. His arms barely touched her, their strength held in reserve. He was giving her a way out, the chance to retreat, and that was what made her press forward.

His breath stirred her hair, and he rubbed the back of her shoulder gently. "You'll be all right. Someday."

"Someday," she echoed, surprised at her own tone. She almost sounded like she agreed with him.

13

Maybe she should have known better, but the last thing Lex expected was for Dallas to waltz right into her room without even fucking knocking.

Her heart shuddered and then started to pound as he stood in the open bathroom door, his gaze tracing every bit of naked skin visible above the water of her bath. Smiling slowly, he dropped one hand to his belt and quirked an eyebrow. "Got room for one more in that tub?"

The question might have ruined the fantasy of intrusion—if he'd meant it as a question at all. Dallas owned everything, and that ownership showed in every easy line of his body.

The steaming water sloshed as Lex lifted one leg to rest on the edge of the tub. "We might have to get close."

"That better be a promise." He'd already discarded his boots somewhere, and the rest of his clothing ended up in a messy pile twenty seconds later. He prowled over to sink his hand into her hair, tangling the damp strands around his fingers as he leaned down to kiss her once, hard. "Scoot forward," he said against her lips.

He slipped into the tub behind her, driving the water level up almost to the lip of the ancient porcelain tub, and Lex leaned back against his chest. "Did you want something, O'Kane?"

"Needed to tell you I won't be around tonight." He splayed his hand across her abdomen under the water, right over the ink spelling out his name. "Jas and I are meeting up with some guys from Three."

"Routine shit, or is something going down?"

"Just testing the waters. Trent had a few men who kept their heads low and seemed half reasonable. I think I can talk them into making themselves useful."

"Ah." Lex dipped one hand under the water to stroke his leg, then raked her nails over his skin. "I wouldn't have cried myself to sleep because you weren't here to hold my hand."

He chuckled against her ear. "No, you probably would've crawled into Noelle's bed to keep her warm. You still can, if you want, but only if you tell me everything you do to her afterwards."

"Dirty fucker," Lex breathed. "She's been expanding her sweet little horizons lately, you know. She'd probably be on me, not the other way around."

"Oh yeah?" Dallas gathered her hair in his free hand and twisted it aside, leaving the back of her neck vulnerable to the warmth of his breath. "No wonder Jas is so fucking smug. He doesn't have to imagine it, does he? He's been watching."

"Jealousy's an ugly thing." She kept her voice light in spite of the dangerous heat curling through her belly.

"Is it?" The hand in her hair jerked tight without warning, craning her head to the side. He licked her throat with a low laugh that prickled over her skin. "I don't believe you."

He probably shouldn't, either. "So tell me what *you* want to see."

"Hard to pick." He trailed his fingers up between her breasts to cup her throat, replacing the collar she'd set aside before climbing into the bath. "You're hot when you're topping Noelle, and I get hotter imagining how I'll tame you. But you know what's even better?"

When she shifted in his grip, his fingers slipped over her skin with a delicious, wet friction. "What's that?"

"Watching you come."

The moment when pleasure stripped away control. Watching a lover succumb to that rush turned her on too, fast and fierce. "I've come for you plenty, just in the last few days alone."

He bit her this time, closing his teeth on the spot where her shoulder met her throat. "No such thing as plenty. When it comes to you and orgasms, Lexie love, it's never enough."

"Uh-huh. So what are you gonna do about that?"

"What do you *want* me to do about it?" Low words, straddling the line between promise and threat. "Give me a fantasy. A nice, filthy one."

She rarely considered it. Other people's fantasies were enough, especially since Lex had been taught how to cater to them. She fulfilled them, and everyone had fun. Simple enough.

But this wasn't simple at all. Dallas was asking

for a piece of her, a revelation that could tell him so, so much, and the end result was the same as if she carried a thousand fantasies locked away in her mind. She shied away. "I haven't really thought about it."

"Bullshit." There was the threat, in the hard-edged word and the slight tightening of his hand around her throat. "Everyone has fantasies. You can tell me to go fuck myself, but don't lie."

"I haven't *thought* about it." She swallowed hard beneath his hand. "Mine aren't important, that's what I learned. It's crap, but even the stupid lessons die hard sometimes."

Silence. His chest rose and fell against her back in three ragged breaths before he growled something she couldn't understand and curled both arms around her. "Christ, Lex. That lesson needs to die *now*."

"It isn't—" Her throat ached, not from his fingers but from the gentle touch, a tenderness at odds with his rough words. "I would have lied to you. That much is true."

"I know, but don't think admitting it's gonna get you off the hook." He drew her more snugly against his chest. "You're stuck here until you cough up a lurid fantasy. And no cheating by telling me something you think I want to hear, or I'll just make you start over."

"You know one," she whispered. "Don't tell me you forgot already."

"Still cheating. You've got to say it out loud. Admit it. Own it. That's part of the journey." His voice dropped to a rasping whisper as he pressed his lips to her ear again. "Want me to go first?"

She held her breath and nodded.

"Fight night," he said. "That's where it starts. I haven't hit the cage in years, but I do in my fantasy. I kick the shit out of some asshole, and there you are.

Sometimes you blow me right there, on your knees in the cage, and sometimes you taunt me. You dare me to take you, and I do. Just shove up your skirt and fuck you up against the bars with half the sector watching."

He never fucked his women in public. He might mess around with the fight groupies or the women in the gang—even Lex herself—but when it came to the ones he'd collared, everything went down behind closed doors.

She could imagine it, though, hot and frantic and so, so sweet. His hands under her ass and steel biting into her back with every hard, mind-blowing thrust.

"Yeah, you're seeing it now." Laughter and smug arrogance lurked beneath his words. He stroked his fingers up her side and stopped just shy of her breast. "Though I'm only getting started. A good fantasy is in the details. Like how you're not wearing panties, and your pussy's so fucking wet when I slide into you. How I pin your hands to the bars of the cage and make you admit that watching me fight got you that damn hot, and you want the whole sector to know it."

Her blood thrummed in her veins, both racing like mad and lingering with the heaviness of arousal. "I like it."

"Good to know," he drawled, his cock heavy and erect against the small of her back. "So now it's your turn. And take a page out of my book, love. That fantasy was all about me. I wanna hear one that's all about *you*."

The real challenge, since too many of her half-formed fantasies revolved around him. "A party," she murmured finally. "We're celebrating something, and everyone's horny. Starving. But you won't let them touch each other until they touch me."

"Yeah?" Rough fingertips grazed her inner thigh.

"A good start, but pretty light on the details."

"I'm not finished." She closed her eyes and focused on the lapping water. "They're supposed to tie me up, but no one can find anything, so they hold me down instead. Wrists and ankles, even my knees while they're pulling my legs apart." The image throbbed through her, driving her legs open under Dallas's fingers. "That's when they start. Their hands first, then their mouths."

He slid his fingers over her pussy, parting her outer lips as his middle finger teased her entrance. "Do you struggle?"

"At first. Until they get their tongues in on the action." Lex arched her hips. "My neck, my nipples. My clit. Everywhere you tell them to lick me."

"That's what I'm doing?" Pleasure sparked as he worked his finger in and out in a slow rhythm. "Telling them what to do?"

"Everyone belongs to you. The woman pulling my hair and sucking my nipples. The men fighting over who gets to fuck me with his fingers and tongue." Her voice slipped into a husky whisper. "Especially me. That's what they're doing, Dallas. Getting me ready."

His breathing hitched. "Ready for what?"

"For you to fuck me so hard I can't stand up afterwards."

Groaning, he touched her clit. Lightly at first, just enough to make her squirm, but when she tried to push closer, he moved his hand with her hips. "How well did they prepare you? What if I want to fuck more than your pussy? Did someone get your ass all slick and ready, maybe decorate you with one of those jeweled plugs you love so much?"

"Ready, yes." Her ears were buzzing now, dampening the sound of her own voice. "But nothing inside me you didn't tell them to put there."

One hand stayed between her thighs. The other slid up her body, wet fingers clamping over a nipple to tug and twist, sparking her banked arousal into flame. "It's your fantasy, honey. What do I do? Do I tell them to fill you with toys and suck your clit until you're sobbing? Or do I not even let them use their fingers? Do I tell them I want your pussy nice and tight when I ram my dick into it?"

There was only one thing she could see when she closed her eyes—Dallas, blazing with jealous, possessive lust. "Fingers," she managed faintly. "But barely. You don't like it. You don't want anything in me but *you*."

"Do they hold you down for me?" He accompanied the words with the firm touch she'd been dying for, fingers moving in rough, quick circles over her clit as the water splashed around them. "Do they hold you open? Or am I so possessive I won't let them do anything but watch?"

Fuck. *Fuck.* "You let them, but only because you know it'll make me come again and again."

"Is that what'd do it?" Hot breath against her ear. Strong fingers between her legs. He stroked and teased and kept whispering filthy words, each one a promise. "Ace and Mad pinning your hands. Jasper and Noelle holding your knees apart while I fuck you. Everyone watching you take my cock, every fucking inch of it, and listening to you beg for me to fuck you harder."

Every word was another caress, a promise. Her nipples ached, and sweat sheened her skin under the water and steam. "I need you to want me so much you can't stand it. Can't even stop."

He whispered three words that sent her crashing toward the edge. "I already do."

As much as she did. *Too much.* Lex turned in his arms and fit her hips to his—easy as breathing, like there'd never been a time when her body hadn't known exactly how to take his. "Now?"

Water cascaded over the edge of the tub as he laughed and thrust up into her. "We're gonna trash your bathroom."

The hard, sudden stretch stole her breath *and* her witty rejoinder, so she yanked his hair and bucked her hips. His laugh was lower, with an edge this time, one that sharpened as he dug his fingertips into her waist and ground against her.

Lex shuddered. "Tell me another one. One more fantasy."

"Just one?" Something dark stirred behind his eyes. "Mine starts where yours did. Except there's a blindfold. And chains."

"You want to lock me up?"

"Mmm." He pressed his thumb to her clit again. "I will chain you up, love. Soon. Only question is where and how."

She couldn't hold back her pleasure—or her plea. "Yes." The first tiny waves trembled through her, and she welcomed them. Rode them higher. "Any way you want, baby."

"Fuck." His head fell back as he arched, sloshing more water around them.

The brink. He was right there with her, maybe always had been, and it was enough to shake loose what was left of her control. Enough to tumble her into the sort of ecstasy that left her clinging to the only solid thing in the storm surrounding her.

Dallas.

As if she'd said his name out loud, he answered with a groan of release.

The water settled along with Lex's frantic breaths, and she lifted her face from the crook of Dallas's neck. "Jesus."

Grinning, Dallas pushed damp hair back from her cheek. "Yeah, that got a little out of hand. I can't seem to keep my cock out of you."

"I've noticed," she teased. "I was talking about all the damn water on my floor."

"It does seem like there's a whole lot less of it in the tub."

As if she really gave a shit about the water with him inside her and hot aftershocks still pulsing through her. "You wrecked me and my bathroom. And I feel pretty good about it."

He leaned up to claim a lazy kiss before biting her lip. "Hope you still feel good when I give you homework to do while I'm out conquering."

"Will I get detention if I slack off?"

"Sector Four-style detention. You'll be bending over the teacher's desk for sure."

She smiled slowly. "I'll be sure not to do my assignments, then."

"Bad girl." Dallas caught her chin and gave her a faux-stern glare. "A good girl would spend the night thinking of more fantasies. And if getting bent over a desk counted, it could top what needs to be a very long list."

"How long of a list are we talking about here?"

"Fewer than ten would be disappointing."

"And what do you plan to do with all these fantasies?"

He smiled.

No words, but the question had been rhetorical anyway. There was only one thing he'd ever do with a literal list of her deepest desires clutched in his fist.

He'd make every single one happen.

Lex arched an eyebrow. "Should I have Noelle help me with them?"

14

Dusk was a perfect time to survey his new empire.

Standing atop the tallest building left in Three, Dallas watched the twisted maze of alleys and broken-down streets come to life as the sun dipped behind the distant hills. Eden was already alight, of course, its looming walls dominating the skyline, a constant reminder of the avalanche of power waiting to descend upon them.

Not that Three needed a reminder. Entire city blocks were nothing but rubble-filled ruins here, silent testament to what happened when councilmen felt threatened. The first man to claim Three had moved too fast, consolidating profit and power with blind greed. He'd thought possession of the largest surviving electronics factory made him immune to reprisals.

And it had—for as long as it took Jim Jernigan

to bring a competing factory online in Eight. The next night, Eden blew a third of Sector Three back to the Dark Ages.

And most of the sector hadn't managed to claw their way out of it yet. Dallas watched fires spring to life in barrels up and down the uneven roads. Here and there, signs of electricity flickered on, a soft glow spilling from windows or the flickering neon of a prized bar sign. But the streetlights remained dark, even in sections that clearly had power.

Fucking figured. Nobody who'd set foot outside after dark in this hellhole would want the streets well lit.

Dallas glanced at the silent man at his side. "Quite a prize I won us, huh?"

Jasper snorted and clapped him on the shoulder. "It's a pile of shit, but now it's *your* pile of shit. Time to get to work, I guess."

True enough. "Don't worry, Jas. If these guys we're meeting aren't complete idiots, you'll have plenty of time left over to play with your girl."

"Tonight's business. I'm good with that." Jasper surveyed the growing darkness. "Ace got that intel on Gareth Woods from his friend with connections in the city. You won't like it."

"Yeah?" Tension knotted Dallas's shoulders, but he refused to let it bleed into his voice. "So rip the Band-Aid off."

"Looks like he's back in play."

"Fuck." His hands ached, and he realized he'd clenched his fists. All the time he'd spent chasing the ghost Woods had become, and of course he surfaced now, when there was no time. "What's our old friend up to?"

Jasper met his gaze, grave and serious. "The

rumor? He's climbing in bed with Fleming over in Five."

It would take all night to untangle the implications—and the enemies. Trent, who'd died trying to kill Dallas. Fleming, who'd always been a knife at Dallas's back. Gareth Woods, who'd tried to settle a score with Noelle's father by framing the man for his own daughter's death.

How the hell were they all connected? Woods and Trent had attacked within a week of each other, but had that been a sign of collusion or merely coincidence? Trent had had a backer, no doubt, someone with access to city resources.

Sighing, he rubbed at the back of his neck. All the good Lex had done with her clever fingers was long gone. "What a fucking mess."

"Uh-huh." Jasper stretched his neck to one side until it cracked. "First Trent in Three, and now Sector Five. Starts to look like a flanking maneuver. Like Woods wants to choke you out, nice and slow."

"I should have seen this coming." Woods had tried to assassinate Noelle—and had shot Lex instead. From that moment, he'd been marked for death, and Dallas was pretty fucking sure he knew it, judging by how paranoid he'd gotten about his security. "He probably thinks Noelle's darling daddy and I are plotting against him. If he wasn't in bed with a sector leader before this, I should have figured he'd find one."

Jasper grunted. "He's blown the biggest advantage he had—we can see him coming."

"They always do underestimate us." He nodded to the broken streets spread out beneath them. "Which could very well make this a distraction, if Cerys is in on it."

"Eh, they handed you Three because they have nothing to lose. You take all the risks, do all the work, and they sit back and collect. It's a no-brainer."

"There's your problem, Jas. You're talking lots of sense and only a little bit of greed." Movement below caught his eyes, and he watched a group make its way through the shadows. "Do you know what it takes to run a sector?"

He answered with a low laugh. "If I did, you'd have to watch your back."

"Damn right." Excitement was building in Dallas's gut now, anticipation of the thrill that came with matching wits against an enemy. The men from Three would be here soon, and he'd get to play his favorite game. "We're all fucking insane, and damn near suicidally obsessed with *more*. Nothing's ever enough for us."

Jasper leaned against the wall of a small hut that had been built on the rooftop. "So I'm learning."

More than a little chiding in his tone, or maybe Dallas only imagined it. He bared his teeth in a grin. "Is this where I tell you I can quit any time I want?"

"Come on, man. You know it's a lie. You love this too much."

It was true, but that wasn't the whole reason. "And I can't stomach the idea of taking orders from anyone dumb enough to want my job."

Jasper grinned. "We all like you well enough, raging insanity and all."

"Gee, thanks. I love you, too."

He raised both eyebrows and pulled his cigarette case out of his vest pocket. "Don't let Lex hear that. She'll get jealous."

Somehow, Dallas doubted it. "Man, she'd sell tickets. And since she's probably going down on your woman right now, I think you and I are fucking well stuck with each other."

"So that's that. You and Lex." Jasper struck his

lighter and touched the flame to the end of his cigarette. "You gonna go ahead and mark her? Enough with this collar bullshit?"

"When she's ready." Which wasn't the same thing as willing. Sometimes he thought he might be able to talk her into wearing ink now, but one thing held him back.

Do you trust me?

As much as I trust anyone.

He'd get a *yes* out of her. And then he'd claim her.

"She'll get there." Jasper offered the lit cigarette to Dallas and pulled another from the case. "Even when she's not with you, she's thinking about you."

Words to make any man smug. "She damn well better be."

Jas blew out a sharp breath that almost sounded like a laugh. "Asshole."

Grinning, Dallas slapped his second on the shoulder. "Whatever. Tell me you wouldn't say the same thing."

"I'd only say that about a chick if I couldn't get her the hell out of my head, either."

Lex had been carving out a permanent place in his subconscious since the day he'd caught her trying to steal from him. So fucking young, so unrepentantly brazen. He'd told her she'd be the death of him, and she'd blithely agreed.

They'd both meant it. He hadn't changed his mind.

And he *still* wanted to be back in that bathtub with her, danger be damned. "She's not just in my head. She's in my blood."

Both of Jasper's eyebrows shot up at that. "Christ, you're serious, aren't you?"

Ignoring the wide-eyed incredulity, Dallas took a long drag from his cigarette and blew smoke up toward the night sky. "I was talking marks. Damn right I'm serious. You of all people should know."

"Guess I never thought I'd see it." Jasper rubbed his chest through his shirt, right over the spot where Noelle's name had been inked into his skin. "You've collared other women, but you never really wanted to, did you?"

"Sure I did. I wanted sex, and I needed it to be simple." Not quite a lie. Once Lex had pushed him to start accepting women into the gang, he'd had to draw a line to keep applicants off his dick. Nothing killed his hard-on faster than a woman counting the ceiling tiles—or mentally counting the money she hoped to get.

"Simple," Jasper echoed in agreement. "Yeah, that's the last damn word I'd use to describe Lex."

"Guess I got tired of it." He snuffed out the cigarette on the wall and turned to face Jasper. "Gonna have to learn to be flexible again."

"Uh-huh. Your woman doesn't play by anyone else's rules."

She'd play by his, if he was smart enough to keep the game too addictive to quit. And she'd given him a good idea of where to start. "Speaking of playing, I think she misses you and Noelle. Next time we have a night off, we should fix that."

He shrugged. "I'm down for it. Don't think I need to check with Noelle."

"What if it wasn't just the four of us?"

Jasper choked on a lungful of smoke. "You mean, like a party?"

"A little more exclusive than that," Dallas grumbled. Sharing Lex with Noelle was tolerable, and Jas was damn near an extension of her. As for the rest... Well, at least Lex's fantasy included a jealous rampage. That was pretty much a guarantee. "Lex wants something. I wanna give it to her. That's all there is to it."

He nodded slowly. "I'm down," he said again. "Just let us know where and when."

"Soon." The sooner the better. He'd tested plenty of Lex's boundaries, shoving her to the edge of her comfort zone and coaxing her beyond. Time to find out if he could do the same.

A trio of shadows parted from the darkness below, and Dallas put thoughts of Lex and pleasure aside as they approached the building. "At least they're punctual. Now we just have to worry about whether or not they're here to kill us."

"I won't be impressed unless they try."

Grinning, Dallas turned to the propped-open door that led into the abandoned building. They'd already cleared out a room and righted a beat-up old conference table and a few rickety chairs. He'd meet them here, in their territory, and feel out their motivations. If he was lucky, he'd find that same mixture that made Jasper so valuable—greed tempered by sense and a healthy dose of self-preservation.

If he wasn't, he'd stare across that table and see his own suicidal ambition reflected back at him. And he'd grant their death wish.

There was only room for one crazy bastard in his territory.

15

Someone was at her door.

Lex heard the latch and saw the door swing open, reflected in the large mirror backing her vanity. It had to be Dallas, a fleeting thought confirmed when he stepped across the threshold, dressed in jeans and a simple dark T-shirt.

Just as presumptuous as before, and she made him wait until she finished sweeping blush across her cheeks before speaking ruefully. "Come on in, O'Kane."

He leaned against the wall behind her and met her eyes in the mirror. "Not gonna throw something at my head and tell me to knock?"

"Have I ever?" She spun around on her stool. "Wait—don't answer that."

"Mmm, best not to." He studied her face for a silent moment as his smile settled into a more serious expression. "I need you to pull off one of your miracles this weekend."

That sounded ominous as hell. "It doesn't involve a trip to another sector, does it?"

"No. But it involves bringing people from another sector here."

It could only be one thing. "A party for the prospects from Three?"

"Yep." Dallas pushed away from the wall and strolled toward her with all the lazy arrogance of a man secure in his welcome. "We'll invite others. Allies and friends of the gang, a few fighters from all over. But they already know what we're about. The guys from Three are the ones who need the right first impression."

The ones who could round out Dallas's power base in their home sector. He could take over in Three and lead with fear alone, but if they could be trusted and useful, bringing some of Trent's former men into the fold would be smarter. "No problem," Lex agreed.

He traced one fingertip along her jaw before sinking his hand into her hair. "I want to close down the club for the night and hold it in the Broken Circle. Dancers, but not any of our girls. Everyone needs to be shined up pretty, but I want you to double-check the lieutenants and their women. And no sweet white lace for Noelle. The two of you will be front and center, and I want you both as fierce as you get."

"Dallas," she chided softly. "I know how recruitment works."

"I know. But this is a whole new playing field." His fingers curled around the back of her neck, commanding and possessive. "For all of us."

Lex shivered. "I'll get it done."

"Tomorrow." A word that allowed no argument, and he didn't give her a chance to make one. "You got plans tonight?"

"Asks the man who just barged into my bedroom," she whispered. "Would it matter if I did?"

"Maybe." His grin returned, edged in wicked promise this time. "But mine are better."

"Yeah? Why don't you tell me about them?"

He reached into his pocket and dragged out a two-foot length of black silk. "Were you telling the truth about your fantasy?"

Her mouth went dry as the implications of the silk hit her. "I wouldn't make something like that up."

"The blindfold is for me," he admitted, watching her with dangerous intent. "But the hands and the mouths and all that comes after... That'll be for you, if you trust me and take it."

If you trust me. There was no going back. If she denied him now, they'd lose the careful, fragile balance they'd fought so hard to find. And if she said yes...

Could she say yes?

Lex swallowed hard, held his gaze in the mirror, and nodded. "You won't let anything happen that I don't want."

He smiled and settled the silk over her eyes, dropping her world into darkness. His breath danced over her ear as he tied it, and his words...

Wicked words. *Evil* words. "Jasper and Noelle know all about what you want. They're waiting for you already, and you're right. She's so hungry to touch you. So are Ace and Mad. But they still know you're mine."

"Six of us?" she asked, her voice hitching over the question.

"Two of us." The knot pulled tight, and he dragged her head back. "Don't ever forget it, Lex. I don't care how many people are piled on a bed, in the end it's still about me giving you what you want and getting off on getting you off."

No, it would always come down to just them. Everyone else, no matter how cherished a companion, was secondary. No one else could compete because no one else was Dallas.

No one else was *her*.

Lex relaxed against him. "They can touch me," she murmured, "but they can't have me. Only you."

"Damn straight," he said, then hauled her out of her chair and into the air.

The world spun around her, all the more dizzying from behind the blindfold. She landed across his shoulder a heartbeat later, pinned by a strong, unforgiving hand dead center on her ass.

Lex dug her nails into the small of his back through his shirt. She could only track their progress through the disorienting dip of his steps and the sway of his turns. It seemed to take an eternity, but finally he paused, and she heard his boot thump against a door.

The next thing she heard was Noelle's familiar laughter, low and sultry. Dallas strode forward, and footsteps whispered past her to the right before the door clicked shut.

Were they all there already, watching? Waiting? Lex tried to slow her breathing, but the anticipation that prickled along her skin had kicked everything else into high gear, too.

He stopped after half a dozen paces—too few to be near his bed—and let her body slide along his as he lowered her to the floor. "Kitten, I know how you love to undress Lex. How about you crawl on over here and get started?"

Hands. A touch she would have recognized, even without Dallas's pet name, tugging at the belt on her robe. The satin slithered to the floor, and Noelle traced her fingers up Lex's sides. "You're so beautiful."

Lex opened her mouth, but the hot sensation of lips grazing her hipbone turned her words to a gasp. Not Noelle, not with the rough rasp of beard that chafed as the mouth moved, opened, followed by the wet heat of a tongue soothing her skin.

"Jasper thinks so, too." Noelle's fingertip brushed the edge of Lex's bra and followed the line of lace until she reached the bow nestled between her breasts. "I'm mad at him now. I wanted to taste you first."

If Dallas's goal was to fulfill her fantasy, they'd all get their chance. "Plenty of other things you could do," Lex said, catching Noelle's hand. "But you'd better hurry before the others beat you to it. There *are* others, right?"

"There's—"

A strong hand curled around the back of her neck, its touch so possessive and sure it had to be Dallas. "Don't answer that," he drawled, pressing his thumb over her pulse for a moment before sliding it under her chin to force her head back. "Are you doubting my word, Lexie?"

"Yes." The word escaped her before she could think to lie.

"You think I only invited Noelle and Jas, because they're safe."

"Aren't they?"

No answer, just that firm hand curved around her throat—and another hand, a different one, grazing the small of her back. Long, graceful fingers instead of blunt and rough like Dallas's, clever fingers that twisted the catch on her bra free in one deft move. And those were different still from the strong, work-hardened hands sliding up her leg toward her panties.

Noelle's fingers were the softest, and they stroked

her cheek. "We're all safe," she whispered as the two new pairs of hands set to stripping her bare. "He knows what's his."

Lex's knees went weak. "*Do* you know, Dallas?"

"Every fucking thing I see," he replied, close enough for his breath to stir the hair at her temple. "But you most of all. You above everyone."

Her bra fell away, and Jasper—it *had* to be Jasper, with that same scratch of beard she'd felt on her hip—licked her nipple. Once, twice, then he drew it into his mouth and sucked hard.

Lex whimpered and tried to lift her hands, but someone caught them. She didn't know who held her arms out to the side, but it was Noelle who buckled the cuffs around each wrist, and Dallas who stripped her collar from her throat only to replace it with something heavier. Leather closed around her throat, a collar that latched in the back with a long, narrow strip that settled over her spine like a promise.

Cool metal tickled, D-rings that brushed her skin as someone folded her arms at the small of her back. Noelle claimed her other nipple as the cuffs snapped into place, leaving her unable to move.

Helpless.

Her panties slid down her legs, and she lifted each foot automatically to allow the fabric to be stripped away. The air in the room felt heavy, heavy enough to press in on her as surely as all the hands.

"Like this." A low whisper, one she recognized as Jasper instructing Noelle. A moment later, their tongues tangled together around one of her nipples in a wet, open kiss—with her between them.

The low buzz of anticipation turned to a very real buzz of pleasure in her ears, and Lex exhaled slowly. "Fuck."

Wood scraped the floor behind her, something weighty being shifted into place. Fingers twisted in her hair, and Dallas's voice skittered over her. "Spread her legs."

A masculine pair of hands obeyed, dragging her legs apart. Sure, strong, but with enough deference to identify it as Mad who buckled her into a pair of ankle cuffs. Someone caught her shoulders, someone else gripped her waist, every touch designed to tease as they urged her back and down until her thighs touched padded leather.

Plenty of surfaces in Dallas's room fit that description, but when Mad's hands returned to coax her legs apart, she knew what she was sitting on. The custom-built chair Dallas usually kept in the corner, the one designed to hold its occupant captive, exposed, legs wide open.

Jasper's ever-present leather wrist cuff brushed her collarbone as he guided her to lie on the reclined chair, midway between sitting straight up and lying flat on her back. In moments she was trapped, ankles locked to the base of the chair, her arms folded behind her.

And all of the touch stopped.

Lex clenched her teeth. Dallas wanted her to break—to squirm, even beg, What startled her was how much she wanted to, to hear the catch in his breathing when she finally gave in.

She bit her lip and arched on the chair. "Please."

Someone pulled off her blindfold, and at first all she could see was Dallas.

He sprawled a few feet away, his arms resting along the back of the couch and his legs stretched out in front of him. He'd lost the black T-shirt at some point, leaving him in dark jeans, a heavy belt and not a goddamn thing else except his ink and his arrogance.

And his smile... *God*, his smile. Slow and lazy, but the edge beneath it matched the one in his eyes, matched the leashed tension that made all his attempts at laziness a lie. Already he was digging his fingers into the leather of the couch, as if he needed a reminder to keep from lunging for her.

Or lunging at the people who surrounded her. Four of them, with Noelle already kneeling between Lex's thighs, Jasper looming behind her, and Mad and Ace standing to either side. No one moved to touch her, not yet, and she knew they were waiting on Dallas's command.

It came soon enough, low, hoarse words that started a dangerous game. "Jas. Get her ready for her new adornments."

"Yeah?" He rubbed his thumb over the corner of Ace's mouth, then slipped it between his lips. Ace licked it, swirling his tongue around and around until it was wet and gleaming.

Lex sucked in a breath as Jasper dropped his hand to her breast and flicked his wet thumb across her nipple. It tightened, tingling under his touch.

But he shook his head. "Not enough, sweetheart." He cupped her breast, spread his fingers wide and then closed them, pinching her nipple to the point of pain.

She didn't moan, but Noelle did. And then slender, soft fingers closed on Lex's other nipple, Noelle mirroring Jasper with breathless glee. She tugged gently— too gently until Mad's hand slid over hers, pressing her fingers together hard enough to drag a cry from Lex.

Jasper rumbled his approval. "Ace, get the rings."

He melted away, and Dallas caught Lex's gaze, holding it through intensity alone. "Not just for your nipples, love. Not this time. I bet Jasper's trying to decide whether he's going to shove Noelle's face between your thighs or just suck your clit himself. Someone's got to get it nice and hard."

But Jasper didn't do either. He bent close to Lex and licked her cheek before whispering in her ear. "Your man doesn't have enough faith in my creativity."

Lex shuddered as he straightened. "You—"

The words dissolved into a groan as Jasper landed a sharp slap on her pussy. Lex shifted on the chair, the warm haze of pleasure already solidifying into a throb of need as she lifted her hips and waited for him to do it again.

He grabbed Noelle's hair and pulled instead. "Spread her open and spank her clit, just like I did. And get your ass in the air so Dallas can watch how wet it makes you."

Noelle's hands trembled as she petted Lex. Slow, soothing strokes at first, then deeper. As exposed as Lex had been before, this was a hundred times more intense. Noelle's ass might have been on display, but Dallas's burning gaze fixed on her fingers as they parted Lex's pussy lips.

As they opened her.

He inhaled sharply, his fingers carving dents into the couch as Noelle's fingers fell in a gentle slap.

Jasper twisted his hand, pulling Noelle's hair so hard it had to hurt. "What did I say?"

She panted, her neck craned awkwardly back but her expression blissful. "I tried, I promise. Show me how, and I'll be good. I'll be so good."

Dallas laughed low enough to send shivers through Lex. "No one believes you, kitten. You're always bad. And you've got two seconds to work that clit like you mean it, or I'll make sure no one punishes you tonight."

Noelle groaned, licked her fingers, and brought

them down on Lex's pussy with a smack. The sensation buzzed through Lex, a pain so hot and sweet it left her heavy, aching.

Jasper moved, one shoulder brushing the inside of Lex's thigh as he knelt beside Noelle. "Touch her like you would if it were just the two of you," he commanded. "Let Mad and Ace see how you make her come when you're not putting on a show."

That made Noelle laugh as she nuzzled Lex's belly, her lips a warm tickle. "The only difference is how fast I make her come. Or how slow…"

"Is that true, Lex?" Mad's familiar face filled her vision, mischief in his dark eyes and his hair as rakishly disheveled as ever. He'd lost his shirt, too, revealing sinuous tattoos that started just below his collarbone on either side of his body and wrapped down his arms, arms that flexed as he tugged at her hair and grinned. "Did you teach her your trick? It's never about who's watching, is it?"

No, the shows were about the truth at the heart of desire. Fake was exactly that, and no amount of acting could make it real. But if you started with something honest—attraction, affection, *lust*—then all you had to do was dress it up in naughty little costumes and let them watch you get off.

The men and women watching might not know why it worked so well, but they sure as hell knew it did.

Two wet fingers—one delicate, one wide and blunt—circled her clit, and Lex shuddered as the haze surged over her. "It is now," she whispered. "Dallas is watching."

"Yeah, he is." Mad traced a path down her throat and around one nipple, teasing it with touches just as soft as the ones between her thighs. "You can feel it, can't you? Fuck, *I* can feel it. If I make one wrong move, he'll be over here, breaking my fingers off one at a time."

"So make the right ones." Lex *could* feel it, the weight of Dallas's fierce stare, as she leaned up as far as she could reach and bit Mad's shoulder.

It drove a rasping curse from him as his fingers tightened in her hair, but Ace returned before she could savor her triumph. "I love these nipple rings," he said, dangling one in front of her. The delicate silver circle was decorated with stylized flames and the outline of a fierce-looking skull that almost matched the one inked on their wrists. He winked at her before addressing Dallas. "Tell me I get to be the one to put them on, boss."

Mad didn't loosen his grip on her hair, but Lex didn't need to see Dallas to imagine the look on his face, not when his voice carried such heat and promise. "Well, Lexie? Do you want Ace's mouth on your tits? That's how he wants to do it, you know. Nestle that ring around the tip of your nipple and suck until it's all snug and tight."

She tried to answer, but the sudden, wet rasp of a tongue over the hood of her clit stole her breath. The constant stimulation coupled with the distraction had her spinning, struggling to keep up with her body's reactions.

The chains around her wrists rattled as she arched, seeking the promise of Dallas's words. "I want it." An answer to the question, and a declaration of so much more.

Cool silver nestled around the tip of one nipple and then the other with barely enough pressure to tingle. Her only warning was Mad's hand releasing her hair before two mouths latched on to her.

No, *four*. Noelle and Jasper licking her pussy, Mad

and Ace sucking her nipples to aching, caged points. Panting, Lex lifted her head far enough to see Dallas.

He smiled and pressed one hand against his fly, where his cock strained his jeans. "They can lick you, darling. They can stroke you and suck you and pet you, but they can't have you. The only question now is how many times I'm gonna watch you come before I get my cock in you."

Lex didn't know what would be worse—if he made her wait through orgasm after orgasm, or if he jumped in before the others had wrung every ounce of pleasure from her limp body.

She swallowed hard, every nerve ending alive, electric. "You want me over the edge before you fuck me. You know you do."

"Yeah. Doesn't make you any less greedy, but I like you that way." He slid his thumb over his belt, like he was considering unbuckling it, then stretched his arm out along the back of the couch again. "Jas? Show Noelle how to put on Lex's last bit of jewelry."

His answering rumble vibrated through Lex as he licked her one last time and sucked on her clit. Not hard enough to get her off, but enough to make her muscles ache as she chased his retreating mouth with a buck of her hips. "Fuck, Jasper, don't stop."

He ignored her entreaty in favor of pinching the slick inner lips of her pussy. "Just...like this," he whispered, guiding Noelle's hesitant fingers.

A different sort of pinch sent a shudder ripping through Lex. Cool metal on hot flesh, the unyielding bite of the jewelry holding her clit exposed and hard.

As if it wasn't intense enough, Ace slipped one hand down her body to tug gently on her new adornment. "Poor Lex. All dolled up, and no chance to come."

An honest-to-Christ whimper escaped her, and

she bit her tongue.

"Lex." Dallas's voice, rough and commanding. "Look at me, Lex."

Her body moved, an instantaneous obedience that required no thought. No will but his.

He was leaning forward, almost straining toward her, his eyes glazed and heavy. Hungry. "Every touch is because of me. Their hands, their mouths. My gift to you. Let me see how much you love it, Lexie. Let me see you let go."

Ace bent his head to her breasts again, and Noelle teased Lex with another slow, leisurely lick. A rush of pleasure tilted her head back, but Mad clenched his hand in her hair and forced her gaze back to Dallas.

Pure lust burned in his eyes, a need that matched her own. His words were truth—others were touching her, bringing her pleasure, but every bit of it ultimately came from Dallas.

Everything.

Mad sucked a tiny line of kisses up the side of her neck, then closed his teeth in a sharp bite that shocked her into a shudder that didn't stop. It couldn't, not with every inch of her body on high alert and vibrating with the promise of a painfully intense orgasm.

Dallas inclined his head as if nodding permission, but his echoed words were nothing short of command. "Let go."

It wasn't until Jasper pushed her hips down that Lex realized she'd arched off the chair. Her muscles shook, everything *throbbed*—and then it all snapped in a screaming rush of relief and release. The almost electric shock of it sizzled through her in jagged, clutching waves, carried and prolonged by tongues, whispers. Groans.

"That's right," a feminine voice finally murmured

against her cheek. Soft fingers stroked Lex's face as she trembled through the aftermath of pleasure. Bliss, warmth—and smooth skin sliding over hers. When she opened her eyes Noelle was there, straddling her lap and tracing Lex's lower lip with her thumb. "That was so hot."

Lex could barely breathe. "Christ. Dallas doesn't fuck around."

"No, he doesn't." Noelle glanced over her shoulder, and Lex caught a hint of the teasing smile the younger woman flashed at him. "I wonder if we can get him off the couch if we play a little..."

Ace laughed from where he'd sprawled out on a cushion next to the chair. "Princess, no one's going to interrupt if you start giving Lex a lap dance. Except Jas, maybe, because he's a joy killer."

Jasper responded with a lazy stretch. "You know you want a piece of me, you jealous asshole."

"Of course he does," Noelle said blithely. Her eyes lit with hungry excitement as she brushed her thumb over Lex's nipple, pinching it against the silver ring nestled around it. "Do *you*, Lex? Do you want Jas and Dallas to fuck you at the same time?"

So much anticipation in those breathless words, but Lex didn't get a chance to respond. A low growl rumbled over them from the direction of the couch, and leather creaked. "Jas knows better than to get his dick anywhere near Lex."

"Someday, honey," she promised instead, the whisper as much for Dallas as it was for Noelle.

Laughing, Noelle ducked her head. Her tongue circled Lex's nipple, tracing the ring before flicking over the tight peak.

Lex shivered. If she'd had her hands free, she'd have cradled Noelle's head, though whether she would have pulled her closer or pushed her away, she didn't know. "I need a damn cigarette."

"Cigarettes are for afterwards," Dallas drawled. A tiny smile played at the corner of his mouth. "And if you've still got brains enough to string words together, then we're just getting started. Ace?"

"Yeah, boss?"

Dallas crooked a finger, and Ace rolled to his feet and padded toward the couch. The whispers they exchanged were low, too low for Lex to hear.

A renewed surge of heat distracted her as Mad dragged Noelle's head over to her other nipple and urged her to suck harder. She obeyed eagerly, and Mad laughed hoarsely when Lex cursed through clenched teeth. "God, girl. You were wasted in Eden. So much hunger. No wonder Lex snatched you up."

Noelle's lips curved into a smile against her breast, and a heartbeat later soft fingers stroked down her belly. "Dallas wants her to come," Noelle replied innocently. "I'm just being obedient."

But Lex recognized the look on Dallas's face, calculating and already smug. "Oh, he has plans for you, baby girl."

His grin widened. "Back off, Mad. I want Noelle to show us just how obedient she is. How long should we give her—two minutes? One?" Dallas's stare burned through Lex. "What do you say, Jas? How fast can your girl get Lex off?"

"Lex is revved up." Jasper surveyed her, his lazy appraisal raising goose bumps on her skin. "One minute, tops. Faster if you let Noelle use her fingers."

"No fingers," Dallas countered. "You feeling confident, kitten?"

Noelle hovered over Lex, their mouths barely an inch apart. "Do you want my fingers?" she whispered.

"Do you want something inside you as badly as I do?"

"You know it," Lex answered, just as quietly. "Like I know you're hoping Dallas spanks your ass."

"As long as we're all getting what we want." She grinned before kissing Lex soundly. Her next kiss landed on Lex's chin, then her throat. She skated over the leather collar and worked her way down, leaving Lex with an unobstructed view of Dallas.

He was watching her. Not them—*her*, as if the woman sliding to her knees had ceased to exist. Dallas had never held himself back from admiring Noelle before, but there was something different in him tonight. He was holding himself back from everything, saving every scrap of intensity and every bit of focus for her.

His cock still strained his jeans, but he didn't touch it this time. Just held her gaze as Noelle made herself comfortable between Lex's thighs, then spoke a single word. "Go."

Noelle went. Slick. Wet. Hot and clever. Lex had taught her all the ways to tease arousal to life, and Noelle used them all, alternating firm licks with light flicks of her tongue, and making evil use of the fact that Lex's clit was still pinched and exposed. In seconds, Lex was lifting her hips, rocking up to meet every clever, delicious caress.

But Dallas shook his head, and she saw the command in his eyes. *Don't come.*

"Oh, fuck you," she moaned, stilling her movements. "You can't be serious."

He didn't get a chance to answer. Either Noelle guessed his game, or she'd simply had enough of behaving. Her lips closed around Lex's clit as her fingers slipped inside. Two and then three, pumping fast and sure enough to drive Lex over the edge.

And yet.

Lex clenched her hands into fists that dug into her lower back, distracting her from the pleasure. She wanted to ignore his imperious, unspoken demand, but her body wouldn't let her. Any other time, she'd have been coming in Noelle's mouth already.

But here, now, all she could do was think, *Dallas told me not to.* In that moment she hated herself, hated him.

Shaking, she opened her eyes. Dallas hissed out a sharp breath, and then he was *there*. He looped one arm around Noelle and hauled her out of the way, ignoring her startled noise.

Lex barely had time to draw in a breath before it was Dallas's hand between her thighs, Dallas's fingers pumping a fast, demanding rhythm. His other hand sank into her hair, dragging her head back until she stared up into his eyes. "It's okay, Lexie. Let go now."

He was beautiful, gorgeous—hers. "You suck," she managed, her voice hoarse from strain.

He smiled, feral and smug and somehow still fond. "I know."

Then he crooked his fingers inside her, rubbing over her G-spot, and a second orgasm crashed through her. No slow buildup, not this time. It was quick and hard, from start to finish, like getting thrown against the door of a car that was spinning out of control.

By the time the thundering waves began to recede, she was dizzy. Her jaw ached from clenching it, and she wanted to wrap her arms around Dallas and hold on tight. Instead *he* wrapped his arms around *her*, and someone must have unclipped her ankle cuffs from the chair, because he plucked her up and brought her back to the couch with him.

He settled down with her tucked sideways across

his lap and her head resting under his chin. "Jas, do something about your little troublemaker."

"You knew what you were getting when you invited us," Jasper replied, idly stroking Noelle's hair. Suddenly, his hand followed the line of her back and landed on her ass in a quick, hard slap.

Noelle moaned, then turned to face Lex with a breathless laugh. "See? Everybody wins."

"Everybody," Lex agreed weakly. Her limbs felt heavy, her arms still trapped behind her back and her legs shaking.

Laughter tickled over Lex as Dallas's chest rumbled under her. He stroked her hair, trailing his fingers through the disheveled strands as if combing them into place. "I'm not finished with you, kitten. You're full of wicked ideas tonight. Putting your fingers where they don't belong, trying to get Jas to fuck Lex with me. Like the idea, do you?"

Noelle flushed and squirmed self-consciously, but she didn't lie. "It sounds intense."

"Mmm." Dallas's next stroke smoothed past the end of Lex's hair, sliding down until his fingertips traced the curve of her breast. "Has Jas ever fucked your ass, kitten?"

The pink in Noelle's cheeks deepened to red. "No."

Dallas laughed. "She has no idea, does she, Lexie?"

"Not yet." But she could, so easily.

"You'd like to watch that, wouldn't you?" Dallas caught Lex's chin and tilted her head back, forcing her to meet his gaze. "No," he amended after a moment. "You wouldn't want to just watch. You'd want to be the one preparing her, working her open, seeing how big you could make those eyes get."

Noelle's eyes still went wide when Lex could manage to shock her—big and blue, darkening all too soon with pleasure and newfound lust. "I'd help," she said. "If Noelle wanted me to be a part of it."

One brow jumped up, as if Dallas couldn't imagine that being a consideration. "Why wouldn't she?"

Noelle choked on a laugh, but her expression was more eager than amused. "Jas never seems to mind, does he?"

Lex licked her lips. "Only if I don't do it right."

Dallas curled a hand under one of her thighs and dragged it wide, twisting her in his lap until she sat with her back snug against his chest and her legs spread open, held apart by his knees. Her hands still nestled behind her, her fingers brushing his rock-hard erection.

"Tonight, you watch," he told her, cupping her breasts. The rings on her nipples weren't tight enough to hurt, but they were still sensitive, and the flick of his thumbs left her squirming. "If you can focus."

She flexed her hands and snagged his zipper with her fingertip. It would serve him right if she managed to get her hand around his dick and jerk him off. See how well he could focus then.

He stiffened, but he didn't stop her questing fingers. Now that she was facing forward again, she could see why Ace and Mad had fallen silent—and why Noelle seemed so flustered. Ace was sprawled out next to Jasper and Noelle, his head tilted back as Mad stroked a lazy hand over his cock. Noelle watched, wide-eyed, her lower lip caught between her teeth.

Jasper chuckled and spoke, close to her ear. "Want to help, sweetheart? Turn the tables on Ace and get your sweet little tongue on him?"

Oh, she wanted to. Belonging to Jasper had made her so bold. She rolled from his lap and crawled across the intervening space, turning what should have been a submissive movement into a fierce predator's stalk.

Lex had seen that promise in her long before anyone else had.

Mad greeted Noelle with a smile and gripped the base of Ace's shaft, holding his cock steady as Noelle flicked her tongue over the head. Ace groaned, his muscles standing out as he tensed, and Dallas chuckled. "Look at what you created, Lexie."

Lex curled her fingers around his erection through his pants. "I didn't create anything. I just set it free."

"Like you're trying to do with my cock?"

Who could blame her? She'd been teased and stroked to the brink and beyond—but he still hadn't given her what she really craved. "You know what I want."

"You don't want it yet." He licked his fingers before sliding them back to her nipple. Wet. Rough. He circled and tugged, building sensation slowly this time, as if he knew exactly what she could take and what was too much. "I'm gonna make you come. I'm gonna feel your ass squirming against my dick, and maybe I'll watch Jas fuck Noelle into next week while I'm at it. I'm gonna hold on to my self-control as long as I fucking can. And when I can't..."

She held her breath until her lungs burned, but he didn't elaborate. "When you can't? What happens then?"

His mouth brushed the sensitive spot where her neck joined her shoulder. Teeth grazed her skin. "Then Lord have mercy on you, Lexie love. Because I won't."

No, he wouldn't, because now she understood. He may have set out to fulfill this fantasy for her, but there was something he needed from it, too. Something beyond the bondage and the games, beyond the orgasms. Even beyond Jasper absently rubbing his thumb over the inside of Lex's ankle as Noelle and Mad traced their tongues up and down the glistening length of Ace's dick.

Dallas was testing himself.

Lex flexed her leg in Jasper's grip and opened her thighs wider.

Dallas laughed. "Legs up," he instructed, lifting her high enough for her to obey. She wound up kneeling, her knees pressing into the cushions as his legs urged hers wide.

As Dallas slid his hands up to her arms, Noelle raised her head and met Lex's gaze over the gleaming, wet head of Ace's cock. Ace protested wordlessly, tangling his fingers in loose strands of her dark hair, but Noelle ignored the insistent tugging and smiled. "Make her come, Jas. For me?"

Ace groaned. "You inked fuckers are impossible. Can't even get through a blowjob without stopping to coo at each other. Where're your damn *manners*?"

Mad shut him up by swallowing half his dick, the strong column of his throat working. Lex held her breath until Ace flexed his hips with a groan, driving deeper into his mouth. "Fuck yeah, you clever bastard."

Clever. So was Dallas as he unfastened Lex's wrists only to guide them back toward her ankles. The metal clips on her cuffs hooked neatly onto the sturdy leather wrapped around her ankles, and suddenly she was trapped again, held not just open but motionless.

No leverage. No way to escape or even squirm as he curled hot, forceful hands around her inner thighs and scooted her forward, as if offering her to Jasper. "You heard your woman. But if you think you can get away with her trick with the fingers, I'll break your fucking hand."

Jas turned his gaze up to Lex. "He's even bossier

than usual when you're naked."

From his smug, easy smile, he knew exactly why. "Takes a possessive bastard to know one," she murmured.

"That's right." He smoothed both hands up the front of her body, plucking each silver ring off her nipples. Before she had a chance to recover from the stinging rush of sensation, he doubled it by dropping his fingers to the metal hugging her clit and working it free, slowly and carefully. He tossed the metal aside and licked his lower lip.

Oh God. It was one thing to have Jasper lick her pussy, and another to have him do it with the hard heat of Dallas's body at her back. She could feel every movement, every intake of breath, and it twisted up inside her, forming a knot of anticipation.

Jasper eased his hands over Dallas's, then worked his thumb through her folds to nudge her clit. "Nice and slow?"

It wasn't a question meant for her, and they all knew it. "Slow," Dallas agreed. "Don't push her over the edge until I tell you to."

Jasper had already bent his head, and his rumble of assent vibrated through her. Lex tensed and looked past him, over to where Noelle had completely abandoned Ace to Mad's deep-throating attentions. Noelle smiled at her as she knelt behind Jasper and stroked her hands up the flexing muscles of his back. "It feels good, doesn't it? His tongue? Sometimes it feels so good I think I'll die."

"It's not *that* good," Lex muttered, prompting Jasper to suck her clit—hard. "Fuck!" Only Dallas's arms wrapped around her like unforgiving steel kept her from jerking straight off his lap as pleasure cut so sharp it teetered toward pain.

Noelle slipped her hand through Jasper's hair, cupping the back of his head. Urging him on. "He tied me up once and did this for hours. So slow, and I thought it was going to be sweet and gentle, but when I was panting and begging..." Her eyelids drooped, and Lex watched her nipples tighten beneath her frilly bra, as if the memory alone aroused her unbearably. "His fingers. God, Dallas, you've got to let him use his fingers."

Tension trembled in Dallas's arms, and Lex swore he growled. "I said no, girl."

Reckless—or just oblivious to the danger—Noelle gave Dallas a baffled look. "*Why?* What is there to be jealous about? Ace could put his fingers in me—"

"Anytime, princess," Ace broke in, voice coarse with mounting pleasure.

Noelle wrinkled her nose. "It doesn't mean he owns me. I already made that choice." Leaning against Jasper's back, she touched the heavy leather buckled around Lex's throat. Not her usual collar, but a symbol just the same. "So did Lex."

Jasper raised his arm and slipped his fingers into Noelle's hair. "Dallas is Dallas, sweetheart. Not me."

Noelle looked so *earnest*, and Dallas's rueful laughter shook through Lex. "Christ, now I'm getting sex advice from a city girl."

"Because I listened to you." Noelle turned her face into Jasper's hand, licking the inside of his wrist above his cuff with a delicate shiver. "Bodies are just bodies. They can feel so good, but they're not the part you should get jealous over."

Dallas cupped a hand under Lex's chin and tilted her head. "Do I have anything to be jealous about, love?"

It sounded lighthearted, almost like a joke, but it didn't look like one. He stared at her, darkly curious.

Intense, as if her answer mattered beyond what Jas was allowed to do to her.

Lex exhaled shakily. No lies. No hiding, not when he'd opened himself to her with the question in the first place. "Never. If I could have anyone or anything, it'd be you."

Moving with painfully gentle precision, he stripped the leather from her throat and replaced it with his hand. Four strong fingers and his thumb riding the side of her neck. "Make her come, Jas. As hard as you fucking can, whatever it takes."

Jasper moved, but only to put Noelle on her knees over the couch, right beside Lex's leg, her cheek pressed to the leather. He stripped off the pink panties she still wore and bit the curve of her ass with a growl, then dragged her arm back. "Give me your hand."

She stretched it out willingly, her thumb rubbing over Dallas's leg, and Jasper guided her fingers to Lex's pussy. "Just two," he instructed as he gripped Noelle's hips.

A soft touch. Noelle's fingers danced over her clit before sliding lower. No disobedience this time, just the luscious slide of two fingers pushing deep.

Holy fuck.

Lex jerked, pressing closer into Dallas's steely grip around her throat. The reminder of his dominance dragged a moan from her, but the sound was eclipsed by Noelle's grateful cry as Jasper drove into her.

"Jasper's getting creative," Dallas whispered against her cheek, the words warm and approving. "Or maybe he thinks you'll come faster if you're watching him ride Noelle. Will you?"

"I like to watch." It turned her on, being close enough to feel the other woman's skin heat as her arousal built, to feel the sharp exhalations of breath on her calf every time Jasper slammed home.

Jasper wound a hand in Noelle's hair, holding her still, then reached out to push her fingers deeper into Lex. "Make her come," he rasped. "Get her off and I'll fuck you harder."

Noelle obeyed, stroking Lex with a determined rhythm that faltered when Jasper drove his cock into her and resumed with renewed effort when he pulled back. Dallas let Lex watch, but only for a moment before using his thumb to turn her head.

Ace met her gaze, his eyes full of sleepy, sated pleasure. Beside him, Mad stared at her intently, his dark eyes heavy with hunger and anticipation, a look that said it all. Ace might have been languishing in the warm aftermath of a hard orgasm, but Mad...

Mad would jump in. All Dallas had to do was say the word.

"How about being watched, love?" he asked instead, holding her chin tightly. "Do you like that?"

"I like—" The words cut off with a hissed curse as Jasper thrust two of his fingers into her along with Noelle's. It burned for a split second, but she was so wet, so ready that the pain faded almost instantly into bliss. She could feel every finger pressed tight against her inner walls, each individual movement as they moved and slicked over and against one another.

Dallas spoke his next words against her ear, low and dark. "Or would you like it more if you could get your lips around someone's cock?"

Debauchery. The kind of sex she'd told herself she'd have to give up to truly belong to Dallas—and here he was, offering it to her.

"I need it," she confessed in a rush. "I need to know." The words kept spilling out, and she was babbling, but she couldn't stop. It was all so much, *too* much, especially when Jasper growled and pushed at Noelle's fingers inside her, curving them to rub her G-spot with every rocking thrust.

Lex tensed, flexing her hands in the cuffs that still held her bound. Release was a heartbeat away, curling up in a dark wave that could crash at any moment. But it didn't matter, because this was what Dallas had wanted—her helpless, undeniable pleasure—and no way in hell would he let it stop now.

"Oh fuck, *yes*." It started as a low cry but built to a scream as Lex shook through the first tremors of orgasm. Not the peak, not yet, but so, *so* good. "More. Christ, Dallas, please—"

"Come here."

A clear summons, and then Mad was there, looming above her, his usually playful exterior stripped away in a moment of naked intensity. His belt already hung open, and in seconds he had his pants jerked open and his cock in hand, his fist clenched around the shaft and the blunt head hovering just before her mouth.

"It's his lucky day," Dallas rasped as he smoothed his hand around her throat and up into her hair. He nudged her head forward, until her lips brushed the tip of Mad's dick. "Because when he's buried halfway down your throat, you'll know *I* gave you that. I'll give you anything you need."

Anything. Lex clenched around the fingers inside her as she sucked Mad into her mouth.

He was so hard it had to ache, the head of his erection already slick and hot, and he groaned his pleasure at the first touch of her tongue. As if the sound had electrified her, Noelle redoubled her efforts, sending another bolt of sensation shooting through Lex.

The couch dipped as Ace settled on the couch opposite of Jas and Noelle, leaving Lex surrounded. His clever artist's fingers stroked the curve of her breast as Dallas tightened his grip in her hair and pushed her head forward. "This is what you wanted all along, isn't it?" Ace asked softly. "Everyone tangled together. All getting off on each other, you getting off on all of them?"

They all belonged there, right alongside Lex. There wasn't a person in the room who didn't belong to Dallas. They wore his ink, fought for him, trusted him with their lives.

It hit her, really *hit* her, along with a dizzy rush of ecstasy. This fantasy, every last harsh, sweet moment, wasn't about her at all, but about *him*—her body for his pleasure, readied by those he trusted most. She'd known that, but not what it meant.

Her fantasies didn't *mostly* revolve around Dallas. They *were* Dallas, start to finish. Trust and belonging and a longing so razor-sharp it could carve you into a million pieces and leave you begging for more.

Love.

She moaned around Mad's cock as her shaking intensified, driven by the hard thrusts and soft caresses and possession. They were touching her everywhere, inside and out. Completely focused on her release, on an orgasm that finally seized her in its grip and twisted, wrenching a muffled scream from her throat.

Dallas moaned, as rough and desperate as the hand in her hair, and then his mouth was on the nape of her neck, teeth closing tight. "That's right, love. You're almost ready for me. Keep squirming. Keep coming."

She already couldn't separate the rise and fall of pleasure. Her vision blurred, and she clenched her fists until her nails bit into her palms. Distantly, she realized Mad had pulled away and Jas and Noelle's fingers were gone, but Dallas was still stroking her, still whispering filthy promises against her skin.

He gave her no chance to recover. She sobbed in a breath as Dallas released her wrists with two flicks of his thumbs, and then they were both moving, the room dipping dizzily as he rose and swung her up into his arms in the same graceful movement.

Lex hit the floor, carpet under her shoulders and one plush cushion under her hips. Dallas knelt between her thighs, sliding his belt free of the buckle.

Yes. Lex reached for him, but Mad caught her wrists in a firm grip. He guided them back to the floor above her head as Dallas jerked his belt loose, the leather rasping through each loop in turn. "What do you want, Lexie?"

She stared at him, at the flex and play of muscle beneath skin. "I want you."

"Damn right you do." He pulled open his jeans and spoke to Mad without releasing Lex's gaze. "Sharing time's over. Go make Noelle's night."

Not quite *get your hands the fuck off my woman,* but the undertone was there, the dangerous edge that wasn't play at all. Dallas had gotten off on giving her what she wanted, but now he was ready to take what he needed.

She could struggle. He'd get off on that, too. But all she wanted was to open for him, body and soul.

She reached for him again, and he caught her hips and drove into her. Hard enough to hurt, and Lex bit her lip until it bled. "Don't stop—"

Another thrust cut her off. Rougher, almost violent. His fingers pressed bruises into her ass as he hoisted her hips higher. "Don't stop what? Don't stop fucking you?"

She tried to nod but banged her head against the floor instead. He was already so deep, huge and stretching inside her, and then he stopped *moving,* just clutched her hips and shifted them in tiny rolling movements that taunted her with too little friction.

And his words... "You want my cock?" Another thrust, short and abrupt, but so much sharper because he hauled her hips to meet it, slapping their bodies together with a deliciously crude sound. "You want me to fuck your pussy?"

Her ears were buzzing again. He could have made her come already, but he was holding back. Lex wrapped her hands around his wrists, digging her nails into his skin. "More. Fuck me hard."

"Quit giving orders." It took him forever to pull back, an eternity enduring the loss of him, and his return was almost as torturous. Deep, quick, but not hard at all. "What do you really want?"

"I want *you*."

"No." He lunged over her, hands splayed on either side of her head, pinning her hair, his body pressing down on hers with strength and heat. "You want whatever I wanna give you."

Lex caught her breath. He'd said he'd give her anything, the world...but she had to trust him to do it.

Did she?

Dallas's mouth descended on hers before she could decide. Hot, abrupt, teeth scraping her lips as his tongue plunged past them. A claiming kiss that turned gentle once she parted for him, turned lazy and warm, and he finished by licking her lower lip with a low groan. "When you admit it to yourself, you can admit it to me," he murmured.

And pulled away.

No. She reached blindly for him, only to have her hands brushed aside as he gripped her hips and flipped her onto her knees in one deft movement.

Pleasure jolted up her spine as he plunged two

blunt fingers into her, but after two lazy pumps he slipped them down to rub her clit. "You wanted me to lose control, love. Didn't know what you were asking for, did you?"

Somehow, she found her voice. "You haven't lost it. Not yet."

He laughed. Laughed and bent over her, cupping her jaw with one hand to force her face up and back. "Oh yes, I have. We left your fantasy back at the couch, darling. This is mine. And in this one, you don't get fucked because you want it. You get fucked because I want to fuck you, and you take it because you love everything I do to you."

His mouth was close enough to lick. To bite. Lex focused on his lower lip and licked her own. "I do love it. More when you stop playing. When you give in."

"Look at me, Lex. Am I playing?"

She met his gaze. It *burned* with unsated lust—and something more. "You sure the hell seem to think this is funny. Leaving me waiting on my knees."

His chest rumbled—a growl or a laugh, she wasn't even sure. He rocked his hips, sliding his shaft against her pussy. Taunting her. "I'm not the one keeping you waiting."

Frustrated, she twisted in his grasp. Only a few feet away, Noelle and Jasper were tangled together again, rocking together in a slow, intense grind. Ace and Mad were wrapped around them both, licking and stroking even as they touched each other.

But it was Noelle who drew her gaze again and again. The look of sheer, utter abandon on the woman's face made Lex's heart seize, and she found herself whispering, "I don't know what else to give you, Declan. I don't know how."

His touch gentled as his fingers drifted from her

jaw up toward her hair. It took him forever to wrap his fist in the strands, but abruptly he pulled his hand tight, dragging her head up until her back bowed. "All right, Lexie love. I'll take it."

That was all the warning she got before he kneed her thighs apart and thrust into her. Her hands slipped, and her teeth clacked shut as her elbows banged to the floor. Even that pain couldn't detract from the pleasure, the pure, goddamned satisfaction of it.

Of being taken.

"This is it. What you won't ask for." He punctuated every sentence with another vicious thrust, driving home the last word hard enough to wring a choked noise from her. He kept moving, kept talking, his words twisting her almost as tight as the sensation of his cock stretching her. "No choices. No responsibility. No having to admit you like being owned."

Because she didn't. No one else had ever come close to giving her a reason to want it, but Dallas was a force of nature, beautiful and brutal. Unstoppable. Only for him could she ever imagine opening herself up so completely.

No, Lex hated the thought of being owned. For him, she'd do it anyway.

"You." Her nails scratched over the floor. "Just you."

"Just me." Between one thrust and the next he was over her, hands planted on either side of her shoulders, the hair on his chest tickling over her back as he fucked into her with long, rough strokes. Over and over again, in her and on her, surrounding her and taking her, all accompanied by a never-ending string of beautiful obscenities.

She quivered in the scant moments between thrusts and cried out when he came back to her, each time harder than before. Each time with less control, more naked need. There was no room left for fighting, herself *or* him.

Lex let go.

Above her, Dallas groaned. His mouth found her ear, teeth rough as they closed on the lobe, tongue wet and warm as he licked in time with his next demanding rock. "I'll give you everything," he promised, each word a panting rasp as his tempo increased. "Everyone. It's all yours, even me."

Especially him.

Lex was floating, awash in an incandescent heat that spread through her, all the way into her fingers and toes. It wasn't an orgasm—that, she could still feel building, growing stronger, like a voice lifting in a scream. This was warmth, safety, all the glimpses she'd allowed herself of what could be.

Dallas slipped one hand under her to cup the front of her shoulder. It shifted the angle of her hips, and one more thrust washed her away, drowning that warmth in a volcanic pleasure that curled her toes and went on and on, until he growled her name against the back of her shoulder and set his teeth in her skin as he came.

16

Most nights, Dallas would have been happy to collapse in a pile on his bed. Six people might have made for close quarters, but he'd slept in closer.

Tonight, he didn't even want Jas and Noelle around.

None of them seemed to mind. Lex was still trembling in his arms when Jasper rounded up the others and herded them out the door, undoubtedly to continue the party—or expand it.

Dallas's party was warm and pliant. Wobbly limbed, too, which was something he could relate to. Pride alone got him to his feet with Lex cradled to his chest, and the need to see to her carried him across the room. After laying her on the bed, he took a few moments to strip the leather cuffs from her wrists and ankles, rubbing softly at the red marks left from her struggles.

Her eyes remained shut, but a slow smile curved her lips. "You're petting me again."

Satisfied that she wasn't injured, Dallas kicked free of his pants and joined her on the bed. "I like petting you. Get used to it."

"Not a complaint." She rubbed one bare leg over his. "Just saying."

She was sated and relaxed, which was quickly becoming his favorite look on her. Her sleepy smile wasn't meant to charm or soothe him. It wasn't a mask. This was Lex, stripped of all that bullshit she'd learned in Two. Not trying to be anyone's fantasy.

It made her his.

He kissed the inside of her wrist. "You mind that I broke up the party?"

"Did you?" Her lashes finally fluttered up as she opened her eyes. "I'm half-conscious. They'll have more fun without me."

"I doubt that." He looped an arm around her waist and hauled her back until she was snuggled soft and warm against his chest. "But I'm done sharing you."

"For now, or forever?"

The game they were playing was too high stakes for lies, even little ones. "I don't know. For tonight, at least."

"I'd do it," she said quietly. "For you."

Those were the words he'd never expected to hear. Or maybe he had, but only wrenched from her, a grudging trade for some ambiguous promise he'd never been able to figure out. "You'd give it all up? Even Noelle?"

"I don't want to. Not because I have to have sex with her or anyone else, but..." Lex turned her head toward him, leaving him staring at her profile. "It makes me feel like you don't trust me. Like you think it means you mean less, or that I won't come back to you."

Of course she'd come back to him. That possibility never bothered him as much as the reasons she'd leave to begin with. The implication that he wasn't enough.

Easy to think. Admitting it out loud—*shit*. The thought alone made him cringe, so he shifted the conversation to something less embarrassing. "It's not about trust, but yeah. I get jealous. And not just over sex, love. I got jealous as hell when Gideon started running his mouth like you two have some big secret."

She exhaled a short laugh. "Only because of his cousin. Mad's been helping me funnel money into some of the other sectors, a little aid for people who need it."

Not the answer he'd been expecting. "Why don't I know about this?"

"Because of how I get the money."

In the earliest days—days when she was new to the gang and he was still wondering if she was a trap Cerys had set for him—he'd kept an eye on her. Followed her.

Watched her steal a whole lot of shit.

In the beginning, he'd thought it was about security. She had no reason to trust him, and anyone who'd come off the streets in Sector Three was liable to hoard anything they could get their hands on. Time had passed and Lex had taken ink, and the bouts of thievery had come to an end.

Or maybe they hadn't. He'd stopped watching so closely after she'd quietly paid off Cerys. That was another secret he wasn't supposed to know about, but it had been the turning point. The proof she wasn't a trap—or, if she was, that the endgame was so subtle and convoluted he'd never uncover it by shadowing her.

So he'd stopped, and he'd assumed she'd given up climbing through third-story windows in search of valuable items. After all, he gave her any fucking thing she wanted.

The silence had stretched out uncomfortably, so Dallas shifted Lex in his arms until she was facing him. "You steal." Not quite a question.

She held his gaze unflinchingly. "Yes."

"From where?"

"Three, mostly. But I've been into Five and Six a few times."

Emotion churned in his gut, and he honestly didn't know if it was anger or fear. Three was bad enough, but at least he knew she could handle herself against low-lifes and thugs. Five, on the other hand...

He curled his hand around the back of her neck. "Do you know what Fleming does to pretty women who cross him?"

Her lips pressed together in a tense line. "I'm not stupid, Dallas. I know what I'm doing."

As if that made it okay. "Then what the hell could be worth risking your foolish fucking neck?"

"I want to *help*." Her voice dropped, low and almost ashamed. "Most people don't get as lucky as I did."

Christ. He lifted her chin to force her to look at him. "Did you think I wouldn't let you?"

"No. But I didn't want you to feel like you needed to take over and do it for me, either."

He didn't know what was worse—that she assumed he would, or that he was half-convinced he wouldn't. It was the first lesson he'd learned growing up, the one that had always seemed to weigh heaviest on his mother's shoulders. You picked your people, and you held them close. You didn't have to go out of your way to hurt anyone else, but you couldn't save them all, either. It had been true on a tiny ranch in Texas, and it was true in the sectors surrounding Eden.

Lex had always given him too much fucking credit—and it always made him want to try harder, to be worthy of it. "You do help. Jesus, Lex. You've changed the lives of every woman in this fucking sector."

Her brows drew together in a frown, and she reached up to rub her thumbs over his cheeks. "But is it enough? I don't know anymore."

"We're about to change a few lives in Three, too. That's a quarter of the sectors, love. It's a lot."

Mollified, she pressed her forehead to his chin. "I swore Mad to secrecy. Dr. Jordan, too."

Doc didn't wear his ink, so he owed him no loyalty—nothing beyond what any man in Four showed him out of sheer practicality, anyway. But Mad... Dallas sighed as he sank his fingers into Lex's hair. He knew what Mad's defense would be, as if he'd already heard it. *What, O'Kane? You want her out there without backup?*

Dallas doubted she even knew how deep Mad's scars ran, but those old wounds made it easy for Dallas to understand his motivations. Mad had suffered the backlash that came from standing too close to power. He knew all the ways an enemy could use a hostage as leverage—and that the truest loyalty to any leader meant protecting them from the hard choices that followed.

Didn't mean Dallas wouldn't scream at him. But for now, he pressed a kiss to Lex's forehead. "They're big boys. Not your responsibility."

Her fingers brushed her throat, where her collar usually lay. "That's not exactly true anymore."

No, it wasn't. "Is that a weight you wanna carry, Lexie? You of all people know the state my shoulders are in most nights."

"Yeah, I do. Which is why I'd have to be a selfish

ass to stick you with all the work."

He touched her collarbone, tracing his finger over the skin he planned to mark. Thick black ink, a design fit for a queen. *The* queen. "Do you trust me?"

Her eyes locked with his—for once, clear and unguarded. "Yes."

Finally.

His blood pumped fire through his veins as he splayed his fingers across her chest, his thumb canted toward one shoulder and his pinky brushing the other. She looked deceptively delicate in moments like this, small under his hand, but there was nothing fragile about the heart beating under his palm.

And it belonged to him. "Ink," he said, the word edged with all his desire. "O'Kane for life."

"For life," she echoed, covering his hand with hers.

He couldn't stop his feral grin, the triumph and satisfaction. "All of you."

"Mmm." She arched an eyebrow. "What's that look for?"

The fire in his veins settled as a burning heat in his gut, stoked higher by the mental image of Lex wearing his ink. Lex, his.

He lifted his hand to trace her lips and let his imagination run wild. She was soft and sweet, her defenses swept away. How much hotter would it be now, fucking her when she was already open and trusting? When he could show her that he didn't need an orgy to overwhelm her senses, to claim every goddamn part of her?

Still smiling, he edged one finger between her lips. "Maybe I'm not done with you for the night."

Lex closed her eyes and bit him. "I won't be able to walk tomorrow, and neither will you. You realize that, right?"

The world could survive the day without them.

Bracing his thumb against her jaw, he pushed his finger deeper, savoring the sharp scrape of teeth almost as much as the quick heat of her tongue. "If you can walk before sundown, it means I didn't get the job done."

She shivered and licked his fingertip with a moan.

He couldn't stop himself from pumping his finger in and out, fascinated by the way her lips looked wrapped around any part of him. "Tonight, you're mine to play with. This mouth..." He added another finger, pushed them both in to the second knuckle. "Mine to kiss, mine to defile."

Her eyes lit up at the word, amusement and lust in equal measure. The back of her hand brushed his stomach, and she walked her fingers slowly up to scratch her nails across his chest.

Oh yeah, she liked that. Liked it even more when he withdrew his fingers, slapped her cheek in teasing warning, and smoothed his hand down her throat.

He smacked her breast next, and the firm flesh swayed enticingly. Made his dick ache, too, and his next words sounded rough. "I could play with these tits for hours. Sucking, pinching..." He tweaked her nipple just to watch her jerk. "Making them bounce."

Her skin flushed, and her breathing quickened. "Yours to play with. Whatever you want."

Three simple words, but the *layers* in them. A man could go dizzy trying to untangle the subtle shifts in power. He owned her the same way he owned them all, as a benevolent dictator who enforced his ownership lightly. Someone who didn't understand would think her submission solidified that claim, would think she'd yanked her own collar tight and handed him a leash.

Blind fools. Submission snapped the leash. Here she was, flushed at the sudden freedom, and he was the one weighed down by the responsibilities that came with her gift. He was the one who had to walk that razor-thin line, knowing one misstep could cut them both.

Trust went both ways, a fact that held him in its grasp as he smacked her other breast hard enough to feel the sting of impact in his fingers. He had to trust that her moan of pleasure was honest, that she wouldn't hold back or hide discomfort. All it would take was one lie on her part to turn him into a monster.

Especially when her fantasy was being taken by one.

Lex shuddered through a soft sigh and framed his face with gentle hands. "You don't have to. Not if it's too much."

Of course she saw. Of course she *understood*, which was why it would never be too much. Growling, he caught her face, his thumb and fingers digging in to her cheeks just enough to serve as a quiet warning. "Are you going to be a good girl?"

Her answer was quiet, serious. "You know me better than that."

He knew she fought back, but sometimes it was hard to tell how much was a struggle to hold on to her defenses, and how much was a silent plea for him to fulfill a need she could barely articulate.

Maybe she couldn't articulate it, but he understood it. Leaning closer, he licked her lips. "Tell me you'll be good tonight."

She stilled and then moved, sliding her inner thigh up the outside of his leg. "I'll be good. Only for you."

He rewarded her with a rough whack on the hip before rolling away, his mind already stumbling over what part of her to claim first. With a few clever toys and a little patience, he could reduce her to limp, trembling bliss.

"On your knees," he ordered as he moved to the open cabinet. A fortune in tools of debauchery lined the shelves, a mix of custom pieces and pre-Flare relics, things meant to bind, to penetrate, to cause pleasure and pain.

He bypassed the whips and floggers, uninterested in striking her with anything but his bare hands. Pain wasn't Lex's trigger, for all that he'd seen her transported by the hazy rush of it. She thrived on sensation, on roughness that stemmed from too much desire, from the feeling of being overwhelmed.

That made his selection easy. When Dallas retrieved the items and turned back to the bed, Lex was kneeling near the end of it, facing him.

Waiting.

God, she was striking. Beautiful, from her disheveled hair straight down to her perfect toes. Sleek, but not soft. She had the strength of a dancer, toned muscles under dangerous curves, and sometimes it was hard not to just *stare* at her.

But staring wasn't enough tonight. He dropped the toys to the bed and traced the luscious line of her thigh before curling his fingers to cup her pussy. "Ready to get back to that talk about the things that belong to me, love?"

Her head fell back, and she clutched his arms with trembling hands. "Yes."

He delved between her outer lips and bit back a groan at how wet she was. Wet and hot, even more so when he thrust his finger deep inside her. Not only for the pleasure of hearing her moan, but for the satisfaction of feeling her muscles clench with arousal when he lifted his other hand to lightly slap her face again. "Open your knees, Lexie. Keep 'em spread wide, so I can play with this pussy however I want."

She shifted on the bed, her knees parting, hips tilting toward his touch. So obedient, so eager, and the naked trust in her eyes was as delicious as the way she squirmed, like she couldn't *not* ride his hand.

Edging closer, Dallas dragged her head back, forcing her to stare up into his eyes as he fucked her lazily with that one finger. "Good girl. You do everything I tell you, and I'll let you decide where I fuck you. And how hard."

Her eyes flashed, dark and hungry. "Surprise me," she rasped.

Possessive heat skated under his skin. This was the part of her he never wanted to share. The others could line up and beg for the privilege of pleasuring their queen, as long as no one else saw *Alexa*, stripped bare and willing to do anything to please him.

His secret pleasure. His gift. And goddamn, was he ready to play with her.

He didn't bother with orders, not when they'd both get off on the alternative. Locking rough hands around her waist, he lifted her bodily and flipped her, sprawling her face down across the mattress as he smacked her ass. "Up on your knees."

Her hands clenched in the bedspread, but she arched her back and obeyed.

Anticipation wouldn't hurt her, so he stayed silent as he retrieved the heavy silver plug. It was wicked, blunt at the tip and sharply flared, with a green jewel flashing from the flat, circular base. Not the sort of adornment you tried with someone inexperienced, but the complete set with their differently colored gems were among Lex's favorite toys.

He took his time with the lube, slicking it over the cool silver before spilling it onto Lex's ass without a word of warning. She hissed in a breath and wiggled under the stream of clear, viscous liquid.

"You know what's coming, don't you?" He massaged the lube into her ass with one hand while he used the other to tease the plug between her pussy lips to rub against her clit.

"Mm-hmm." A lazy answer, at odds with the way her legs trembled.

He could get her off like this, but it would be quick and fleeting, the kind of pleasure that melted through you and vanished, forgotten. This wasn't any other night. This was the night she'd agreed to take his ink, to belong to him.

Patience would reward them both. At least, that's how he justified it to his aching cock when he placed the tip of the plug against her ass and watched her shudder as the slight pressure stimulated all those tiny nerves. "Hands back here," he ordered, his voice hoarsely menacing even to his own ears. "Hold yourself open so I can watch your greedy little ass take anything I put in it."

She slid her hands over her thighs, slowly stroking her way up to the swell of her ass. Her nails dug into her skin as she spread her cheeks and pushed back toward the plug in his hand.

Eager. She was always so damn eager, but it had never shredded his self-control like this. The possessiveness throbbing in his veins was barely human. He wanted to rasp darker words. Cruder words, just to see how far she'd let him go, how completely she'd play this game.

All the way. He knew the answer even as he pushed the plug deeper. Her tight little asshole tensed at the invasion, but he soothed it by working the toy in a careful circle, gently stretching her as his other hand centered on her clit. "Are you scared of me?"

She turned her head, her brow furrowed, and pressed her cheek to the bed. "Not even close, honey."

He worked his fingers faster, dragging a moan from her as her ass finally yielded to the mix of pleasure and pressure. The plug slipped in, and the jewel nestled tight between her ass cheeks. He couldn't stop himself from slapping her hip just to watch her clench. "You're never afraid of me. No matter how much I demand from you. No matter how crazy I get."

Her gaze locked with his as a shudder took her. "I'll always want more of you, Declan."

His final prize from the cabinet lay a few feet from her knee, and he caught the end loop with one finger and lifted it to dangle in front of her. Three smooth, silver balls dangled from the thin silicone casing that connected them, each swaying in odd counterpoint to the smaller round weight trapped inside.

They were large enough that two would have teased her plenty, even without the plug, and she knew it. So he let them dangle there as he stroked her clit too lightly to do anything but keep her on edge. "I want you to take all three of them."

Lex groaned, long and low. "Please."

"That's my girl." He gave her clit one final slap, unable to resist the sound she made or the way her hips jerked. She was so wet he probably didn't need more lube, but he used it anyway before pushing the first ball into her pussy. Dark satisfaction filled him as he watched her body take it, as he watched her writhe and listened to her moan. As he gently pushed the second into place.

He could do anything to her, *anything*, and she'd let him. Maybe even love it, as long as it got him off. It was ridiculous. It was humbling.

It was the hottest fucking realization of his life.

He stroked her trembling thighs and slid the final ball into place, pushing it deep with one finger and shuddering as she cried out. "My dirty, perfect girl. So good."

She shifted her hips, just a little, and stopped short with a strangled cry. "Fuck."

"That's the idea, love." He gave her one last soothing stroke and circled the bed to stand opposite her. A vast expanse of mattress separated them, at least five feet, but it gave him a lovely view of her flushed face and wild hair and her ass still in the air.

Beautiful. Beautiful, and his. Wetting his lips, he finally gave himself permission to curl a hand around his aching cock and stroke it. "Tell me how you feel."

She watched his hand, her own tongue darting out to lick her lower lip, as if she could taste him already. "I feel full," she whispered as she started across the space between them on her hands and knees. "Every time I move, something shifts inside me. Like when Jas and Noelle were fucking me with their fingers."

"You liked that, did you? Are you the one putting all those ideas in her head?" He licked his palm and gripped his shaft again, already imagining himself between Lex's lips. Soon, so soon. "Jasper fucking your pussy and me taking your ass? Or was it the other way around?"

"Does it matter?" She arched her back, bending her upper body low to the bed with another sharp inhalation.

Not really, but watching her like this made it clear that something else did. There was no hesitation in her body now, no self-consciousness. He shouldn't have demanded her submission in front of the people she helped lead. No wonder he'd been viciously jealous, and protective on top of it. This sweet vulnerability was his, not to be shared or showed off, but to be savored in privacy.

He'd show her what mattered. "Crawl to me."

Lex smiled slowly. "Or what?"

He braced both hands on the mattress. "Or I'll drag you over here and spank your ass until you're so wrung out from all the orgasms that you can't do anything but whimper while I fuck you."

That got her going. She bit her lip and eased across the bed. "Where could you possibly fuck me? I'm all filled up."

Breathless, gleeful words, and he laughed as he reached out to free her lower lip from the sharp edge of her teeth, only to replace the pressure with his thumb. "You will be," he agreed, making his voice as low and dangerous as hers was light and innocent. "You'll be so full when I'm fucking this sweet mouth."

"There's nothing you can't give me." Acknowledgment. Confession. "I figured that out a long time ago."

"Nothing I *won't* give you." He took his time wrapping the wild strands of her hair around his hands, letting her savor the slow slide from gentle to brutal as his grip tightened and he tilted her head up. "Tonight was the last time. I'll never ask for submission in front of anyone else again. You're my queen. They can crawl on their hands and knees and beg for the chance to fuck you, and we'll decide if they deserve the honor. But no one else sees you like this. This is just for me."

Her eyes sparked, warm and inviting. "Dallas..."

He knew that look. She wanted his cock, and he wanted to give it to her. Was *dying* to give it to her, as rough and uncontrolled as even she could hope for. "Open your mouth."

Lex curled her fingers around the edge of the bed, wiggled her ass one more time, and parted her lips.

He gave himself a few blissful seconds to admire her, from her hungry eyes and flushed cheeks to the swollen lushness of her lips and the pink flash of her tongue. Visual overload, but not half as stirring as the way she tugged against his grip in her hair, straining toward him.

So he gave her what she wanted, pressing into the heat of her mouth with a low groan. Heaven, especially when she wasted no time in teasing her tongue over the sensitive spot under the crown of his cock. But he only gave her a moment before dragging her head back. "Do you want to make me come?"

No hesitation. "Yes. I want all of you."

Another thrust. Deeper this time, taunting her with a hint of force, the first warning of his unraveling control. "If it's too much, slap my hip three times. Understood?"

She hummed around him and lifted a hand to his hip, but only to stroke the backs of her fingers lightly over his skin. It was permission and a plea rolled in one, so he did the only thing he could.

He let go.

Clutching her hair in his fists, he fixed her head in place and pushed deep with a satisfied groan, finally letting himself focus on the rough rasp of her tongue and the heat of her mouth. "Suck me. Show me how grateful you are to be so very, very full."

Her eyes drifted shut. Her free hand closed around the base of his cock, squeezing and stroking, but she didn't move her mouth, not beyond the gentle flutter of her tongue. Not that he'd have let her if she tried, but the fact that she didn't twisted lust around him, driving his hips forward until he bumped the back of her throat.

She wanted to be used, and he wanted to defile

her—two needs that clicked together like puzzle pieces, turning unacceptable urges into something beautiful. A communion between outsiders, a moment of damn near spiritual understanding. Forget the hollow pomp and circumstance of Eden, this moment, feeling Lex's body vibrate with pleasure as he fucked her throat—*this* was a religious experience.

Blasphemous, maybe, to compare a higher power to the delicious depravity of choking a woman with his cock.

Dallas didn't give a fuck.

"Put your hands back on the bed," he growled, pulling back far enough to let her gasp in a breath. "And open your eyes. Look at me."

She obeyed, dropping her hands to twist into the bedspread. Her eyes were almost black now—stormy, burning with lust and affection and something that was more than either. More than both.

Holding her gaze, he pushed between her lips, pushed until she struggled to swallow him, pushed until her lips stretched wide around the base of his shaft and everything was tight, luscious heat and the sizzling knowledge that this wild, dangerous creature trusted him with her body, trusted him to take his pleasure but still leave her sated.

Too good. He wouldn't last long, but he didn't need to. He might not be twenty anymore, but the plans he had for her would have him hard enough to fuck her one more time before the night was over. This was for both of them, one moment of fractured self-control, so he tightened his grip and let himself revel in it.

Let himself fuck that perfect, willing mouth.

He pulled back to let her take another breath, but Lex leaned in, chasing him with a rough, hoarse moan. "Greedy bitch," he murmured affectionately as he thrust deep again, in and out, over and over, clutching the back of her head to hold her in place and dragging her back by the hair, just to enjoy the way she strained for his cock, begging with everything but words.

She couldn't use them, so he found enough for both of them. Fond and filthy, coarse compliments and lewd promises. He didn't have to think, only had to hold her gaze as each rough thrust brought him closer and closer, and the obscenities spilled, unbidden, from his lips. "That's right, take it all. Take my dick until you fucking choke on it and beg for more. You want more, don't you? Want me to come in your mouth?"

She managed one short whimper and a quick, frantic nod. He indulged himself with one last moment enjoying the hot depths of her throat before hauling her head back and transferring his grip to the slender column of her throat. "Use your hands," he commanded, squeezing tight enough to give her a taste of danger without cutting off her breath. "Jerk me off on your tongue."

"Fucking *hell*." Lex wrapped both hands around him, end to end, and twisted lightly. The barest tease, but it dragged a groan out of him, all the same. His shaft was slick from her mouth, slick enough for her to switch to one fist and pump it smoothly over him, base to tip and back again.

That was all it took. The tight clasp of her hand and the sight of her parted lips, her ready tongue. When pleasure tightened at the base of his spine and rolled outward, he gave in to it, growling with each stroke until the sight of his semen spilling across her tongue forced her name from him in a tortured moan.

She milked his cock with a shudder, lapping at him between swallows. Dallas watched her, buzzing on the afterglow, and she was the most magnificent thing he'd ever seen. "You're perfect," he said roughly, stroking his thumb along her throat as it worked under his palm. "You don't have to try to be my fucking fantasy. Everything you are is perfect."

With a wordless moan, she leaned in and pressed her cheek to his stomach. "I needed this tonight. So much."

"I'll take care of all your needs," he promised, smoothing her hair into place. It caught on his fingers, and he took the time to work through the tangles left behind by his clutching fists. Just a few moments of quiet stroking while her breath fell hot on his skin, and he knew she must be wondering if the game was over.

He hoped it never was.

Dallas coaxed her head back, smiling down at her. He traced his fingertips over her lips and then seized her chin in a rough grip. He slid onto the bed, forcing her upright as he crowded her space. With her knees splayed wide, it was easy to loom over her, and he reached down to slap her pussy. "You've got a lot of needs, don't you, love? Desperate, aching needs."

"Oh, God." She grabbed his shoulders, her nails scoring his skin.

Sweet pain, and it'd be even better when those nails were digging into his scalp. Twisting, he spilled her to the bed on her back, with her head near the edge and her hair trailing over the side. Her tits swayed temptingly, but he had only one goal in mind as he swept both hands down her body to shove her slick thighs wide. "Christ, Lex, I've never seen you this wet. You sure you haven't come?"

"Not yet." The sudden movement had rocked her, though, leaving her eyes glazed and her chest heaving.

"Then I'll have to fix that." Simple enough, but he took his time, sitting back on his heels before tugging her closer. With her lower back on his knees and her legs splayed on either side of his, she was spread before him like a banquet. A helpless, trembling feast, and he loved the way she shuddered as she watched him lick his own thumb.

Her reaction when he swept it over her clit was immediate, electric. Her hips bucked, and she ground out a fierce curse. "Mother*fucker*."

Laughing hoarsely, he pinned her in place with one hand spread across her abdomen and flicked his thumb over her clit again. Watching her writhe would have him hard in minutes, but he'd counted on that. Nothing sent blood rushing to his cock like the noises Lex made when she was close to coming.

Her eyes rolled back, and he swatted her hip. "Look at me. Look at me, Lex."

"I can't." Her head hit the bed, and she twisted under his hand.

Lunging upward, he pinned her hair to the mattress and loomed over her, his shaft settling so sweet in the cleft of her pussy. "Look at me," he commanded a second time, holding her gaze as he ground against her. "You look at me while you're coming."

Desperate noises escaped her with every harsh, staccato breath. She shook beneath him, her body molding to his as her skin heated to burning—and beyond. Her fingers slipped into his hair, gripping and releasing in time with the rough rhythm of her rocking hips.

But her eyes were what held him captive. Dark, unfocused, lids drooping with the force of her climax only to snap open with the next shudder, as if pleasure had taken hold of her body and she was lost somewhere beyond obedience, beyond thought.

It could only be better if he was actually inside her.

The bottle of lube sat discarded a few feet from her head. Reaching for it slid the length of his dick over her clit, and he thrilled at her choked, hungry noises. By the time he closed his hand around the bottle, she was twisting through another peak, reduced to whimpers and clutching fingers, oblivious to his intentions as he freed his hair from her grip and drew himself upright.

She was still panting when he caught the jeweled end of the plug and gave it a gentle tug. "Stay with me, Lex."

She twitched as the plug eased free of her body. "Christ, Dallas—"

Lube, plenty of it, sliding over her ass and covering his cock. He pumped his fist over his erection. "You know what I want. Pull those legs up and open for me."

Lex wrapped her hands behind her knees and eased them back, her gaze riveted to his hand around his dick. He stroked again, slowly, just to taunt her, then gripped his shaft and guided the head over her pussy and lower, pressing against her ass. So tight, even slippery with lubrication and prepared for him.

"How does it feel, love?" he ground out, driving a moan from them both as he eased the crown of his erection past the ring of muscle and into her body. "How does it feel to have my cock in your ass? You've had it everywhere else tonight."

She sighed, a long exhalation that turned into his name. "Don't stop."

He didn't. Hell, he *couldn't*, not with her so fucking tight around his dick, clenching eagerly and pulling him deeper. Release had done its work on her muscles, melting away tension so that it seemed like no time at all before he was balls-deep and shivering at the sensation of being inside her while those damn clever toys rocked in her pussy with every jerk of her hips.

No wonder she was trembling so hard she could barely hold her legs up.

His own hands were none too steady, but he fought through the throbbing pleasure and the need to *move*. He replaced her hands with his own, spreading his fingers wide across her thighs before pushing her knees toward her chest.

He answered her guttural whimper with a soothing rumble. "Just like this, love. Full and tight and nothing you can do but close your eyes and take it. You want to take it, don't you?"

"All of you," she whispered, her voice thick with pleasure. "Every goddamn inch."

His laughter sounded as jagged as his control as he eased back and slid home again. "You've already got every goddamn inch, you greedy bitch." He pushed her knees closer to her chest and thrust harder, knowing the sort of pleasurable chaos it would set off in her pussy. "Nothing's enough for you, is it?"

"Me?" She moved beneath him, arching to meet his thrusts. "One thing. That's all I want."

She didn't have to say it. The answer bloomed in every touch, every movement, it took root in her voice and grew with her cries. *You, you, you.*

All she wanted was him.

So he gave her exactly that, with rough thrusts that sent her flying into release. He gave her *himself*, stripped of control, focused on nothing but fucking them both into a blind stupor, riding the maddening rhythm of her body as it spasmed and contracted with climaxes that came closer and harder and reduced her to breathless sobbing. There was nothing to do but close his eyes and let her drag him down into sweet, filthy oblivion, her screams echoing in his ears.

The world grayed around the edges as he came,

and it took forever for the shuddering aftershocks to stop, buried as he was inside her, her hips twitching helplessly with every breath. Clenching his jaw, he slipped out of her and lowered her legs.

He'd never seen her so debauched. Her skin was flushed and damp, her eyes still clenched tight, and she moaned as he eased her hips to the bed. "Lex, honey? Can you open your eyes?"

"Yeah." But she didn't, just lay there, sweaty and panting.

He didn't have that luxury, not while she needed tending. Moving carefully, he caught the loop at the end of the string of balls and pulled the first one free, but all the gentleness in the world couldn't stop her hoarse cry or the jerk of her hips.

Murmuring soothing noises, Dallas settled himself between her thighs and pressed a soft kiss to her clit. "You're all right." He eased the second sphere out of her. "I've got you."

She laughed and covered her face with her hands. "No, you don't. I can't stop spinning."

He dropped another kiss, this time to her inner thigh. "Nothing wrong with spinning." One final tug and another full-body shudder from Lex, and he tossed the toy aside. "I'll catch you, love. I'll always catch you."

"Will you?" She traced his jaw. "Even when you're spinning with me?"

"Especially then." Because that was the sweetest thing, the truth no one seemed to understand unless they lived it. Responsibility wasn't an unpleasant duty he tolerated just to get to the good parts. It *was* the good part, the essential one. It was the feeling of satisfaction and smug pride that grew with every moment she sprawled boneless, trusting him to care for her.

Physical pleasure was a fucking beautiful thing,

but it was fleeting. The thrill of having her curl trustingly against his chest as he lifted her from the bed would linger.

Maybe even forever.

17

The potential recruits from Three looked like they'd just stumbled across the lost city of El Dorado—if they'd been looking for tits and ass instead of gold.

Lex sat up straighter and tugged at the bottom of her velvet corset. From her vantage point beside Dallas, she watched the new guys weave their way through the crowd. They didn't speak unless spoken to, but they seemed relaxed, their heads occasionally bobbing in time with the throbbing music.

At least they had manners enough not to be grabbing ass already. It was damn near the most a woman could hope for, especially out of Wilson Trent's old sector.

"They don't seem so bad," Noelle observed, shifting closer to Jasper nonetheless. She looked unusually fierce in leather and chains, but the dark style and dramatic makeup suited her every bit as much as her usual ruffles and lace. She'd braided her hair up off her neck, leaving Jasper's ink winding across her skin in elegant, deadly warning.

There was a lot of ink on display tonight, including Dallas's. Spiked bands clasped his wrists below his O'Kane cuffs, but his arms were left bare by his heavy leather vest, and he draped one across the booth behind Lex as their three visitors drifted closer. "They're careful," Dallas corrected, "which just means they're not idiots."

Jasper huffed out a laugh. "Or they're careful idiots."

Dallas snorted. "Six said these were the brightest of the bunch, but that's like saying they're the softest rocks. The one on the left is Cain. I'd bet on him being the brains of the operation."

The man was tall, dark, with a look of deceptively relaxed concentration on his smooth brown face. It reminded her of Bren, the way he watched the world, registering everything and filing it away for later.

"The other two are Riff and Elvis." Dallas's lips twitched. "One of them's a musician. And it ain't Elvis."

Lex had seen enough musicians in her time to spot Riff, with his long black hair and scowl. Which left Elvis as the pretty boy, the one licking his lips and eyeballing the women like he was making a fucking grocery list for later. "He thinks highly of himself, doesn't he?"

"Presumably. He wants to run things, and that takes a certain amount of arrogance."

Lex leaned her head back against his arm. "You would know, honey."

"Damn straight."

Elvis turned toward their corner, and Dallas tensed as the man's gaze slid over Lex and Noelle in turn. He mostly kept the expectant lust from his face as he approached, but Lex could see it in his eyes. Hear it in his voice. "Dallas. Jasper. Quite a party."

Dallas settled a hand on Lex's shoulder as he nodded to the chairs on the opposite side of the table. "Oh, we're just getting started. Take a seat."

He did, sprawling out to take up as much space as possible. Cain was the last to sit, choosing the chair that would leave him with his back against the wall.

Lex liked him already.

She offered him a smile as she slid a whiskey shot closer to him. "Cain, right?"

He nodded and accepted the tiny glass, but didn't drink. His gaze flicked briefly to her collar—and no lower. "And you'd be Lex?"

"I would." She glanced at the other two men. "Noelle and I were sorry to miss the trip into your sector. Introduce us to your friends?"

Cain opened his mouth only to close it as Elvis leaned forward and swiped the shot of whiskey. He knocked it back without fuss and grinned. "This is Riff, and I'm Elvis. I guess that kind of makes me a king."

Riff's derisive snort was the only sound he made. Lex longed to echo it as she placed a drink in front of him before sliding another shot to rest near Cain's hand.

Since he hadn't gotten whatever he was clearly after, Elvis tried again. "I've always wanted to meet the infamous Lex Parrino. I caught your show once. Never forgot it, either."

He said it with a leer that left everyone at the table uncomfortably sure he'd spent more than a few nights jerking off to the memory of her dancing. Dallas tensed to the point of anger beside her. Before he could explode, Cain stepped into the awkward pause. "That would make you Miss Cunningham," he told Noelle, managing not to stare at her tits, either.

"Noelle," she corrected with a smile sweet enough to ruin the effect of the wardrobe. "Just Noelle. I'm an O'Kane."

His gaze flickered to Jasper. "Right. I met your man the other night."

"Jas is my right hand," Dallas said in his best lazy voice, relaxed and easy despite the strain Lex could feel in every muscle of his body. "Bren's my left. You'll meet him later."

Riff stirred but said nothing. Elvis transferred his leer to Noelle. "I'm more interested in this little lady here. Not every sector has their own Eden royalty. I heard Jas plucked her out of her daddy's house in the middle of the night and taught her to be bad."

Jasper drew on his cigarette and blew smoke in the man's face. "Maybe she doesn't want to talk about it."

Coughing, Elvis waved his hand in front of his face. "Just curious, man. No judgment. If she's any indication of what they're hiding behind those walls, sign me up for salvation."

Noelle's expression had frozen into that sweet, smiling mask, but her words were edged in frost. "You never know. Eden might welcome a man of your character."

Elvis's eyes narrowed, and Cain slapped him across the arm. "Shut up. We're here to talk business." He arched a brow. "Aren't we?"

Jasper crushed out his cigarette, slid out of the end of the booth, and held out his hand to Noelle. "Let's dance, sweetheart."

Under the table, Noelle wrapped her fingers around Lex's in a brief, encouraging squeeze. She murmured a polite farewell to Cain and smiled at Riff before slipping her hand into Jasper's and abandoning the table without so much as a glance at Elvis.

That only seemed to encourage him. He twisted in his chair, watched Jas and Noelle disappear into the crowd, and whistled. "Tits or not, that is one frigid sister. But I bet it's fun, sticking it to Eden every night."

"That's an O'Kane," Dallas replied mildly as he stroked his fingers over Lex's hair. "And all O'Kane ladies have one thing in common, *brother*. They don't let you stick much of anything in them if you can't be assed to learn some manners."

"Might even stick something in you." Through the velvet of her skirt, Lex traced the knife strapped to the thigh. "If you know what I mean."

Riff's lips twitched, disrupting his scowl. "If he doesn't figure it out, he deserves it."

Silence fell around the table. Cain stared at Lex, not out of particular interest or even disdain, but almost as if waiting for her to do something.

She refused to fidget, lifting her drink instead. "Yes?"

He cleared his throat and prompted, "Business?"

And that's when Lex realized he expected her to leave.

She froze with her glass to her lips, goose bumps rising on her arms. The reasonable one—the *smart* one—and he still figured she shouldn't hang around while the big boys talked. "Excuse me?"

The men looked at Dallas. Elvis even went so far as to smile snidely. "Where're *your* manners, O'Kane? The shit we have to discuss isn't any sort of talk for pretty ladies."

One heartbeat. Two. That was all the time it took for Dallas O'Kane to dismiss her like she was nothing.

He lifted his arm from around her shoulders. "You really don't want to listen to any of this, love."

Maybe he really was trying to spare her, but it cut deep. When faced with ugly words, he'd responded quickly enough, but now, confronted with actual disrespect, he caved. Easier not to argue and risk driving away potential recruits.

So much for being the queen.

Whatever, O'Kane. She slipped her hand under her skirt and drew the knife. She slammed it down on the table as she rose, embedding the tip half an inch into the already scarred wood. "I'll see you boys around."

Without waiting for a response from Dallas—she knew better—Lex stalked off into the throng of bodies, righteous anger driving every quick step. She wanted to get drunk, get stupid, but she had a crowd to manage and work to do.

And goddamn it, she was going to do it.

The knife quivered in the table.

Elvis quivered in his chair.

Okay, maybe that was taking things a bit far, but it figured that *now* the bastard had decided to shut his fucking mouth. Maybe that was a good sign, after all, one that showed he could learn. He wouldn't be the first O'Kane to learn manners from Lex at knife-point.

Dallas would be lucky if she didn't cut him tonight.

Resisting the urge to sigh, Dallas shifted position, sprawling out on his side of the booth. "I'll tell you straight up, boys. Some things about Three are going to change, and you can roll with me or get your asses rolled over. The way you treat the ladies better top that fucking list, or the boys will bury you."

Cain eyed the knife. "Got it. He'll do better."

Might as well get the ugly stuff out of the way first. "Our women aren't the only ones used to a basic level of decency. Whoring's an honest job, and if the men in Three can't charm their way into sex, they're gonna start paying for it. Maybe it'll inspire people to work on those manners we value so much."

"Elvis might be crass, but he's stand-up when it comes to that shit," Cain shot back.

Dallas lifted an eyebrow and pinned the pretty boy with a look.

"What?" the man snarled, apparently bored of attempting charm. "Jesus Christ, if telling a woman she's got nice tits is a crime, I don't wanna live anymore. And you're awful high and mighty for a man whose club features naked girls fucking each other for tips."

"Consent," Riff muttered. "He doesn't think we know what the word means."

"I think anyone who worked with Trent could use a refresher," Dallas agreed. "Or did you folks forget he threw Six at me like a secondhand couch? I've seen how stand-up his operation was when it comes to that shit."

Cain shook his head. "None of us were involved with that. The guys who were got pretty damn dead. Or did *you* forget that you killed them?"

"As long as we're all on the same page." Dallas poured another round of shots himself, using the time to scan the floor for Lex. He found her standing with Ace's friend Jared, the dangerously handsome man who was probably the richest free agent in Four.

Dallas had tried to convince Ace to recruit Jared into the fold more than once—mostly because the man earned his wealth screwing rich, lonely ladies behind their neglectful husbands' backs. He knew enough secrets to bring a quarter of the wealthiest families in

Eden to their knees.

Dallas wanted those damn secrets.

Jared was laughing now, clearly amused by something Lex had said. She knew how badly Dallas wanted the man charmed. Driving him away would have been a suitable revenge, but petulance wasn't Lex's style. She wouldn't risk the gang and its interests. When the time came for her temper to slip free, Dallas would be the only target. And she'd make him pay.

It was probably sick to find the prospect a little arousing.

With the liquor served, he turned his attention back to the three men seated across from him. Time would tell if they could learn enough to be useful, but Cain had one point. The worst offenders under Trent's reign had been the men loyal to him, and those sorry bastards were really fucking dead.

Sometimes you had to work with people you didn't like toward goals that were good for everyone. Lex would have to get used to it, if she wanted to be queen. You couldn't force men like these to respect women, and trying would only make you look weak. No, you had to step on them until they behaved, and let them see for themselves how much nicer life got when the ladies were on your side. That would change their minds.

The money and willing pussy wouldn't hurt.

She fucking *dared* him to walk into her room uninvited tonight.

And yet, that's exactly what he did. The door swung open as she sat at her vanity, removing her jewelry, and Lex was so taken aback that she almost laughed. Almost.

The man really had no sense of self-preservation

at all.

Dallas draped both arms across his chest and sighed as he watched her drop her rings into a bowl. "Well?"

"Well, what?" she asked.

"Are we gonna do this or not?"

Lex slid the clip from her hair and reached for her brush. "Do what? Should I whine and complain like the little bitch I am so you can pat me on the head and buy me something pretty to shut me up?"

He pulled her knife from his belt and flipped it over in his hand. "I sorta figured this was an invitation to fight. Don't back down now, honey. Tell me how you really feel."

She turned around and snatched the knife. "I'm *not* your little bitch. Don't treat me like one, especially in front of potentials. It sets a shitty example, O'Kane."

"I slapped them down good, Lex. Before you left *and* after. But I can't erase a lifetime of learning in one fucking meeting."

A handy deflection—if it were true. "You're full of shit. You didn't slap them down."

He frowned. "Of course I did. They're untrained puppies, Lex. You rub their noses in it when they piss on the floor, and eventually they learn. I didn't drown them in the river over it, no."

She stared at him, dumbfounded. "You have no idea what I'm talking about, do you?"

Dallas was too smart to reply quickly. She could almost see him turning inward, struggling to replay the short conversation and figure out what he'd missed. "The guys made asses of themselves," he said finally, a diplomatic, evasive answer.

"Uh-huh. About...?"

Another pause. "Noelle?"

Lex swallowed past the lump in her throat. It was one thing for Dallas to take the path of least resistance when it suited him, even if it meant shoving her aside as useless and purely decorative, but to not understand what he'd done? That was different. Worse.

She turned back to the mirror and pulled the brush through her hair.

Dallas snarled and slapped a hand against the wall. "Not okay, Alexa. You can shout at me, you can throw things at me, you can do your fucking best to slip that knife between my ribs, but you *do not ignore me.*"

"Are you listening to yourself?" She dropped the brush and the knife to the vanity with a clatter and rose, facing him. "You don't like being dismissed, so what in hell makes you think it wouldn't piss me off just as much?"

"You wanted to stay?" he scoffed. "Shit, woman, *Jas* didn't want to stay."

"He isn't your partner." Lex lowered her voice. "He also could have hung around without making any of you blink. Not just those assholes, but you, too."

That drew him up short. "Cain. It was Cain, wasn't it?"

To her horror, angry tears burned her eyes. "There's more to respecting the women around here than not groping them or saying disgusting shit they don't want to hear. Way more."

"Jesus, Lex. I know." He took a step forward, but didn't crowd her space. "But I can't reach into the man's head and make him realize you can think circles around him."

"No, I could have done that on my own." She met his gaze reproachfully. "*If* you'd had my back. But you didn't. You told me to run along like a good girl while the menfolk had their talk. And don't think that didn't tell them something about you, Dallas."

"You're blowing one little thing out of proportion. I didn't even kick you out. I gave you the choice, because listening to them was always gonna suck until we smacked some manners into them. I gave you an out, and you took it."

Sincerity laced the words. Whatever else, he believed them. "Those little things? They build up in the long run."

He shoved his fingers through his hair and exhaled sharply. "I don't want there to be a long run. If they can't come around all the way, things will change. But fuck, Lex. I can't write off every bastard who isn't housetrained from minute one."

Her self-control snapped. "I'm not talking about them, Declan. You asked me to take your fucking ink, and tonight you acted like I was some random girl you peeled off your dick after a cage fight." She stalked to the door and jerked it open. "I'm talking about *you*."

Dallas whirled on her. "What should I have done? If it's so obvious to you, tell me."

Her anger melted into something else, something determined and insistent. She could do this, make him hear her and understand. "For starters? You could have treated me like I needed to be at that meeting. Like I helped you build this place, because you know what? I damn well did."

At least he was listening. He took in her words, turned them over, and then nodded. "Yeah, but the shit tonight? That's not your thing. You don't sit in meetings with our guys, either. I get that it felt like a snub, but if you hadn't needed to prove a point, would you have really wanted to stay?"

As if that mattered. "It's part of my job now. Isn't that what you wanted?"

He tilted his head. "You wanna come to all the meetings?"

"Yes." She'd taken on a new role, one she couldn't fill without keeping up with everything that happened.

Dallas sighed and rubbed a hand over his arm. "It means change. It means putting a target on your back. I'm not saying no...but can we talk over the danger when we're not pissed and fighting?"

Plenty of things already made her a target—her association with him, her *collar*—and he wanted her to have ink. The biggest target of all if you wanted to bring down a ruthless man like Dallas O'Kane. "All I need is for you to understand. Don't try to protect me from things I need to do."

"And I need you to give me the benefit of the doubt." He caught her wrist and ran a thumb over the O'Kane ink wrapped around it. "This right here? This is proof I'll listen."

It had taken her six months to convince him it was a bad idea to exclude women from his gang. "You're not bleeding. That's proof *I'll* listen."

He crooked a smile. "I'm a little disappointed. What's that a sign of?"

Lex pushed away the tendrils of uneasiness still curling through her. He didn't understand, but he would listen. It would be enough. It *had* to be enough.

She touched his hand. "It's a sign that this just might work out after all."

18

Dallas had never been able to bring himself to entirely trust city tech.

The banged-up tablet on his desk was clever enough. He liked the fact that he could speak words instead of writing them and see his notes transcribed into clean lines of text, as if by magic. It was quick to manage and easy to organize. And it could all go away with the blink of an eye.

It had happened before, after all.

The thing was on the fritz again, mangling the words he spoke and locking him out every time he tried to save the file. He tossed it aside and was starting his list of most likely recruits over on paper when a knock rattled the door.

A mass of red curls appeared as Trix stuck her head into his office. "You have a visitor."

Her appearance reminded him he needed to add women to the list of potential recruits—with her at the top of it. "What kind of visitor?"

She hesitated. "Dressed like she's from Eden, but she seems pretty comfortable out here. She walked in like she owned the place."

Dallas could only think of one person who could possibly qualify—and he couldn't think of a damn reason for her to be in his sector. "She didn't give you a name?" he asked, but he was already on his feet.

Trix shook her head. "I asked, but she didn't answer. Just said you were expecting her. Business."

"Like hell." He followed Trix into the hallway, tugged his office door shut, and locked it for good measure. "Is Lex still out with Noelle and Rachel?"

"As far as I know." She tilted her head. "You want me to get rid of this lady?"

"No, she's for me to deal with." But not in his office, where he had papers scattered about and too much private shit. "Give me five minutes and bring her to the meeting room. And whatever the hell else you do, keep Lex away from there."

Her pale brow creased in a frown, but she backed away with a nod. "Sure, I can handle that."

He waved Trix away as the corridor split, sending her back toward the front of the club as he climbed the stairs to the second floor. The building that housed the Broken Circle was still the heart of their operations, even though the compound had expanded into a sprawl that covered four sector blocks. He was in his element here, on home turf so familiar it lent him an extra edge, a confidence he'd need for this meeting.

It was Cerys, it had to be. Come to take the next step toward whatever endgame she'd envisioned when maneuvering him into a position of greater power.

Smart as he was, Dallas had zero confidence in his ability to think circles around a woman who played politics with Cerys's skill and intensity.

But that didn't mean he couldn't use her own game against her.

By the time Trix showed Cerys into the meeting room, Dallas was sprawled in his customary chair at the head of the table, a bottle of whiskey and two shot glasses on the table in front of him. He looked up from trimming his nails with his pocketknife and—like a good uncultured barbarian—kept his ass planted firmly in his seat. "Cerys."

She unwrapped a deep brown fur from around her neck and draped it over the back of a chair at the opposite end of the table. "Mr. O'Kane."

Yeah, she could make a man feel like a misbehaving boy with nothing but the inflection in her voice. Ignoring the twinge, he committed to his rudeness. "You're a long way from home. What brings you south of the fence?"

She stood still but glanced around the room, taking it all in. "I came to talk about Alexa."

He damn near cut off the tip of one finger as his fist clenched. "That so?"

"Don't get all excited." She sank gracefully into a plush, padded chair set against the wall. "You know her as well as I. She's your woman, and happy to be that—for now. But she'll want to do more. *Be* more."

"Could be." That was how women like Cerys laid traps—with the truth, the bitter, painful truths that niggled at a man. You had to make him bleed before you offered to kiss it all better. "Could be you don't know her half so well as you think."

"It's possible," she admitted. "That's why I'm here instead of talking to Lex."

"Yeah, she'll love that."

Cerys smiled. "No, she won't be happy with me. She does prefer to ignore the reality of her situation sometimes."

Leading words. He wanted to be too stubborn to ask. Wanted to. "And what's the reality of her situation?"

"You own her, and she's not a woman who can be comfortable with that."

"I own Lex exactly as much as she lets me," Dallas replied, baring his teeth in his own sort of grin. "You of all people should appreciate the pitfalls of trying to own Alexa Parrino."

"I do, which is why I now realize that I should have been grooming her for something special." Cerys shifted on the chair and crossed her legs. "I should have been readying her to take over Orchid House."

Well, shit. He hadn't seen *that* coming. "You getting bored of politics, Cerys?"

For a moment, her serene mask slipped, and she looked *tired*. "I'm getting too old for the games, O'Kane. The bickering between the sectors, the threats." She shrugged. "I have money. I want to enjoy it."

"And you want to hand your business over to the one that got away?" The perverse part was that it made a sort of sense. The girls who stayed to be trained into docile little puppets wouldn't have the ruthless fire necessary to lead. *If* he could trust that the weariness he'd seen in Cerys's eyes was truth and not simply another mask.

"I'd still benefit. I'll receive a healthy cut of the profits until I die, that's tradition. The way things are done." Her smile turned cunning. Jaded. "Do you think my predecessor liked me? She loathed me, but she knew I could make money. So here I am."

Still not the right answer. "What makes you think Lex would turn a profit? She doesn't just hate you. She hates what you do."

"For the girls' sakes, of course. So she knows they'll have someone looking out for them."

He thought about Lex's whispered confession, the need to help, and he hated Cerys a little more. Not only for knowing where to stick the knife, but for knowing better than he had. With Lex under his nose day in and day out, he'd still found a way to be oblivious to the need gnawing her up from the inside.

Cerys hadn't. "Even if that pitch worked on her, who says it'll work on me? I happen to like Lex right where she is, not off playing hero in some other sector."

She responded with an unladylike snort. "Right where she is for now, you mean."

"You know some travel plans of hers that I don't?"

"Cut the shit. You know what I'm talking about."

She'd already said it once: Lex would want to do more, be more. The only thing he hated more than this meeting was having it after that fucking fight over the prospects from Three. Lex already wanted to be more. Could Cerys smell that weakness on him? Hear it in his voice?

Fuck that. "Lex is a lot happier as my queen than she would be running a damn whorehouse."

"You say that with such derision, but isn't that what she is? Your whore?" Cerys shook her head. "Perhaps she'd be even happier as your equal."

Rage overwhelmed good sense, and he slammed the knife down on the table. "You watch your fucking mouth, unless you want me to drag you back to the fence by your hair and throw you over it."

She held up a placating hand. "I meant no offense."

"Bullshit, you didn't." Bracing both hands on the

scarred wood, he rose and leaned forward, pinning her in place with the force of his anger. "You pretty it up over there. Flowers and nice dresses and *training*, but you're a pimp, Cerys. A grasping, greedy pimp. If anyone running a brothel in my sector tried to take a third of the percentage you do, I'd let Ace pound their face into the cement. You meant for me to be fucking offended, but you know what? Calling her a whore's still not as big an insult as turning her into you."

Cerys stared back, unmoving. "I've upset you."

Which had probably been the damn point, but he couldn't reel it in. "We haven't even gotten started on how you plan to make her my equal. All the other house heads will just step aside and let you pick the next sector leader, too?"

That got her back up. "Orchid House rules Two. It always has, and it always will."

"Why?" He pressed his advantage, needling her pride. "If you want me to get Lex on board with this, you're gonna have to sell your product a hell of a lot better. What makes Orchid House so damn special? Why should I give a shit about Lex having it?"

She stood. "Save me some time here. Is it a sales pitch you need, or an excuse?"

"A what?"

"An excuse," she repeated mildly. "Something convenient to tell yourself so you feel better about wanting control of my sector."

Oh, he didn't hate her. Hate was too mild a word for this, for his furious embarrassment at having the ugly truth of him stripped bare. She was the dark mirror of Lex, a woman who saw into his heart just as clearly and never gave him any credit at all—because he didn't fucking deserve it.

"I have an excuse," he replied in a quiet, deadly

voice. "Getting you out is all the excuse I need. But I need a *reason*."

"Power," she whispered. "Think of everything you could do with it, yes?"

He could think of one thing Two could give him, beyond their well-trained crafters and hearty business in long-distance trade. "How much juice do you have in Eden?"

A mirthless smile twisted her lips. "How many horny, desperate bastards are there in the city?"

His heartbeat sped. "I'm only interested in one of them right now. Gareth Woods."

The tiny wrinkle in her brow smoothed. She approached the table, lifted the whiskey, and began to pour it. "Interested in him, or in his painful demise?"

"In causing it, mostly." He settled back into his chair and watched her. "What do you really want, Cerys? You'll never be satisfied sitting on a porch swing and counting your money. For once in your life, speak truth to a man. Maybe the results will shock you."

She drained a shot and poured a second before answering. "Do you have any idea how exhausting it is, catering to men? I don't promise to take up knitting or raise cats in my old age, but believe me, Mr. O'Kane. I wouldn't mind being able to tell a few of you fuckers exactly what I think of you."

Dallas laughed as he picked up his own glass. "Now that? Is a motivation I believe. So maybe we can find common ground without giving up hating each other."

"I like the sound of that," Cerys said with a smirk. "I think Lex will, too."

"Why don't we try a deal without Lex first? We both have something the other wants, don't we? Let's start with an alliance of neighbors."

She clicked her shot glass against his. "Agreed."

How to phrase it? No outlandish lies, promising things she'd know he'd never deliver. Just the right amount of opportunity and reluctance. "I'll bring your proposal to my woman. I'll even do my best to see she considers it. But I want a show of good faith in return."

"What you want is Gareth Woods on a silver platter. I understand."

"Access to him." He studied her over the edge of his glass. "He knows I'm hunting him. He's played a good game at staying out of my way, but I only need to find him once."

"I can make that happen," she assured him.

"How soon?"

She considered it as she finished her second drink. "It'll take a little time. Be patient."

Be patient. Words he hated, but they'd be worth it if he could put a bullet in the head of the man who'd been responsible for Lex's near death. Oh, he'd have to let Jasper come along, since the assassin had been gunning for Noelle. But that kill, that retribution— it would balance the scales. It would be the ultimate proof that no one crossed the O'Kanes and lived. Not a scummy sector leader like Wilson Trent, not a councilman straight out of Eden.

Hell, if he played his cards right, Lex might not ever have to know. Not about the kill, and not how he'd agreed to pay for it. He just had to snatch the bait out of Cerys's trap without letting himself get snared by the promise of power.

"All right," he agreed. "I assume you have a contingency if I can't talk Lex around?"

"She's not my only possibility." Cerys set down her glass and retrieved her fur. "Merely my first choice."

She didn't seem worried about going out on a limb

without a guaranteed return, which could mean any-thing. That it wasn't a limb. That she wanted Gareth Woods dead for her own reasons. Or that she really did believe he had Lex under his thumb.

Or that she was planning to betray him. Dallas had to figure that possibility into his plans. "How far in advance can you send me a location and time?"

"Far enough that you'll be able to get your men into place."

But not so far that *he* could betray *her*. He screwed the top back on to the whiskey bottle and held it out to her with a grin. "Why don't you take it with you? That stuff you call liquor in Two could use some bite."

Cerys threw back her head with a laugh. "Thank you, but no. Don't take this the wrong way, but I'd like to be able to deny I was ever here."

That made two of them.

19

For the ruthless kingpin of a bootleg liquor operation, Dallas O'Kane lied for shit.

He was even worse at hiding things, though Lex had to admit that might just be her. She'd spent so many years getting to know him, working with him—and yes, frankly, infatuated with him—that she'd memorized his moods. She recognized the tiny shifts in his expression, the way his eyes seemed to change color depending on his moods.

Right now, his mood was foul. Dark. Lex laid down her fork and studied him over the rim of her beer. "You've been quiet."

Dallas didn't lift his gaze from his steak. "Have I?"

Evasion—yet another sign something was wrong. "You have, and I'm starting to think it's about me."

That goaded him into addressing her, but his

too-charming Dallas O'Kane grin seemed hollow. "You make me a lot of things, love. Quiet ain't one of them."

"Uh-huh. Gonna tell me what's on your mind?"

"I wasn't planning on it." Sighing, he let his fork clatter to his plate. "Which probably makes me a damn fool, thinking I could pull this off."

She forced herself to relax her fingers and set down her beer bottle. "You're starting to scare me, Dallas, and I don't like it."

"It's not—" He swore and shoved back from the table. "I didn't want you to have to think about it. You've got enough to deal with, helping with the recruiting efforts."

Or he just didn't want to tell her. "What is it?"

Dallas met her eyes, and she knew from the tension in his gaze that the words would be bad. She just didn't realize how bad. "Cerys came to see me a few days ago."

Lex crossed her arms over her chest. "What the hell did she want?" Even as she spoke, she suspected she already knew.

"What did she want, or what did she say she wanted?"

Cut the shit. Lex bit back the words and shivered. "She did it, didn't she? She brought it to you."

He frowned. "If you mean she offered us her sector on a silver platter...yeah. But shit, Lex. I wasn't gonna fall for it. Nothing in life is that easy."

"That's where you're wrong." She shivered again, her chill subsiding into a strange sort of numbness. "What if it *was* that simple?"

"What, if we could just take over Two and own all of it?" He snorted. "Sure. In that world where puppies shit rainbows, I'd be stupid not to take it. I'd know all the dirty secrets about every bastard in Eden, and you'd have the resources to rescue people from dawn 'til dusk. At least until the other sector leaders wiped me off the map for thinking I could own three territories."

And they'd be right about one thing—he'd be thinking *he* owned it, not Lex.

She blinked at him, struggling to work through his offhand words and her own raging thoughts. "You say *we*, but you don't mean it. *You'd* take over, *you'd* own three territories. You."

Frustration twisted his features as he pushed himself to his feet. "Fuck, quit nitpicking my words. You're taking my ink. What I own, you own."

"Horseshit." Lex lashed out, knocking her beer bottle over to crash into his plate. "What I own, you own, and you can't turn that around on me. I'm not willing to sell your soul for some damn power."

"Back the hell on up, woman." Ignoring the beer spilling over the edge of the table and onto the floor, Dallas clenched both hands around the back of his chair. Wood creaked, and his knuckles stood out stark and white. "I didn't trade your soul. I didn't even put it on the table."

"Only because you don't think you could get away with it." She stood and held his gaze challengingly. "But you would if you could. You said it yourself—you'd be stupid not to."

"In a world without consequences," he snarled. "You wouldn't be tempted? Not even a little? You could decide how the houses run, and you wouldn't have to be my queen. You could be queen all on your own."

They sounded like Cerys's words from his lips. The perfect justification for why it would all be in her best interests as well as his. She could help, change things. Pretty lies, because no one really wanted things to change. The men in power benefited from the situation, and the women in Two knew nothing else. The only way to really change it would be to burn it all to the ground.

Pretty lies. Dallas had to know that on some level, but he'd still considered Cerys's offer, honestly *considered* it, and Lex's anger died, choked out of existence by the misery that overwhelmed her.

She focused on a thin sheen of bubbles tracking across the table. "I was fifteen when I left Sector Two. One of the maids told me Cerys had found my buyer— sorry, my *patron*. So I ran. I lived on the streets. I starved, I stole. I did everything but sell myself because I saw how that went down and I swore it wasn't worth it. Even if I died instead, it could never be worth it." Her eyes burned, and her vision blurred. "Shows what I know. I did it anyway, right? Sold myself."

Dallas exploded.

That was the only word for it. The chair shattered under his hands, and he flung the pieces away, upending the table in the process. Plates crashed and shattered, the bottles clattered and rolled, spilling beer across the carpet as Dallas bit off one word at a time. "You are *not* a whore."

She stood there in the mess, bits of food and broken glass on her shoes, as the first tears fell. "No, I'm worse. I didn't give you anything as simple as my body." He had her heart, her soul, *everything*.

Glass crunched under his boots as he took a step toward her, but he stopped with a jerk when she backed away. A scowl twisted his features. "Don't you fucking do that."

It wrenched a laugh from her. "Do what? Cry like a girl?"

"Don't twist everything." He took another step, slow and careful this time. "Don't back away from me like I'm some dangerous animal. You haven't even seen me scary."

She wasn't worried he would harm her—partly because he never had, and partly because no blow could ever hurt as much as his words had.

And if she told him that, he really would lose it. "How?" she asked instead. "How could you ever want to ask me to go back there?"

"Because it's not the same," he snapped, and finally it was honesty pouring from his mouth. Painful, brutal honesty. "You'd have the power over all of them. You'd be my equal!"

The icy chill seized up, solidified, leaving Lex frozen. Her wrist itched, and she absently rubbed her thumb over the ink marring her skin.

His equal. Someone who brought enough value to the transaction, who was good enough for him. If he'd made those kinds of judgments about her before, he'd never admitted them. But maybe now was different, now that he wanted to do more than collar her.

The leather was suddenly constricting, unbearable. She couldn't breathe, couldn't even think until she reached up and unbuckled it.

Dallas's teeth clacked together. "What are you doing?" he asked too quietly.

The collar fell away in her hand. "If grabbing at power just to have it is what it takes, I'll never be your equal."

"You're doing it again." He wasn't looking at her, not anymore. His gaze was fixed on her hand. On that scrap of leather. "You're looking for a fucking excuse. You're chickening out."

"Oh, honey. I wish I was." She could get angry, yell at him about this like she had the party for the prospects from Three. But she'd hate herself for giving in, because it would only happen all over again. "You have no idea, Declan."

He growled, his hands curling into fists. "So you're gonna walk away over something I didn't even ask you to do? What the hell else would you call that?"

"Don't act like you were thinking about me. You were just trying to figure out Cerys's game." Her voice cracked, and she steadied herself. "Here's the hard truth. It may not be a game. It might be legit. Can you still say you wouldn't ask me to do it?"

He hesitated. Not long, no more than the span of a few heartbeats. But he hesitated, and they both knew it.

The look on his face, hurt and confused, floored her. He still didn't understand, but he would, eventually. He'd know why. But that didn't help as she stood there, collar in hand. Her chest actually ached, which was fucking stupid.

Hearts didn't literally break.

She held out the collar. "Take it. Please."

"No." A storm was brewing behind his eyes, one that would swallow the pain and unleash something far more dangerous. "Not unless you're planning to replace it with my ink."

It hurt so much more, having a glimpse of something perfect only to realize it couldn't exist, that it fell apart when times got hard. "I have to find someplace, but I'll go." Yet another way she'd betrayed herself. It had been years since she'd kept up a place outside the compound, somewhere to go if things went bad. "If you can give me a few days—"

"*No.*" He advanced on her, and she could hear the thunder. "This isn't how it ends. This isn't what kills us. Not stupid, fucking *words.*"

"What else could it be?" They'd always lived loud,

almost violently. Screaming and shouting. It made sense for their relationship to die quietly.

He stopped toe-to-toe with her, looming over her, taking up all the air, all the light. "Not this. Not her."

"Dallas..." All she had left were harsh words, damning ones, and she had to soften them by lifting her hand to his cheek. "It wasn't her."

Pain flashed across his face, jagged as lightning as the storm broke.

And he kissed her.

No, not a kiss. Nothing as gentle as that. His fingers snagged in her hair, yanking her head back as his mouth came down, forceful and desperate. Bruising.

He'd always touched her with care, even when he gave it to her rough, but not now. This wasn't desire but punishment, not need but some twisted version of it.

Not possession but confinement.

Lex let her hands hang by her sides, and the collar fell to the floor. No matter what, she couldn't fight. A dark thread of longing was already unfurling in her belly, and if she fought him, it would all get tangled up in sex.

His teeth dug into her lip, and he growled. "Gonna pretend you don't feel it? You don't feel *us*?"

Of course she did. She'd felt it the moment she first laid eyes on him, the zing of awareness that hadn't faded over time but deepened into something inescapable, and strong enough to tear them both to shreds.

She shuddered and gripped his shirt, clenching her fingers in the fabric. "This part isn't the problem."

"But this part is so good." He backed her toward the wall, every step pushing her deeper into his room, deeper into him. "Worth fighting through the rest of it. What happened to trusting me?"

She'd given it all to him, and he'd let her down. Because there was a flip side to that trust, an implicit promise that if she handed him her heart, he'd always put her first. And he hadn't.

"I'll hate both of us," she whispered. "Can't you see that? If I keep letting you do these things to me without standing up for myself, it won't matter. There won't be enough of me left to love you."

Her back thumped against the wall. He was smothering her. So warm, so strong, so familiar. "So stand up for yourself. Just don't walk away."

She put her hands flat on his chest and pushed. "Stop it."

"That's it." He slapped his hands to the wall on either side of her head. "Stand up to me."

She'd finally given in, opened herself. Trusted him. "Not like this, Dallas."

"Fucking *fight* me, Lex."

"I shouldn't *have* to!" Shaking, she ducked under his arm.

She only made it two steps before his fingers closed around her shoulder. Desperation drove her to slap away his hand, then dive for one of the knives on the floor.

His expression hardened as she held the blade in front of her. Furrowed brow, compressed lips, narrowed eyes—but she couldn't tell what was going on behind that dark gaze. "Would you stab me, Lex?"

"Only if you make me."

His lips twisted into a terrible smile. "Good. Get out before you have to."

Her eyes stung, and her throat burned. Maybe he understood and maybe he didn't, but more words would get her nowhere. "Fine." She dropped the knife and turned for the door.

As she reached for the doorknob, his voice rolled over her again. "This doesn't mean I'm giving up. Cerys and Two can burn. I'll show you, Lexie. Somehow, I'll fucking well show you. I'm not letting you go."

"I know," she said as she slipped out the door.

It was what she was afraid of.

bren

She was trying to be sneaky, but she was watching the show.

The door behind the unofficial VIP section led to the back staircase, and stood mostly in shadows. Bren doubted anyone else had noticed her there, braced against the jamb with the fingers of one hand on the doorknob, as if she needed her escape route ready to go.

Out on the stage, beneath the garish lights, Ace was flogging a woman. He had her bent over a low table, completely naked and tied so that all he had to do was turn his wrist to flick the leather tails against her exposed pussy.

And Six was watching every quick slap.

Bren studied her profile in the low light. "Do you like the idea?"

She started at his voice and jerked her gaze from

the stage, as if she'd gotten caught doing something far more incriminating than watching. "What idea? Getting whipped?"

"That," he agreed easily, "or being on the stage. Not all the shows involve pain."

She folded her arms across her chest, under her breasts. Defensive and wary, and he knew the answer before she spoke. "No, not really. I've never liked being the entertainment."

He stopped beside the curtain and listened to the woman onstage moan and plead. "Is that what you see out there?"

"Maybe. I don't know." She shivered and glanced at him, her expression torn by honest confusion. "Is she acting?"

"Nope." He vaguely recognized the woman as one of Ace's regulars. "She likes it like this. Sometimes he stops when she's ready to fuck, and other times he keeps on whipping her."

"Oh." She seemed flustered, maybe more so when she realized how close she'd drifted to him. No matter how many careful feet he put between them, Six always seemed to cover the distance in a dozen shifts of position or tiny shuffling steps, and she never really relaxed until they stood shoulder to shoulder.

So shy—not about sex, necessarily, but pleasure. Bren held her gaze but tilted his head. "Tell me what you see when you look at that."

She hesitated. "You're not gonna like it."

"Probably not." But he couldn't counter it with his own point of view if she never said it.

Wetting her lips, she glanced at the stage again, just in time to watch Ace drive a choked plea from his lover's lips with a skillful application of leather. Six flinched at the woman's throaty cries and looked away.

"A man whipping a woman. And a bunch of other men getting off on it."

"Abso-fucking-lutely. What else?"

Her expression tightened. "That's it. I didn't even see that she liked the pain. You told me that."

"What if I told you that was part of the fantasy for her? Being watched?"

She didn't say anything at first. She took his words and digested them, then turned back to the stage and studied it again, a tiny furrow of concentration appearing between her brows. "So she's using the men to get her fantasy?"

So careful, too, those little leaps in logic. "In a way. She isn't making the best of being on the stage, Six. It's what she wants."

"I don't think I could want that," she admitted after a moment, and there was apology in the glance she threw him. "The people watching, I mean. That was always the part I hated most."

A tiny slip, the kind of glimpse into her former life that made him want to dig up Wilson Trent and kill him some more. Instead, he smiled. "No shows for you, then."

Her slight exhale of relief sounded almost sad. But her gaze swung back to the stage with renewed curiosity, as if the words had freed her from a sense of foreboding. "The pain... Does it feel good because she always likes it, or because Ace is doing something special?"

"To hear Ace tell it, everything he does is special." Bren leaned closer. "Have you ever had an itch, one of those crazy ones that you can't stop thinking about? On your back or your arm, wherever, but all you could fucking think about was scratching it?"

Still watching the stage, she nodded.

"That's just pain. You scratch your skin and it confuses all the nerves, scrambles them so they can't feel the itch anymore."

"I didn't know that." She shivered, tickling where her arm brushed his, and changed the subject so abruptly he wasn't sure he'd heard her right at first. "You can fuck me if you want to."

Bren blinked at her. Instead of an invitation, it felt more like paying the executioner before laying your head on his chopping block. "Don't take this the wrong way, but if you really wanted to fuck me, you wouldn't need to tell me it was okay."

She winced and looked away. "I don't know if I *want* to fuck," she admitted after an awkward moment. "But I don't mind it. And the fucking comes with other stuff here. Everyone's always touching."

Comfort. Connection. "If that's what you want, ask for that. I'll give it to you."

It took her two deep breaths and a wary glance at him to form the words, and they came in a whisper. "Do you mind? If you don't want to..."

He pulled her close with one arm, wrapping it around her body as he moved her in front of him. Her body nestled against his, curvy and strong. He stroked his other hand down her arm and whispered in her ear. "Watch."

Ace had moved on to fucking the blonde on stage. She moaned and thrashed fitfully against her bindings, more so every time Ace slammed deep and paused to work her reddened shoulders with the flogger. He had a sense of theatrics suited to the stage, and a finely tuned understanding of the woman beneath him.

Six squirmed, goose bumps rising beneath Bren's fingers. "I believe you now. She's...definitely not faking."

"Not even a little."

"And you like watching?"

"I like pleasure." Her skin heated, and he slowed his strokes. "Everything about it."

"Oh." A sound, caught somewhere between a gasp and a moan. On the stage, Ace's blonde tipped over the edge into a screaming orgasm, and Six turned her cheek toward Bren's shoulder and closed her eyes.

As if she couldn't watch.

But that was okay. He soothed her with a soft noise and whispered the promise he'd made himself, the one he kept giving her over and over. "Plenty of time."

20

No one had ever really understood Dallas's reluctance to screw one of the women in the gang. Oh, they pretended to, nodded and smiled, but most of them thought he was fucking crazy for not riding every willing girl who crawled into his lap. God knew there were some smoking hot ladies sporting his ink, but aside from Lex, he'd never been all that tempted.

The guys didn't think he was crazy anymore.

Word spread. He didn't know how, but it always did. The first whispers had popped up the moment Lex set foot outside his room without the collar, and they'd swelled from there. By the next morning, everyone in the gang knew that Lex and Dallas were fighting, and not in their usual way.

Dallas had expected the girls to turn on him. He hadn't anticipated how cold they could get, but their disapproval didn't shock him. The number of men who'd joined them in expressing protective anger did.

Maybe it shouldn't have. Lex championed the women, to be sure, but she was just as prominent a presence in the men's lives. She was the one who dealt with all the details that made life comfortable, the one who kept everyone happy and healthy and harmoniously fucking at frequent parties.

In retrospect, he probably should have expected the men to turn on him first.

The worst part was agreeing with them. He *had* fucked up. He'd told Lex all the wrong things at exactly the wrong time. Trying to keep his plan from her had been a fool's game. It might have worked before, when they'd lived parallel lives, but not now that they were all tangled up in each other day and night.

Well. They *had* been.

The knock on his door startled him so much he clenched his fist and snapped a pencil in half. No one had willingly gotten within ten damn feet of him all day—the ones that weren't pissed at him were wary of his temper—which made him wonder what the hell could drive someone into his domain. "Come in!"

The door popped open, and Dylan Jordan strolled into his office. "Good evening to you too, O'Kane."

"Doc." A chill shivered down Dallas's spine as he studied the doctor—whose presence usually meant bad shit had gone down. "You here on business?"

"Sort of." The man dropped into a chair on the other side of the desk and tried to smooth his dark hair into some semblance of order. It didn't work. "I came by to see what the hell's going on around here."

Christ. If the whispers had turned to grumbles that were rippling beyond the gang already, he really was in deep shit. "Who's been shooting off their mouth?"

Doc arched an eyebrow. "Lex sent me a message."

The chill turned to ice. "Saying?"

"She asked me what the process would be for removing her tattoos."

"*What?*"

"Her cuffs." The man said it like he was talking about the weather. About nothing. "And something about a new one. A name."

The name hurt like a knife in the gut, but even that had nothing on the cuffs. Lex *was* O'Kane. She'd helped shape what they had become, had helped touch the life of every person wearing O'Kane marks. "You're fucking kidding me."

Doc snorted. "I told her I wouldn't touch the ink unless you said so, but a wise man would make sure she didn't ask me again. I don't know if I'll say no next time."

If it had been anyone else, Dallas would have snarled. He still wanted to, but threats and intimidation were wasted on Dylan Jordan. No matter how many women threw themselves at him, desperate to save him, the man was as self-destructive an asshole as Dallas had ever met. Sometimes he thought Doc pitted himself against dangerous men in the hopes that one would eventually put him out of his enduring misery.

Dallas didn't plan on it. The man was too damn useful to kill. Of course, telling Lex he wouldn't remove the ink without Dallas's permission was damn near suicidal on its own. "You must not have told her no in person, because I don't see any stab wounds."

For a long moment, all the man did was stare at him. "You're pretty goddamn despicable, aren't you?"

"I run a gang of bootleggers," he replied, fighting to keep his temper and his panic on a tight leash. Pretty damn difficult when he could feel his perfect fucking life crumbling beneath him. "I am what I am."

"Yeah? Well, what you are is an ass." Doc rose, shaking his head. "Lex didn't try to cut me when I told her. She just cried."

A knife in the gut? A pinprick compared to how those three words felt. *She just cried.* Lex, indomitable, unbreakable Lex. He'd coaxed her into trust, shoved and pushed until she let down all those cold, hard walls—

And then he'd crushed her.

Christ.

"Uh-huh." The man dragged a tin from his pocket and popped a small white tablet into his mouth. "Fix it, would you? I don't like it when you kids fight."

Kids, as if Jordan was some kind of fucking sage elder instead of three or four years older than him. Dallas didn't know whether to laugh or strangle the motherfucker. "Gee, Doc, I was having a great fucking time, but if you insist."

"Sarcasm doesn't suit you nearly as well as you think, O'Kane."

"I save my heartfelt confessions for the people wearing my ink." He said it without thinking and damn near winced. Nobody wearing ink wanted to hear his heartfelt confessions. They didn't even want to look at him. He'd always stood slightly apart, but this feeling of standing alone was new. And miserable.

And if Lex was crying, he deserved it.

History fucking loved to repeat itself.

This time, it was Lex shoving her belongings into a bag as Noelle looked on, horrified and outraged. "You don't have to do this, Lex. It isn't fair. It isn't *right*."

At least she wasn't trying to talk her off the ledge.

"Damn right it isn't fair. But it is what it is."

"Bullshit." Crossing the room, Noelle grabbed Lex's arm and held it up, forced her to stare at the ink Doc had refused to remove. "That is a promise. You're the one who taught me that. It's a promise, and being in Dallas's bed has nothing to do with it. This is your home and we're your family."

A truth that had changed the moment she'd accepted his claim. Lex closed her eyes. "Now you know why his women were always outsiders. It's easier for them to leave eventually."

"Because he drives them away?" Noelle's hands framed Lex's face. "Don't let him. He doesn't get to do that, not to you and not to us. If you don't want to stay in your room, come stay with us."

"This is me, all me," she countered. "Dallas isn't making me go. He doesn't even want me to. But I have to."

"Oh, Lex. No." Noelle released her only to curl an arm around her waist, tugging her toward the couch. "Come on and sit with me for a few minutes. Tell me why you think this is your fault."

"Not *fault*, not like that." She sank to the cushions and leaned her head against Noelle's shoulder. Support had been hard to come by the last couple of days, mostly because Lex had to hold back from accepting it. It only reminded her of all she'd be leaving behind. "There are just so many things, so many reasons it would be easier to stay. And I *can't*."

"You should be able to," Noelle whispered. "What Dallas did to you was wrong. You say he's not driving you away, but he is."

It was hard to know for certain when Dallas seemed so oblivious to the real problem, and so sure of himself that she couldn't help but second-guess herself.

Noelle had reacted with gratifying outrage, but even that couldn't erase the doubt.

It drove her to grip Noelle's hand. "You understand, don't you? Dallas has no idea what he did, and it's making me wonder if I'm just crazy."

"He put his ambition before you," Noelle said immediately. She traced one of the ink marks swirling across her own shoulder before reaching out to touch Lex's throat. "He asked you to give up all your defenses, and then he didn't protect you. It's *wrong*. Jasper tried to send me to Eden, but he was cutting out his own heart because he thought it'd keep me safe. Even if he didn't do it, Dallas was considering cutting out yours, just to get more of something he has too much of already."

Lex's throat went tight. It was everything she'd been too wounded and twisted up to say, every reason she'd been betrayed not only by Dallas's actions, but by his confusion. Hearing it all laid bare hurt, so much she couldn't breathe.

She finally managed to drag in a breath that sounded more like a sob. "Jasper was thinking of you. He screwed up, but he did it for you."

Noelle dragged her closer, wrapped her in her arms and her love and made soothing, sympathetic noises. "I know, Lex. I know."

"Dallas doesn't get it. He has no idea what he did wrong."

Noelle rested her cheek on top of Lex's head with a sigh. "Maybe he does, and he can't admit it. He tried to offer you something he values—power. But Dallas is an intuitive man. A *smart* man. I think he knows you better than that."

He did, of course. He'd kept Cerys's visit from her and skated around the issue long enough for Lex to realize he knew she wouldn't be happy about any of it.

"He wants it all. Sector Two *and* me."

"Then he's not only greedy, he's stupid." Noelle's voice held no room for argument. "But that doesn't mean he gets to take everything you've built and all the people you love away from you."

Her home, her family. "I should have known it would go down like this. Dallas and I have never been easy."

"Maybe this'll teach him." Noelle cupped Lex's cheek and tilted her head up. "I've never been sure if I think he deserves you. But it's not about me. What do *you* want?"

The impossible question, because the answer made her sound weak. "I love this place. I've been here so long—Jesus, I helped build it. I want to stay here, Noelle. I've never wanted anything more." A lie, but just a little one.

She wanted Dallas the most.

And Noelle knew it. The other woman had grown in more than one way in the time she'd been free of Eden. She pressed her forehead to Lex's and lowered her voice to a whisper. "Are you afraid to stay because you're afraid you'll go back to him, no matter what?"

Lex had to stop fucking *crying*. "I know I will. It's not even a question. What kind of idiot does that make me?"

"The kind who's in love." Noelle's lips feathered over Lex's cheeks, kissing away the tears. "But you've got people who care about you. I won't let you go back. Hell, every woman wearing cuffs will line up and take turns sitting on you. You're ours."

She couldn't make that promise, not with Dallas's words still shivering through her. *Somehow, I'll fucking well show you. I'm not letting you go.* "I can't leave right away—it's been a few years since I kept up anyplace else to go. But I was wondering if I could take your old room for now."

"You should stay with us," Noelle protested immediately. "With me'n Jas. You shouldn't be alone."

"I need to be, at least for a while."

"Okay." Pulling back, Noelle swiped tears from Lex's cheeks with her thumbs. "My room's yours. Anything you need is yours."

"Thanks, Noelle." She drew in a calming breath. "One step at a time. I'll get through this."

"Yes, you will. In better shape than Dallas will, too." Noelle's tiny smile was a little mean. "Just remember how much we all love you. Dallas may be the king of this gang, but you're its heart. If he doesn't appreciate that yet, he will."

"No." Lex shook her head. "He's still your leader, and a good one. I don't want anyone to make trouble for him, not on my behalf."

Noelle touched her cheek, her blue eyes dark with resentment. "I'll follow my leader. I'll obey my boss. But you can't make me be nice to the bastard who hurt my friend."

"Thank you," Lex whispered. Dallas had broken her heart with his unthinking ambition, and he'd do it all over again when she had to leave other people who were dear to her. People like Noelle, who were as much a part of her as Dallas, if only in a different way. "I love you and Jas, you know."

"Of course you do," Noelle replied, voice light and teasing. "I'm adorable, and Jas is irresistible. But we love you back."

The silliness lifted her spirits, her first taste of hope in days. "We'll see, okay?" Maybe she and Dallas could come to an understanding. Maybe she didn't *have* to leave. "Just...we'll see."

"Good. And, Lex?"

"Yeah?"

"Even if you have to go, I'll still love you. And I'll still be in your life. It's not about this." Her fingers curled around Lex's wrist, covering the O'Kane cuff as she pressed Lex's splayed hand to her own chest. Over her heart. "It's about this."

About love. Belonging. Lex slid her arms around Noelle and hugged her tight. "No matter what. I promise."

For the fourth time in as many minutes, Lex caught herself staring blankly down at the inventory sheet in her hand.

Disgusted, she rubbed her eyes and started over with the top line. "Focus, goddammit. You're not helping anyone like this."

"It's okay." The quiet voice came from the doorway. Lex barely managed not to flinch, startled, as Rachel swung in to kneel beside her. "Amira and I can handle the inventory before opening."

"I need to do something," Lex argued.

"Plenty to do." Rachel plucked the clipboard out of her hand and nodded to the door. "Start with picking up your phone call. Someone's on the line for you."

"Which phone?"

"End of the hall."

Lex wiped her hands on her jeans and headed for the extension. Maybe it was Doc, calling to say he'd changed his mind about her tattoos, or Walt Misham, with a line on transports out of the city.

But it was neither. "Hello?"

"Lex." A female voice, soft and nervous, and it took her a moment to recognize it as Jade, the woman who'd waylaid her outside of Cerys's quarters.

Apparently, word hadn't traveled outside the sector yet. "Sorry, honey. If you're looking for a ride out, it'll have to be with someone else. I'm kinda in the doghouse over here at the moment."

"Oh." A world of disappointment in that one word, too much for even a professional to hide. "I'm sorry for your trouble. I'd just thought... I'll be traveling to Five tonight, and if I disappeared on the way back tomorrow, Woods wouldn't miss me for another two weeks—"

Lex froze. It was too much of a coincidence to *be* a coincidence, so it had to be a trap instead. "Gareth Woods? That's your client?"

The pause was perfect. Hesitation, and then a muffled curse, as if the woman had let too much slip. "Now you know how desperate my situation is."

"And why you came to me." Lex tucked the receiver between her ear and her shoulder and dug her cigarette case out of her pocket. "I mean, that's the deal, right? You figure I'll off him for you?"

Jade exhaled sharply and began to laugh. "It was clumsy, wasn't it? Slipping his name into the conversation that quickly. Pacing has always been my problem. I start off so patiently, and then I wait too long and have to rush."

"Don't feel bad. I'm really fucking paranoid at the moment."

"I meant everything I said, you know. About being friends with your sister, and that you're a legend." The amusement in Jade's voice faded. "I just didn't tell you everything. I know Woods tried to kill one of your people, and I know you're taking him down tonight. I don't want to die in the crossfire."

Lex's heart skipped a beat. It all made sense suddenly, the one thing Cerys could have handed Dallas to ensure he'd consider her crazy fucking offer. Something he wanted more than power or money, more than air. And even, in a perverse way, more than her.

Gareth Woods.

Tonight. Cerys must have come through with the setup. Maybe she was about to clue Dallas in, or maybe he already knew. Either way...

"Can you get me in?" She glanced around quickly, confirming she was alone in the hall. "Tell him you're bringing a friend?"

Jade inhaled sharply. "You don't know what you're asking."

She didn't give a damn. She was tired of Dallas and his excuses. He could claim he was going after Woods to protect her, but it boiled down to plain, old-fashioned vengeance. "Yes or no, Jade?"

"You can't come here. But I could convince my driver to stop on the way, if you can be ready and waiting."

Only one more question, one that dug its claws into her and wouldn't let go. "Is it a trap? Is she trying to get rid of Dallas, or dealing with him square?"

Jade hesitated long enough to cinch fear tight before whispering, "I don't know. But Cerys will win either way. She always does."

"No shit." Lex crumbled her unlit cigarette with a grimace. "Pick me up on the east side of the bridge, near the border between Two and Three. I'll find a way."

"All right. Dress like a rose." A pause. "You remember what that means, don't you?"

It meant she'd be raiding Noelle's closet to get her frilly white dresses and lingerie back. "I remember."

"Five o'clock. Lex?"

"What?"

"If you can't get me out, don't leave me to a slow

death. Tonight I want to be free, one way or another."

"Damn, girl. Don't be so morbid." Frowning, Lex hung up.

Jade could still be playing her, counting on her need to one-up Cerys—or, worse, to protect Dallas. It wasn't hard to connect the dots on a foolproof plan to get them out of the picture, and with the perfect justification: interfering with Cerys's rightful business.

And in Sector Five, no less. Woods probably chose the locale because he needed to make a drug run anyway, but she'd have to tread carefully. Mac Fleming would recognize her in a heartbeat, and it could blow everything to hell.

They might need backup. Damn near suicidal backup.

Lex picked up the phone and dialed.

21

She might have underestimated exactly how much money Gareth Woods put in Mac Fleming's pockets.

Oh, she'd anticipated that Fleming probably had a honey hole somewhere that he lent to Woods when the man needed a place to lay low, get high, and abuse some women, but she'd never dreamed he'd let Woods do it *in his house*. And yet that was exactly where the driver stopped, outside the stately white mansion Fleming had spent years—and a fortune—building.

Lex adjusted the wide bracelets covering her cuffs and clenched her hands in the frilly lace of her short skirt. "You get that Mac Fleming knows my face, right?"

"He's never here when Woods is," Jade replied, staring out the window. Her own hands rested in her lap, clamped together so tightly that her knuckles stood out, pale and sharp. Her ashen face and strained eyes could have been nerves, but Lex had seen people on the edge of withdrawal before.

The woman was about to freak out.

Lex swatted her arm. "Hey, keep it together. What about Fleming's guards? Anyone he might have taken to the summit in Sector Two?"

"No, just Finn," she said after a moment, shaking her head. Her thumb brushed compulsively over the inside of her wrist. "He's the guard who brings the drugs. No one's allowed to handle them but him." She finally looked at Lex with a wan smile. "It used to just be me and Woods in the house for the night, once Finn left. Now he brings guards. A lot of them. He's terrified of Dallas O'Kane."

"He should be." After all, Dallas wanted him dead badly enough to make deals with the devil.

Through the divider, Lex heard the driver's door open and close again. Jade took a deep breath. "Finn won't come in right away. Gareth likes to watch me deal with the withdrawal symptoms. The timing is quite precise. I suppose I'd be impressed with Mac Fleming under other circumstances."

The back door opened, and they climbed out. Jade wobbled a little, and Lex steadied her. "Just do everything you're supposed to do. I'll work it out."

"Remember to smile," Jade replied as the driver took her other arm with a gentleness that spoke of loyalty. The old man had given Lex one long, searching inspection when they stopped to pick her up, but hadn't spoken a word then or since.

Two bulky guards in uniforms so cleanly pressed they screamed *Eden* moved aside as they made their way up the steps. More guards leapt to open the main doors. They performed their job in efficient silence, keeping their hands and gazes to themselves.

And then there he was.

Lex had only seen pictures. She'd looked him up herself, but she'd also stumbled across papers Dallas had left lying around, files still open on his tablets. Gareth Woods, polished and urbane. A cultured, bloodthirsty monster.

His gaze flicked over her, appreciative but dismissive, and the intent stare he turned on Jade warped the very concept of affection. When he stepped forward to sink his fingers into her hair, it made a mockery of the caress Lex had seen a thousand times. This was ownership, stripped of any choice or chance of escape.

He tightened his fingers and wrenched Jade's head back, lifting his other hand to her cheek. "You brought a friend for me. What a sweet girl you are. A sweet, thoughtful girl."

As tense as Jade had been in the car, she was serene now. And she was *good*, steel nerves beneath a honeyed smile as she played her game. "I'm your rose, sir. But she's something special. Something most men will never taste."

Gareth glanced at Lex again, his eyes heavy with speculation and dark lust. "And what's that?"

"A rose with thorns."

The whispered words hung in the air like a tantalizing challenge. Gareth released Jade and slowly turned. "Is that what you are?"

"Barely." Lex lifted her hair and tilted her head to bare the back of her neck—and the tiny, ancient scar that nestled there, a legacy of Cerys's training. "If you have thorns, they burn them off."

He touched the scar, lingering with a chilling reverence that only got creepier when he lifted his thumb to his lips and licked it. "Jade is such a lovely girl. She struggles at first, but she pants for it before it's over.

Do you struggle? Or is the prick of your thorns more subtle?"

Lex kept her gaze fixed on the far wall. "You'll have to find out."

He laughed, delighted, and dragged Jade to his side for a quick, rough kiss that she endured placidly. "You bring me the best gifts," Gareth crooned. "You deserve a reward. Would you like that?"

Jade's breathing hitched, and the sudden raw scratch in her voice wasn't an act. Full of desperation and self-loathing, deep enough to fill an ocean. "Please."

Woods released her so abruptly she stumbled and shook his head with a chiding sound. "That's not how you ask."

Shuddering, Jade folded her knees and sank to the floor. Her hands trembled until she laced them together, pressing them to her stomach. "Please, Gareth. Give me relief from this pain."

"Fine." He nudged her leg with his shoe. "Scoot to the door and call for Finn. I'll be getting to know our new friend."

Jade started to rise, but he moved fast, planting his foot in the small of her back and driving her roughly to the floor. "Crawl."

Woods was at the wrong angle to see it, but Lex caught the searing hatred in Jade's eyes, the fury that would have burned him alive if thoughts were weapons. She lifted her gaze, just for a moment, and Lex could almost hear the words, as if they'd been spoken out loud.

End him.

And then Jade crawled.

Lex searched the room behind Woods's back. Any sort of blade, even something heavy she could use to knock him out until she could crack his worthless neck—but there was nothing she could lay hands on without alerting him.

And she was running out of time. When Fleming's bodyguard showed up, the odds would tilt, and not in her favor.

She drifted toward the line of vintage pipes and pre-Flare drug paraphernalia on display behind the table. "I've never taken any of the stuff Jade is on. Is it good?"

His interest sharpened as he watched her, but his smile was so damn smug she wanted to punch it off his face. "She's crawling, isn't she?"

"I know she thinks it's good." Lex turned and eased up to sit on the table. "I'm asking about you. That's what I'm interested in."

His brow knotted slightly, and he slipped his hand into his jacket. "I could buy you a dozen times for what Finn's about to give her. She's earned it by being good." He withdrew a tiny plastic bottle that rattled when he shook it. "But these. Slip one under your tongue, and you'll forget all about your thorns."

"I don't want to forget them." She leaned back, bracing her arms behind her, and her fingers brushed the long stem of a pipe. "They make me interesting."

Irritation flashed in his eyes. "A modest struggle to protect one's virtue is charming. Disobedience isn't. If you want a chance at the rewards Jade enjoys, show yourself her equal by following her example. A decent girl kneels to her superiors."

Oh, hell no. "Did you know that men with no patience for conversation tend to fuck the same way?" Lex closed her hand around the pipe, which wasn't a pipe at all, but a heavy length of blown glass. "And that's not nearly as fun as it sounds."

His face turned red as he took a threatening

step forward. Over his shoulder, Lex saw Jade braced against the door, her eyes closed and her face drawn. No one would interrupt this moment.

Not if she moved fast.

Woods made the decision for her. He raised one arm to strike her, and Lex swung the length of glass around—a fucking *bong*, of all things. It hit his shoulder and shattered.

Roaring, he flung a hand up to his face. Blood trickled from between his fingers and another cut marred his forehead. "You bitch!" he bellowed.

But not at her.

The door rattled as Woods whirled and lunged toward Jade, who was struggling to drag herself to shaking knees as her patron barreled toward her, damn near frothing at the mouth. "You traitorous, treacherous *whore*—"

Footsteps thudded in the hall, heavy and quick. The world narrowed to the cool glass in Lex's hand, the warm blood trickling down her wrist, and slowed to a crawl. By the time she slid off the table, Woods had his hands around Jade's throat.

Lex had trained for this. Every week at Orchid House had brought a new trainer, a new situation. A new way to kill. It would make sense to hear Cerys guiding her. Instructing her.

But the words that drifted through her mind now belonged to Dallas. *Throat. It's soft, lots of bleeders, and you don't have to do much damage to straight-up kill a motherfucker.*

The anatomy lessons at Orchid House did the rest. She reached around and grabbed his upper arm, but he didn't even seem to notice. All his attention was on Jade, on her red face and bulging eyes. On ending her life.

Lex stabbed the broken glass into the right front side of his throat, thrusting it home with all her strength. The wicked shards dug deep into his flesh, and she dragged her makeshift weapon back toward her, slicing through the large blood vessels in his neck.

He released Jade, backhanding Lex as he flailed. She stumbled back, fell, and then he was on her, snarling and wild-eyed as blood gushed from his throat.

He wedged his forearm across her throat and leaned on it—hard. Lex sputtered and pushed back, but her feet slipped on the blood-soaked tile. Woods outweighed her by a good sixty pounds, and without any leverage, she couldn't shove him off. But she could outlast him, maybe.

Hold on, Lex. Just fucking hold on.

Jade wept, her back against the door as the blood pulsing from Woods's jagged, gaping wound began to slow and his skin went pallid, gray. He was cursing, the words coming slower and slower, like a battery-powered toy losing its charge. He slumped, the pressure from his arm intensifying.

Dead weight.

With growing horror, Lex bucked and tried to roll, but she couldn't budge him. *This is it,* she thought vaguely. *This is where I die.* The world was already fuzzy, bright white but darkening by the second, and she was tired, so tired...

One more mighty shove and she flung him off her, gasping for breath. Jade screamed as something hit the wall. Lex struggled to sit, only to find herself staring down the muzzle of a pistol.

It was Fleming's bodyguard—the one Jade had called Finn—who stared back, his dark eyes unreadable.

"Lady, you just fucked up my night."

22

Gareth Woods really was well and truly terrified.

From the trees at the edge of the property, Dallas watched the house through a pair of zoom lenses and listened to Bren's report. "Looks like Fleming cleared out pretty good. Most of the guards left seem to have come with Woods. Cruz and I can go in, work together, kill the ones from Eden, neutralize the ones from Five."

Maybe not the most satisfying approach, but Fleming wouldn't appreciate having his guards murdered, and Woods was less likely to slip through Dallas's fingers if his guards died quick, silent deaths. "Anyone from Two?"

"One driver. No guards."

And no sign of Cerys. Hard to say if that was good or bad, but it did simplify things. "Take Cruz and get as many as you can out of the way without being seen."

"Got it." Bren dropped his rifle, checked the pistols in his holsters, and drew a knife from his boot. "Give us a lead. Two, three minutes."

Dallas watched the two men disappear, following them with his gaze as he spoke to Jasper. "You ready to put this bastard down?" Easier to ask the question without having to look the man in the eyes. Something fragile had almost snapped between them, something that had been strained for a while. Jasper was a man of divided loyalties now, and the person who held his heart might cheerfully sink a knife into Dallas's.

"Would've thought you'd be more excited." Jas knelt beside him and lifted his own binoculars. "This is what you wanted, right? Gareth Woods's blood?"

"Sure it is." It had been his obsession for damn near a month, but he'd hardly thought about it from the moment he'd wrapped that collar around Lex's throat. Hell, he hadn't even worked up half the excitement he should have over getting his hands on Three. Sending Bren to do recon, recruiting new members when a little extra legwork could have resulted in more money...

Lazy. He'd been lazy, because he wanted to keep his ass in bed, preferably with Lex under him. Or riding him.

If he hadn't been so hot to blow a hole in Woods's brain, Lex might be under him right now. So he had to make this the highlight of his goddamn year.

A branch snapped behind them. Jasper spun, already drawing his hunting knife as the foliage parted.

A bleary, red-eyed Dylan Jordan held up both hands. "I surrender."

Jas sheathed his blade. "You almost got hurt there, Doc."

"Almost." The man snorted out a laugh. "Only counts in horseshoes and hand grenades, isn't that what they used to say?"

Dallas groaned and rubbed his thumb and forefinger over his eyes. Whatever pills the man popped like candy didn't do a damn thing to fix the fact that he was fucknuts crazy. "What the hell are you doing here?"

Both of his eyebrows shot up. "Lex told me to meet her. When I saw you over here, I figured you were in on it."

"Lex told you to meet her *here*?" Dallas echoed, his brain struggling to process the words.

His body moved.

Dodging Jasper's attempt to grab him, he snatched up a gun and jammed it under Doc's chin, adrenaline and fear graying out the edges of the world. "How long ago? How fucking long ago?"

He didn't flinch. "This afternoon. She said it was a pickup—a girl who needed help to detox."

Which meant she'd known almost as long as he had, and had made her own choices about what to do with the information. Just imagining what that choice was likely to be—

Dallas bit off a curse as he shoved Doc to the side and whirled to snarl at Jasper, who was blocking his path. "I *will* go through you."

"No, you won't." Jas glanced at his watch. "Not for thirty more seconds."

Thirty seconds of knowing Lex was trapped inside with a monster and his guards. Thirty seconds of wondering what she'd had to sacrifice to get there, what she'd endured because Dallas hadn't found a way to finish this bastard off weeks ago.

Thirty seconds of rage that she would willingly walk into a trap *he'd* helped to set, knowing it could spring shut on her. Christ, they were in Sector Five. How many ways could Fleming administer drugs? They could be in the water, in the food, in the fucking *air*.

"I'm going to strangle her," he growled, shaking with the effort it took to restrain himself. Raising an alarm could get her dead, but he wanted her in his arms *now*, so he could examine every goddamn inch of her for the slightest injury and then skin whoever had put it there.

Slowly.

"No one would blame you." Jasper held out his pistol, butt first, offering it to the doctor. "Ten seconds, and you're gonna make yourself useful."

"I'm not stupid." Jordan pulled a semiautomatic from the small of his back. "I don't wander around unarmed."

Dallas barely heard them. He was a rubber band stretched too tight, seconds from shooting forward or snapping back on the idiots trying to hold him in place. Clutching his gun in one hand, he rested the other on the hilt of his knife.

Eight...seven...

Lex was in there. His *heart* was in there.

Five...

He needed to tell her that.

Three...two...

God, let her still be alive to tell.

"One," he growled, and started running.

Doc and Jasper kept pace with him as he raced across the open area. They found proof of Cruz and Bren's handiwork as soon as they cleared the edge of the building. Two men lay dead, and a third leaned over them, his fingers pressed to one bloody neck as if seeking a pulse.

He was still reaching for his gun when Dallas slit his throat.

True to Bren's promise, most of the guards were

down, and they only ran into stragglers as they followed Cerys's directions through the labyrinthine halls. Dallas plowed through them, Jasper at his side. One guard, two, four—

They rounded a corner, but the man at the other end wasn't a guard. He was too damn old, for one, though he held a gun in both shaking hands.

"Drop it," Jasper ordered flatly.

The old man's hands wavered as he stared at Jasper's wrists. A moment later, the gun clattered to the floor. "She had those," he said in a shaking voice, pointing to Jas's cuffs. "Lady Jade's friend. Are you here for her?"

The name meant nothing to Dallas, but it wasn't hard to guess that this was the driver from Two. "You picked up a woman tonight?"

He nodded and edged carefully to the side, both hands held upright. "A friend of the lady's, she was."

"And she's through here?" Dallas gestured to the huge double doors.

Another nod.

He couldn't hear anything on the other side. No sounds of fighting or fucking, just a chilling sort of silence that could mean anything or nothing. For all he knew, the damn room was soundproofed so no one would know what Fleming's high rollers got up to on the other side.

Only one way to find out. Dallas passed his knife to Doc and pulled his favorite pistol. "On three?"

Jasper counted it off under his breath, then splintered the door's latch with one solid kick. Lifting his weapon, Dallas spilled into the room only to freeze three steps later.

A gigantic man he vaguely recognized was holding a gun to Lex's head. Finn, a silent, severe hulk who ran drugs for Mac Fleming.

Beyond that, all Dallas could register was the blood. It covered Lex, slicking her skin and drenching the ruffled white negligee she wore. His heart seized until he realized there was too much blood for her to be sitting upright, tense and alert and noticeably fuming.

Not hers, then. A brief glance at the woman sprawled beside her made it clear it wasn't hers, either. Her white gown was splattered, but her worst injuries seemed to be the vivid red marks around her throat.

As if he could read Dallas's thoughts, Finn sighed. "If this woman belongs to you, she's been busy," he said, gesturing briefly with the gun. Dallas looked to the left and saw Woods sprawled on his back, glassy-eyed, with a giant shard of glass sticking out of his throat.

"He had it coming," Lex spat.

"No argument here, dollface." Finn dug through his pocket without taking his eyes off Dallas and came up with a bent cigarette. "But you put me between a rock and a real damn hard place. Also known as my boss and yours."

"I'm not her boss," Dallas drawled, fighting to keep his temper leashed. One wrong move could end Lex. "But I am thinking I might shoot your balls off if you don't point that gun someplace else."

Snorting, Finn lit his cigarette. "If I point it someplace else, I'm dead. Lackeys have eyes too, O'Kane."

"Easy answer?" Lex rose slowly, her hands held out to her sides. "You weren't here. Woods brought plenty of guards, and something else needed your attention. Business, or even some pretty little thing with a powerful need to see you."

The barrel of the gun followed Lex as she moved,

and Dallas fought to keep his voice lazy. "Lex is right. My only grudge with you at the moment is your shitty taste in where to point your weapon."

"Yeah, except lying to the boss tends to come back and kill a guy." Finn took a long drag from his cigarette before dropping his arm and letting his gun point toward the floor. "But hey, I'm dead anyway. Just don't shoot me before I finish my last smoke, eh?"

Leaving the bastard to Jasper, Dallas crossed the intervening space in three paces and dragged Lex to him. "Jesus Christ, woman, you will be the death of me."

"Jade," she muttered, clutching his arms. "She's already hurting."

He couldn't unlock his arms from around Lex. Not until Finn was gone, maybe not until they were back in their own damn sector. "Doc's here."

"A doctor can't help her," Finn said in a dull voice. He watched Jade tremble on the floor with dark eyes devoid of satisfaction or sympathy, devoid of anything but a numb sort of exhaustion. "I can give her the dose I brought to take the edge off, but she'll be going through this again in two weeks unless you send her off peacefully before that."

Doc knelt next to the woman, tilted her head back, and peered into her eyes. "Is this that shit Fleming's been pushing? The habit-forming additive?"

"Insurance in a bottle." Finn looked away, and Dallas could hear his distaste.

Distaste wasn't enough, not for this. Chilling rage had burned away everything except the need to be touching Lex, to remember she was safe and their enemy was dead. "Give the last dose to the doctor."

The man retrieved a plastic container the size of Dallas's thumb and tossed it to Doc. Dallas waited until the doctor had checked it and nodded before gesturing with his gun. "Time to finish that cigarette."

"Dallas, no." Lex curled her fingers in his shirt. "He could have killed me and Jade and been gone already."

He hesitated, because she was right. Even if Finn hadn't wanted to kill two women, he could have gotten out before Dallas showed up with the cavalry. "So why *did* you stick around?"

Finn snuffed out his cigarette against the bedpost. "I was hoping to make a deal. You all clear out and pretend you were never here, and the boss and I pin this on Cerys." His gaze tracked over Lex. "It's not entirely a lie."

"No one's gonna believe a junkie whore wiped out a squad of Eden-trained guards," Jasper observed.

Dallas tended to agree, but Finn just laughed and flicked the butt of his cigarette into a pool of Woods's blood. "I've pulled off more complicated frame jobs with zero sleep and tripping on acid. What sort of cushy life do you fuckers live in Four?"

"The kind where we work smarter, not harder."

"Enough," Dallas snapped. "If you wanna stay behind and play with the dead bodies, be my guest. I'm not gonna piss my name on the wall to prove I was here. Doc, the girl?"

The man pocketed the inhaler. "Want to have one of your goons carry her?"

Bren and Cruz had arrived, so Dallas directed Jasper to help the doctor and had Bren cover their retreat so Finn couldn't shoot them in the back. His gaze snagged on Gareth Woods as he turned, and he hesitated, half expecting thwarted rage to roar through him. That kill—that *vengeance*—should have been his.

The dead didn't matter. Lex did. He swept her up into his arms, surprised when she didn't struggle or protest. Something different rose in his chest as he carried her out of the bloodstained room.

Hope.

23

Dallas's good mood lasted until he got Lex to his room. It had taken too long to get from Five back to Four, especially when Jade had roused just enough to protest at leaving her driver behind. Still riding the buzz of having Lex curled trustingly against his chest, Dallas had ended up being too charitable, and Noelle was currently hovering over a dotty old refugee from a Victorian novel who had earnestly asked if Dallas could use a valet.

A gang leader with a valet. Jesus *Christ*, he hated Cerys.

At least the new arrivals had somewhat distracted Noelle. Dallas figured he could thank Jasper for that, one way or another. But all of the delays meant that by the time he helped Lex out of her blood-soaked clothes, bruises had begun to form on her body.

And that made him rage.

"I just need a bath," she protested. "And some gel for my hand."

"Shh." He turned on the shower and climbed in with her, blocking the worst of the spray with his body as he eased her hair aside and started a slow exploration. "Your face is swelling up, too. What happened?"

"I got smacked, what do you think?" She twisted away from his touch. "I'm covered in blood, that's the bad part."

"*Lex.*" It came out as a snarl that echoed off the tile, and he fought to moderate his tone. Fought and failed. "Let me take care of you, for Christ's sake. Let me do this."

"I—" A shudder wracked her. "Okay, fine."

Seizing hold of his frayed self-control with both hands, Dallas edged her under the showerhead. "I'm sorry. I didn't mean to snap. You just scared the hell out of me."

"I know." The water plastered her hair to her head and ran red with the blood that hadn't quite dried.

He poured shampoo in his hands and worked it into her hair. "Why'd you do it?"

"The opportunity presented itself," she answered dourly.

That simple. That cool. For all that she was tolerating his attentions, Lex was still pissed at him. "Because I dealt with Cerys."

"I took him out," she said stormily. And I did it on *my* terms, not yours."

"Okay." He cupped her cheeks and tilted her head back. "Look at me, Lex. Believe me when I say this. I don't give a fuck. As long as you're okay, Cerys and Fleming and everyone in both their sectors can burn. And Gareth fucking Woods, too."

She stared dully back. "Stop it, Dallas."

He opened his mouth and shut it again without speaking. Talking wasn't getting it done, so he'd listen. He'd prove he *could* listen. Maybe that was what she needed, to know she could draw a line and ask him not to cross it, even if the line was this simple.

Stop it.

In silence, he washed the blood from her hair and body, taking careful note of her injuries. When the water finally ran clear, he turned it off and wrapped her in an oversized towel, using a second to work the water from her hair. "Will you let me bandage your hand?"

Lex nodded and tugged the towel higher on her chest. "I need something to wear."

Because there wasn't anything else, he found her a clean T-shirt and toweled himself off while she pulled it on. He took just enough time to drag on a pair of jeans and went in search of the med kit.

Impossible not to compare this to the last time someone had gotten patched up in his suite. Noelle had babied Jasper's tiny cut before kissing every part the man had to make it all better. That had been a night of dedicated debauchery, a night he'd almost crossed the near-invisible line he'd drawn for himself and fucked Lex cross-eyed, even though he hadn't collared her.

She'd been pissed at him the next morning, pissed that he'd gotten her off but refused to get in her, pissed over his arbitrary line and how ridiculous she found it. *Dicks aren't required for fucking, Declan.* A certain proclamation, delivered with a tilted brow that invited him to imagine a whole world of scenarios that didn't require dicks even before she added, *I should know.*

Having watched her fuck Noelle on a dimly lit stage more than once now, he suspected she'd been right about that, too.

When he returned to the couch, he found Lex curled up on one end, her legs tucked beneath her, rubbing her fingers over the tattoo on her wrist.

He thought of what Doc had said and damn near bit through his tongue to keep from commenting. Instead, he set the kit on the couch and knelt in front of her. Slow and easy. That's what he had to do.

Gentle.

"Do you want Jade to stay here?" he asked as he examined the cut on her hand. A safe, neutral topic to test the waters with. If Lex wasn't planning to stay, she'd be less likely to make long-term plans involving the gang. Assuming any plans concerning Jade could be long-term.

"That was *my* deal," she whispered. "Her freedom for Woods's life."

He'd grumbled over Noelle. He didn't have the heart to do it about Jade now, not with Lex looking so bruised and hurt and sad. "She'll have a place," he promised, "and whatever Doc needs to make her comfortable. But, Lex..."

She shook her head stubbornly. "Trix. She came from Five—you know that. What you don't know is that she kicked that shit, too. She did it, and she'll know how to help Jade."

Maybe he should have been surprised, but he wasn't. Trix was sexy curves over steel, the kind of tough that only came from surviving hell. It was most of the reason she fit in with the O'Kanes. "Is Trix gonna go for ink?"

"I don't know." Lex pulled away slightly, her eyes shuttered. "I won't know, Dallas. That's not who I am, not anymore."

Unable to stop himself, he wrapped his arms

around her and pressed his mouth to her temple. "I'm sorry, Lex. I'm fucking sorry. I'll do better. I *need* you. We all do."

She stiffened. "I did everything, Dallas. I gave you all those things you wanted. I played my part, I did my job—I even killed that man. Not for myself, because I was scared or pissed off, but *for you*. So you could rest. I'm here, in your room and in your fucking clothes...and you still don't understand."

"I hurt you." Even the admission grated, but it was the truth. "I've never had to do this before. The submission, all of it—it was always about the bed. I should have been more careful. I should have protected you better."

"Protected me from yourself?" Shaking her head, she pushed against his chest. "It's on me. I should have known how wrong this would go."

His arms tightened instinctively, and he couldn't stop them. This was it. This was where fear overcame him, fear of losing the person he needed more than air, more than the blood in his veins. Fear of letting her slip away only to find that nothing would satisfy him ever again.

This was the moment he would close his hands around the one thing he should have cherished and crush the light out of it, because he was too selfish to let something beautiful escape.

He could keep her here. No one would stop him, not if he played it right. He could wear her down, use what he knew of her body and her needs, break down those walls so completely she wouldn't be able to find two bricks to stack together.

He was Dallas fucking O'Kane, king of Sector Four. She belonged to him.

"One kiss," he whispered. "Give me one kiss."

Silence. Then she wrenched out of his arms so fast she almost tumbled to the floor. "This is why," she whispered hoarsely. "Noelle wanted me to tell her I'd stay, but I can't, and *this is why.*"

He clenched his fists until his fingers ached to keep from reaching for her. "You can stay. I won't—" The words were broken glass in his throat, cutting him as he forced each one free. "It was goodbye, Lex. Just a kiss goodbye."

She eyed him warily before finally taking a step back. "I can't right now. Not tonight."

Fear. There was fear in her eyes, and that was when he recognized the horrifying truth. This wasn't the moment. The moment had come and gone, and he hadn't seen it. He'd closed his fingers tight enough to crush the trust out of her, and he hadn't even realized it.

Closing his eyes spared him the sight of her, but not the guilt. Not the pain. "Okay. Just go. You can go."

Her breath caught on a sob, but the only other sounds were of soft, quick footsteps...and the slamming of the door.

He waited long enough for her to be well and gone before rocking to his feet. Mechanically, he pulled on socks and boots, buckled his belt and found a T-shirt. Familiar motions, things his body could do without thought.

He wasn't going to think. Couldn't afford to, not while he was still sober enough to chase Lex down and try to change her mind.

There might not be enough whiskey in the world to drown out the knowledge that he'd put fear in Lex's eyes, but he was damn sure going to find out. After all, he *was* Dallas fucking O'Kane.

And Dallas O'Kane was all he'd ever be. Declan

had to die tonight, and take all those messy personal feelings with him. Weakness and vulnerability and love.

Whiskey oblivion was a fitting way to start the rest of his lonely, miserable life.

jasper

When people split up, it always ricocheted like a fucking bullet, ripping through everyone who happened to be close by.

You couldn't get much closer to Lex than Noelle. Jasper was closer to Dallas, which left him shit out of luck, pushed out of his own bed while Lex cried on his girlfriend's shoulder.

He went to the warehouse. Dallas liked to work with his hands when shit got to be too much, and there were always crates to be built and piles of salvage to be picked apart and sorted.

Not tonight.

He heard the crashing sounds from outside the building, and they only got worse when he slipped inside. Louder. Lights flickered in the workroom, and the crack of shattering wood punctuated rhythmic thuds as Dallas smashed a sledgehammer into what had probably been a stack of newly built crates not so long ago.

Jasper rubbed the knot forming at the base of his neck and groaned. "Come on, man. What the fuck?"

Dallas paused, but only to snag a half-empty bottle of whiskey off the table. He took a healthy swig before waving it at Jasper. "My fucking booze. My fucking crates. I can smash them all day long because I'm *Dallas O'Kane*."

"Sure." Jasper bent to retrieve a jagged splinter of wood from the floor. "But someone's gonna have to rebuild it all."

"Is that why you're here?" Dallas drank again, still clutching the sledgehammer in one white-knuckled fist. "Because your girlfriend's busy rebuilding things?"

Dallas O'Kane didn't fish for information, he demanded it. So this halting, roundabout question meant the world really *was* ending. "Why don't you ask me what you really want to know?"

The tortured noise Dallas made was that of a wounded animal. "Because I *don't* want to know. I don't want to know if I broke her so bad even Noelle can't fix it." Swinging the sledgehammer, he sent a shattered piece of wood flying toward the salvage pile. "You didn't see the look on her face, Jas. Lex was afraid of me. *Lex*."

There were a million ways to fear, and at least as many reasons why. "Should she have been?"

"I don't know." An admission. A plea for help. "Fuck, man. I don't fucking know."

Jasper caught the handle of the sledgehammer and twisted it away from Dallas. "I don't know a lot about women, but I've been watching you and Lex for years."

"Yeah?" Dallas snapped. "Ever seen her terrified

of me before?"

Christ help him not to beat his best friend's ass. "When I lived out on the farm, there was this dog there. Mean bastard, crazy. Must have bit a couple kids a year, but old Robbins kept him around because he was a damn good guard dog. Once the mutt got it in his head something was his, he'd rip up anyone who tried to take it."

Drunk as he was, Dallas eyed him suspiciously. "Robbins? The bastard with one hand torn to hell and back?"

"Uh-huh. Dog got him." Jasper hesitated. "I'm not good with words, but I know you have a crazy, mean dog in you. If you can't keep it in check, it'll bite the shit out of you."

"Don't worry about me. Worry about the rest of you." Dallas lifted the bottle again but didn't drink. Instead he stared at the label as the amber liquid sloshed back and forth. "I can't keep it in check. Never really could. Lex was the one wearing a collar, but she's had me on a leash for years. And now she's leaving."

"Maybe it's what she needs to do." Jasper snatched the bottle this time. "Maybe you need to let her. Because all I keep hearing is how low you are, how bad you fucked up. How you don't want her to go. You haven't said jack shit about what's good for Lex."

"Because everything I try makes it worse," he roared, lunging across the space separating them. Dallas's hand closed around the bottle as they stood toe-to-toe, the potential for violence seething in the air between them. "Everything I do hurts her more," he repeated in a quiet, chilling voice. "So if I have to drink myself halfway to dead to find a way to let her leave, that's what I'm going to do."

"You can't," Jasper reminded him softly. "You're

Dallas O'Kane."

"Not tonight." He closed his eyes, but not before Jasper got a glimpse of bleak, utter hopelessness. "Tonight I'm a man who has to figure out how to let go."

If he could figure out how to do that, then he might not have to. It didn't take a genius to see Lex didn't want to leave—if she did, she'd be long gone already, and none of them would ever hear from her again.

It didn't change the problem at hand. "Come on, then," Jasper said.

Sighing, Dallas let his hand fall away from the whiskey, but he didn't move. "I'm not going back to my room. It's full of her."

"Then where? Name the place, and I'll drive."

"I'll sleep in my office." Sudden, jagged laughter spilled free. "Funny, huh?"

Not much amused Jasper at the moment. "How's that?"

"Dallas O'Kane," he muttered. "Better get used to the bastard, because he's all that's left."

He'd started swaying, so Jasper pulled one arm up around his shoulders to support him. "No middle ground with you, is there?" Everything would work out fine, or the fucking world was falling down. Nothing in between.

"That's what makes a winner, Jas. That's what makes a *leader*. You fight to get it all, or you go down trying. Accept nothing less."

"You know you're full of shit, right?"

Dallas took a half-hearted swing at him, listing them both to the side. "Fuck you."

"Yeah, okay." He stopped at the back exit and hesitated before reaching for the doorknob. "We're still here. No one's going anywhere."

"Everyone's always going somewhere. You've been

gone since that girl passed out at your feet."

"That's crap," Jasper said firmly. "I'm right here, where I've always been."

Dallas swayed and put one hand against the doorjamb to hold himself up as he squinted at Jasper. "You're right there, but you're not where you've always been. And that's okay. I'm glad you're blissful, man. I just miss my brother."

Well, shit. "You're a chatty drunk." Jasper eased open the door. "You always wanna talk about your damn *feelings*."

Dallas snorted. "Enjoy it while I've got 'em."

"Scratch that. You're a *weepy* drunk."

"I fucking well earned it tonight," he grumbled. "I went for all and got nothing."

"Finally, you're starting to get it."

Dallas mumbled something incoherent—probably the last couple swigs of whiskey hitting his bloodstream. Sloppy drunk, all right, and all Jas could do was lead him down the hall to his office and dump him on the couch.

And fetch him a cup of water. Dallas swatted at it, so Jasper poured it over his head and listened to him sputter as he settled in for the night on the rickety lounge chair in the corner.

24

"How about this color?" Amira held up another small bottle, this one red with gold flecks.

Six eyed it with the same wariness she had the previous offerings, but Lex could tell she was trying for politeness when she shook her head slightly. "I don't know if red's my color."

The girl was still awkward and crap at socialization, but she'd get better. And most of the O'Kane women had taken note of Bren's fondness for her and acted out of their own fondness for him, making it their mission to put Six at ease.

It might work, if the overdose of sisterhood didn't give her a panic attack first. Six started when Nessa flopped down on the couch beside her, waving another bottle over her head. "I've got it, I've got the winner. She's a girl after my own heart, so she needs something dark." She dropped her voice to an ominous whisper. "Like our *souls*."

Noelle choked on her beer. Six was staring, her eyes wide, and Lex finally nudged Nessa with her foot. "You're scaring the piss out of her."

Nessa tossed her brightly colored bangs—purple, this week—out of her eyes and grinned. "Just lightening the mood until someone interesting climbs into the cage. Look here, Six." She held up her own nails, which were a shimmery black with golden sparkle. "It's the best of all worlds, right? It says, *yeah, I'd cut you* but also *I like shiny things*. Just let me try it on you."

Six extended her hand with all the enthusiasm of someone reaching into a bear trap, but the corner of her mouth tugged up a little. "Are there good fights coming up?"

Both of Amira's eyebrows rose. "Flash said something about Ace fighting the new guy. Bren's friend."

"Ace?" Noelle demanded. "Does he fight? I've never seen him fight."

"He steers clear of it. Usually." Lex leaned forward, distracted from her brooding. "What's up? Ace all mad that Cruz moved in on Rachel?"

"Rachel dumped Cruz," Six said abruptly. "While you guys were still in Sector Two."

"I heard it was right after she got her new tat," Nessa added without looking up from Six's nails. "And we all know *that's* been on slow boil just about forever."

Lex stared. "You're shitting me." How had she been so wrapped up in her drama with Dallas that she hadn't even noticed?

"It's true." Noelle dropped a hand to her shoulder. "At least, I know the part about them breaking up is. I meant to tell you, but things have been hectic."

"Jesus." Lex glanced over at Rachel, who was

pouring drinks. She didn't look happy, not in the least. Certainly not like she'd been hopping on Ace's dick every night. "So she and Ace...?"

Nessa shook her head. "I don't think so. If he'd finally caught her, we'd all know, because we'd be watching it every time we turned around."

"That's the truth," Amira said.

Which meant something had gone horribly wrong. Lex should have been there, if only for moral support. Instead, she'd been too busy indulging her own pain.

"I should check on her," she said as she started to stand.

"Check on who?" Rachel shoved a mug of beer at Nessa, then drew it back. "You're not going to drink this *before* you finish painting people's nails, are you?"

But Nessa wasn't looking at Six's nails anymore. Her gaze had strayed to the cage. "Oh boy."

Lex turned to see Ace, barefoot and shirtless, stretching his tattooed arms over his head on one side of the cage as Cruz climbed in the other side.

Rachel dropped to the couch. Noelle rescued the beer, and Lex rubbed the blonde's shoulder as she stared at the two men in the cage. "This is so stupid," she mumbled. "What the hell are they doing?"

"Blowing off manly steam." Nessa finished painting Six's last nail and closed the bottle before patting Rachel's leg. "You can't stop them, so pretend this is some ancient arena and they're... What did they call them? The guys in the metal suits?"

"Knights," Noelle supplied. "But only men think a duel over a woman is actually about the woman."

Lex sighed. No, this was about ego. The bell rang, and the two men circled each other slowly. "Nessa's right, Rach. Let them beat each other stupid like a couple of little boys. No harm, no foul."

"Unless Cruz breaks Ace's fingers," Nessa whispered too softly for Rachel to hear.

From the first jab, it was clear that Ace's fingers were the last thing on his mind. The two men clashed with matching snarls, Cruz's power and speed only partially countered by the fact that Ace fought dirtier than anyone Lex had ever seen.

Cruz was dangerous. He was good. He was *pissed*.

But he was holding back. Maybe out of respect for Ace's place in the gang, or maybe because he really did think Dallas would shut him out if he injured their artist's precious hands. Cruz checked his strength more than once, hesitating with a kick, pulling a punch.

And Ace took advantage of it. Mercilessly.

Lex couldn't hear them over the shouts of the crowd, but words were being exchanged. Ace ducked an unsteady punch and came up under Cruz's arm, slamming into him and ramming them both back against the bars. His mouth moved in some incomprehensible taunt, and Cruz roared and flung Ace across the cage, seemingly more enraged by Ace's smug little smile.

They crashed together again, locked face-to-face, arms straining, muscles bulging, teeth bared in matching growls, and Lex wasn't the only one who saw the pressure begin to shift. Nessa reached blindly for a beer and ended up grabbing Noelle's arm instead. "Uh, is it just me, or is it *hot* in here?"

The two men were steaming up the cage, all right, exuding a palpable sexual tension that had people staring as the fight went on. The crowd buzzed, with more than a few curious gazes landing on the couch—on Rachel.

Judging from the flush creeping up her cheeks, she knew exactly what people were saying.

She stood suddenly. "I need to get a few more

bottles from the storeroom. I'm just—yeah."

"I'll go with you." Amira climbed to her feet more clumsily, one hand around her pregnant belly.

When they were gone, Noelle scooted into Amira's spot, her gaze never leaving the cage. "I know I'm still pretty new at this, but that looks a little bit like foreplay."

"Yeah. Someone better get them a do-not-disturb sign for the night."

"Someone better get us *all* one," Nessa retorted, flinching as Cruz got his arm around Ace's neck and ended up elbowed in the side for his trouble. "See, Six? This is what makes life worth living. Men who don't know if they wanna fight or fuck, but will climb into a cage to figure it out in front of everyone in the sector."

Six squinted and tilted her head. "Ace fights dirty. No rules, no mercy. And he's got a nice jab."

"A nice *jab*?" Nessa shook her head. "Oh, honey."

Noelle took a sip of her beer to cover her smile and leaned closer to Lex. "I think I see why Bren's fond of her."

Lex's answering smile faded as she caught sight of Trix across the room. The redhead had covered the discoloration with makeup, but there was no mistaking the swelling around her eye. She had one hell of a shiner—and, unlike Cruz and Ace, no reason for it. "What the hell happened to Trix?"

Noelle's brow furrowed. "I don't know. I hadn't seen her all day until just now."

"Jesus *Christ*," Nessa whispered. "Dallas can't have seen that yet, or someone would be dead."

"Someone's about to be. Stay here." Lex elbowed through the crowd.

Trix saw her coming and turned away, angling her face down to cover her cheek, but Lex caught her arm and shook her head. "That's not how it works, honey. Who was it?"

Trix's eyes widened. "Tell Dallas I'm not trying to cause trouble—"

"I need a name." A name Lex could connect with a face, which she could then connect with her boot.

She didn't answer, but her gaze skittered tellingly to the corner, where Dom was holding court with a handful of the punks who came to fight in the cage, hungry for a little of Dallas's attention.

If they thought listening to Dom was the way to get it, they were right...in the very worst way.

He tensed as she approached, but Lex couldn't manage to wipe the anger from her features. "You're in deep shit this time, Dom."

Dom jeered at her, puffing out his chest in a useless attempt to look unconcerned. "Yeah? Says who?"

She slapped the drink out of his hand. "I'm not fucking around. If Dallas doesn't kill you, I'll do it myself."

"You better watch your mouth, *bitch*." He leaned close enough for his breath to wash over her, reeking of tequila. "I hear you're not so high and mighty now. Just another piece of ass who doesn't know when to shut up, strip down, and spread 'em."

Rage swelled, closing off her throat. Not at the personal insult, but at his implication—that women were only good for one thing, and worthless for anything else. Worse than worthless. Subhuman, nothing but disembodied parts waiting for his slavering, short-lived attention.

He'd already shed his shoes in anticipation of a fight in the cage. Lex stomped down on the bridge of his foot, then slammed the heel of her hand up against his nose.

He howled and swung a fist toward her, but it went wide. Not because she'd dodged, but because an iron arm had locked around her waist and hauled her out of the way.

Jas and Bren appeared on either side of Dom, sending his companions scattering. No doubt none of them wanted to be associated with the beatdown to come, especially when Dallas's voice tickled Lex's ear. "Lexie love, were you about to throw an ass-stomping party and not invite me?"

Easy words, lazy, at complete odds with the rigid tension in his body. He was playing his part, king of Sector Four, and she found herself going along with it. "Had to. I would have saved his head for you, though. You'll want it when you see Trix's face."

Dallas lowered her carefully to the floor. "Jas? Make sure Dom doesn't get any ideas about moving."

The crowd had gone silent, and Lex looked up. Her eyes locked with Trix's big blue ones, and she motioned her over. "Come here, honey."

The woman's chest heaved, but she obeyed, crossing the room with her hands clenched at her sides. "I'm sorry, Dallas."

He caught her chin with gentle fingers and tilted her head back, angling her bruised eye toward the light. "Only thing you need to be sorry about is not coming straight to me. You work for us, girl. You're protected."

She bit her lip and nodded.

Dallas released her and turned to Lex. They'd known each other so long it was easy to read the silent plea in his gaze. For this night, for this *moment*, he had to be the king, and he desperately needed her. Not Lex, his lover, or even Alexa.

He needed his queen.

Dallas didn't look away, even when he spoke. "Get

in the cage, Dom."

Bren stepped forward, but Lex cut off his protest with an upraised hand. "You heard the man. He's ready to settle this."

Dom bit off a curse. "Fuck that. I won't."

"O'Kane for life," Dallas drawled, the painful edge under the words sharp enough to cut. "You wanted to punch someone, I'll give you someone to punch. If you're one of us, do what you're fucking told and get in that cage. If you're not, I'll let Bren put two bullets in your head right now. Trust me, he wants to, just to spare me the fight."

Jasper nudged him, and Dom stumbled forward. "Have it your way, O'Kane. I'll kick your ass." He stomped toward the cage.

A queen wouldn't let her king go into a fight without her favors. Lex hesitated for a half-second before curving her hand around the back of Dallas's neck and drawing him close for a quick, hard kiss.

His lips moved against hers, but not in a kiss. In a whisper. "Thank you."

Let them all think the rumors were just that. They'd find no weakness here, no dissension. "Go."

He went, stripping off his leather vest as he walked. The harsh warehouse lights allowed for nothing to be hidden. Not the proud swirl of ink dominating one arm and shoulder, not the scars that marked his chest and back.

He was rough, hard and unforgiving. A force of nature.

And, like a storm, he had no mercy.

The cage door had barely shut when he hit Dom for the first time, smashing a fist into the man's unprotected face. He fought back, but he was no match for Dallas's cold fury.

Lex watched, every breath burning in and out of her lungs. The fight could have been over in a few minutes of brutal punches and well-placed kicks, but Dallas was holding back, almost toying with Dom. Going as much for pain as for victory.

He was putting on a show. Sending a message. Every time Dom staggered to his feet only to be knocked back down, Dallas reinforced the line he'd drawn. You didn't hurt Dallas's women. You didn't touch his people. Not the ones wearing ink, not the ones who worked for him. Because if he'd do this to one of his own men, no one else had a hope in hell of survival.

The fight had started with cheers, but as it dragged on, the warehouse grew still around Lex. O'Kanes watched in solemn pride. The rest of Sector Four watched with a mixture of satisfaction and fear.

Dallas carried the weight of everyone's safety on his shoulders, and he won it with violence and blood, taking one last swing to lay a staggering Dom out before flexing his bruised knuckles.

Dom thudded to the concrete, and Dallas lifted his head to meet Lex's gaze. Frustration. Satisfaction. Heat, as his adrenaline pumped and one sort of arousal melted into another.

He was thinking of his fantasy, the one he'd laid out so bluntly in her bathtub. The one where he celebrated his victory inside her, right there in front of everyone.

Not now, after everything that had happened. But turning away wasn't an option for Lex, either. So she stepped forward and held out her hand. Dallas hopped out of the cage and clasped her fingers. Kissed them.

Then he walked away.

As he neared Jas, he jerked a thumb toward Dom's prone figure. "Strip his cuffs," he said, raising his voice so his words carried back to them. "And then dump him with the trash."

Lex winced. As loathsome as Dom was, stripping tattoos was nasty business. The doctor had lasers, but he saved them for people he liked, or when his work had to be neat. Dom would get acid, and then he'd get turned out into the streets.

"I'll call Doc," Jasper said brusquely.

Dallas took one last look back, and Lex froze. A *last* look, that's exactly what it was—him drinking in the sight of her, fixing it in his mind because soon it would be gone.

She would be gone.

He turned and slammed through the back door nearest the garage.

Her mind fluttered, struggling to light on why she felt sick inside. She'd *known* this. The decision had been made. Plans begun. And yet something inside Lex still shrank away from the thought. Her friends, her family—

But that wasn't what twisted a cold knot in her gut. She didn't have to leave Sector Four, or even the O'Kane compound. She could stay right where she was, be as close to any of them as she'd ever been.

But not Dallas.

Her hands began to shake. He'd spent days waiting for her to come around, to tell him it would be all right, but it seemed that now he understood the one thing she needed more than apologies, more than promises.

He was finally letting her go.

25

The garage was dark, and the slamming of the door echoed behind her. "Dallas?"

A clatter came from the far side, where tools lined a low wooden workbench. Light flared, sudden illumination that offered her the sight of Dallas's back in silhouette. "Go back to the warehouse, Lex." He bit off each word, as if he had to measure them one at a time to keep his control. "I need to cool off."

"I can't." She was drawn to him, always. Unable to walk away. "Are you all right? Your hands?"

His snarl echoed through the darkness. "I'm not fucking around."

"I *can't*," she said again, desperation almost choking her. "I can't leave. No matter what's going on between us, you need me here. I'm not just an O'Kane."

Dallas spun, still mostly backlit. She could barely

make out his face, only sharp shadows playing over a fierce expression. "If you touch me, I can't promise I'll let you go again. Not right now."

She couldn't go, but she couldn't stay, either. Couldn't push or retreat. Love him or hate him.

Something had to give.

"All I wanted was you." Her voice broke on the confession. "To be as important to you as you were to me."

Silence. Heartbreaking, humiliating silence, until Dallas shifted his weight. "Would you stab me, Lex?"

An exact echo of his words from their horrible, horrible fight. She shuddered. "Only if you make me."

He was still wearing his boots. He hadn't taken them off before fighting Dom, and now he bent and jerked a knife free from the left one. He flipped it around so he was holding it by the blade and offered it to her.

His way of providing her an escape. If she couldn't walk out the door, she could still stop him.

As soon as she touched the hilt, Dallas was on her.

It was harder and different and *more* than the night she'd stripped off his collar. Rough hands, intense kisses, his mouth slanting over hers as he immobilized her with an unforgiving grip in her hair. But it wasn't angry. It wasn't punishment.

It was hunger, pure and simple. Unchecked, uncontrolled desire, spilling out of him without finesse or thought, drowning her in the truth of how much he wanted her. How much he *needed* her.

This was what she couldn't walk away from, the reason she'd stay, no matter what. Her longing reflected in the trembling clench of his fingers.

Lex let the knife clatter to the table and wrapped her arms around his neck.

Groaning, he slid his hands down to her thighs

and hoisted her against him. "I can't do this without you. I can't be Dallas without Lex."

The night had driven that home already. "We can't wind up hating each other, either. The damn sector won't survive it."

"I know. I *know*." One hand caught her hair and dragged her head back again. "If you can't stay and be Lex, I'll be Declan and go. Anywhere you want, anywhere you can be happy. None of this is worth a damn if you're not here."

The world stopped. He couldn't do it, could never give up what he wanted so much and had worked so hard to build—and yet there was no deception on his face, just an earnestness that almost hurt to see.

He'd leave it all. For her.

"I want you to be happy," she whispered. "With Four, with the gang. With me."

His grip relaxed in her hair, shifting to cradle the back of her head as he turned and set her on the workbench. The knife glinted a few inches away from her fingers as he lifted his other hand to her cheek. "With you. That's the only way I'll ever be happy, Lex. I thought it didn't matter if you left, that it *couldn't* matter, but I'm a goddamn liar. I'm too fucking selfish to stay here and suffer like some noble fucking martyr. They're my people, but you're everything."

Power was one thing, but his people were another entirely. "You need them, too. But that's okay. So do I."

Dallas exhaled and rested his forehead against hers. "Yeah, okay. Maybe I need them. That's what's gotta change, isn't it? No more lying. Not to you, and not to myself."

"No more," she agreed. But he wasn't the only one who'd hidden things, from himself or her. "If you can do that, so can I. Because I love you."

"I've always loved you." A shudder worked through him, and he pulled her closer. "I've always wanted you. They don't have a word for how much I need you. Everything good I am, everything good I've ever done… it's all you. You make me a king. Without you, I'm just another psychotic thug."

She framed his face with her hands and kissed him through a laugh. "I hope I don't make the thug in you disappear completely. I like him."

His answering laugh was low, relieved—and a little dangerous. Cuffing one of her wrists with his fingers, he dragged her hand down until it covered the hilt of the knife. "How much do you like him?"

Enough to give him what he needed, forever. Even if that meant promising violence to keep him from crossing her lines. She closed her hand around the handle of the knife. "Enough to stop him if it's too much."

He stroked a warm path down the side of her neck before gripping her throat, his hand settling high enough to tilt her chin back. "You're worth getting a little cut up. Just don't stab anything you'll want in working order later."

"Smartass."

He just laughed. He was still laughing when he snapped the braided straps on her tank top and jerked the fabric free of her breasts. He caught one nipple in his mouth and sucked hard, the edge of his teeth scraping her flesh.

Lex abandoned the knife and scratched her nails across his bare back with a shiver. "I saw you in that cage. Thinking about this."

"No you didn't." He lifted his head, giving her the full impact of his half-crazed eyes. Need and triumph and *bloodlust,* and he licked his lips as he thumbed her damp nipple, as if the taste of her lingered on his mouth. "I was thinking about you on your knees, so hot for my cock you'd suck it all night long. Because I'm a psychotic thug *and* a goddamn barbarian."

"And a horny bastard." She skated her fingers around his rib cage and reached for his belt buckle.

He let her get his belt open before stepping back to lean against the side of one of his favorite cars, a sleek little pre-Flare antique he'd lovingly restored with years of tinkering. Spreading his arms along the roof of the vehicle, he grinned lazily at her. "You can bring the knife with you if you want. It's fucking hot."

Instead, she left it on the worktable and walked toward him. "I used to do this all the time. Right here in the garage, remember?"

"Your mouth isn't the sort of thing a man forgets, love."

"So you've told me." She slipped to her knees and looked up at him, unable to resist rubbing her palm over the hard bulge beneath his fly. "Sometimes I think you don't even care how it feels, you just want to see it. Me, on my knees, with my lips sliding around your cock."

He inhaled sharply as his eyelids drooped. "It doesn't suck."

"Then watch me." Her voice dropped to a yearning whisper as she tugged at his zipper. He had to know what this did to her, being able to wrap her hand around him and hear his breath catch. To see every muscle in his body tense when she freed him from his pants, to hear him groan when she stroked him.

"Only one thing could improve the view," he rasped as she licked small circles around the head of his cock.

She squeezed his shaft and lifted her head. "What's that, honey?"

He bared his teeth in a feral smile. "Ink. Marks."

"Ink." Her nipples tightened as heat rushed through her to settle between her thighs. "Tell me what you want. And try not to scratch the car." She took him deep but not hard, gripping the base of his shaft as she sucked him lightly.

"*Fuck*." His hand fell to the back of her head, impatient desperation clear in the hard press of his fingertips. "Matching ink, you and me. Something fitting for a king and queen. For Dallas and Lex."

She hummed, the image already forming in her mind—an early version of the O'Kane symbol, stripped down and simple, with a crown for each of them.

Beautiful. *Right.* She sucked harder, flicking her tongue against him.

"And I want your name on my skin," he continued. "*Yours.* Alexa."

His fantasy, and she couldn't fulfill it without words. She pulled away and coaxed another curse from him with one smooth glide of her fist. "And your name on me. Do you want everyone to see it...or just you?"

"Just me." The words were a growl. "Declan is yours."

"Mine." She licked him again, base to tip, and moaned.

Growling, he thumped his free hand against the car hard enough to rattle it. "Quit teasing, or I swear to *Christ*—"

Her heart skipped and stuttered as hunger seized her. "You'll what?"

He tugged at her hair and leaned down. "You give me my fantasy, or I'm gonna give you yours. And you know which one I'm talking about."

It should be here, in the garage, surrounded by the scents of motor oil and tire rubber and metal. This was where she'd watched him work on the salvaged cars, listened to him talk about his grand plans for the gang. Where she'd first begun to wonder if there was a place in all of it for her.

Her fantasy *and* his. They'd have both.

She took him again, closing her eyes with abandon when he thrust against her mouth with a ragged groan. "That's right." He threaded both hands through her hair to hold her in place. "You like it like this. Dirty and rough, getting fucked by a man who wants you so bad he'll risk all your sharp edges. Who fucking *loves* your sharp edges."

Because he had them, too, the quiet, sneaky kind that would cut you before you realized what was happening. Lex knew that now.

And it didn't matter. All she gave a damn about was her people, her family. Her man. She'd fight to protect and love them all, even if she had to fight them.

Or herself.

She reached up to grip his ass, and he hissed as his head fell back. "I know you wanna suck me off. It gets you hot, doesn't it? Deciding when I come." He thrust forward, pushing deep enough to choke her. "Which one of us is in control now? I never fucking know."

She didn't need to breathe. She'd never need anything else, ever. Just this.

He surrounded her, overwhelming her. Sweat and leather and whiskey and even the metallic scent of blood, from where his bruised knuckles lay wrapped beneath strands of her hair. When the world began to swim he drew back, stroked her hair and said that she was beautiful, that her mouth made him crazy, just long enough for her to catch her breath before rocking forward again.

Lex pulled away, heedless of the sharp tug of his fingers in her hair. "You're in control," she gasped.

Dallas stared down at her, his eyes intent. "That an observation or a request?"

The cool, easy words flew right the hell out of her head. "Please."

He moved so fast her head spun. One second she was on her knees, the next he had her up and moving. Three stumbling steps back with him looming over her, only to spin her when her ass bumped the worktable.

His slick shaft jutted against the small of her back. The wooden bench pressed against her hips, just the right height to bend over. But instead of pushing her forward, he curled his fingers in the remains of her tank top and jerked at it. "Arms up."

Anticipation raised goose bumps on her skin, but Lex didn't move.

Growling, Dallas kicked her feet apart. She swayed, and he used her momentary distraction to haul the front of the shirt up and over her head, dragging it to tangle around her upper arms behind her back.

"You can be bad." The words didn't quite cover the sound of leather rasping against denim. His belt sliding free of its loops, one at a time. "You can fight. You know what it'll get you?"

She couldn't hold back her moan. "No, what?"

"Fucked harder." He planted a hand between her shoulder blades and shoved her down until her only option was to turn her head and rest her cheek on the scuffed wooden table.

Just like that, every ounce of her attention was riveted to the sweet pressure of his hand, and how much she could push against it before he eased up. Gave up. She struggled carefully, unwilling to risk losing the heat of him at her back and the rough bite of the bench beneath her.

He laughed and dropped his belt across her lower

back, the leather a dangerous threat—or promise. "Is that the best you've got?"

She jerked hard, panting when his splayed hand shoved her closer to the table. "Oh, Jesus." The words escaped her in a hoarse, pleading rasp.

"Not quite," he murmured, sliding his hand up over her shoulder and around her throat. He dragged her upright, her arms trapped between them, and wrenched open her jeans. "But you can pray to me for mercy, if you want."

Lex arched her hips. "You're a tease."

He responded by shoving his hand into her panties, his fingers slicking over her pussy. "And you're wet. I bet I can get you wetter."

She started to respond, but the hand around her throat began to tighten. At the same time, he grazed her clit with a rough enough touch to send pleasure rippling up her spine.

"Oh, yeah." He whispered the words against her ear as his fingers found a quick, unforgiving rhythm, blunt fingertips slicking back and forth until blood pounded in her ears and her vision blurred. "Such a hot, wet pussy. If I weren't such a tease, I'd already be fucking it."

"Dallas—" Lex barely managed to rasp his name before his rhythm quickened. She rocked as much as she could, and it was almost enough.

Almost.

"Declan," he corrected, easing his grip so that she could speak. "Say it. Say it while you're coming."

"De—" Her hips jolted in a shudder that spread through the rest of her along with a blaze of heat that melted her. "Fuck, Declan!"

"Shh," he soothed, keeping her on edge with another clever twist of his fingers. "Sweet, sweet Alexa.

My Alexa. Do you trust me?"

A current of fear flowed beneath the words. Lex longed to hold him, but she was trapped against his chest. All she could do was turn her head with a shaky sigh. "I trust you." She rubbed her cheek against his chin. "I love you."

He caught her mouth in one quick, tender kiss, then sharpened it by biting her lower lip with a groan. "Want me to stop teasing?"

More than anything. More than *life*. "I need it."

One more taunting stroke before his touch vanished, and she was bent over the table again. She stretched her arms against her bonds as he hooked his fingers in the waistband of her jeans and panties and hauled both down just far enough to bare her ass. He didn't give her time to savor the anticipation or even think before the broad head of his cock pressed against and then inside her.

No teasing. No mercy. With one hand forcing her to the table and the other bracing her hips, he pushed into her in one raw advance. He felt huge, bigger with her jeans trapping her legs together, and he filled her one relentless inch at a time.

Lex's head spun, all thoughts of struggling to regain control of the situation gone. He'd take what he wanted—and in return give her everything she never knew existed.

As if he sensed her submission, his fingers drifted up to smooth through her hair. He withdrew a few inches before rocking back, pushing deeper and a little harder. "Does it scare you, love? Knowing you're stuck with me?" His hand tightened suddenly, hauling her head back. "Does it scare you to know I'd burn it all to the ground if that'd make you happy?"

Pleasure clashed with satisfaction. "Hell, no."

Nothing less would be enough.

He thrust harder, angling to hit all the right spots. "It should. I couldn't let you go. I knew I had to, and I couldn't. I'll be any man you want. A king or a beggar or a farmer or a killer. But I'll never be the man who can let you walk away."

It hurt where he pulled her hair, painful tingles that shimmered down her spine and melted until her body clutched greedily at his cock. "No more leaving," she gasped, a promise and a warning.

And because he was Dallas, because he *knew* her, he understood both. "What'll you do instead?"

"Make you pay," she growled. "Make you mine all over again."

Groaning, he slapped a hand on the table and bent low enough to speak in her ear. "Your threats get me so fucking hot."

The angle shifted his thrusts to a subdued grind, and Lex smacked her head back against his shoulder. "Sharp edges, remember?"

"Uh-huh." Every thrust was a little rougher, a little quicker, as if his self-control was fraying at the edges for all the lazy drawl of his words. His body told the truth—the hardness in his tensed muscles, the growing urgency every time his cock plunged into her.

He reached for the knife as he straightened. The tangle of her shirt around her upper arms loosened and fell away, and he jammed the blade back into the table in front of her. Catching her hand, he guided it to curl around the hilt. "If you let go, I'll stop."

"Kinky bastard." She gripped the knife with one hand and the edge of the worktable with the other.

Dark laughter spilled over her as he slapped her ass. "It's not kinky until I tell you to stab me," he corrected.

Before she could respond, he clutched her hips and drove into her so hard that she pitched forward into the table. She bit her tongue, but the pain vanished in an instant, consumed by the fire sparked by his next thrust.

Deep and unforgiving, the kind of merciless fucking she'd had to coax out of him before. Rough grunts punctuated each thrust, along with the slick sound of his cock slamming into her, their bodies slapping together.

It *should* have been selfish, Dallas using her body, wrenching his pleasure from it too fast and hard to give her any in return, but his hands held her hips at that desperate angle, and the sparks multiplied, turned to fire.

He cracked one open palm against her hip. "Is this what you wanted?"

Yes. The word didn't come, but she did. The knife wrenched free and clattered to the wood, but Lex couldn't help it. Her entire body shook, trembled on the edge of something *more*, so she pressed her forehead to the table and whispered his name.

"Christ," he groaned, dragging her back to meet his cock. "I love fucking your pussy while you're coming. So fucking tight and hot."

She swept one arm out, desperate for something to hold on to, and the knife skittered away and flipped onto the floor. "Don't stop—"

"Never," he promised, riding her faster. "I'll never stop fucking you. Never stop needing you. Loving you."

Something crashed off the pegboard above the table, and the impact vibrated through the wood, up through her body. In the midst of a storm of ecstasy, that small, quiet sensation centered her.

Never stop.

Dallas had always known how to get her off, but this was different. Having him *with her*—and knowing she always would—tripped something primal deep in her brain. Every nerve ending lit up, and she tensed again with a mounting pleasure that went on and on, tighter and tighter as his movements grew less and less controlled.

A rumbling noise started in his chest, twisting feral possession with satisfaction, and gave way to a string of snarled encouragements, words bitten off between fast jerks of his hips. Things like *fuck yeah* and *so good*, commands that stroked inside her. "Take me," he growled, barely audible over the rattle of the table and the blood pounding in her ears. "Love it. Tell me you love this."

"I love—" Something snapped, just fucking *snapped*, and her brain locked down. The waves turned to bolts, lightning strikes that curled her toes and left her gasping for enough breath to scream.

He did it for her, a wordless shout of triumph as he rode her clenching pussy to his own orgasm. He slammed home a final time before freezing there, his body locked within hers, his forehead dropping to rest between her shoulder blades.

He panted, his skin slicking over hers with every breath. Lex tried to lift a hand to his hair, but her limbs felt too heavy. So she licked her lips and shivered beneath him.

Lips brushed her nape, a soft kiss through her hair. "You all right, love?"

"I can't move."

"Me neither." But he did anyway, levering himself up before easing his cock from her body with a soft hiss. His hands were gentle as he eased her panties and jeans back into place, relentless possession in every touch.

He turned her, lifted her onto the table, and grabbed her arm with a curse. "Shit, you're bleeding."

There was a shallow, harmless gash running along the outside of her forearm. Lex stared at it and laughed. "I don't even feel it."

Dallas still frowned, sparing only a few seconds to straighten his pants before ordering, "Stay here."

He stomped out of the easy circle of light only to return with a small med kit. He fussed over her arm, applying med-gel and frowning even harder when she winced at the contact.

Lex watched him, rapt. "I was willing to stay and be her, you know. The queen. For you and the gang. That's what I had decided tonight."

Dallas froze in the act of opening a bandage, his gaze suddenly wary. "And now?"

She touched his face, every last shred of doubt gone. "I still want to be her for everyone else. For you, it's different. I can be all of me."

He fixed the bandage in place before catching her hand and turning to kiss her palm. "Christ knows I'm not going to stop being dumb, Lex. And I'll always want power. To keep us safe, and because it's who I am. But I'll come to you first, and be honest about it. Because I'll always choose you. Over power, over money, over everyone and everything. You just have to believe it, okay?"

"I do." Part of her always had—the part that had held her back from seeking more of Dallas's attention over the years. It was safer, in a way, to flirt with that devotion rather than submit herself to it…and then have it snatched away. "I need to come first. Well, me and the gang."

"Hey." He caught her chin. "Everyone and everything. Get it straight in your head, woman, 'cause it's too late to back out.”

“Stubborn ass.”

“Whose stubborn ass?”

Lex wrapped her arms around him, relishing the heat of his bare skin against hers. “All mine.”

26

Ace had always had a hard-on for symbolism and subtext.

With the bulk of Lex's hair wrapped around his fist to keep it out of the way, Dallas watched Ace lay the final lines on Lex's new marks. His own throat and shoulders still stung with the reminder that he'd gone first, and the knowledge that they'd soon be a matched pair pleased the darkest, most possessive urges Dallas had.

Or maybe it was just seeing his name—his given name, his *real* one—curled across the nape of her neck in stark black ink, a private claim no one could refute. Ace had risen to the challenge of marking his king and queen, crowning an elegantly understated version of the O'Kane logo. Dallas's was set in bloody barbed wire and Lex's in thorny rosebuds, but both faux-collars ended the same way—with the name of the person who held them together.

Knowing ALEXA stretched across the back of his neck was almost as satisfying as watching DECLAN take shape across hers. Ace might be a cocky pain in the ass, but sometimes Dallas was reminded how much the bastard deserved that attitude.

Ace swiped a hand across the back of Lex's neck and patted her shoulder. "Almost done. You hanging in there, sister?"

"It doesn't tickle," she murmured, "but I'll make it."

Dallas shifted his grip on her hair and bent down to meet her gaze. "It looks fucking fantastic. And hot."

The corner of her mouth kicked up in a smile. "You'd better think it's hot. That's my skin he's marking up."

With the way she was bent forward over the chair, he could have stood up and given her an eyeful of just how hot he found it. Not that a blowjob was his top fantasy right now, as sexy as Lex could make it. He wanted to stare at that ink as he rode her, every thrust made sweeter by the promise staring back at him, the one that said *forever*.

"Uh-uh," Ace said loudly enough to interrupt his fantasy. "I recognize that look. I'm glad as hell you two aren't fighting anymore, but no getting frisky while my needle's near someone's neck."

With a laugh, Lex reached out and wrapped her fingers around Dallas's. "I recognize that look, too. And he has a point."

Dallas spared Ace a glare and turned his attention on Lex. "No sex," he agreed before lifting her hand to his lips. He kissed one fingertip, then sucked it between his lips to flick his tongue over it in the most suggestive way he could manage.

Her laughter died, and she released a shaky breath. "Have it your way, but it's on you if Ace fucks up my ink because you had me squirming."

"Christ, you're worse than Jas and Noelle," Ace muttered, swiping a cloth over the back of Lex's neck. "Thank God I'm done. Let me slap some gel on there, and you crazy kids can go fuck each other silly."

Ignoring him, Dallas crouched down to bring his gaze level with Lex's. "Hi, darling."

"Hi." She grinned. "Isn't it cute how he seems to think we're going to clear out of here before we get dirty?"

"Oh, I don't think he'll mind until he realizes he *does* have to clear out."

Ace's head popped around the side of Lex's body. "Wait, what? You're gonna screw in my studio, and I don't even get to watch?"

Dallas cupped Lex's cheek. He'd come so close to losing everything, but because of her strength and her heart and her willingness to trust again, he'd never have to face the world alone. "Our studio," he corrected absently, smiling as he rubbed his thumb over Lex's lower lip. "Isn't that right, love?"

"Ours," she whispered, leaning into his touch.

Nothing in a life of scrabbling for power had prepared him for how good it felt to watch her lips form that word, one simple sound that erased a future of lonely decisions and replaced it with companionship and shared responsibility.

Ours.

"Damn right," he confirmed, and sealed the bargain with a kiss.

about the author

Kit Rocha is the pseudonym for co-writing team Donna Herren and Bree Bridges. After penning dozens of par-anormal novels, novellas and stories as Moira Rogers, they branched out into gritty, sexy dystopian romance.

The Beyond series has appeared on the New York Times and USA Today bestseller lists, and was honored with 2013 and 2017 RT Reviewer's Choice awards.

acknowledgments

As always, we owe eternal thanks and gratitude to the many people who helped us get through this book.

First to the ever-patient Sasha Knight, who has been a partner in this adventure above and beyond the call of editorial duty. Thank you for making us fight to be better, and for summoning excitement, dispensing encouragement and handing out hugs at all hours of the day and night. Additional thanks go to Sharon Muha, the sharpest proofreader one could hope to find. Any mistakes that have wiggled by these two are well and truly our own.

Many thanks as well go to the friends who held our hands through panic and frustration, especially when we weren't entirely sure we'd survive our hero and heroine—or that they'd survive each other. We owe the finest bottle of whiskey we can find to Vivian Arend, Alisha Rai, Ann Aguirre, Eliza Gayle, Lauren Dane, Lillie Applegarth and Edie Harris for alternately propping us up, pinning us down, slapping us silly, and hugging us cross-eyed. And two bottles go to Sophia for holding Bree's hand through a million website redesigns and checking two million versions of these ebooks until the formatting was just right.

the beyond series

Beyond Shame
Beyond Control
Beyond Pain
Beyond Temptation
Beyond Jealousy
Beyond Solitude
Beyond Addiction
Beyond Possession
Beyond Innocence
Beyond Ruin
Beyond Ecstasy
Beyond Surrender

gideon's riders

Ashwin
Deacon
Ivan
Hunter

mercenary librarians

Deal With the Devil
The Devil You Know
Dance With the Devil

www.kitrocha.com